Advance Praise

"A Future Library project in reverse, the prescient stories of *Dispatches from Anarres* give the impression of having been published a hundred years before they could have been written, providing readers with a rare glimpse into the future—both its potential dangers and its new ways of honoring luminaries like Le Guin. Stories like "The Night Bazaar for Women Turning into Reptiles" show us how the mission of expanding and exploding what's traditionally celebrated in the genres of science fiction and fantasy is entwined with the dismantling of ideological containers. I'll be recommending this book forever."

—Joe Sacksteder, author of *The Driftless Quintet*

"Dispatches from Anarres is why I read. This remarkable anthology of short stories in tribute to Ursula K. Le Guin is filled with thoughtful, heartbreaking, funny tales. Some will remind you of Le Guin and others of her spirit. I found myself pausing to think and breathe after many of the stories. This book is both readable and deep."

Doug Chase, bookseller, Powell's Books

"In the spirit of Ursula K. Le Guin's own 'Carrier Bag Theory of Fiction,' in which she envisioned a storytelling beyond the old fixation on conflict and battles, *Dispatches from Anarres* gathers a beautiful collection of healing stories. From the whimsical to the political, these Portland writers' magical imaginations and commitment to social justice shine on every page."

—Ariel Gore, author of *Hexing the Patriarchy*

"Dispatches from Anarres is a beautiful homage to the late Ursula K. Le Guin. It's also a tribute to her beloved city of Portland and the surrounding earth and water. Each story is its own magnificent offering to be scooped up and savored by readers."

—Annie Carl, bookseller, The Neverending Bookshop

"The work of Ursula K. Le Guin echoes across our time like a chorus sung by a mighty voice. *Dispatches from Anarres* gives other voices the chance to answer back with mighty verse. Offerings from Curtis C. Chen and Lidia Yuknavitch ring with the tone of writers who learned from Le Guin, while Rene Denfeld and Fonda Lee look to continue Le Guin's legacy of holding a mirror up to our world. A truly gorgeous anthology, with voices the world needs to hear calling the tune."

—Meg Elison, author of *The Book of the Unnamed Midwife*

"Ursula K. Le Guin never inspired others to write like her; she inspired them to find their own imaginative powers. These deeply original stories are the result: magical, moral, wise, beautiful, and full of surprises."

—Julie Phillips, author of *The Baby on the Fire Escape: Motherhood, Creativity, and the Mind-Baby Problem*, and of a forthcoming biography of Le Guin

"*Dispatches from Anarres* is what happens when a bunch of brilliant writers come together to pay tribute to a singular literary giant. This polyphony of voices from real and imagined worlds is timely, audacious, and teeming with style."

—Kimberly King Parsons, author of *Black Light*

Dispatches from Anarres

TALES IN TRIBUTE TO URSULA K. LE GUIN

Dispatches *from* *A*narres

TALES IN TRIBUTE TO
Ursula K. Le Guin

edited by
Susan DeFreitas

FOREST AVENUE PRESS
Portland, Oregon

Library of Congress Cataloging-in-Publication Data

Names: DeFreitas, Susan, 1977- editor.
Title: Dispatches from Anarres : tales in tribute to Ursula K. Le Guin / edited by Susan DeFreitas.
Description: Portland, Oregon : Forest Avenue Press, [2021] | Summary: "Named for the anarchist utopia in Ursula K. Le Guin's science fiction classic The Dispossessed, Dispatches from Anarres embodies the anarchic spirit of Le Guin's hometown, Portland, Oregon, while paying tribute to her enduring vision. In stories that range from fantasy to sci fi to realism, some of Portland's most vital voices have come together to celebrate Le Guin's lasting legacy and influence on that most subversive of human faculties: the imagination. Fonda Lee's "Old Souls" explores the role of violence and redemption across time and space; Rachael K. Jones's "The Night Bazaar for Women Becoming Reptiles" touches on gender oppression and a woman's right to choose; Molly Gloss's "Wenonah's Gift" imagines coming-of-age in a post-collapse culture determined to avoid past wrongs; and Lidia Yuknavitch's "Neuron" reveals that fairy tales may, in fact, be the best way to understand the paradoxes of science. Other contributors include Curtis Chen, Kesha Ajose-Fisher, Juhea Kim, Tina Connolly, David D. Levine, Leni Zumas, Rene Denfeld, and Michelle Ruiz Keil, with a foreword by David Naimon, co-author (with Le Guin) of Ursula K. Le Guin: Conversations on Writing"-- Provided by publisher.
Identifiers: LCCN 2021015177 (print) | LCCN 2021015178 (ebook) | ISBN 9781942436485 (paperback) | ISBN 9781942436492 (epub)
Subjects: LCSH: Short stories, American--21st century. | Le Guin, Ursula K., 1929-2018--Influence.
Classification: LCC PS648.S5 D58 2021 (print) | LCC PS648.S5 (ebook) | DDC 813/.0108--dc23
LC record available at https://lccn.loc.gov/2021015177
LC ebook record available at https://lccn.loc.gov/2021015178

Distributed by Publishers Group West

Printed in the United States

Forest Avenue Press LLC
P.O. Box 80134
Portland, OR 97280
forestavenuepress.com

1 2 3 4 5 6 7 8 9

In memory of Ursula Kroeber Le Guin
(1929-2018)

Contents

I. Magelight

Interlude

Interlude

III. On Time and Darkness

Postlude

Credits

An Oregon Literary Fellowship helped finance this project. We are grateful to Literary Arts for the support.

Lao Tzu, excerpt from "Returning to the Root" from *Tao Te Ching: A New English Version*, by Ursula K. Le Guin. Copyright © 1997 by Ursula K. Le Guin. Reprinted by arrangement with The Permissions Company, LLC on behalf of Shambhala Publications, Inc., www.shambhala.com.

Excerpt from *The Left Hand of Darkness*: 50th Anniversary Edition by Ursula K. Le Guin, copyright © 1969 by Ursula K. Le Guin. Used by permission of Ace, an imprint of Penguin Publishing Group, a division of Penguin Random House LLC. All rights reserved.

Excerpt from *A Wizard of Earthsea* approved as fair use by HMH Books and Media.

"The Night Bazaar for Women Becoming Reptiles" by Rachael K. Jones was originally published in *Beneath Ceaseless Skies* and is a 2017 Tiptree Award honoree.

"Old Souls" by Fonda Lee was originally published in *Where the Stars Rise: Asian Science Fiction and Fantasy*, edited by Lucas K. Law and Derwin Mak, and was nominated for a World Fantasy Award and an Aurora Award.

"Birds" by Benjamin Parzybok was originally published in *Strange Horizons*.

"Finding Joan" by David D. Levine was originally published in *Daily Science Fiction*.

"Laddie Come Home" by Curtis C. Chen was originally published in the 2016 *Young Explorers Adventure Guide*, edited by Corie and Sean Weaver.

"The Way Things Were" by Jonah Barrett was originally published in *Moss Covered Claws* (Blue Cactus Press).

"Hard Choices" by Tina Connolly was originally published in *Brain Harvest*.

"When Strangers Meet" by Sonia Orin Lyris was originally published in the anthology *New Legends*, edited by Greg Bear.

"Wenonah's Gift" by Molly Gloss was originally published in *Isaac Asimov's Science Fiction Magazine*.

Foreword

DISPATCHES FROM ANARRES IS a tribute to the vision of Ursula K. Le Guin from writers who either live in or have a strong connection to Portland, Oregon, the city Le Guin called home for sixty of her eighty-eight years. The premise behind this book is not only that Portland shaped Le Guin's writing but also that writers who live in Portland, who walk the same streets Le Guin once walked, in turn have been shaped by Le Guin, arguably Oregon's greatest writer.

But are either of these notions, when examined, actually true?

Yes, one of Le Guin's canonical science fiction novels, *The Lathe of Heaven*, is set in a future Portland, but for the most part her science fiction and fantasy novels are set in imagined other worlds. Should we therefore consider Le Guin's relationship to Portland in the same way we do Alice Munro's to southwestern Ontario or Gwendolyn Brooks's to Bronzeville, Chicago—places these writers' work seemed to emerge from, be fed by, and grow out of?

Le Guin often wrote about the importance of the imagination and put forth a philosophy that, interestingly, did not place the imagination in opposition to the real. Can a book be truly called "realistic" if it does not include the imaginative, given that our imaginative faculties are so central to what makes us human? Or as Ursula put it (more pithily than I ever could): "People who deny the existence of dragons are often eaten by dragons. From within." And: "Children know perfectly well that unicorns aren't real. But they also know that books about unicorns, if they are good books, are true books." Le Guin was quick to point out that many of our foundational cultural texts, from *Beowulf* to *Don Quixote*, from *The Odyssey* to *Hamlet*, are in fact fantastical, imaginative works that are also true and real ones.

Outside of science fiction and fantasy, Le Guin did directly engage with "the real world." Her poetry and nonfiction often explicitly spoke to the geography, culture, and ecology of Oregon and northern California. From a meditation on the street where she lived to poems written from her favorite cabin in the remote Steens Mountain region (where her family briefly home-steaded generations ago), these writings are rooted in the "here" of place. But when it came to her fiction, she said: "I seldom exploit experience directly. I do what the poet Gary Snyder calls 'composting'—you let everything you do or think or read or feel sink down inside yourself and stay in the dark, and then (years later, maybe) something entirely new grows up out of that rich darkness. This takes patience."

If everything Le Guin did or thought is part of this composting process—the process that led to the world of Earthsea and the planets of the Hainish cycle—then the metaphor of composting seems not a metaphor at all. Le Guin and the landscape she inhabited, literary and geographic, were inseparable. A founder of Oregon Institute of Literary Arts (the precursor to Portland's most prominent literary organization, Literary Arts), she also taught writing workshops at Portland State University, at the Malheur Field Station in remote Harney County, Oregon, and at Fishtrap in the Wallowa Mountains. She was an enduring supporter of Portland's KBOO community radio and of West Coast small presses, from the feminist sci-fi press Aqueduct in Seattle to Tin House in Portland to the anarchist AK Press in Chico, California. She explicitly credits the landscape of the Steens Mountain region of Oregon as an inspiration for *The Tombs of Atuan*, and that of northern California for *Always Coming Home*—and one could imagine, standing atop the high point of Orcas Island, Mount Constitution, in northern Washington, overlooking the watery wonderland of that island archipelago, that it too could've been a wellspring, if not the wellspring, for the world of Earthsea. Le Guin's imagination arose from the Cascadia bioregion, and she continued to weave herself from it and back into it again. Her imaginative composting came from and returned to this land, this earth in particular. Taken in this light, Susan DeFreitas's twinning of Portland and Anarres—not as a reductive one-to-one correspondence, but as a mysterious union of the real and the imaginative—makes sense.

In Le Guin's *The Dispossessed*, Anarres, the smaller planet in the double planetary system it shares with Urras, is considered lesser, not a planet at all, but rather a moon, a "rebel moon," by its larger, wealthier, capitalistic, patriarchal neighbor. Long ago, in order to stop an anarchist rebellion, Urras agreed to allow the revolutionaries to live as they saw fit on Anarres, signing a noninterference pact to that effect. The anarchist society that arose on Anarres considered itself free and independent of the old world largely thanks to this pact.

For the longest time, Portland too was left alone, the forgotten big city on the West Coast. Without the immediately dramatic and stunning settings of San Francisco, Seattle, and Vancouver, Portland was a quiet inland port, one that lacked the scope of international commerce and cosmopolitan cultural influence of its outward-facing neighbor cities. And it was here, out of the spotlight, far from the hype, that artists and writers and dreamers, attracted by the cheap rent and affordable cost of living, were drawn to reinvent themselves. Whether it was the DIY ethos that developed here, the farm-to-table relationships that supported the local food movement, the family-like network of writers that emerged, or the radical acts of civil disobedience to protect the environment or protest the latest war (so prevalent that the first President Bush called Portland "Little Beirut"), the city emerged in many ways as a rebel moon.

Le Guin believed the notion of home was both imaginary and very real. "Home isn't where they have to let you in. It's not a place at all. Home is imaginary. Home, imagined, comes to be," she said. "It is real, realer than any other place, but you can't get to it unless your people show you how to imagine it—whoever your people are." It is easy to imagine that these people—the tree sitters, the DIY artists, the community organizers—were not only inspired by Le Guin's writing but also showed her how to imagine it. Le Guin was a listener, and a composter of what she heard. She advocated fellow feeling for the nonhuman "other," for plants, animals, rocks, rivers, and even the tools we have fashioned from what the world has given us.

No wonder the stories of her fellow Portlanders, these dispatches from Anarres, include tales of women coming of age, women coming into their power, of tree-like networks in our brains, of tree-like networks *as* our brains, of the inquisitive and nostalgic remembrance of humans by ant collectives, and discussions of rebellion among bees. But there are tales that reveal the darker side of Portland as well. There is a reason Le Guin subtitled *The Dispossessed* "an ambiguous utopia." Le Guin didn't see the world through rose-colored glasses. Nor did she see Anarres or Portland this way.

As Jo Walton has pointed out, "Anarres could so easily be irritatingly perfect, but it isn't. There are droughts and famines, petty bureaucrats and growing centralization of power." And Portland's self-regard, its self-mythologizing, its imagining itself into being as a place of self-reinvention, has often been fueled by historical and cultural amnesia. Founded on stolen indigenous land, built on the idea of racial exclusion, many Portlanders live here without a sense of the city's history of redlining and displacement, of lash laws and internment. And as Portland has entered the spotlight, succumbing to a hype it had avoided for so long, housing prices have skyrocketed, the homeless population has exploded, communities of color have been pushed to its periphery, and Portland's own utopic mythology has rightfully been called into question.

Samuel Delany suggests that the term "ambiguous utopia" is not meant to apply to Anarres in particular. That the peoples of Urras and Anarres both mistakenly believe they are living in a utopia. That Le Guin is questioning the notion of utopic visions altogether. "It's only by problematizing the utopian notion," Delany said, "by rendering its hard, hard perimeters somehow permeable, even undecidable, that you make it yield anything interesting."

This is what Le Guin has done. And under her spell, there are stories here that root the imaginative deeply in place, that suggest that there is no walking away from difficulty to create a happiness "over there." Here we are, as in so many of Le Guin's novels, in a place where people are imagining worlds into being that suggest both dystopic and utopic possible futures. Here we are with choices to make. About where to be, how to be, and what to imagine. Welcome to *Dispatches from Anarres*.

—David Naimon, co-author of
Ursula K. Le Guin: Conversations on Writing

Introduction

IN PREPARING THIS INTRODUCTION, I am reminded of a journey I took in the spring of 2018, when I was in the midst of editing this anthology. This was before the Covid-19 pandemic hit, when travel was something we didn't have to think twice about, and travel I had, to a writer's residency in Joseph, Oregon. The organization that had offered me the residency was honoring 2018 as "the Year of Ursula," with a whole calendar year's worth of events honoring Oregon's grand dame of speculative fiction. It seemed a fitting time to be editing an anthology in tribute to her, and a fitting time to be "living in Le Guin," as I had for many months at that point, reading and rereading her many extraordinary novels, works of criticism, and poetry.

I was driving to Portland from Joseph for a break in this two-month residency, headed north on 82, with the full moon rising over the Wallowa Mountains. All along that drive, through snowcapped peaks rolling down to velvet green meadows, with cattle dreaming in the blue shadows, Ursula K. Le Guin kept me company. I was thinking of her affinity for the landscape of eastern Oregon, and for landscapes in general—thinking of her travel journals, detailed in *Dancing at the Edge of the World*.

I was thinking too of the teenagers I'd taught that week. Part of my job as the writer-in-residence that spring with Fishtrap—a nonprofit dedicated to "good writing and clear thinking about the West"—was to appear there in these kids' English classrooms and ask strange things of them: *Think of someone you know and the way they speak. Now try to write as if you were that person.* And: *Take the point of view of an animal. Describe something the animal loves and something it hates. Try to use the specific body language of this species.*

In her Catwings series, and in many of her short stories, Le Guin handled animal points of view with uncommon respect, enlarging our circle of sympathy without succumbing to easy assumptions. That's what I was challenging these kids to do with that second exercise of mine—challenging them to extend the reader's sense of empathy through the art of fiction, as Le Guin did.

Also, let's be honest: these are divided times, and I thought writing about animals might be a safely nonpolitical subject for the youth of Wallowa County, population 7,000. These were ranch kids, mountain kids, kids who grew up hiking in the Eagle Cap Wilderness—I thought they might have some interesting perspectives on the inner lives of animals, and they did. (My favorite story was told from the point of view of a miniature horse.) But one of my students that week essentially crossed his boots at the ankle and said, "I'm not going to take the point of view of a cow. A cow is just money to me."

As I drove, I wondered what Le Guin would have had to say about that—on one hand, about the conveniences of the capitalist worldview, and on the other, about the way sensitive artists like me tend to romanticize animals they only see from the side of the road. One of the finest things, to my mind, about Le Guin's critical work is its nuance, the product of her riprap of influences: pastoral, intellectual, scientific, moral, and spiritual. There are no easy answers in her work, and it serves to keep us from getting too comfortable with our own.

Swinging down along the Wallowa River, the Lostine River, and the Minam, the moonlit mountains loomed close to my little car and then stepped off lightly into the plains around Elgin and Imbler—and then, with a shock, I arrived among the great bright lights of La Grande.

Driving from there on through to Pendleton and then The Dalles, I was struck by an odd sort of déjà vu, the sense that I'd seen these small cities as big cities, in a dream, maybe, or, impossibly, in a memory, as if these places really might have been big cities in the past. It took me a moment, on this late-night drive, to realize I was remembering these cities as dreamed by George Orr, the protagonist of Le Guin's *The Lathe of Heaven*.

How extraordinary, I thought, the way she inhabits this landscape. How lucky for us that her vision was so strong, her voice so clear, that she is still here among us, challenging us to avoid easy assumptions in our own lives, and in our work as artists as well.

At one of Fishtrap's literary events that spring that I was lucky enough to attend, Rich Wandschneider, the organization's founder, noted that Ursula K. Le Guin was "quite simply, the intellectual leader of our state." She was also a great American writer, and one whose influence on the genres of science fiction and fantasy cannot be overstated. But as the great lady herself told us in her essay collection *The Wave in the Mind*, the "denigration, omission, and exception" the female writer faces during her lifetime "are preparations for her disappearance after her death."

Le Guin certainly stacked the decks against that eventuality, with a stunning seventy-one published books to her name. But even so, who's to say that the forces of white capitalist patriarchy will not converge to crush that hard-won legacy? After all, there are few bibliographies more subversive than Le Guin's, more challenging to that power structure in all of its forms. Those of us whose job it is to tell stories, among them the story known as history, and literary history in particular, simply cannot allow that to happen.

In *Dispatches from Anarres*, each story reminds me of something different about Le Guin's work. Fonda Lee's "Old Souls" explores the role of violence and redemption across time and space;

Rachael K. Jones's "The Night Bazaar for Women Becoming Reptiles" touches on gender oppression and a woman's right to choose; Molly Gloss's "Wenonah's Gift" imagines coming-of-age in a post-collapse culture determined to avoid past wrongs; Lidia Yuknavitch's "Neuron" reveals that fairy tales may, in fact, be the best way to understand the paradoxes of science; and Stevan Allred's tales of Ib and Nib speak not only to Le Guin's penchant for the songs and myths and folktales that make an imagined world feel real but also to her respect for the paradoxical truths of the trickster.

The trickster was certainly with me every time I actually met Le Guin: I was always too tongue-tied in her presence to tell her what she and her work have meant to me, as both a writer and a reader. This anthology, in many ways, is an attempt to make up for that, and also my attempt as an editor, as a literary storyteller, to share what it has meant to others—and what it might yet mean for all of us.

Le Guin is a giant of American letters, but her place in the canon will only be assured if we insist upon it. *Dispatches from Anarres* is one way of insisting upon it—one way of saying, *look at the worlds she left us!*

Those worlds she imagined, to my mind, are like winged seeds adrift on the wind. Many of them landed in her own city, the Rose City, and took root in that fertile soil, giving birth in turn to other worlds, and other ways of thinking about this one.

In Le Guin's 2014 National Book Award speech, which quickly went viral online, she said, "I think hard times are coming when we will be wanting the voices of writers who can see alternatives to how we live now and can see through our fear-stricken society and its obsessive technologies to other ways of being, and even imagine some real grounds for hope. We will need writers who can remember freedom. Poets, visionaries, the realists of a larger reality."

You'll find them in these pages.

—Susan DeFreitas, January 2021

I. Magelight

Only in silence the word,
only in dark the light,
only in dying life:
bright the hawk's flight
on the empty sky.
—The Creation of Eà,
from *A Wizard of Earthsea*

A Lay of Light and Anger

STEWART C. BAKER

Listen!

Listen, you wealthy with your spell-song towers and glimmering gardens, you noble poets with your fawning admirers.

Listen, citizens of Chak-ley, favored of the Dux, and I shall tell you a tale.

On the eve of my seventeenth birthday, my favorite parent, Creiya, died.

The power of their death-dirge struck me from a dozen provinces away, cutting through the strands of the idle poem I had been weaving out of spell-song and knocking the air from my lungs. I scrabbled at the pendant they had spelled for me, which burnt hot against my skin, and flung it across my chamber, where it shattered into a dozen couplets against the hearth.

The pendant was the last thing I would ever have of Creiya. I had asked them for it when they left for the interior at the Dux's command, had clung to their consonant armor as they gathered their troops and begged them for it, a pretty thing shaped like a bird.

Minhu—my other parent, whose family had been landowners for generations, and who had never known hardship—had called it foolish, a spoiled child's wish, but Creiya had not denied me. They had simply spoken a few half-rhymes, then looped the chord that formed around my neck.

In truth, Minhu had been right. I had wanted the bird pendant as soon as I learned that Creiya would wear a token from the Dux, a sharp-edged pin shaped like a dragon that glared out from their uniform, spell-sworn to keep the Dux informed of their movements. Seeing that dragon as Creiya made ready to leave us, I had wanted a memento of my own. A way to ensure that some part of my favorite parent's thoughts stayed at home with me while they travelled. While they warred.

The bird Creiya crafted was blue and purple, all smoothly shaped wings and prettier by far than the Dux's dragon pin. Only now, as I picked the remnants of their spell-song from the hearth with shaking fingers, did I realize what I had done. Spell-song costs attention always, constant thought on the speller's behalf. Creiya was not the Dux, with scores of spell-singers to keep watch on their workings, and I felt certain that maintaining my bird pendant had distracted them in battle. That it had caused their death.

Already the couplets of the pendant were fading—their letters losing their form, their rhyme becoming dissonant. My parent's spell-song was vanishing, along with their life. Yet I could not stop myself from picking up those pieces, trying to coax them back together with spell-song of my own.

This was how Minhu found me, huddled over the hearth and sobbing my love into a ruined mess of broken lines.

They approached me with heavy footfalls and laid one hand on my shoulder. "I'm sorry, Ahrei," they said.

I sobbed harder, holding the remnants close. "I killed them!" I gasped. "*Me.*"

They blinked, ran one hand through their short-cropped, greying hair. "You did not, and Creiya wouldn't want you to think it. They wanted your safety. Your happiness. Not this." There was no anger in their words, no hurt. Their voice was measured and even, as sturdy and unfeeling as stone—the same as always. They still wore the dun-and-silver robes of their station, rather than the mourning white we would now dress in.

"What would *you* know?" I snapped.

"I know plenty," they said, smiling sadly. "And I know it was Loi who killed Creiya, not you."

Loi, the spell-singer who used their powers to steal from rich landowners like my parents instead of taking their proper place in the social order. Loi, the renegade whose hardscrabble army had been the talk of the fifteen provinces since they'd routed the Dux's army a sennight ago. Loi, against whom the Dux had sent my parent—the renowned spell-singer and general Creiya of Tenbridge, crafter of epics and terror of the wildlands.

"Then why don't you go after Loi?" I shouted. "Why are you still here, instead of *doing* something?"

"I am not Creiya," Minhu said with a sigh. "It is not for me to do such things."

Which was stupid. Minhu may have been only a landowner, but hadn't their parents drilled them in spell and sword as well as society, just as my parents had me?

Minhu had walked to the window while I fumed, to look down on our sprawling gardens. When they spoke again their voice was soft. "And killing Loi would not bring Creiya back to us."

Their voice broke on the last phrase, ever so slightly, and for a moment I thought some emotion would break through their shield. That I'd see the hurt they must feel, to know that their lover was dead. But they just took a deep, ragged breath. "At least," they said, "we have each other."

Once they were gone, my despair morphed into anger—at Loi, at myself, at the Dux, and especially at my parents. At Creiya who had gone off to war and died, and—even more so—at Minhu, who was too much a coward to even show their feelings, let alone seek revenge.

Clenching the remnants of the broken pendant tight, I poured every bit of power I could into spell-song, twisting and folding all the grief I'd been holding into hate, jealousy, blame. Every little slight Minhu had dealt me over the years—every misunderstood cry for help I'd given them, every well-intentioned reply, every shielded emotion they had never shown me.

And as I wove my words, the beautiful thing my dead parent had given me shimmered with power, blackened with despair, until I held in my hands no longer the wings of a pretty bird but a curse of talons, an invective of beaks that reminded me of the sharp edges on the dragon the Dux had given to Creiya.

I told myself this meant their duties from the Dux now lay with *me*, and swore I would deliver the curse to Loi.

I DIDN'T GO TO supper.

I didn't respond, either, when Minhu returned two hours later with a tray of cooling food. I lay unmoving as they stood at my bedside, listened to their even breathing, to their eventual sigh and the sound of their footsteps retreating.

I waited longer still, until the bells rang out even-song. Until they rang out midnight. Only then did I stir myself from bed and take up my travel-sack.

Abandoning my childhood home and only living family should have been hard, but emotion had always run strong in me, deep and fast like a river. The anger I felt at Minhu, at their cowardice, stayed with me as I stuffed clothing and paper in my travel-sack, as I sneaked to the kitchen and grabbed a waxed bag of rice and dried fish.

I saw no servants. Perhaps Minhu had dismissed them, casting our home into the three-moon period of mourning required by the Dux for the death of a general, when even our servants would be forbidden to work. As I crept through our night-dark gardens, I paused before a sculpted vine of jasmine, its white petals glistening like stars. It would be a shame were they to wither in the absence of our gardener, and I thought briefly of rhyming their roots extra strength. But, remembering what had happened to Creiya—to my pendant—I left the vine to die.

In the stables, I saddled a donkey as quickly as I dared, whispered words of calm waking in the creature's ear, and was on my way.

If Minhu would not avenge their partner, *I* would avenge my parent.

I HAD HEARD THE servants whisper rumors of Loi's encampment in our province, so I rode all night along mountain paths to its supposed location, sustaining the donkey with ditties of courage and clarity. Or maybe these were for myself. I was not used to riding for so long, let alone in the mountains at night, and I had not slept since the morning before.

Worse than the sleepiness, though, worse than the anxiety, was the curse I had crafted of Creiya's pendant. Its malevolent rhyme and sibilant dissonance unsettled me, its weight in my travel-sack and its presence in my mind a constant itch. As the first weak light of sunrise pierced the craggy mountains to the east, I dismounted and pulled it from my travel-sack.

What I saw changed the anxiety to lead in my stomach. During the night, it had changed further. Gone were the talons and beaks— the only remnants of the pendant my parent had given me. All that remained was a fist-sized ball of sharpness and edges that snagged in my travel-sack's fabric as I lifted it free, a tangled mess of bent-in blades that caught the light and cut it to ribbons.

I thought on my promise to deliver it to Loi with misgiving, but I had come too far now to go back. With a shiver, I returned the pendant to its place, then relieved myself in some shrubs and ate my fish and rice while sitting at the edge of the path.

By chance, the place I had stopped overlooked a village, a collection of dirty thatched-roof huts nestled in the valley between the mountains. A village so near to our estate seemed likely to supply some of our servants, and I marveled that they would keep their own homes so mean, so ugly, when they had spell-song enough to craft sculptures of our jasmine, to sing our floors spotless.

I had intended to continue riding, but when I stood and stretched after eating, all the energy drained from my body in a rush.

The long night, I told myself. The stress of losing one parent and leaving the other. And I had not eaten much yesterday, either. Surely it was nothing to do with the curse. Nothing to do with the fact that its glowing blades remained in my mind like an after-image of the sun on a cloudless day.

It might be dangerous to sleep in the wild so close to where Loi's forces had been seen, but I couldn't keep going. I would fall asleep while riding.

Fighting back yawns, I tied the donkey's lead to a windblown cypress, lay down under its dancing needles, and closed my eyes.

Just a short rest, I promised myself. Then I would find Loi. Then I would get my revenge.

I WAS AWOKEN BY a chill of shadow.

When I opened my eyes, two warriors loomed over me, blocking out the glare of afternoon sun. Both wore the bronze plate and red-tasseled helmets of those in the Dux's armies, and wielded the traditional sword and spear.

I was equal parts relieved and disappointed it was not Loi's rebels who had found me. The Dux's warriors would return me to Minhu's estate. To their care. I would never avenge Creiya's death.

The tallest of the two poked my foot with the butt of their spear. "You are Ahrei, child of Creiya and Minhu," they said.

There was no point denying it. I sat, squaring my shoulders, summoning the pride I had heard in my parents' voices when asked their name and status. "I am."

The two glanced at each other, then nodded. The one who had not spoken took up my donkey's lead, while the tallest offered me their hand. When I did not take it, they squatted on their haunches, bringing their head level with mine. "I am sorry for your loss," they said. "It is a loss for all who value justice."

"Thank you," I whispered, blinking back sudden wetness from my eyes.

"Come, now," they said. "Loi has been expecting you."

Where the mention of my parent had brought me to tears, the name of their killer struck me like a blow. Something of it must have shown on my face, as the guards backed away, giving me space.

"Loi means you no harm, child," the tall one said, voice gentle.

"Then why did they kill my parent?" I snapped, scrambling to my feet.

The guards exchanged another glance.

"They did not," said the tallest. "It was the Dux who did that."

FROM THE LAYS THE Dux's travelling poets recited, I had learned that Loi's rebellion was a slovenly, ramshackle collection of malcontents. That they would murder children to laugh at their parents' pain and that they fought amongst each other when Loi did not have them aimed at an innocent.

As the two guards in the Dux's armour walked me and my donkey to where Loi's camp was set, I steeled myself, expecting a dozen unclean rebels in threadbare cloaks as disheveled as their morals.

What I found was as far from the official lays as the curse I had crafted was from my dead parent's pendant. There were far more than a dozen rebels—among them, many others who had defected from the Dux's army—and each of them was cleanly dressed. The encampment was organized like a wheel, with tents arrayed down each spoke and a clearing at the center, the rebels sitting at tent-flaps or around campfires. The smell of saffron rice cooked in butter and spices filled my nostrils, reminding me I'd had nothing to eat but a few handfuls of fish and rice since the morning before.

The thing that took me most aback, though, was the sound. Or rather, the lack of it. For instead of the riot of drunken arguments, the camp was filled with a silence that spoke of focus, of eager attention, as the rebels watched a figure who stood in the center clearing. The figure had long, braided hair that was greyer than Minhu's and a body worn thin by hard living—the slightest hint of paunch at their midsection suggesting a more luxurious past.

As we approached, the guard on my left nudged the one with my donkey and both came to a slow stop. The one with the donkey whispered a quick riddle of silencing into the creature's ear, and the one who had my shoulder gestured that I should sit and listen.

Curious, I knelt in the grass and listened as the person at the center began to recite. I do not remember what they said, only that their words were like sunlight on a cold day, like ice on a hot one. Their meter burrowed through all the lies about Creiya's death and the justness of the Dux's cause I had convinced myself were true. As line after line flowed from their lips, my anguish floated to the surface of my mind and I clutched at my chest with a sob.

The sound drew the speaker's attention. They bowed to their audience, sweeping their braid against the ground. "And that, my friends," they said, "is where we must stop for tonight, for I see we have a guest, and not even poetry is more precious than that."

A chorus of good-natured groans went up from the gathered rebels, and then the gentle murmur of quiet conversations took their place.

I wish I could say I had changed my opinion of the rebels. That I had already been won over to their cause. But I was, in truth, still too stunned by the beauty of the poet's words to be anything other than distraught that they had stopped.

"Who are you?" I asked as they approached. I leaned towards them, carried away by an image of them dressed in the finery of my parents, reciting lays and epics to my jealous friends. "You could be the talk of any court you chose," I continued. "Why are you here, serving Loi? Leave them, and come home with me."

The raucous laughter of the guards beside me made me jump. Too late, I remembered where I was. Not in the stately home of a friend, where poetry was a show of style and grace, and might be bought by the highest bidder. I was smack in the center of a camp filled with renegades. With rebels against the Dux and all that spoke of order. And I could not go home.

My ears flushed with heat.

"Foolish child," said one of my captors, although their voice was amused. "They *are* Loi."

And Loi—renegade leader of an army that had terrorized the fifteen provinces, and the person who had murdered my parent—bowed their head, made a flourish with their hands, and said, "At your service, Ahrei, child of Creiya and Minhu."

I HAVE ALWAYS PRIDED myself on my spell-song. On my poems. On my ability to craft baubles and amusements for my friends and loved ones.

Before Loi, I was like a rivulet who thinks itself a river, iced over in the winter while the waterfall beside it roars on. For the first time, I knew myself a spoiled child of seventeen instead of a great master of the arts. Everything I had planned to say to my parent's killer—every angry word, every promise of death, every anguished entreaty—froze on my lips unspoken.

Loi did not rush me, did not goad me to speaking. They stood, face politely neutral, and waited for me to speak.

During their recitation, the curse in my travel-sack had shifted. I lay one hand on it, feeling the changes in its tangled blades, suddenly uncertain whom I hated. Whom I had intended it for. At the realization, the words of the guard that afternoon returned to me, and my tongue thawed.

"The Dux," I said, then floundered.

It was enough. Loi's expression sharpened. "They give their generals a charm," they said, "and anyone they think cannot be trusted. They claim it as a blessing, as a way to communicate. It can take any form—a bracelet, a necklace, a knife."

"A pin," I whispered, the memory of that dragon rising in my gorge like bile.

"Just so," Loi continued. "And when the people who have been given these charms stand up to the Dux, they use it to kill them. To reach out and stop their hearts with all their stolen, pent-up power. That is what happened to Creiya, when they met me here to plan our next campaign."

I shuddered, the tears breaking free again.

"I knew Creiya," Loi said, their voice gentle. "I called them friend. In their travels and their warring, they had come to understand the suffering of the people, and a year ago they sought me out, determined to end the Dux's tyranny. For a long time, they were able to decline the charms the Dux offered their warriors. This time, they could not say no.

"We thought we had been careful, that their counter-song could fool the Dux while we planned our next campaign. But it was not enough." Loi paused, looked away for a moment, then continued. "I am sorry for their death—truly, Ahrei, I am. But know that it is not the worst of the Dux's sins. They have caused the hunger of the people, and the starving of the land, for many years."

I could only stare. Loi had called my parent *friend*. Co-conspirator. Then the rest of their words hit home, and I remembered the village I had seen. Its huts. Its disarray.

"Hunger," I repeated, dumbly. "Discontent."

Loi nodded, their face serious. "The people suffer, Ahrei. The Dux's guard takes their livelihoods, arrests any who resist, kills anyone who disdains them. Harsh laws refuse all but those of noble blood the right to craft spell-song as they wish."

I flushed, again, to think of the idle poems I had crafted in my chambers. Of how I had amused myself by folding synonym into synecdoche, rhythm into rhyme. Never had I thought to question why the people who tended our gardens and saw to our needs wore such plain clothing when they came from beyond our walls. Never had I thought to ask why we *needed* walls.

Loi waited for me to respond, then spoke when I did not: "It is wrong," they said.

Again, that subtle shift of the curse. I nodded, sick to my stomach, not trusting myself to speak.

"I would like you to join us," Loi continued, taking my hand between theirs. "I would like you to help us fight the Dux."

I swallowed, and again I felt that shift in my travel-sack. Although a small part of me wondered at the feeling, I knew suddenly I would do anything for Loi, for their cause. Even if they could not bring my parent back, they had shown me the truth about Creiya's death, about what they held dear.

"I will," I managed, voice raw. "I will join your ranks, and gladly."

Loi's smile deepened. "You are of noble blood, Ahrei, and can find ears where we cannot. I would have you take my song to others like you. I would have you tell them of our purpose, and win them to our cause." They paused, set their mouth in a grim line. "I will not lie, it is dangerous work—at least as treacherous as battle. If the Dux's guard catch you, they will kill you, favored status or no."

I opened my mouth to agree, to tell Loi I would go to the ends of the earth for them, speak to anyone they chose even if it meant my death. Before I could speak, though, a vast shadow fell over the camp, and a voice I knew better than my own yelled out my name.

Minhu, my parent, had come for me.

MINHU RODE A SONG-SPELLED griffin, dark of fur and feather. It was massive, its lion's body as large as ten horses abreast, and as it circled the camp on its powerful wings, it roared in echo of my parent's anger.

Many of the people in the camp scattered at that roar. Loi, however, made no move to flee. While I shrank to the ground, they turned in one fluid motion, shielding their eyes against the glare of the sun with one hand, their other resting on one hip.

Their stance must have made their identity obvious, because

my parent turned the griffin towards us and—as it beat its wings heavily to keep its place—pointed down at them with one shaking hand.

"Devil!" Minhu shouted, their voice carrying clearly through the tumult of the griffin's wing beats. "Destroyer! Was it not enough to kill Creiya? You had to take my child as well? I will see you dead!"

On the final word, they raised both hands high overhead, mouth forming the words of a short, sibilant poem. Although I could not hear the words, I felt sure that the blow it caused would be fatal. Loi didn't move, didn't so much as cringe away. Instead, they brought up a barrier, word-strong and shimmering.

I, who knew Minhu's anger and fury, which lay always beneath the ice of their surface, knew it would not be enough. Before they could speak the final line of their casting, I pulled the curse free of my travel-sack. From the way it had shifted and warped during my discussion with Loi, I knew it had changed, but still I was surprised by what I drew out—the curse was no longer a tangle of blades, but a spear, straight and fleet and sharp enough to cut through a lifetime of lies.

I hesitated only an instant, then threw it at the griffin, screaming a shanty of speed and surety. The blade struck true, slamming into the griffin's belly so that it reared back in the air, shattering into dissonant whispers and unseating Minhu, who spat the final words as they tumbled off its dissipating back, bringing their hands down at Loi. Minhu landed hard on one leg and half-collapsed to their knees.

The blast of their words went wild, scattering bursts of energy through the camp. The largest hit Loi full on. They took the attack with a grunt, muttering words I could not hear that sent the bolt ricocheting away, tearing a gouge in the earth at their feet that spread, crackling, to one of the guards who had served under my dead parent.

The hate of the poem sliced through the unfortunate rebel like a plough through spring soil. The guard went down, screaming in pain, the stink of their charred flesh mixing with the fresh-rot smell of overturned dirt.

I bent and retched, to think I had played a part in it, and only thanked the gods that Loi did not seem harmed. The stench of death and dirt and vomit did not give Minhu pause. They limped towards us, their mouth pulled in a rictus of hate and pain.

As though they were not there, Loi turned to the wounded guard and, with a whisper, turned their screams to the deep, even breathing of sleep. Then they dragged themself between Minhu and me, one hand held out before them and the other clenched over their stomach.

With a visceral shock, I realized that Loi had been hurt after all. They stank of blood, of bowels; they could barely stand. All around, there was only the silence of the camp, the stillness of twice times a hundred people cowering in fear. I wanted to scream at Loi's followers, to call them all cowards for not acting, to beg them to help. To step forward and restrain my parent, who was mad with grief.

But they were not cowering. They were watching Loi, hands on their weapons, words unspoken on their lips, their muscles taut as bowstrings. They trusted their leader to solve this, to bring my second parent, too, over to their cause.

They did not know Minhu. Their power when they raged.

Finally, I found my voice. "Stop," I gasped. "Stop!"

"I will not," my parent said. "All I ever wanted was to keep you safe. I tried to keep you out of this, but you left me—you *left* me, after Creiya, after . . ."

Their voice broke, and for a moment they just sobbed, gesturing for words that wouldn't come. I wondered to see Minhu cry, who had never shown me so much as a kind word. But was that right? I cast back through my mind, wondering if I had simply misunderstood my living parent all these years.

Then Minhu spoke again, their voice calm as a frozen lake. "Loi has turned you against me," they said. "Loi will see you dead. I will not allow it." They raised their hands above their head again, advancing, the words of another casting clear in the quiet of the camp.

"Loi," I begged, gripping one shoulder, trying to coax them to the ground, to my rear, to safety. "Loi, please. I will go with them. You need to rest. To heal."

They looked back at me, shook their head, then turned away, whispering words just beyond hearing. A shimmering shield flickered into being around Minhu.

Minhu snarled. Their words rang out more loudly, their consonants hissing in the air.

With my hand on Loi's shoulder, I could feel the strength flowing from them as they kept up their counter-spell. They staggered to one knee, nearly falling, and for a moment the shield flickered off.

Barely able to breathe, I pulled words of my own from the back of my mind, grasping at whatever I could reach—my feelings for my parents dead and living, the Dux's betrayal, my newfound love for Loi and their cause, my fears and hopes and dreams. I squeezed Loi's shoulder and spoke my own prayer of shielding just a hair's breadth before my parent's next twisted bolt of anguish slammed into us, crackling like fireworks against our combined protection.

Loi's smile deepened. "Protect the people like this, when I am gone," they whispered. "And forgive your parent. They love you."

The words carried no sense of poetry. No rhythm, no rhyme, no particular meter. They did not allude to anything. And yet those words broke my heart as surely as the most tragic epic. They shifted my view of the world.

And then Loi died.

As they sagged to the ground, I stayed standing, stunned into inaction until my parent's attack faltered and my shield fizzled out.

"It was the Dux," I stammered, looking to my parent as they limped towards me, their eyes red with grief, with anger, with I knew not what. "It was the Dux who killed Creiya, not Loi. It was the Dux."

MUCH MORE COULD I tell you, people of Chak-ley. Much of Minhu's sorrow, more of my own. Of the way our tears mingled with those of the rebels for their dead leader, and of how we slowly, steadily grew closer in the days that followed, united in our cause.

Were I a better poet, I would weave with words an image of the funeral we held for Loi and Creiya, tell you how their bodies burned, the smoke of their spirits rising straight up into the heavens.

But I can hear the distant sounds of hoofbeats, the martial clamour of the Dux's guards approaching. Time grows short, and I—amidst your wealth and splendor—am armed only with words.

So, people of Chak-ley, as I leave you, I ask you of your hearts.

Will you stand with the Dux, who has walled you up with your pride in your spell-song towers, or will you look past your finely manicured gardens and see the suffering of the people?

Will you close your eyes to wickedness, or will you heed my words, learn my lessons, lift your voice with mine?

This story owes a debt to Earthsea's focus on naming and the power of words. But it also touches on two themes that commonly appear in Hainish Cycle stories: resistance and how we can change for the better when our understanding of the universe shifts.

The Night Bazaar for Women Becoming Reptiles

RACHAEL K. JONES

IN THE DESERT, ALL the footprints lead into Oasis, and none lead out again. They come for water, and once they find it, no one returns to the endless sand. The city is a prison with bars of thirst and heat.

Outside the gates, the reptiles roam: asps and cobras, great lazing skinks, tortoises who lie down to doze in the heat. Where they go as they pad and swish and claw their way through the sand, no one knows, save the women who look over the walls and feel the deep itching pressure in their bones, the weight of skin in need of sloughing.

THOUGH HESTER HAS SOLD asp eggs at the night bazaar for five years, she has never become a reptile herself, no matter what she tries.

She takes eggs wherever she finds them. She has eaten those

of skinks and geckos. She has tasted sun-warmed iguana eggs. She has traced water-snake paths through Oasis and dug for their nests. She has braved the king cobra's sway and dart, and devoured its offspring too. Once, she found an alligator egg, and poked a hole in the top and sucked out the insides. But no matter what she tries, Hester has never broken free and escaped the city like the other women do.

She even tried the asp eggs once, the ones that were her livelihood. It was the day after Marick the mango seller asked to take her as his sunside lover. Hester left home and dug asp eggs from the clay by the river. The sun spilled long red tongues across the sand, over the footprints always entering the city, never leaving, and Hester's skin itched all over, and her flesh grew hot and heavy, and she longed for cool sand sliding against her bare belly.

One, two, three eggs into her mouth, one sharp bite, and the clear, viscous glair ran down her throat. The shells were tougher than she expected. They tasted tart, like spoiled goat's milk. She waited for the change, but the sun crawled higher and nothing happened.

She has never told anyone about the day with the asp eggs. Not her mother the batik dyer, who spatters linen in hot running wax and crafts her famous purple cloth. Not Marick, her sunside lover, who sells indigo cactus flowers and mango slices on a wooden tray. Not Shayna the butcher, her moonside lover, whose honey-gold verses roll from her tongue, smooth and rounded as sand-polished pebbles. Hester hasn't told them, because they are why she longs to leave.

THE NIGHT BAZAAR MEETS on a different street each week. Each morning before, at sunrise, Hester finds three blue chalk symbols sketched on the doorjamb behind the perfumed jasmine bush. Sometimes she sees a falcon, a crane beneath a full moon, and a viper climbing a triple-columned temple portico. This means *We*

assemble where the Street of Upholsterers intersects the Street of Priests,
when the Crane rises. Or it might be a hand holding an eye, a wavy
river, and a kneeling woman, which would mean *Meet where Oasis*
runs to mud, and beware the police. Hester memorizes the message
and wipes off the chalk with her sleeve.

They meet in secret, because the night bazaar was outlawed
when the Emperor stepped down from her throne and became a
snapping turtle. No one knew if she chose to change, or if a traitor
had slipped her the eggs unawares. These days, vendors caught
selling such goods moonside are made to drink poison sunside.
Even possessing the eggs earns a speedy execution. But in Oasis,
women at their wits' end have always eaten the eggs, and fled.

Hester packs the asp eggs in damp red clay and binds them, in
sets of three. Any more would be a waste, and any less, insufficient
to cause the change. At the meeting point, booths have already
popped up in the dark. Hester drapes her bamboo frame in purple
and gold batik, fringed with the shiny onyx hair of some young
customer who bought eggs long ago.

She lays out packets in three reed baskets and lights a lamp
that burns tallow made from women's fat. At moonrise, Hester's
chin lifts, and over vendors hawking their wares, she sings:

> *Eggs of the asp*
> *collected riverside*
> *in the new moon dark*
> *Come, buy, and eat!*
>
> *Opal-white eggs*
> *cool as desert's night*
> *against your belly*
> *Come, buy, and eat!*

The customers arrive, ghosts cut from darkness by moonlight's
blade. They are no two alike. They are old and young. They are

blind and deaf and whole of body. They have hats and sandals, sunburns and calluses. They come singing and weeping and completely silent. The vendors sing to them all, a cacophony and a tapestry. Hester's bones buzz from the dissonance, her skin as a quivering lizard bolting from rock to rock.

On slow nights, Hester bargains for rare eggs, which she devours on the spot. They never work. *A waste of good coin*, the merchants say, clucking their tongues, but they take payment anyway. *Traders should not eat their wares.* Most vendors prosper from the illegal trade, but Hester barely makes ends meet because she spends so much on eggs. Shayna, her moonside lover, often teases her about her bad business sense.

Marick never asks what she does moonside. By this, Hester has come to fear him. He does not ask because he already knows.

HESTER HAS TO WAIT for sundown to pack for the next bazaar, since Marick won't leave for work before then. People often compliment her attentive sunside lover—how he won't leave her side until sunset requires it. When they are alone, he keeps his distance. He has not once touched her, not as a lover does. Perhaps he mistakes her distance for demure shyness, the way she lies still in bed, how she curls into herself during the midday nap.

Ever since they met, Hester has a recurring dream where her body is a golden pot with an amethyst lid and she an asp inside it. In the dream, Marick plays the oboe, charming her out with music. She slithers to him, and he grabs her and devours her.

When she wakes, she feels hollow and hungry inside. Her mouth tastes sour, like the eggs that will not change her.

Truthfully, her shoulders relax when Marick leaves for moonside life, and she can go to the night bazaar. Hester wonders if Marick's moonside lover is any different from her. Perhaps he loves Marick better. Perhaps he likes mangoes. Perhaps Marick touches him. Perhaps he is less afraid than she is.

HESTER'S FIRST CUSTOMER THAT night wears a priest's robe tied all wrong, knotted at the shoulder like they do on the Street of Blacksmiths to keep their sleeves from the hot anvil. People often pretend to be another thing when they come to the night bazaar. The woman's fingers stroke a linen packet, thumb caressing the round bulges.

After payment, the woman unwraps the eggs and eats them. The moon glints on her teeth. Hester cannot hear the eggs burst above the din, but her insides quiver anyway.

The woman falls into a heap before Hester's booth. Her flesh splits open and she slithers out from her own breastbone, her shining black length cutting crescents in the sand. The newborn asp slithers through the gutter, making westward toward the desert.

Hester drags the blacksmith's sloughed-off body behind her booth for later processing. There will be more before the night's end.

They seem so sure when they approach the booth, like they know it will work for them. They often stop to browse the other wares, but their eyes slide until their fingers find the asp eggs. They do not waver. Assurance steadies their voices. She used to ask them why, back when she first started selling. *Why the bazaar? Why tonight? Why this shape?*

"Because this body has grown too tight around me."

"Because breathing weighs me down, and I am exhausted."

"Because each night, I dream of walking into the desert and not returning."

"Because each morning, I watch the merchants pass into the gates, and I want to scream, 'Stay away!'"

At the night bazaar, they shed their skin and leave as asps and tortoises and crocodiles. They pass the gates unimpeded. They go out into the desert and erase the footprints leading inward.

～

THE NIGHT HESTER MET Marick, the bazaar assembled where the Street of Cobblers bisected the Street of Zither Players. Someone must have betrayed them. Perhaps a sharp-eyed officer traced the steady stream of determined lizards and serpents and tortoises scampering through the gutters and under the gates and out into the darkness. A cry cut through the selling-songs: *Run! Run!*

It had happened before. It was why the booths collapsed so easily. Hester grabbed her basket and yanked the batik down. The crowd surged toward the Street of Cobblers, pressed from the rear by police with battering sticks. The cloth sheet tangled in the bamboo bars, and Hester wrestled with it.

"Hester?" It was a young policeman, stick in hand. "The batik dyer's daughter. I would know you anywhere." She knew him too: Marick the mango seller. Now moonside, his crooked teeth became a cobra's fangs. "Wait. I need to speak with you."

His boot pinned the batik sheet to the cobblestone. Hester yanked harder, heart thudding against her ribs. *Poison,* she thought. *Bloated bodies at the wall.* The sheet ripped, and she fled into the crowd.

The next day, Marick arrived at her mother's shop with six ripe mangoes wrapped in a tattered batik scrap, and a proposition.

To mark her as his sunside lover, he gave Hester a gold earring shaped like a pot set with an amethyst for a lid. It was heavy for its size.

Marick never mentioned that night at the bazaar. What happened moonside wasn't discussed sunside. She could not tell if the coercion was deliberate or accidental on his part.

It all amounted to the same for Hester. Marick's love was a prison. His smile tightened when she glanced out the window to check the sun's position. *Test me, and you shall learn my nature,* said that tightness. His gaze followed her everywhere. She always checked the doorjamb for the chalk signs before sunrise and erased them. Propriety forced him to stay away until dawn touched the rooftop.

When they were alone together, she mirrored his smile, and the woman who gathered asp eggs curled in on herself, deep down where no one could ever find her sunside. She dreamed and dreamed of being consumed, of escape.

NEAR MOONSET, AS THE crowd thins to a trickle and the reptiles depart, a hand rests on Hester's shoulder. "Never trust a woman who gathers asp eggs, for she may become one," Shayna whispers, breath warm and licorice-scented.

"They don't work for me, I'm afraid." Hester turns so Shayna's kiss falls on her cheek.

"You cannot become what you already are," she jokes. Shayna stops trying to steal kisses and counts the shedded bodies. Eight women lie bisected and cold: a good night. Shayna's blades flick and twist, opening seams, probing apart joints. The hair goes to the weavers, the bones to the lemon tree growers and to the scribes, and the meat goes to the vulture breeders and the candlemakers.

The two women work quickly, distributing the haul to runners who buy for the sunside merchants. If any time remains, they slip off to Shayna's bower on the Street of Butchers for a few hours in the dark together before sunrise. Their infant son, too young for a name yet, sleeps in a basket nearby. He has hair like damp sand. "He gets it from his father," Shayna explains when Hester pets his soft head. Shayna talks about her sunside lover more than anyone Hester has ever met. It was especially tiresome during her pregnancy last year.

Hester rolls over in the hammock in the dark. "Shayna, have you ever wished to leave Oasis?"

Shayna turns, and the hammock sways. "I prefer not dying of thirst and exposure, thank you. I like my life here. I have my family, and business. Why?"

"Sometimes I wonder where the reptiles go. They say there is an ocean out there, beyond the desert."

Shayna yawns wide. "You spend too much time at the night bazaar. You should start a proper family. When are you going to give me a moonside baby of my own?"

"You sound like my mother." With Marick and Shayna in her life, it is what everyone expects. Children thrive best with two mothers and a father. Hester only has one mother, though. Perhaps that is why she cannot become a reptile.

"You haven't answered my question," Shayna points out, stirring, and the baby wakes and cries.

Hester climbs from the hammock and rocks him until he calms. Outside, the dark sky is gray and heavy. Softly it starts to rain. Too late, she realizes her mistake. "Oh, damnation! It's morning, Shayna." She dresses and sprints out the door, through the rain, toward the Street of Dyers.

An oil lamp sits lit on the stoop when Hester gets home, and the door is ajar. Marick, home from his moonside life, curls in bed with his back toward the door. Hester listens to his breathing for ten heartbeats, slow and regular like wind in the olive tree branches. When she is sure he is asleep, she stows her basket of asp eggs beneath the bed and lies down beside him. Marick always smells like incense and cinnamon at dawn, the way Hester smells faintly of butcher's blood. In this way, they bring their moonside lovers home with them. At sunrise, the scents make a family.

She dreams of Shayna and Marick and the unknown men who love them. Of her mother, alone by sunside, and Hester a child only half-mothered, now half-mother again to the nameless baby with the damp sand hair. If only she had hatched from an egg. Reptiles needed no mothers or father. They birthed themselves and named themselves and no one kept them from the desert.

She is dreaming of the desert when she wakes in the evening, the day's heat slipping away. Marick isn't in bed, nor is he in the kitchen cutting up mangoes. It is only then she realizes: in her hurry to return from Shayna's home, she forgot to erase the chalk from the doorjamb. Marick's muddy footprints squat below that spot, the jasmine branches forced back, but he is already gone.

So is her bundle of asp eggs.

THE MOMENT HESTER NOTICES, she ransacks their home, searching for the missing eggs. She strips the bed and shakes out the linen sheets. She dumps the reed baskets piled by the door. She plunges both hands elbow deep into the refuse heap outside the window. Worms ooze around her knuckles.

Never in all this time has she left evidence of the night bazaar. Never so much as a glance toward the doorjamb and its tiny chalk symbols. Her bones quiver inside the bag of her skin. The sky is streaked angry red, and moonrise bears down with vicious weight. Marick could return at any time with the other policemen, with the poison.

Her fingers dig into her palms so hard they draw blood. It is against every rule for him to police her by day: against law, against custom, against decency. But poison makes no such distinctions, and if he found the eggs, she would have no defense. She could beg Shayna to hide her, but how would she explain it without exposing her sunside life?

Hester wraps her head in batik and hurries to the western wall, where the reptiles emerge in a thin, long line across the sands. Above them, bodies swing to and fro over the gates, dry and mummified by weather and time. It was always a major affair when they hung out a new one. Marick took Hester to watch once. He held her hand, and neither smiled.

If she could be that kind of creature. If she could cross the desert. If she could break free of the spidersilk bonds Oasis imposed, the thin invisible obligations tying woman to man to woman to child, a web which caught and snared.

Hester finds herself at home again, standing before the darkened door. Behind the jasmine bush, she finds the chalk symbols: a pot, an oboe, and an egg.

We gather in the alley on the Street of Midwives where the Emperor was born.

She considers going into the house, lying down in the dark, and waiting for Marick, but her feet are already drawing her back toward the night bazaar.

HESTER'S MONEY BUYS HER half a dozen crocodile eggs, two cobra eggs, and a large speckled monitor lizard egg still warm to the touch. She swallows them down and will not let her stomach vomit them up, no matter how much her guts twist. Her head buzzes like when she drinks too much palm wine. Her hands tingle as if the poison courses inside her veins already. She hurries from booth to booth, begging for more eggs, but her colleagues only cluck their tongues and offer her rose petal tea, or silken shawls, or cool hands to the forehead.

"I am not sick," Hester insists. "I need to buy more eggs." But they will not sell them to her.

At last she hunches behind her booth, shivering in the chill, waiting, hoping yet for transformation. She has no asp eggs to sell, so the customers pass her by, until at last one does not.

Despite his broad-brimmed veiled hat, Hester recognizes Marick, when he sets the missing eggs on the booth's counter. He smells like incense and cinnamon. "Do not try to run now. Not this time."

Fear twists her gut hard, and all the raw eggs roil in her stomach. She gags and vomits into the sand behind the booth. The slimy white glair pools with her bile, studded with chunks of undigested shell. Her last hope of transformation, absorbed into the sand. The desert will take even this before it will take her. As her hope dribbles away, so does the fear. Hester laughs a short, sharp hyena bark.

"Everyone pretends to be something different at the night bazaar, Marick. What are you supposed to be?"

He hesitates, then twitches the veil up. Rose-colored moonlight bathes his face, a rare lunar eclipse. He looks small and fragile as a pressed flower, not at all like the man she has feared for five years.

He leans forward, voice low and secret. "I need to know how the eggs work. Is there a spell?"

Hester snorts. "You want our secrets before you betray me. You think you can ask, and I will tell you, as if this is not my bazaar and you are not a customer. As though the price is not my life."

Marick shakes his head hard. "No, no, you've got it all wrong, Hester. Have the police found the night bazaar since we became lovers? Do you think that is a coincidence? Whatever I am, I am no traitor."

It has the ring of truth to it, though she does not want to trust him. "What do you want from me? You take me for a lover and do not touch me. You follow me here and do not arrest me. You say you've been protecting me. What do you want?"

He casts his eyes toward the gutter, which is littered with tiny reptile prints. When he speaks, his voice is not a mango-seller's cries or a policeman's growl but trembling and weak, a flute cracked and leaking air. "I am done, trying to live in this body. It doesn't fit. Not with dayside lovers, or nightside lovers. Touches do not reach me. I wear my own flesh like a cloak, and I am alone inside. It isn't mine. Maybe I was supposed to be a reptile? A woman? Half a mother to complete some child? I do not know. I only know that if I don't shed this body, I will suffocate in it. Do you understand?"

He sounds just as sure as every woman who has come before. "You just eat them, Marick. There is no spell. The eggs don't work for men, though."

He shrugs, and the corner of his mouth lifts. "I will try, anyway. I don't know any other way." Marick unwraps the eggs and rubs off the clay. He cracks them one by one, sucks out their insides, chews and swallows the shells. Around his ankles, women skitter and slither westward on scaled claw and belly.

Hester waits for his disappointment, but instead he collapses before her booth. An asp springs from his breastbone, a fine golden-eyed creature damp from heart's-blood, and it joins the reptile exodus in the gutter. As she watches him go, a hollow place inside her rips open, as though the last of her hope has also left her and slithered into the desert.

Mechanically she drags his unwanted body behind the booth. It has been many years since this chore unsettled her, since a customer's discarded eyes fixed upon her face, but Marick was her dayside lover, the only one she had. For the first time since she joined the bazaar, a body becomes a corpse.

WHEN SHAYNA SEES MARICK, she steadies her head between her hands. "Oh, Hester, what have you done? The law might turn a blind eye to the night bazaar as long as we're discreet, but it won't ignore a dead policeman."

"He isn't dead. He became an asp, Shayna!"

The two women slump together behind the booth while Hester confesses everything. "What did he do? Why did it work for him?"

Shayna jerks her chin toward the sky. "Eclipses are strange. Moonside and sunside join hands and pass. Perhaps the desert calls to its own."

Hester curls up tight and tries not to retch. No eggs for her, because she is already empty inside. She does not say, *Why won't it work for me?*

Shayna holds her at arm's length. "You think I don't know. You think I don't pay attention." She undoes Marick's earring, holds the matching golden pot to Hester's ear. "Tell me, lover, what makes you so afraid? Afraid enough to piss away your profit on all those eggs? Scared enough to leave me too?"

"You are so happy here," Hester manages through hitching breath.

Shayna's eyebrows pinch together like when she is considering the best way to slice open a ribcage. "Maybe the eggs do not work for you because you do not need them. You're practically an asp already. You spend enough time among their nests."

Somehow, the thought comforts her. "And you, Shayna? What are you?"

Shayna's smile is all teeth. "I am a butcher, of course."

They drag Marick's shell into an alley. In the night bazaar's bustle, no one notices. Hester grabs the booth's batik fabric and drapes it over the ground. Shayna is a good butcher, well-practiced and quick, skilled at separating muscle from skin and meat from bone. The waxed batik absorbs the blood in brown-bordered swirls.

Shayna cuts, and Hester sorts the pieces. Hester lays Marick's heart in the pile for the vulture breeders. It is soft and round like a ripe mango on a plate, plum-red as an amethyst, tattered where the asp ripped through the flesh.

As the heart drips onto the batik, Hester sees maybe there is another path to freedom, one she never considered before Marick transformed. How she could leave behind the mass of bodies— the heralds, the upholsterers, the weavers, the potmakers, the herbalists, the papyrus-rollers, the inksetters—all the close, warm mammalian musks, the raised voices, the songs and tambourines. How she could slip beneath the gates, slither into the desert, the sand burning her belly into hard scales; her tongue flickering, testing the air. Some irresistible pull inside knows exactly where lies the ocean she has never seen, beating on a far shore. Her flesh feels heavy and cumbersome, and she thinks she could shake it loose, leave it behind to mummify in the heat and sand.

If this other path will work for her.

Hester saves Marick's heart carefully, wrapped tight in stained batik until the blood no longer soaks through. They sell the meat and bones to the vendors, but the skin they burn at Shayna's bower on the Street of Butchers. Its wetness makes the fire smoke and sputter.

"I can hide you for tonight, but you'll have to leave tomorrow,"

Shayna says as they wash up at home. "We can slow down their investigation, but they will find you. There were witnesses. Someone will talk eventually."

"Yes, of course. I understand." Hester inhales Shayna's familiar licorice smell, and longing prickles down her back. If this path works for her, there will be no more sunside or moonside, no lovers to fear and tend to and worry over. There will be no night bazaar, because in the desert, everyone is a reptile. Asps are asps by day or night.

HESTER WAITS UNTIL SHAYNA sleeps before she draws her last gift in chalk on the doorjamb: two stones, a dead woman's eye, and an asp. *Find me at the wall where criminals are made to drink poison, and come alone.* Then she kisses her sleeping lover and their moonside baby, and she leaves.

At this hour, the night bazaar must be packing up. A few snakes and lizards skitter through the gutters. Hester follows them to the gouge in the sand where they have dug a hole beneath the wall. They slither and wriggle and just slip through. Overhead, ropes creak as the mummified corpses swing.

Before she can lose her courage, Hester unwraps Marick's heart, sliced into strips like a mango, her final hope on a wooden tray.

Hearts are eggs, she realized when Shayna slit open Marick's body and piled his organs on the stained batik. Hester wonders what will hatch from hers.

Hester eats it, piece by piece. If this fails, the police will find her. Her body will swing overhead with the rest, always within sight of the desert, but never able to go there.

The heart slides into her belly, easier than glair, and settles in the empty space which once held fear. The quivering in her bones becomes a violent shudder. A change is coming, churning her like a sandstorm. She slips and twists inside her own flesh, full to the brim, a straining wineskin, a sated leech, an egg about to burst.

It does not hurt much, the hatching, the shedding. No worse than picking off a scab. When it is over, she slides free onto her segmented belly, the sand warm, the wind drying her damp newborn back. Her tongue tests the air, and tastes water far to the west, beyond the husk of her old body, through the gouge beneath the wall.

Over the wall the bodies swing and creak on their ropes, but they are only shells, and the poison rests between her teeth now, a gift for those she chooses to kiss. Oasis shrinks toy-like under her unblinking reptilian gaze. It is a nest, a golden pot with an amethyst lid, trapping asps until the music plays, but it cannot hold her anymore. All over the city, people pitch and turn inside themselves, sliding against the smooth walls of their prison, but only a few buck against the shell and break it.

But the desert is a city too, vaster than Oasis, and the reptiles are its people. Hester tastes them on the wind. Blood and incense, jasmine and mango, they call to her, all the ones who went before, the peasants and merchants, the old women and the young, the Emperor and Marick all, now fully themselves, unchanging day or night. Their prints erase the footsteps trailing into Oasis. Their bodies are arrows which point to the sea. They are waiting for her. It is almost time to go.

Hester waits beside her cooling body until sunrise breaks upon the city. Oasis turns over in its old familiar rhythm. Moonside lovers kiss and part. Footsteps hurry from house to house, and chalk symbols are found and read and quickly erased. And then, for the first time sunside, Hester sees her: Shayna the moonside butcher, come to unseam her body.

Hester knows Shayna will sell the parts piece by piece, a last providence for her Oasis family. A family can live for a month on the price a human body would fetch. Her hair will go to the weavers, her bones to feed the lemon tree groves, her fat to fuel the lamps, everything given back to the city that bore her.

Except her heart.

Shayna saves it in the same scrap of bloodstained batik that once held Marick's. Hester hopes it will be enough.

But now, the part of her that cannot be bought or sold slips beneath the wall, tastes the distant water, and goes to find it.

As a young teen, I first ran across Ursula Le Guin's work in a science fiction anthology at the public library. That story was "The Matter of Seggri," a novelette that explored the anthropological consequences of extreme gender segregation on a planet where three women are born for every two men. "The Night Bazaar for Women Becoming Reptiles" is my tribute to what that story evoked in me, especially in how changing expectations of gender and sexual orientation may play out on the stage of a self-contained society, and how these expectations can be both freeing and constricting.

The Wake

JAMES MAPES

AT THE START OF my journey west, a little god in a stone spire told me I'd be witness to three heralds of a great change.

I found the first in a city of ancient, stepped pyramids. The citizens there were being tormented by their protector god, a hawk-being dwelling in the tallest tower. Instead of giving them good harvests and healthy children, it was scattering locusts on their fields. I passed far around the city, not daring to walk its empty, dusty streets.

A week later, I came to a small settlement carved out of a colossal chunk of granite, the only stone in sight on a vast, yellow plain. The people were all mute. Their elder wrote in ochre on the stone, explaining to me that the wind had taken both their god and their voices as it tore across the grass. They stared hard at me, suspicious, and I moved on quickly, camping a few miles down the road.

Finally, I reached the edge of the Crescent Sea, and found myself in need of a boat.

By the plume of their cooking fire against the morning sky,

I found a homestead a couple of miles up the coast. The three women who lived there had several boats pulled up on the rocky shore not far from their house. The biggest woman bargained with me for the smallest boat, making no effort to hide that she wanted to cheat me; if I was so desperate to go north, then it would cost more than my horse and my last coins to do so. In the end, though, the smaller of her wives emerged from the shadows of their home and whispered in her ear. At this, she softened and agreed to the trade, even leaving me with two little coppers in my purse. She also gave me a bag of salt and three good nectarines to speed my sailing. I thanked all three of them, smiled at the small one, and said goodbye to my horse.

My new purchase was a battered little dinghy, sorely in need of pitch and paint. Despite this, I judged it ready for a day's sailing to the City of Song.

Before I set sail, I built a fire to make my offering to Numos of the Crescent Sea—trying to ignore the homesteaders peeking over the little cliff behind me as I did.

First, the salt, and the miracle of Numos: when I emptied the bag into the fire, the salt burst into a weak cloud of green and blue flame, sizzling like the waves. The effect was somewhat less than I remembered, but the sign was clear.

I stood and faced the water.

"Numos!" I called out. "Lord of this great sea! I have always been grateful to you. Many years ago, far to the east where the river Iron meets your waters, I slipped and fell into you. You plucked me from your waves and put me back on my boat. Please accept this gift, and give me safe passage!" And then I cast the nectarines, one by one, into the water. I waited to see if one of the god's servants would reply. The Sea God left me waiting, and doubt began to gnaw at my stomach.

"He's been sluggish of late," the big woman called over the hill. "Pay it no mind." I waved to her as she ambled away. I felt the stirrings of misgiving, but there was nothing I could do but go on.

I kicked sand over my fire, slung my pack into the dinghy,

then pushed it out into the Crescent Sea. I rowed out a little ways, bumping over the lapping waves, then shipped the oars and raised the little patch of sail. Soon I caught a cold, fast wind that sent me skimming across the water to the northwest.

I found myself unable to relax, especially when I lost sight of land. The slapping of the waves against my boat's hull carried a strange rhythm—or maybe I was still smarting at the god's silence? When the gods no longer speak to us, I thought, there would surely be trouble on the horizon.

It didn't take long for me to curse how right I was. As the sun rose towards its apex, clouds rolled in from the south to block its rays, turning the whole sea gray.

I leaned out over the gunwale. "Were they not good nectarines?" I asked the water. But the sea did not reply; I heard only the creaking of the mast and the staggered slaps of the waves against the hull. I flipped the last two coins in my purse, a pair of little copper sparks, into the waves.

But the storm still came. The clouds darkened like ink spilled across paper, and the little waves of the sea shattered into dips and swells. The lands I'd marched across for months were far out of sight, but I'd not yet neared the rocky peninsula to the north and west; all around me was water, growing ever darker.

Then the rain arrived, and the wind turned.

"Green-bearded bastard," I swore as I fought to get the sail down. Crosswinds battled around me, catching the jib and swinging it at me.

The icy rain came harder and harder as I fought the sail and battened down the oars; by the time I was done, the wind had caught the vessel and turned me about. It was no use, I thought. All I could do was get through it.

I broke out my last rations: half a piece of hardtack, almost impossible to chew, and a warming sip from my flask, that glowing liquor I'd been given in the Valley of Light by their local priest. It restored some strength to me.

I tipped the last bit of it over the side, too, just in case, and watched it glimmer as it flowed down into the depths. "Don't bother me anymore, you brine-headed fish-herder," I said. "I've had enough for one day."

Still nothing—no fish, no otter, no seabird. Did Numos even know I was here, I wondered? I wished I'd saved at least one nectarine for myself.

The air became charged, as though I'd be struck by lightning at any second. I bent myself against the wind, my hands clenching on the tiller against the force of the current.

As the storm grew, I felt a coldness in my heart, totally separate from the rain and water pelting me. It wasn't just the weather, but the mindlessness of its fury, as though nothing I did meant anything to it.

The waves grew higher and the rain colder. I do not know how long I fought the sea—I could only concentrate on riding out each wave and pushing my boat into each crest.

Time passed, and I felt my strength flag. Suddenly, a great wave reached up and over my bow, throwing me off the tiller. I made a wild lunge at it as the boat careened. "Go on, salt-sucker!" I yelled into the wind. "Bring me down to see you! I'll kick off your frigid blue balls!" My words flew away, lost in the spray. I got ahold of the wooden handle and threw my full weight against it, bringing my boat around into the waves.

Then, in the distance, I saw the impossible. The water was rising up out of the sea, a dozen whirlpools coalescing into spinning funnels reaching up into the sky.

My whole body felt like a rope about to snap. "So, you are here," I muttered between grinding teeth. "And you're trying to kill me." But why would the gods, great and small, bring me this far just to drown me?

I stood up in my boat before the whirling spires and cupped my hands to my mouth. "Not today, you bastard!"

I found myself in a canyon of water, walls of foaming brine looming above me, threatening to drop on my head. My muscles shook with exhaustion as I steered my craft around and through their impossible geographies, holding tight to the tiller, eyes narrowed against the icy rain, hating Numos with all my heart.

Suddenly, a terrible noise tore forth from the depths of the water, shaking my bones. The whole surface of the sea vibrated with tiny spikes as the scream continued—and then, just as suddenly, it cut off.

All around me, the mountains of water began to collapse. I struggled to turn my boat, but my arms wouldn't obey. The tiller was like a stone, unmovable. The Lord of the Crescent Sea had me at last.

Then the canyon before me opened up, the walls of water to either side falling away, and I saw a glimmer of gray clouds above. I willed myself to hold fast, clinging to the tiller with whatever iron I had left in me.

When the great wave hit me, it lifted my little boat and carried both of us out into the open in a wild and twisting rush. My little craft stayed true and upright, and I held the course. After minutes, days, years, the wave set us smoothly down with a crash on a calm sea.

I crumpled against the tiller of my boat, legs splayed in the puddle of cold saltwater that pooled in the bilge. Next time, I resolved, I'd give the god of the sea at least four nectarines—and perhaps an apple or two as well.

I felt my eyelids close. The last thing I saw was a single ray of sun shining down out of the clouds.

THE MAST SWUNG AGAINST the blue sky like a slow metronome.

I sat up, and the sea around me was calm. I saw a bird flying in the distance; the storm was like a dream, already gone.

Someone was peeking at me over the gunwale of my boat: the big brown eyes and water-slicked head of a sea otter.

"Go tell your master I am still alive," I mumbled, chapped lips not forming the words quite correctly. "And find out if I should thank him."

The otter cocked its head and slipped away into the sea.

I scanned the horizon and saw, in the hazy distance, the dark rearing of land.

Every muscle screamed as I got the sail back up and the rudder turned. Once I did, the wind was brisk, and I made good progress. Assuming I had only dozed a few hours and it was late afternoon, I was headed west, still, and that rocky mount was the peninsula that shaped this arm of the Crescent Sea. If so, I hoped I could find a fishing village or some other harbor; I had nothing left to offer Numos for another day's sailing.

It was not long until I spotted a village on the shore among the twisted, stunted trees. Out in front was a single dock made of big, thick trunks, the villagers' boats beached on the rocks behind it. I brought my dinghy in with hands that were beginning to shake.

At the end of the dock were three people in coarse clothing, tunics dyed dark blue. They sat on the rough wood, feet dangling over the side, a bottle between them. As my boat approached, they stared at me in open wonder.

One of them, an older woman, spoke to me as I came closer; her words sounded like water running across stones.

"I don't understand, I am from far away," I called back in the common tongue. "What is this village?"

"Doomed," the woman answered, accent heavy, then took a great swig from the bottle. The boy with them caught my line as I tossed it, hauled my craft in, and made it fast to the dock. I saw him make a sign with his hands at the rope, probably the start of some ritual dedicated to the village's god, but then the older woman gave his hands a slap. He looked down.

"You were out there when it happened?" the younger of the two women asked me. She had a curious accent, not like people to the east; the words of the common speech were curved in her mouth.

"I was," I said. "I was caught in the storm as I sailed from the eastern shore this morning. I am Aul Ferria, a traveler."

"Anka," the younger woman said, indicating the older woman.

"And I am Ketevan." She peered down at me from her perch on the dock. "Do you need a hand?"

"Perhaps more than that, my lady." I held up both hands to her, and she braced herself against the timbers and hauled me up like a net full of fish. As she let go, I collapsed to the dock, my legs giving out beneath me.

"You'll have to excuse me," I said, "The seas were a bit rough, here and there." They nodded, wary, and I opted to stay seated.

The pier ran a dozen paces to the wharf, a stout bulwark of stone along this short stretch of rocky coast. A half dozen little structures related to the fishing trade made up the first row of buildings, all made of the same dark gray stone. Beyond those was a great hall in the middle of a square, mostly stone but finished with a tall timber roof. Its high windows glowed with firelight, and I thought I could hear mournful singing within. A funeral? Then what were these three doing out here?

"Where come from?" the older one, Anka, asked, tripping over the words.

"Far to the east. But please—do you have a god of this village? I should offer something if I'm coming ashore."

The lad, still unintroduced, choked. Ketevan shot him a look, then said to me by way of explanation, "Our only god was Numos."

"Well, pardon my offense," I said, "but he gave me a hard time of it just to get across this bit of water—and that was after taking my damned fruit and coin, can you believe it?"

Ketevan and the boy looked at their elder, who stared at me, cold and disbelieving; it was clear I'd said the wrong thing.

"Maybe he doesn't know," Ketevan said to her companions. She turned back to me. "That wasn't just a storm, Aul Ferria of the East. The god Numos died today."

A cold fist gripped my heart.

"Impossible," I said. "The sea spans a dozen countries."

"The fish brought word to our priest at dawn that the god lay dying," she replied. "We laid up the ships and gathered in prayer on this dock. The storm almost claimed us all."

"Got the priest," the boy added, and the two women shot him withering looks.

"Now the rest of them sit around that damned fire in the hall and throw salt into the flames, but it no longer burns."

"It doesn't burn?" I repeated, wondering if she had misspoken.

"It just sits there in the embers. We'll have no salt left in the village by nightfall if the idiots carry on. And then what?"

And these three were sick of it, I gathered, given the bottle sitting there on the dock beside them.

I swallowed, trying to lift the weight in my chest, but I only found it heavier. "Then I truly have been brought here," I said to them. "I have a tale to share with your people."

"They'll curse you back out into the sea, the mood they're in," Ketevan replied.

"Then I will tell you, and you will figure out how to tell them." I leaned back against the old timber posts of the dock, feeling the chill breeze through my still-damp clothes. "I come from a valley high in the hills above the sea—this same sea. A strong river ran through my village; both it and its god were called Iron. Half a year ago, that changed. There is still a river, of sorts, but the god Iron is dead. It started with a great flood, washing away half my people; as Iron died, the river ran rust-red with its blood. Our own priest stepped into the flow and was carried away—perhaps the way yours was."

I broke off, my throat burning. Ketevan barked a string of commands to the nameless boy, who got me a dipper of water from a barrel at the end of the dock. The water stung my lips at first, but it cooled me all the way down my chest, lightening my heart.

"Thank you," I told him. For the briefest moment, his eyes—a strange, deep blue—met mine. He took the dipper back to the barrel, then disappeared into the village, towards the mournful singing and flickering lights of the great hall, leaving me with the two women.

"I do not know what is happening to our gods," I continued. "I buried the bodies of my kin and my friends, and I watched the ones who were left waste away, standing in the shallows of the river, holding their fish baskets and singing to a dead god. Without Iron, the fish wouldn't listen. Our crops died, my people starved, and our village broke apart. So take my warning: do not look to Numos. He is gone. No one will answer you with a favorable tide, nor send fish to your nets. Never again will this sea care for you. And if your people are like mine, then soon they will be talking of other gods. Some who survived left to find other valleys, other rivers where a god would take them in. But now . . . if the gods are all dying, one after another, what refuge remains?"

"We have endured the god's displeasure before," Ketevan said, quietly, "but never his indifference. I do not know what we will do."

"You will live," I replied. "That's all you can do."

She nodded back, her mouth tight.

"And you?" Anka asked me.

"I will continue on to the City of Song in the north and tell my tales there."

Anka half turned to Ketevan and placed her hand on the younger woman's shoulder. She said something in their own language, and Ketevan smiled. Then Anka nodded to me and left, stomping her way up the dock and into the village.

"What did she say?" I asked.

"She thinks there must be some little god following you, guiding your footsteps—otherwise, how could you come to us?"

I thought of the path through the maelstrom and said nothing.

She added, glowering, "Anka is going to tell the village what you told us. We will see how the fools take it." She cast a glare towards the shore, and said, "Ah, he comes."

The boy was staggering down the dock with a big basket crooked up into one armpit and a stout barrel under the other. He came to me first, laying the basket across my legs, then took the barrel to Ketevan.

Inside the basket was a pair of worn, blue-dyed trousers and a shirt—clothes that were wonderfully, beautifully dry. Beneath that were provisions: a loaf of hard, brown bread, cheese wrapped in cloth, some sort of smoked fish, and two good apples.

It took a moment before I could speak. "From the bottom of my heart, thank you."

"We could hardly do less," Ketevan said, then added, "I will see to your boat. Hurry up and change."

"Ah." I shucked off my shirt and creaked to my feet, then paused before taking off my pants.

"Don't worry, traveler," Ketevan added with a wink, "you're not the first half-drowned fish I've seen." Then she jumped down into my boat and started bailing out the water with the old bowl I kept there, facing away from the shore. I changed.

Then, moving stiffly, I went to the boy. He was filling three wooden mugs from the barrel.

"You didn't bring enough," I said gently. "My lady, would you pass me up that bag?" Ketevan followed my finger and tossed up my pack. From it, I withdrew my own cup, a hollowed-out half of a ram's horn, and held it out to the boy. He filled it.

"We will not forget them simply because they are gone," I said to him, and he nodded. We joined hands over the fourth cup, and Ketevan stopped to watch as we sent the ale over the edge of the dock and down into the water. We were all silent, watching the water, but the scant foam from the beer disappeared with no sign or remark.

The boy passed around the other three cups. We raised them to each other and drank a little, the dark, salty ale going down quietly. After a moment, Ketevan went back to fussing over my boat.

As she worked, the sky beyond her caught fire in great swathes of purple and red. As it began to darken, she pulled the rope out of the pulleys leading from the end of the jib to the top of the little mast and showed me a portion. The stiff, old rope was almost worn through, a moment away from snapping. She smiled up at me and said, "Your little god," then vaulted back onto the dock and trotted off towards one of the other boats.

I found myself alone with the boy.

"What's your name?" I asked.

His face was turned to the water. "I do not want to say, sir."

After a long moment, I said, "In my language, my name honors my village and our river." The boy met my eyes and I knew I had guessed rightly. "When Iron left, those of us who remained found my name uncomfortable. Sometimes, I was made to feel like I was . . . responsible, somehow. Perhaps that's why I had to leave."

In the silence that followed, I took a long drink of ale, then asked, "So what will you do now, my nameless friend?"

"I do not know," he said, his voice almost a whisper.

I stretched out my creaking bones, then filled my cup from the barrel. The boy's cup sat next to it, untouched after the toast; I topped it off and handed it to him.

"Well, drink up, lad, for your namesake if not for you. The dead must have a wake. And if you have nothing else to do in the morning," I added, "then sail with me and we'll brave the next storm together. Maybe we can find you a new name in the north."

The boy kept looking down, but I saw his back straighten, and he nodded. Then, meeting my eyes again, he took the cup from me and struck it against mine, and together we drank them dry.

Ketevan came back with a good, stout rope, wound it through the pulleys, and tied it off to the stay. Then she sat on the edge of the dock with us, and we watched the smaller, rosy moon—the Trickster's Eye, we called it back home—rise over the water. We filled our cups, one for each of us and a fourth for the dead, and stayed on the dock until the new tide came in with the morning.

I was born in Portland and have lived here my whole life. Ursula K. Le Guin is one of our greatest sources of pride. She changed how I saw my city when I read about its many forms in The Lathe of Heaven. *This story is, admittedly, more in the Earthsea vein. I miss her.*

Black as Thread

JESSIE KWAK

JILLI IS SHREDDING DISCARDED headscarves, the gauzy strips curling in along the tear like paper at the edge of a flame. Her lap is heavy with long ribbons of silk dyed lavender and pomegranate and sunshine and lake, the finer ones shot through with iridescent strands of gold. These strands Jilli plucks out and tucks inside a pouch in her bodice. Close to her heart.

The threads of gold aren't much, but nothing is much, these days.

She's singing as she stitches the ribbons end-to-end, singing as her fingers roll the endless strips to twist them tight and smooth, singing as she winds the strands into balls.

The Navu occupiers would forbid these songs if they knew what they were, but the officer examining the wares in the family shoe shop gives Jilli only a passing glance. She tucks her feet beneath her stool, the wooden soles of her shoes clacking against the tile floor.

In her hands, the ball of ribbon breathes in her song, deep and fast and alive.

She'll weave it into a tough, shimmering fabric to serve as the uppers of the shoes her brother Desh cobbles—leather is rationed, like most things, and Jilli and Desh are experimenting with cork and wool and silk.

And shoes are flying off the shelves, as Cazhitlani citizens tend to save their ration chits for rarer goods. Their creations of cork and wood and woven ribbons have been written up breathlessly in the society papers; they've had four orders just this week from women planning their daughters' coming out balls.

Their shoes for men are equally popular, quilted wooden-soled boots as sturdy as the ones Desh used to create out of leather, Jilli's decorative stitching echoing the style of leather carving that had been popular before the Navu invaded. Other cobblers stole her and Desh's quilted-wool-and-wood style almost as soon as the first boots were on display in the window, but Jilli's seen them, the stitches skittering like drunken mouse tracks, unevenly spaced and wayward. Functional, she'll give them that, but Jilli, she'll toss out the entire day's work if she finds a stitch out of place.

The Navu officer in his shop is admiring a pair of boots, though frowning at the underslung heel. "Doesn't that make it difficult to walk?"

"It's the northern style. Riders prefer them." Desh turns on his own underslung heel, executing an abbreviated dance step in the tiny space of his shop, his back-step cut short before a display case. "Dancers, too."

The Navu officer laughs. All the Navu seem to find Cazhitlani fashion and showmanship amusing. Jilli smiles at his back, appreciating his underestimation of her brother.

"I need them for a ball. Don't you have anything less—" The officer waves a hand foppishly.

"Bold?" Desh is used to this question from Navus. Dirt brown and stone gray are the colors of choice in the home country, it seems. Jilli's head hurts to think of the utilitarian deadness.

"For you, of course. I can make something special." Desh turns one of the boots over in his hands, pursing his lips as though thinking over the color scheme.

But Jilli knows what he's thinking. And in the split second his brown eyes meet hers, she screams in her mind for him to send the officer away.

"Jilli, the green wool, please?"

Jilli sets her work aside, careful not to let it tangle, then plucks the pile of green wool scraps off the shelf behind the counter. This fabric had been a nobleman's discarded coat, before Desh found it in an alley trash heap and picked apart the seams.

"Green is a good color. Subdued and professional, but enough to still catch some attention, yes?" Desh winks at the officer. "For the ladies at the ball to know you've got some hidden passion of your own?"

A smile flickers at the corner of the officer's mouth before he tamps it back down; Desh has him. With long brown fingers, Desh fishes through a drawer for a card of brilliant red buttons carved from the plastic of discarded toothbrush handles.

In Cazhitlani color lore, green can be a pleasant surprise, an unwelcome visitor, or a clueless person—good or bad, green is always unexpected. Fleck green with red like a bloodstone, and you have an indicator of unexpected violence. A warning sign to stay away from this one.

Though Jilli suspects Desh is not going to be content only providing a warning.

"A pop of color on the green, of course, or no Cazhitlani debutante will give you a second look," Desh says with a smile. The officer doesn't even notice he's nodding along. "But I promise, we'll keep the embroidery plain. No unnecessary flourishes."

Desh catches her eye while the officer brushes a finger over the buttons, and Jilli's heart sinks. She's singing protection into the ball of yarn meant for Cazhitlani ladies' shoes, but her magic can cut both ways. At a glance, the quilting on the officer's shoes will look precise and professional. But just as the color scheme of these boots contain a warning, every stitch will contain a curse.

The officer shakes her brother's hand.

Fear flutters in Jilli's chest.

It STARTED FAR AWAY, border towns popping inside out like kernels of corn in the searing heat of the passing Navu armies. Towns Jilli had never heard of filled the morning newspapers, seasoning the day's conversation as everyone who walked into the shop suddenly recalled a distant family connection in the border region.

Everyone had agreed the war would advance no farther, but Jilli had changed her charms. Spells for dancing grace and riding prowess were for times of peace. What the people of Cazhitlan needed now was protection.

When the rations started, it was an unexpected boon for those who could adapt to new materials, like Jilli and Desh—and also for Jilli's magic.

She'd never tried to charm headscarves before. Jilli's theory is, once a fabric is made, the magic of the maker is locked in so tight that another's charms can find no purchase—she can't even change her own charms once a piece is done. But unravelling unspells, and the silk ribbon has been an amazing medium for her work. She can feel her songs felting into the fibers of the ribbons as she rolls them in her moist palms.

It's similar with her stitching. Embroidering spells into leather is tough work for fingers and mind, and Jilli's songs have always chafed reluctantly against the tough hides. Wool, though, is a different story.

Tonight she's embroidering by candlelight in the back of the shop, well after midnight, and she should be exhausted, but the dark sharpness of cursing magic scrapes her alert with every syllable. Her fingertips are raw with pinpricks and the black thread she's using is flecked with her blood, though of course it doesn't show. Jilli's skilled with a needle, but curse magic seeks blood. It doesn't matter how careful she is, how slowly she works, how sturdy her thimble. The needle takes a nip when it's thirsty.

Jilli takes a break to stretch her hands while Desh shapes

the sole on his workbench, a delicate lick of blade against wood, butter-gold curls scattering on the floor.

Her little brother's hands are kissed by the gods. If it needs made, Desh will make it, the tools of his craft delving insatiably into his materials in a way that is both poetic and unsettling. One summer their mother mentioned they needed candles, and Desh did them up on a whim that afternoon with an iridescent wax blend that shifted and bloomed into the shape of a rose as it melted.

He finds passion in every art he tries. Jilli may not find pleasure in the craft the same as him, but she appreciates a job done well and a roof over their heads.

When she was younger she was jealous at the ease with which her brother picked up new art forms, but with his genius comes an insatiable restlessness she doesn't share. Before war came to the capital, Desh had been a good night's sleep away from growing bored with cobbling, Jilli, a breath away from watching her livelihood sift out from beneath her like sand in the tide. She'd felt it in her bones, in that slow cave-in of her chest whenever she watched the shop and wondered where he'd disappeared to, which arcane art he'd come home infatuated with. Hoping he was just out bedding some boy or girl, distracted by caramel-sticky sex and not the sultry new businesses of tailoring or window-painting.

Jilli's not a fool; she'd been interviewing replacements for Desh on the side. But she couldn't imagine a world where she shared the family shop with someone who wasn't family.

Tonight Desh draws the blade across wood, and a shaving so translucent it could be a beetle's wing drifts to land on the toe of Jilli's slipper. His tongue darts up to catch a bead of sweat on his upper lip before it falls onto the sole he's shaping. He's grinning.

Jilli would never count the war a blessing, of course, not even with the society paper write-ups and the rapidly growing stash of coins she has hidden in a thick rationed-leather pouch under the hearthstones of the cookstove. But for the first time in months her brother is truly captivated by his job.

Her raw fingers cramp against the thin sharp needle as it dips in and out of the wool, marrying coat-wool to scavenged batting to felt, and Desh looks up as her song falters.

"How goes the work?" he asks.

This magic is wrong, she wants to say, but in actuality she's finished nearly an entire boot in one sitting, her stitches more precise than ever, her patterns more intricate and inspired.

"It's going well," she says.

He frowns at her. "You're bleeding."

The needle's pricked her again. Jilli's impulse is to suck the blood from her finger before it gets to the fabric, but she slides the thread through her fingers instead. Best give the curse song what it wants.

"What if the Navu find out?" Jilli asks.

"Find out what? They don't even believe in fashion, why would they believe in magic?" Desh winks, but his cheerfulness fades as he looks at her. He sets his blade aside. "Let's call it a night."

Jilli is exhausted, her vision watery with candlelight, her throat raw from curse songs, her fingers aching—but she doesn't want to stop. There's something intoxicating about this magic, how easy it is to weave and felt and stitch. For the first time in her life, Jilli realizes giddily, she's found a craft that comes as easily to her as everything else seems to come to her brother.

But she lets Desh take the glittering needle from her and set the fabric gently aside, pull her to her feet and give her a hug.

"We're doing important work," he says, his voice soft in her ear. "But you need to rest."

His voice sounds far away, echoing like a pebble thrown down a well.

THE NAVU OFFICER WHO commissioned the green boots with the red buttons will die a week after he picks them up, thrown by his horse. Later in the month, a Navu lieutenant will choke to death on a lump of potato while wearing his gray-and-lavender house slippers. A few days after that, a Navu general will be stomping back and forth in her black wool boots with the gold buttons, berating her secretary for a misplaced letter, when she'll suddenly clutch her chest, her heart stuttering to a stop.

And Jilli will feel it when every one of them dies.

One success leads to another, and desire for Jilli and Desh's gorgeous shoes spreads like wildfire through the ranks of the occupiers. Greens and blues and purples scavenged from discarded coats, always quilted in black thread—it's become their signature, and it hides the dark stains of magic.

This morning, Jilli enters the shop and sets a new pair of riding boots—ruddy brown with emerald-green buttons—on the counter. She feels curses tugging sticky against her fingertips as she pulls her hand away. She's been up all night but feels exhilarated and light. This is what it's like to find passion in a craft.

Where the first order brought about dread, Jilli's excitement grows with every new one Desh brings her: *This one's a colonel, Jilli, this one's an intelligence officer!* With each pair, Jilli's needle must bite deeper and deeper to find blood past the callused scars of her fingertips. With each pair, the gleam in her brother's eyes dims, and now he's gnawing his lip, staring after the customer who's just exited the shop. Jilli caught only a glimpse of a Navu officer's gray in the broad shoulders as the door shut behind him.

"Another order?" She leans in, hungry. "Who is it this time?"

Her brother doesn't quite meet her gaze. "It can wait," Desh says.

"He looked important. What did he ask for?" Five gold arrowheads on his sleeve—she's never seen a Navu officer with so many. She wants to tell herself it's patriotic duty surging beneath her ribs, not eager pride. Felling such a man would be a powerful blow for the Cazhitlani resistance.

Felling such a man would be such a showcase for my art.

Her brother is frowning at her. When did his brown eyes lose their spark of gold?

"Desh—"

"We're backed up. I have half a dozen pairs of dancing shoes to make first. Can you weave the uppers today? We'll talk about the new order later." His voice is carefully distant; a hand squeezes her heart.

Jilli nods and turns to her pile of headscarves waiting to be shredded, but she suspects before she even starts what will happen. She remembers the words to the songs, but they stick in her throat. She shreds the colorful silk but the edges singe black; she rolls them in her palms but the nervous sweat muddies and dulls the colors.

She almost doesn't care. More interesting, more complicated, more powerful work calls to her. She doesn't remember why singing protections into ribbons used to be satisfying.

When she sets her newest ribbon-yarn ball beside those she rolled a month ago, anyone can see it's a sullen and sickly thing. Jilli stands suddenly, shreds of headscarves cascading from her lap, tumbling to the tile floor in a rainbow snarl. She should clean them up, but she's too afraid to touch the impressionable fibers any more than she already has. She tucks the newest ball in a pocket where its surly magic can't rub off on anything else.

"I'm going to bed," she tells Desh, who's frowning at the rainbow ribbons at her feet.

But she doesn't sleep. She listens to him in the shop below, the constant bell of the door opening, the clack of wooden heels, his forced laughter. After all these years of waiting for him, alone in the shoe shop while he ran off to follow some other passion, she's finally had a taste of what he's found so seductive. And now he wants her to give it up?

At least it's not taking her away from the shop, she thinks, lying awake and listening to her brother chatting with a customer below. It's not taking her away from him.

She's not sleeping—she really doesn't need to sleep much these days—so finally, right before closing, she thinks she'll go see him again. Help with things. Apologize. She pauses inside their family home, a hand on the door that leads to the storefront; she can hear voices inside, her brother talking to the plumber next door.

"After coming out season, we're thinking we may close the shop for a few weeks," Desh is saying. "Take some time to rest. We've both been working nights."

The door handle feels hot under her hand—too hot, callused fingertips searing into now-soft iron, and she pulls her hand away with a hiss of pain. *We're* thinking? Rage spikes in Jilli's heart, because for all his *wes*, Desh has certainly not discussed plans to close up shop with her.

When she was making them a bored living at her craft, it gave her brother leave to wander. But the minute she finds a passion of her own, he can't handle the responsibility of holding down the shop?

She backs away from the steaming door handle and flees back to her room, pretending to sleep as her brother finishes closing up for the evening, as he cooks dinner, as he calls her name gently at her door.

And long after he's gone to bed, she rises. She lights a candle, stokes up the fire in the workshop.

Tonight Jilli drapes her brother's favorite vest—the vest he wears every day—across her lap and threads a needle. Tonight she sings a song of binding, to keep her brother Desh close, keep him safe, keep him from straying somewhere out of her reach.

Keep him tied to the shop he so desperately wants to leave.

She's thought of this before, before the war came to the capital. Plenty of men and women have hinted to her that they would pay good money for such a charm for their partners, but she's always said no. Now she wonders how much of that was out of fear that her skill wouldn't rise to the task. After all, before she began stitching curses into the shoes of Navu officers, she only felt comfortable with the lightest of protection charms.

Now, though, she knows her power is strong. She's proud of it.

Her plan is to embellish the embroidered mandala of protection she stitched years ago on the pocket of Desh's vest. Just a touch of new charm in among the old. She makes the first stitch boldly, the second with gusto, then gasps at the third. This sort of charm should need no blood, but the needle bit deeper than ever, and the tip of her index finger glistens black as thread in the candlelight.

She darts the finger into her mouth, sucking it clean as she's done a hundred times before, but her blood doesn't taste like its usual warm metal. It tastes bitter and is as dark as tar.

When she pulls her finger back to frown at the blood, astonished at the taste, a single drop falls onto the heart of the mandala. The fibers soak the magic up thirstily—she can feel it spreading fast and eager—and to her fascination, the colorful threads of the mandala turn black. An old maker's charm transformed in a heartbeat by her power.

Who knew she could do this?

That simple Jilli's art could be so powerful?

It feels amazing, this power. The knowledge that she can force such a change fills her with pride and curiosity—what else could she accomplish? How much more could her power grow?

Jilli brushes her pricked finger over the mandala, unable to feel the raised threads through her calluses though she can feel the thrum of the dark magic sharp and clear.

When he puts this on he will stay with you he will never want to leave again he will stay.

She knows it, because now she can feel the whole house—all the shop—like it's part of her bones. She feels it when her brother wakes, when he smells the smoke of her fire and leaves his bed, the impression of his slippered feet on the stairs.

Felt-soled slippers, with uppers she knit for him in love, leave soothing traces with every step.

"Jilli?" Desh calls. "Are you up here?"

Jilli throws his vest into the fire before she can think twice. She tosses the ball of muddy yarn in after, followed by her spool of black thread, and watches the flames leap sickly green and angry with magic until they become golden once more and the fabric is a sooty gray husk, collapsing gently over the coals.

"Jilli?" Desh is kneeling in front of her, his smooth hands slipping into hers, his frown deepening as he feels the jagged calluses on her fingers and turns her fingers over to see. "Jilli, come to bed."

"I think we should close the shop after the coming out season," Jilli says. "For a few weeks, at least. We can talk about what to do next."

"'Next?'" Desh's brow furrows. "This shop is your life."

Jilli wraps her arms around his neck.

"No," she says. "It's not."

I've always loved the way Le Guin's stories focus on the small details and overlooked people in a society. Fantasy as a genre is so often centered around traditionally powerful roles like queens and generals, but Le Guin's work put a spotlight on everyday people, household objects, women's work. In this story, I took inspiration from her to explore how something as overlooked as textile arts and frivolous as fashion could turn the tide of a war.

A Woven Womb

C.A. McDONALD

GYNDRE WATCHED AVDRA'S EXPRESSION shift from excitement to eagerness as she entered the grove. The brightness in her friend's ruby eyes sent a thrill of fear down the Weaver's spine; in the past, Gyndre had seen Avdra plunge headlong into decisions without fully weighing the consequences. It was how, as a child, Avdra had broken her leg jumping from the cliffs above the City. Gyndre had nearly followed her and done so herself. Avdra's enthusiasm was a storm one should feel pleased to survive intact.

Speaker Omus loomed behind Avdra like a ghost, his face revealing all of the reservation his wife couldn't feel. Gyndre tried to meet his gaze, to gauge his mood on the eve of the Weaving, but Avdra forced herself into her line of sight, her beaming smile refusing to be ignored.

"I am ready," she gushed. "You were right, the fear did go away." Avdra had never really been afraid, not by Gyndre's assessment, but she had done a good job of feigning the obligatory anxiety of a soon-to-be-mother. Gyndre wished her closest friend could, just for a moment, grasp the enormity of what she was about to do, but it was a familiar, ever-futile wish.

"Are you ready?" Gyndre asked Omus. The Speaker gave a small smile, and his eyes darted to his wife. Seeing a Speaker, who could command the elements—to shout down violent storms, to stand at the foot of an avalanche and will it to rise back up a mountain—now nervously glance at his wife was startling.

"No, but Avdra is ready enough for me, I think." He laughed softly, but Gyndre could see the tension in him. The raw, real worry. Good. One of them needed to have their feet on the ground about the enormity of their undertaking. Gyndre had facilitated Weavings where both parents were naïve fools who came out the other side stumbling and half shattered by the experience, and that was before they had even attempted parenting.

"When do we start?" Avdra asked. A soft breeze lifted her wild red hair from her shoulders.

Gyndre patted her arm where her robe left her bare brown shoulder exposed to the evening air. "If the two of you are ready to begin, then so am I."

Avdra grabbed Omus's hand, and they walked deeper into the grove. Velvet shadows seemed to enfold them.

"Do you remember talking about this when were girls?" Avdra asked.

"Yes," Gyndre said, smiling.

"Will you have your own child someday?"

"It may sound blasphemous, but I feel like all the children I've helped Weave are all the children I'll ever need."

Omus made a scandalized laugh. Like all touched by magic, it was expected for Weavers to have children of their own, to pass their gifts on to the next generation. To not do so would be selfish to the highest degree—a deliberate, purposeful neglect of one's duty. Magic did not flow in the veins of even a tenth of the People, but it was the reason they thrived when others did not.

Yet it was strictly forbidden for Weavers to add any of themselves into the children they made with others. A child must have only two contributors, in order to ensure predictable results (though theoretically, any number of adults could create an offspring). If

Gyndre were to add even a drop of herself to the mix, the Weavers' Order would seek the child's destruction, the parents would be imprisoned, and she could very well be exiled.

This wasn't just academic fact. History was smattered intermittently with the results of multiple unions, some benign, some disastrous. The worst case in recent history, though long before Gyndre's time, had created a Speaker of such skill and nuance that he could commune with almost anything in the natural world, be it living or dead, and command it with a single word. He had been mad, claiming the land itself spoke of the need of balance, that the use of so much magic would have eventual consequences. His most egregious crime had been in rallying a coup against the Speaker's guild. The Temple had taken an even stronger stance against his kind after his execution.

THE TREES ON EITHER side of the path through the grove grew closer then widened apart as they entered the heart of the sacred woods where the ceremony would be performed. The temple's lights behind were all but swallowed by the darkness. Above, the obsidian bowl of the sky arched, star-studded and clear.

The ancient river stone of the Weaving ground was cold under Gyndre's bare feet. They positioned themselves in a rough triangle at the center of the clearing. The preparatory materials were ready for their use, in silver bowls on stands off to the side— salt from the Far Sea, ashes from the Burning Mountain, dried flowers from the temple garden, and incense carrying the salty tang of dragon blood. The aromas of the reagents never failed to excite her, even after so many Weavings. It was like drawing into her body the very scent of creation, opening the womb of the world.

"Be still," she said to Avdra and Omus, softly. She could see the anxiety in his eyes, and the anticipation held taut in Avdra's body. Gyndre let her robe fall to the ground and pool around her feet as she allowed her own thoughts to quiet.

The quietness of the moment settled in her soul—the sacred stillness that courted magic. She moved to the silver bowls and, one by one, smeared the contents across her breasts and belly. Stinging salt, rough ash, and perfumed petals clung to her naked skin as she moved back to form the triangle again, this time lifting her hands as she felt power begin to well from within.

Magic was a whisper of joy within her soul that became a chorus. As it rose within her, she felt it echo in all things, like a tide of unseen brightness creeping up along the trunks of the trees, in the roots of the grass, in the stone under her feet. The joy was the pleasure of pure being and wildest possibility, the sense that if she just reached out, she could hold the wonder of creation inside herself.

Omus and Avdra tapped into their own magic, and the power inside them harmonized with her own. She reached for their power, calling to it with open hands.

"Omus, son of Omlan and Sharus."

His magic flowed to her from the air around him, a strand of light the color of rain flecked with thunder clouds. She accepted it and could almost feel the different natures of the individuals who had contributed to him, winding it around her finger like it was a piece of woolen thread.

"Avdra, daughter of Gaven and Andrad."

Avdra's power joined Omus's, as yellow and bright as a dandelion head.

Their magic together lifted Gyndre up. She could taste Avdra's eagerness like lemon on her tongue. How badly she wanted a child. A daughter. All of that wildness and forward momentum enfleshed, separate from her, giving her space to breath for once. Avdra wanted a child like the possessed craved an exorcism.

The heaviness in Gyndre's gut was Omus's hesitance. It felt like a stone in her body, the weight of reluctance manifested. He was doing this for his wife and his wife alone. Gyndre had seen parents like him before—but she did not need his enthusiasm, only his power, and that he freely gave.

Words fell from her lips. The Weaver's cant, gently tugging more of the essence of Avdra and Omus into her hands.

A flash of memory seared her mind as she gathered their magic in her. Avdra, in the sun with Gyndre, both laughing as girls. Freckles on her nose, flowers woven into her hair. Gyndre could smell the warm grass beneath their young bodies, feel how utterly carefree they were. Soaring like a pair of hawks in an endless sky.

Omus's thoughts raced through the scene. The figments of Avdra and Gyndre shivered under the hand of a cold wind that hadn't been there in the past. His fear was deep. Deeper than the heaviness in Gyndre's stomach. As she pulled his magic from him, she found it woven into every fiber of his being. It was like tearing up a tree and finding every root touched with rot.

She could only do her best with what she had.

Gyndre began to speak the magic into a spool. Golden and fiery with Avdra's essence, bruised and bent by Omus's. Another memory—Avdra hurtling over the edge of the cliff to the clear pond below, shrieking in delight. Gyndre felt her fly. Felt the joy of her fall. The thrill. And then Omus's magic cut through the moment, entangling it with his own memories. Fear choked her. The memory changed, and Avdra fell against the rocks, dying in blood and pain and agony.

Gyndre shuddered. This was not normal. Avdra's and Omus's essences were so different, it was like making cloth of oil and water. The spool gathered and grew in her hands. Black and gold and crackling. Unstable. Gyndre took a deep breath. There was almost enough to begin, almost enough to cast the first threads and form a soul. She just had to keep going and hope she could force the magic into stability.

She was Avdra again. This time, a young woman, dancing by a fire. Drunk. A fond memory. But abandon turned to horror as fingers of smoldering coal erupted from the base of the flames and pulled Avdra apart, limb from limb.

What had happened to Omus to make him this way? She couldn't see, couldn't decipher his memories; his magic was so foreign to her. But the fear was everywhere, in every thought, in every moment he experienced. It curdled her stomach and brought bile to her throat as she tried to begin knitting the soul.

There was a shape, and then it slid apart. She felt Avdra's alarm, and then a cold wave of power from her husband. Avdra and Omus could feel flashes of Gyndre's experience, just as she could feel theirs, and now had to know something was amiss. Gyndre gasped and steadied herself. She tried again, refusing to panic. The threads of the soul formed a lattice in the air between them.

Yes! It stayed true. She didn't know if it was Avdra's or her own relief that filled her.

Gyndre drew on the spool in her hands, shaping the person before her. A daughter it would be, with deep, powerful magic in the vein of her mother. She would be the best Shaper in a generation. Wild. Free. Gyndre smiled. Avemus would be her name, and she would be all of the things her mother was, but her own incarnation of them, playful and . . .

The Weave frayed, and what could be, evaporated. The daughter would be terrified. A shell of a human, afraid to leave her home, afraid to speak, loathe to conflict. Her name was Omendra. She would be scared of her own magic and thus never use it fully, a great majesty left to waste. Terrified of herself, she would withdraw and harm herself or others. Omus's nature took all the fire from the girl and replaced it with cold ashes.

Gyndre wove, trying to keep the darkest parts of his nature from the girl and replacing them with more of Avdra.

She saw the child, running in a field, not with abandon, but terror from imagined demons. Cutting her little feet on brambles until the earth was slick with her blood. Torn apart from the inside. Hands clenched to control emotions that were not real. Insane. She became doomed to paradox.

Gyndre stopped Weaving. In all of her decades she had never encountered this before, two people so wrong for each other, their offspring was fated to a life of horror and heartbreak. A powerful witch the likes of which no one had ever seen, but so ripped apart by her nature, she would be a danger to herself and all who encountered her.

Birthing this child would harm the world.

If her calling was to serve, making this child was not a service.

"Gyndre," Avdra said, her voice shaking with strain. "What do we do?"

Abandon the girl, Gyndre thought. *Let the soul-weave fade into nothing. Never have children with your husband. Give up the very thing you want so badly.* "I don't know."

Tears sprung into Avdra's eyes. "Please, Gyndre. There has to be a way."

The grief in her gaze gutted Gyndre, and the weight of their shared history pulled on her heart. They had been girls together, growing side by side, and here was Avdra's daughter, an echo of the past made flesh. A parallel in time. Part of Gyndre felt like she was losing their own daughter.

In that moment, she could see what would happen to Avdra if she said no. She held so much of her in her hands, Avdra's nature, the vision of it was unstoppable. Avdra would wither. All that brightness gone, like a bonfire doused to boiling, seething ash. And Omus . . . Gyndre had to force herself not to read his reaction in his power, but she could taste the barest hint of it like poison on the back of her tongue. Self-loathing. Hatred. Despair. He would be a man broken beyond repair.

"Please," Omus said. Terror and guilt warred in his eyes. "What can we do? I'll do anything." Tears fell silently down his face. He blamed himself for this failure. Part of Gyndre wanted to think he wasn't wrong, but the truth was, with anyone else he might have been able to make a viable child. He and Avdra were just so different, so opposed—if they had someone who was just slightly more grounded, reserved, balanced . . .

Revelation washed through her on a wave of horror. *What if . . .*

Just imagining it changed the feel of the power in her hands. She felt the triad between the three of them and saw what could be. She could save the girl and her wild magic. She could keep

Avdra's heart from breaking into two. She could save Omus from a living death.

Moreover, the power hummed more perfectly, more harmonically, between them than she had ever felt before. At first, she had thought perhaps it was because she and Avdra had been friends for so long, but it wasn't just Avdra's magic she held. It was the three of them together.

Gyndre allowed her sight to expand once more, this time to a different child—a child of Avdra, Omus, *and* Gyndre. She could give her people the greatest Weaver ever known, with a depth of sight and power so rich she could change history. Not a Weaver like Gyndre, but something more, something else. Not just able to see the hidden threads of spirit that bound all of creation, but able to pluck them like the strings of a harp and draw harmony from them. A balanced, whole heart and a wild soul unfettered by fear. She would not be perfect, but she would be *good*. Achingly, beautifully, imperfectly good in only the way the best humans were.

Gyndre looked at them. She felt like the grief and hope and magic she held in her hands had become a knife, her only choice to either plunge it into their hearts or into her own.

"There might be a way." She could scarce believe she was going to voice the possibility.

"Anything," Avdra said.

"Yes," Omus whispered fearfully.

"See what she could be." Against every instinct in her body, Gyndre pulled the thread of her own magic and held it like she did the others. So close to each other, the harmony rose to a crescendo. She was certain they could feel how perfect the blend would be. "This will resolve the paradox of her being and make her stable. Otherwise . . ." Gyndre shook her head. "Otherwise she will be mad, and a danger to others and herself, and thus I should not Weave her."

"But your order forbids—" Avdra began.

"I know," Gyndre said. "The choice is yours; I'll do my part." For Avdra or her people more, she didn't know in that moment.

"Do it," Avdra said, through gritted teeth. "Please."

"Omus?"

For once, there was no fear on his face, just cold acceptance. Gyndre felt the threads of their fate shifting in her grip.

"Yes," he said. "Whatever you need to do, please do it."

Gyndre nodded. She looked at the three threads, hanging in the air. Blasphemy. Beautiful, heart-breaking blasphemy.

She slid her essence into the Weave.

"Oh," she breathed as the three threads melded together. Just as in every Weaving she had done, the magic was beautiful—only now she could feel the tugging on her soul as it drew on her own power. Her thoughts, feelings, needs, and emotions, spiraling out from her heart and through the air on a strand of stardust to join the other two. Tears poured down her face. She hadn't known this is what it felt like, like she was losing part of her most intimate self and giving it to someone else, freely and with joy.

The child formed before her, the soul expanding and deepening, becoming more real. The lattice of the body began to take shape—small, but strong, a toddler in equivalent age to the flesh-born. Sinew and skin wove the light into being. Curly hair like her father but red like Avdra's—her eyes blue like Gyndre's, set in a dark face. Gyndre could feel part of herself in the child. She prayed it was her best parts.

The name of the child formed on her tongue.

"Ogyndra," she said. A strange name of three parts. To know her would be to know what she was. Forbidden. And yet Avdra and Omus repeated the name with joy on their faces, as if it were the purest thing they had ever uttered.

The magic ebbed as the Weave completed. Light faded into a dim glow all about the grove, leaving a naked child asleep on the stone. Red curls like a crown of fire ringed her head.

Avdra moved toward her first, carefully. Cautious. Omus watched her, worried. Gyndre clutched her hands to her heart as more tears fell, sliding between her naked breasts.

"You have to go, before someone sees," she said. "Anywhere.

Leave the city." She tried to think of anyone who would be willing to harbor a cursed child. Who yet stood who would dare challenge the People? Despair flickered like a dark flame in her heart, but she smothered it.

Omus looked to her. "There are villages in the cold North, yes? All flesh-born. Maybe we can hide her there."

Gyndre nodded, imagining a rocky, desolate coast. A far cry from the golden palaces forged by Shapers and eternal summer bestowed by Speakers. The thought of her daughter being raised there made her ache, but there was no other choice.

Omus's eyes were wet. "What about you? If we flee, they will know what we have done. They will sanction you. Punish you."

Gyndre looked down into the face of her daughter. Her eyes opened and took in the world for the first time. She smiled up at Avdra, and then up at Gyndre.

"They won't have proof, Omus. I'll say . . . I'll say the weaving failed. You were too reluctant to proceed and Advra too unstable. The child died, and it broke you. They might suspect, and I will suffer shame because I should have known better than to proceed, but someone has to stay here for when she comes back. You felt her capacity. Someone has to prepare the world to listen to her one day."

"But the price—"

"A Weaver's duty is foremost to the People, Omus. We need her." Gyndre kneeled down and touched Ogyndra's soft curls. "She belongs to everyone."

Avdra pulled the child into her arms. Her eyes met Gyndre's. The depths of the gratitude and sadness in them cut Gyndre to the bone. If they had been friends before, they were something else now. Mother to the same child. "Thank you, my friend."

"Take care of your daughter." Gyndre tried to ignore the pain in her heart.

"Our daughter," Avdra said. The tears in her eyes didn't fall.

Gyndre could only nod.

Omus and Avdra looked at her, and then Omus put his arm

around Avdra's shoulders and pulled her toward the mouth of the grove. He hung over Avdra, like he was protecting her, no longer cowering in her shadow.

Gyndre watched them go. Her heart broke, but she didn't.

She will need me, Gyndre thought. *And I will be here.*

I see the heart of Ursula K. Le Guin's work as the belief that words have the power to shape the world by revealing irrefutable truth. In my piece I explore this idea through naming magic similar to the cosmology of A Wizard of Earthsea; *what if the fundamental nature of names reveals the ways our innermost identity challenges established structures of power?*

Prothalamion

TRACY MANASTER

IN THE FIRST MONTH of the year, Dreamgiver forgot which bed was which, and we all slept visions meant for others. We troubled over it, first alone, and then at family hearths, then hearth to hearth to hearth, and then as one we went to Grandmother Suttle. Some comfort we found in hearing, yes, she'd weathered such a shifting before, in the long-ago summer when first she'd bled. On her word we cut parsnips for stew and waited. There were some among us who reveled in the change, seeking quilts with chores undone. The schoolmaster was always abed by dusk. Each night he became the baker's youngest daughter and he danced in the village square. Youths queued up to touch his breasts, and fine powder rose on contact, like flour.

IN THE SECOND MONTH, an osprey circled the crescent moon. We went solemn into our houses, knowing what that foretold.

A MOTHER BEYOND THE mountains birthed two wolves in a

single caul, or so we heard. We spoke of it in half-voice, having never spoken of such a thing before.

St. Efrik's Day came. Our unwed dug together for the Blessing Stone buried each year at the Landing Gate. Our mayor stood ready to daub it with her palm blood. Till sunset our young ones dug, and after. Hands blistered then burst. The baker's youngest daughter was first to voice it: The Stone was gone. We said it then as well, all of us, divvying the absence, the weighted words. Timothy Dare offered the yolk-colored luck pebble he'd carried since childhood and we saw it bloodied then buried, but we knew it wasn't the same.

The Sojourners arrived, their painted sledges dull with mud. Smoked fish they had to trade, and dried fish, and clever children's rattles hewn of fish bone. We asked for nets; Grandmother Suttle had seen in the growth of bankmoss that this would be a fine year for quickfin. The Sojourners had no nets, they swore it on the Path itself: no nets, no rope, no tools that were meant for mending.

The wolf twins beyond the mountains died, or so we heard. Their brothers who walked on two legs were no longer able to see the color green.

Our youths lost their shoes at the swimming hole: girls their right shoes, boys their left. Timothy Dare and the baker's youngest daughter discovered their feet were of a size and took it in turns to wear a pair entire. The rest hitched around uneven, like drunks, and the cobbler wouldn't come again till spring.

Early mushrooms came up, every one of them fish colored. None of us could tell vision caps from stew buttons from deathslips, not even Grandmother Suttle.

BY THE NINTH MONTH, our dreams had returned, proper and sorted, well ironed. The baker's youngest daughter, having already exposed her breasts to Timothy Dare, found her righted dreams less potent than wax. The schoolmaster wept and did fractions. Dirty moon pockets bunched beneath his eyes, and we never again saw him eat bread.

INSTEAD OF MILLET, OUR fields yielded grains of glass. These we ground into flour and johnnied into cakes. Though our stomachs bled until quieted with goats' milk, the cakes went down golden-sweet, like honey.

IN THE ELEVENTH MONTH, frost returned and we gave thanks that this at least was uncorrupted. Our mayor turned into a sow, then grew the brutal tusks of a boar. She gored her last lieutenant, and lavender bloomed out of season where he died.

NO ONE BEYOND THE mountains could see the color green now, or so we heard, and the wolf-kin had begun to lose orange. We spoke of this less to speak than to have spoken, gossip a panacea for dread.

AND THIS GRIEF: GRANDMOTHER Suttle dreamed of her own grandmother three nights in a row, and on the fourth night she developed a second mouth. It settled square between her shoulders and had a tongue and a child's set of teeth. We gathered, all of us. We burnt the herbs we'd learned from her to burn. We cracked bones for marrow broth. We placed black river stones at her bedposts and yet. Our oldest and most beloved kinswoman passed from our knowing the night of Autumn's equinox, that *mouth* calling the name of one she had never married.

THOUGH OUR LEECHES SHIED from taking and our rams refused to cover, we still held the plenty feast of St. Goia the Bald. Our children made themselves ill, sneaking sweets.

NO WORD CAME FROM beyond the mountains in the fifteenth month, and no word ever came thereafter.

IT RAINED ON THE nuptial day of Timothy Dare and the baker's youngest daughter. We stood up for them nevertheless, all of us, and sang round them in our eight concentric rings. The schoolmaster sang his part, his voice lower and more rusted than he'd dreamed it. Still, he sang, he did, we heard him; never would we say he shirked. At our circles' center, the couple unbound each other's hair. Doubtful our voices reached them through the storm, but still we sang, as if this were a kinder year, as if our songs themselves were shelter.

The idea of dream incursions and disruptions here is shamelessly lifted from The Lathe of Heaven, *though the mechanism in this piece is steeped more in myth than in science. This speaks to my longstanding preoccupation with the anthropological approaches in Le Guin's work and the ways that received traditions, taboos, kinship structures, and ritual inform the lives of individuals and communities. It would be twee to suggest a one to one ratio, but 'Prothalamion' does get at the unsettled (frankly ominous) slant of the world as I see it these days: what word comes from beyond our mountains is seldom good and often beyond the bounds of moral comprehension. Yet we still live our lives; people fall in love, barter, improvise, gossip, celebrate, and—as with this book—mourn the loss of a visionary matriarch.*

The Kingdom of the Belly

MICHELLE RUIZ KEIL

THE GHOST CATS LIVE in the neighborhood where they died. Regressed to the *we* of the kitten pile, they nest in the roots of towering firs, soothed by the gossip snaking through the fungal web that laces the urban forest.

When the moon is full, they rise, piercing the skin of the night to defy the coyotes, those fanged, merciless gods.

Hate! the cats hiss. *Hate! Hate! Hate!*

Spent, they wane with the moon. One or two drift off. No one knows where. Most pass the time playing at predation. Airborne, they chase birds whose blood once filled their mouths. The birds don't see them. Like the cats, they know that pleasure is for the living.

ONE CAT FOLLOWS A different moon. The girl in white. Every night she calls.

Kitty! Kitty! Kitty!

Kitty! Kitty! Kitty!

ON A NIGHT WHEN the moon is bright and not quite round, a coyote shoulders into the streetlight in her loose forest coat.

Is she the one who snapped his neck? The one who lived another day by tucking all the cat's future days into her hot red gut?

The girl begins to sing, a sad song about a blue-eyed boy.

Coyote listens, head cocked.

The next night, the girl's song carries a challenge.

> *Coyote, my love, I will give to thee*
> *Treasures and treasures and treasures three*
> *If only you bring him*
> *Back to me.*
> *Bring my boy back to me.*

Coyote walks into the light and raises her snout to the moon:

> *Have for me these three things*
> *Your brush of silver*
> *A golden ring*
> *The honey voice you use to sing.*

THE NEXT NIGHT THE full moon bleaches the street white as summer bone, silvering the strange procession to the dead end of the street: girl, ghost cat, coyote.

They follow the forest path to a clearing by a stream. Coyote sits. The girl produces her silver-backed brush from a nightgown pocket. It catches the moon as she smooths her long, dark curls—three strokes. She holds it out to Coyote, who bends her head.

Brush me.

The girl pulls the bristles over the thick ruff: one stroke, two strokes, three.

The ring, Coyote says, and opens her mouth.

The girl slips the gold band from her little finger and places it on Coyote's long red tongue.

Coyote swallows the bright thing into the depths of her.

Now, begins Coyote, licking her chops.

No, says the girl. *First, my boy.*

Me, the ghost cat thinks. *ME!*

Coyote bows her head, shows her teeth, wrinkles her snout and breathes. The great black nose tugs at what is left of the cat, pulling him in. Sucking him down. Down, down, into the kingdom of her belly.

Inside the hot, wet world of the larger animal, the cat lies down and rolls. Flesh of his flesh. Blood of his blood. A bird in his own belly, a place he remembers as heart—he is devourer and devoured.

The coyote rumbles and heaves, quaking, shaking as the earth does when the animals go silent and the soil heaves and trees fling their branches at the street.

Gathering layers of life, the cat is rolled into a ball, compressed. And then—released! Cold! The air too loud in his ears. His body in fours and pairs, familiar and new, aching and wet on the forest floor. The sky is the coyote's golden belly. The space between her long legs frames the girl.

Now, Coyote commands. *Now sing.*

I will if you will, says the girl.

Snouts raised, they sing together, of meat and mouth, loss and hunger. Coyote moves in for the kiss.

Our bargain, she says, moonlight mouth to petal lips.

Coyote pulls away. My girl pulls the furred face back to hers. A second kiss, petal to moonlight.

Fair trade. The girl grins when the kiss is done. *Even Steven.*

The coyote opens her mouth and laughs, raising her high-pitched girlvoice to the moon. *Kitty, kitty, kitty,* she sings.

My girl and I join her, fang-pitched and wild as this place will be when the forest reclaims the houses and all the humans are gone.

I first encountered Ursula K. Le Guin's work deep in the bowels of hell —
a.k.a. the Canyon Middle School library. Her books accompanied me into
adult reading, but the stories closest to my heart are her Catwings books —
royalty among the beloved children's books I read to my two daughters.
They tell a story about being born different, about transcending childhood
trauma, detailing the perils of being trapped and how to get free. I thought
of these books, Le Guin's interest in animal-human communication, and
the sense of ghostly companionship I have when I think of her life and
work when writing "The Kingdom of the Belly."

Interlude

Ib & Nib and the Ice Berries

STEVAN ALLRED

From a sound-tape collection of Central Karhidish "hearth-tales" in the archives of the College of Folklore in Rer, recorded during the reign of Emran VI. Narrator unknown. This "Ib & Nib" tale is one of dozens featuring these two cousins, who are fond of tricking one another. Habben plays based on this and other Ib & Nib tales are popular diversions throughout Karhide. The "kobold" in this tale is understood to be an imaginary companion such as a child invents, for there are no large fauna on Gethen other than the Gethenians themselves.

LONG, LONG AGO, IN a Hearth on the river Arre, south of Rer, there lived two cousins named Ib and Nib, who went out to cut some wood to keep themselves warm in the winter. There were but two trails they could follow to the forest. The longer way was the valley way that went around the mountain, and the shorter way was the mountain way that went over the top.

"The ice berries will be ripe along the mountain way," said Nib, who loved ice berries above all other things.

Ib loved them too, but not so much as Nib. "The mountain way is steep, and I will be too tired to cut wood if we go that way," said Ib. "We should take the valley way."

Well, yes, Nib agreed, they[1] didn't want Ib too tired to cut wood. But all the way to the forest Nib kept looking up the side of the valley to the mountain way. *I must find a way to get to those berries today,* thought Nib, *while they are at peak ripeness, for their season is all too short.*

Nib led the way, but just as they arrived at the spot where the mountain way and the valley way came back together, just there, at the edge of the forest, Nib held their hand up and said, "Stop!"

Ib, surprised, ran into Nib, nearly knocking them down, and Nib hid their smile, for they had stopped so abruptly just to make Ib stumble.

"What is it, cousin Nib?" said Ib.

"Clumsy fool!" Nib said. "Use your eyes. Look at those footprints."

Ib looked, and yes, Nib was right, there were two footprints right in the middle of the path. Footprints all by themselves, with no tracks leading to them, nor from them.

"You see those claw marks?" Nib said. "Kobold!"

"We'd best get on with our woodcutting," said Ib.

"Woodcutting?" said Nib. "There's a kobold about! Don't you understand?"

"I understand about the kobold, yes," said Ib, "but we need wood. Winter is coming."

"You cut the wood," said Nib, "and I'll watch for the kobold."

"*Nusuth,*" said Ib, sounding unperturbed, but Ib knew this was

---

1   Translator's note: given the nonfixed gender of Gethenians, any translation from the autochthonous languages of Gethen must somehow render the ungendered "somer" pronouns into the target language. This translator has elected to use they, them, and their for all Gethenians, imperfect though this solution may be.

Nib's oldest trick, to find a way to loaf while Ib did all the work. *No matter*, thought Ib, *for a trickster can always be tricked.*

So, while Ib chopped wood, and sweat began to drip off their brow, Nib climbed a *hemmens* tree, and made a great show of looking about for the kobold. "No kobold to the north!" said Nib, shading their eyes with their hand. "And none to the west," they said, rounding their voice into the singing tone of a balladeer. "No kobold to the east!" Nib sang out, "and none to the south."

After a few minutes of watching out for kobolds, Nib decided to rest their eyes. *To keep my eyes fresh*, thought Nib, *in case a kobold comes.* A short time later Nib was asleep.

While Nib slept in the tree, Ib cut wood for the both of them, stopping only to sharpen their ax when needed. From time to time they heard rustlings in the forest, and they knew the kobold was about, watching them work. In Hearth, a kobold was mischievous but benign, but a kobold in the wild could be a dangerous thing. Still, Ib did not trouble themself, for they had a long history with the kobold, and they had not been eaten by one yet.

When Nib's snoring grew especially loud, Ib said, "Come out, kobold."

The kobold came out from beneath a bramble and stood upright. They looked much like Ib, or Nib, with the same face as the two cousins, who were themselves as alike as any two elvers you might pull from the River Arre. But the kobold had sharp claws on hands and feet that were more like paws, and they walked as easily on four legs as two. This kobold was accompanied by a whisper of snow moths that flitted lazily all about their head, like drifty snowflakes when there is no wind.

"Hello, cousin Ib," said the kobold. The kobold held a basket full of ice berries in one great paw, and this gave Ib an idea.

"Hello, cousin kobold," said Ib. They leaned in and whispered, "It's time to play a trick on Nib." The kobold nodded and grinned, for they loved to play tricks, as did Ib and Nib. And so they put their heads together, Ib explaining how much Nib wanted ice berries, and the kobold explaining that the ice berries had all been picked and eaten, save for the ones in their basket, and Ib saying that the kobold should walk down the valley way, leaving footprints to show that they had just passed that way. And this the kobold did.

Ib watched the kobold walk away on all fours, the basket of ice berries in their jaws. And then the kobold stood and began to run, faster and faster, until they spread their arms and flew off. *What a thing it is, that a kobold could fly*, thought Ib. And the snow moths that flew off with the kobold—how beautiful they were! Then Ib cut more wood, and when the wood pile was big enough to burden both their backs, Ib called out to Nib, "Time to carry the wood back to the Hearth."

Nib climbed down from the tree, shivering. "Such a cold day it is," they said.

"Yes," Ib said, a sly smile on their lips, "for those who nap instead of chopping wood." But Nib was too busy yawning to pay attention to Ib.

They shouldered their bundles of wood and set out, but came immediately, of course, to the footprints of the kobold, right at the spot where the mountain way and the valley way came together at the edge of the forest. But now there were more footprints, leading back the valley way, and Nib thought, *Here is my chance to get those ice berries.*

"We can't go back that way," said Nib. "The kobold is down that path. Let's take the higher path, over the mountain."

"That way is twice as rocky, and three times as steep, and four times as cold as the valley way," said Ib.

"Even so," said Nib, who was thinking, *All the more ice berries for me.*

"As you wish," said Ib, "but I will take the valley way, and I will be back at the Hearth drinking a mug of hot beer while you are still thawing frostbite from your fingers and toes."

Nib laughed and said, "You'll not be returning at all if you run into the kobold, and I shall claim your firewood as mine."

"*Nusuth*," said Ib, pleased that the kobold's footprints were having the desired effect. And so the two woodcutters parted ways. Ib followed the kobold's footprints down the valley way, hurrying, so they could be first back to the Hearth. And Nib climbed swiftly up the mountain way, eager to get to the ice berries, and to prove how foolish Ib had been.

Nib climbed up the rocky path and soon came to the first of the ice berry patches. But there was not a single berry to be had there. They climbed higher, to the next ice berry patch, and once again, there were no berries. *That greedy kobold has gotten here ahead of me*, thought Nib. But they kept climbing, and they kept looking for ice berries, until they got to the top of the mountain, where the biggest ice berry patch was. Here, again, there were no ice berries on the bushes, but lo and behold! There, right in the middle of the path, was a basket full of ice berries.

"Oh my, oh my, oh my!" said Nib, looking up the trail, where they saw no one, and down the trail, where they saw no one. *Ice berry crisp*, thought Nib. *Breadapple pudding with ice berry topping*, thought Nib, and again they looked about, and still there was no one. *Just plain ice berries*, Nib thought, their mouth watering, *just one! Even if the kobold comes back, they won't miss just one.*

But before Nib's fingers had quite reached the ice berries, the berries all turned into snow moths and flew away in a great whisper. Nib snatched at the moths, and they managed to catch a couple, but they were dry and bitter in their mouth, and they spat them out.

And then the kobold stood up in the thickest part of the ice berry patch—which, as it happened, was right next to Nib.

"Hello, Nib," said the kobold. And then the kobold opened their mouth and roared, their jaws so wide they could have swallowed Nib's head whole.

Nib was so terrified they reared up and screamed, and then they tottered backward, and before they knew it, they were falling noggin over knees all the way down the mountain.

The kobold chortled, thinking, *You can always count on good old Nib for a big old laugh.*

"*Nusuth*," said the kobold, and they whistled to the wind,

and all the whisper of snow moths came back and settled in their basket and became ice berries again.

Back at the village Ib stacked their firewood and then went to the tavern. They ordered a mug of hot beer and sat facing the door, eager for Nib to walk in and see them there, as good as their boast. And indeed, after a few more mugs of hot beer, Nib did appear at the tavern door. Their cheeks were scratched, and one eye was swollen, and Nib walked with a limp.

"Oh my," said Ib, "did you run into the kobold on the mountain way?"

"I did," said Nib.

"How lucky for you," said Ib. "And did you find many ice berries?"

"I did not," said Nib. "Not a single berry, and then the kobold tried to eat me, but I fought them off, and gave them a few good blows to the head, and then I scared them so bad they ran away like a frightened child. And now I am famished, for I have fallen halfway down the mountain, and lost my load of wood."

Ib hid their smile behind their hand, and then they called out to the kitchen. "Bring more hot beer for my cousin and myself."

In scarcely a moment's time, to the astonishment of both Ib and Nib, the kobold appeared in the kitchen door, wearing the apron of a barkeep. In their hands they held a tray, and on the tray were three mugs of hot beer, steaming fragrantly. And on the tray also were three bowls of breadapple pudding, freshly made, topped with generous helpings of ice berries.

"Ice berries and pudding!" shouted Nib. "My favorite!"

Ib, Nib, and the kobold all laughed a great laugh, and then they began to talk all at once.

"I tricked you into doing all the woodcutting," said Nib.

"I tricked you into taking the mountain way," said Ib.

"I tricked you into falling off the mountain," said the kobold.

"Whose idea was the moths?" said Nib. "Was that you, Ib?"

"No!" roared the kobold, "that was all my idea."

"The footprints, that was me," said Ib.

"You lied about beating me up and scaring me away," laughed the kobold.

"I knew you were in the bushes while Ib cut the wood," said Nib.

"You liar," said Ib, laughing.

"Let's order more beer," said Nib.

"Since I tricked last, this round is on me," said the kobold.

Nib took their spoon and dug into the breadapple pudding for a great big bite covered with ice berries.

"I never get tired of this," said Nib. "I could do this every day."

"And we do!" said the kobold. "Shall we trade now?"

"Oh yes!" said Ib and Nib. And they put their hands on the sides of their heads and lifted them off. Ib handed their head to Nib, and Nib handed their head to the kobold, and the kobold handed their head to Ib. They put their new heads on, and they raised their beer mugs, and they drank a toast.

"To us!" they shouted, "to tricky, tricky, tricky us!"

I have been very much under the spell of The Left Hand of Darkness *as I have written these folktales. I love how the cultural anthropology and history of Gethen is suggested by the various side stories Le Guin wrote into her novel. My story intuition told me this: a species that transforms in and out of gendered-ness on a monthly basis will have folktales celebrating bodies that change joyfully, gracefully, fluidly.*

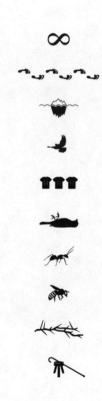

II. Returning to the Root

The ten thousand things arise together;
in their arising is their return.
Now they flower,
and flowering
sink homeward,
returning to the root.

—from Le Guin's *Lao Tzu: Tao Te Ching: A Book about the Way and the Power of the Way*

Old Souls

FONDA LEE

THE FORTUNE-TELLER'S NOSE IS speckled with moles. A tie-dyed scarf is wrapped over her scraggly blond dreadlocks. She takes my left hand and turns it palm upward, tracing its lines with glittery purple fingernails.

"Ahhhh. Hmmm. Yes."

She draws a lungful of incense-thick air and closes her eyes, tilting her head back as if ascending to a higher level of perception. I study her face and focus on the fleshy touch of her hand on mine.

A grave robber glances left and right into the darkness before snatching at a glint of gold.

A carnival ringmaster with a waxed mustache spreads his arms to the crowd.

A man in a pinstripe suit stands at the docks and lights a cigarette, watching silently as casks are unloaded.

"I can see," the fortune-teller says in a breathy voice, "you have a long life ahead of you. There is a man with you, a handsome man. Your husband? Yes! You have children too—"

I pull my hand away. The metal chair scrapes back loudly as I stand.

"What are you doing? The reading isn't finished!"

"Yes, it is." I'm furious at myself. What would compel me to stop in front of a cheap street sign with *PSYCHIC* in big curly silver letters? To take a flight of stairs down to a cramped basement and shell out twenty dollars for nothing?

Desperation.

I sling my messenger bag over my shoulder. "You aren't psychic," I snap. "You're a fraud. You profit from dishonesty. You always have."

She stares at me, mouth agape. Her face reddens, darkening her moles. "Who do you think you are? *You're* the one who came to *me*! No one asked you to come. Get out of here, bitch!"

I don't need further encouragement. I barge through the curtain of black and white beads, past a woman in a long white coat and sunglasses sitting in what passes as the waiting room, and nearly knock over a lava lamp on my way out the door.

Back out on the sidewalk, I pause, blinking back the prickle of angry tears, the weight of disappointment so heavy it seems as if it'll push me through the damp concrete. I zip up my jacket, debating whether to go back to the campus or to skip my last lecture of the day and return to my apartment. My roommate will be gone for the rest of the afternoon, and I'm in no mood to sit through Medieval European History. I start down the sidewalk toward home, arms hugged around myself.

"Old soul," a voice calls from the stairwell. "Wait."

It's the woman in the white coat, the one who was sitting in the fortune-teller's office. She follows me with quick strides until she reaches me. Her hand shoots out and catches me by the arm.

"You see the past, don't you? Yours and others." Her words carry a faint tremor of excitement. She pushes her sunglasses onto the top of her head, pinning me with her gaze.

For a motionless second, I stare at her face, into dark, ancient eyes. Then I look down at the pale hand on my arm, and a shudder of astonishment goes through me. We're close, touching, but nothing happens, the way it does with other people. No images unspool in my mind like a surreal art-house video. She's the person standing in front of me, and no one else. It makes her seem unreal. An illusion of a person. Either I can't read her or there is nothing to read. No past. No other lives besides this one.

I jerk back. My voice comes out high. "Who are you?"

She gives me a small, satisfied smile. "I am one of the Ageless. And I've been searching for someone like you."

WE WALK INTO THE nearest Starbucks. This being Seattle, there's one less than a hundred feet away. She buys a caramel mocha for me and green tea for herself. She tells me her name is Pearl. She's been visiting every self-proclaimed psychic in the city, hoping to find someone like me—someone who can see past lives without trying to, the way artists see color or perfumers detect scents.

"Most psychics are frauds," she explains with an off-handed shrug as we bring our drinks to an empty table, "but once in a while, I find someone who can make reasonable predictions of the future by seeing the past, the way you do." She glances at me. "It's a rare ability."

Not one I'm thrilled to have. I study my mocha. "Do you have it?"

She leans toward me slightly. "No. I don't have your clear sight. I can only sense things about people, including those who can see better than I can."

"Who—*what* are you?"

She takes a long sip of her tea. "Death and rebirth, death and rebirth. So it goes for everyone, except the Ageless. I have had no other life but this one. I will have no other after it."

I'm silent for a long, baffled moment. Everyone I've ever met has past incarnations. It would be hard to believe Pearl if I hadn't seen it—or rather, *not* seen it—for myself. I study her face. She has smooth Asian features that make it hard to judge if she's twenty-five or forty. "How old are you?"

She crosses her legs, resting her chin on her hand. Her gaze grows distant. "Five hundred and thirty-some is as far back as I can remember. I've lost the exact count."

I suck in a breath. I imagine what it must be like to live for so many years without dying, to have the gift of so much time. As my eyes widen with awe, Pearl's mouth tightens. "Trust me," she says, "a life as long as mine isn't something to envy."

"But you must have been through incredible times, seen incredible things."

A shadow crosses her face. "What I've seen is those I love die, while I live on, never changing."

I hadn't thought of it that way. An awkward pause rests between us. Quietly, I ask, "Are there others like you?"

"A few." She doesn't say more. "Enough about me. You must be wondering why I want to talk to you." Her lips curve in a small smile that is beautiful but cool, like the smile on a marble bust. "I think we can help each other. You are searching for something, just as I am. Tell me, what are you searching for?"

I lower my gaze. Customers bustle around us as the baristas call out orders. I'm oddly unsurprised to be sitting in a coffee shop having this unbelievable conversation with a woman even more unusual than myself. Still, I hesitate. I tried to talk about this to my parents when I was ten years old. They put me in therapy until I said what the therapist wanted to hear and was proclaimed "better."

My voice falls to a whisper. "I want to know how to break the pattern."

EVERYONE HAS A PATTERN. A template. No matter how many wildly different lives you've lived, there is always something constant. Some people are always artistic. Some have ill-fated love lives. Some are always born in a certain place. The fortune-teller has been a conniving cheat in every one of her incarnations.

I've had six lives. Seven counting this one.

The first one is as indistinct as a preschool memory. I was named Cael. I lived in a family of six and spent many a day fishing along the banks of the Tyras River, tying knots with my uncle, the sun warm on my back. I was thirteen or fourteen when Scythian raiders rode into my village. I ran out to fight and remember only the speed of the horseman, his tapered metal helmet, and the arc of his battle-ax. It was terrifying, but the end was quick.

I became Hassad, the rich and spoiled youngest son of an Arab sheik. I owned a beautiful falcon that I raised by hand. It sat on my arm when I rode. I remember the smell of mint and thyme mixing with the chatter of my father's wives in the mornings. On my twentieth birthday, I went hunting with my brother and was mauled by a leopard. I hung on for five days before blood loss and infection finished me off.

As Marie Rousseau, I was a midwife-in-training in the Languedoc region. In the foothills near my home there were groves of olives, and in early summer, purple lavender would bloom amid the sun-bleached wild grasses. I made a fatal mistake when I provided herbs to induce a friend's abortion. Her husband accused both of us of witchcraft—and that's why today even birthday candles set my nerves on edge and the sight of a campfire reduces me to a boneless heap of terror.

My soul fled to water. I was Yamada Hasashi, the eldest son of a fisherman in the Kyoto prefecture. I felt the salt wind in my face every day, and grew up on a simple but satisfying routine of daily hard work. Then the daimyo drafted all the men of our town, including my father, leaving me to feed my mother and younger siblings. I took my father's boat out in stormy weather. When I was thrown overboard, I knocked my head on the prow of the boat before going under.

I've pegged my fifth life, as Sikni, down to the 1770s. I was a member of the Yakama tribe in the Northwest plateau. I listened to grandmother's stories of Coyote the trickster around the lodge fire, and I delighted in the softness of my favorite buckskin dress, the one with blue and yellow beads. I was fifteen years old and the medicine woman's apprentice when I succumbed to smallpox.

Then I was born as Andrew Reed. I traveled one hundred and eighty-some years but only a few miles between being Sikni and Andrew. I lived and went to high school in the town of Yakima, Washington. I ran track, made mixed tapes, got to second base with my girlfriend at the drive-in showing of *Mad Max*. Two months before graduation, she and I were at a 7-Eleven when it was held up. Someone else in the store pulled a gun on the robber. He freaked out and started shooting. I took a bullet through the neck.

I've ranged across the world and over thousands of years. I've skipped across race and gender and vocation. There's only one thing that connects my lives: how I die.

Short lives, tragic deaths. That's my pattern. My ages of death are like a lottery number when recited: fourteen, twenty, nineteen, sixteen, fifteen, eighteen. I've never made it past the age of twenty.

This time around, my name is Claire Leung-Hartley. Yesterday was my twentieth birthday.

"I CAN HELP YOU," Pearl says.

"You can?" I lean forward. The paper cup trembles in my hands as I set it down.

"The Ageless know things. We ride the long journey of history. You mortals merely hop in and out."

My voice falls. I feel heavy from having shared so much of myself. "I don't want to keep dying young. I think it would be easier if I was like everyone else and didn't remember it at all. I don't know why I'm different."

Maybe whatever process erases past-life memory randomly glitched when it got to me. But the truth is, I think there *must* be a reason why I can remember all my lives and deaths. Maybe it's so I can finally find a way to escape my fate. Maybe Pearl is part of the reason.

"Tell me," I plead. "How do I break the pattern?"

"Help me, and I will help you," she says. "I am searching for someone. The soul of a man I knew long ago. I promised him I would find him again, no matter when or where it was." She smiles a slow, sad smile. "He lives somewhere in this city. I can feel it. Please help me find him."

I consider what she's asking. It doesn't make sense. "This person you're looking for—he might be anyone now. He might be an old woman or just a baby. Unless he's like me, he won't remember you."

"Love never dies." Sitting across from me, her slim, pale hands clasped around her teacup, she still seems unreal to me. Her dark hair spills over the shoulders of her white coat. Her eyes are bottomlessly old, as if the blackness of her pupils is a window into the universe, stretching back and back and back. How long has she been searching?

"I promised to find him," she says. "I have all the time in the world. When we meet, he'll remember me, I'm sure of it." She sounds absolutely certain, as if she's done this before. Maybe she has.

I used to want to search out my old families. Andrew's parents; they would be very old now, if they were still alive. Sikni's tribe members. I thought about visiting Japan to see if anyone with the family name of Yamada still lived in the fishing village. A great-great nephew or niece of mine perhaps. But even though I wanted to do those things, something held me back. Not just the logistical difficulties, but fear. Fear of reality and memory colliding. Of the past overwhelming the present.

I looked up Jeanne, my old girlfriend—Andrew's girlfriend—on Facebook. She lives in Boise now and is married with three grown kids who are older than me. It was strange to look at her picture. It was her, but it wasn't. Reality didn't match the memories I had of her, memories clouded by a teenage boy's lust. She used to have long hair the color of autumn. Full lips. Devastating eyes.

But that life, like the others, is gone now. Snatched from me before I was done with them. I can't have them back. What good would it do for Jeanne to have some college-aged girl show up at her door, claiming to be the reincarnation of her murdered boyfriend from high school?

This life is what I have now. And Pearl is the first person I've ever met who might know how I can keep on living.

"I would like to help," I say slowly, "but there are millions of people in the city. How can I possibly find one person? Maybe you have all the time in the world, but—"

But I don't. I am on borrowed time.

"I will tell you how to recognize him." She leans forward. "Do you agree to try?"

I ARRANGE TO VOLUNTEER part-time at the Veterans Affairs office. I figure it's my best chance of coming into contact with the person Pearl is looking for. Ethan is surprised and slightly peeved. Between our class schedules and this new commitment, we have less time together than he'd like.

"Where did this come from?" he asks, petulant. "I never knew you had the faintest interest in the military."

"Andrew was thinking of enlisting." I offer a shrug. "Maybe I'm just scratching an old itch."

Ethan and I have been together for a year, but it feels longer than that. We're serious about each other. I know I can trust Ethan. He's the first person I've dated who I dared open up to. I told him almost everything. He didn't call me crazy, and he didn't run away.

"You're serious," he said. At the time, we were sitting on the sofa in his place and he was nuzzling my neck. There's a small red birthmark on the left side of my neck and a much larger, port-wine stain on the right side, behind my ear. Usually, my hair covers the bigger blemish. Ethan calls the small birthmark my "vampire bite" as he pretends to be the vampire. That night, after we'd been together for almost six months, I was feeling reckless. Reckless and vulnerable. "It's not a bite," I said. "It's a bullet hole." I showed him the other side—the exit wound. "Sometimes, when you die tragically in a past life, its mark stays on you."

"You really think you were shot through the neck in a past life?"

I curled in on myself a little. "I don't think I was. I *know* I was."

He came back a few days later, ashen-faced. "I looked up the *Yakima Herald Republic* in the library archive. It's all there—reported the day after you said it happened."

I could tell he was struggling to believe me. I said, "You're thinking that doesn't prove anything. I could have looked up the same article and made up a story to match what's in the newspaper."

"What car was Andrew—were you—driving?"

"A 1969 Pontiac GTO," I said without hesitation. I loved that car.

"What was the mascot of your high school?"

"The Pirates."

He sat down next to me, searching me with his eyes. "Either you're pulling a detailed, elaborate hoax on me for no apparent reason or you're telling the truth." He touched the birthmark on my neck with the tips of his fingers. "As crazy as this is, I believe you."

I hugged him then, and I cried a little. He wanted to know more about what I remembered, not just about Andrew's life but the other ones too. I was still afraid to tell him too much, afraid of driving him away, even though I knew he was drawn to the unknown instead of repelled by it.

Ethan has been a medieval alchemist, a native Peruvian river guide, and a university chaplain, but my favorite of his past incarnations is Moloni, the African tribal wisewoman, whose deep well of wisdom and compassion I sometimes see reflected in Ethan's cornflower blue eyes. I think seeing her in him gave me the courage to trust him. Ethan is a seeker, driven by a desire to know more of the world, especially that which can't be seen. It's why he's majoring in astronomy, which he admits is the "dumbest thing ever as far as job prospects go." It's why I'm falling in love with him.

I trust Ethan more than anyone in the world, but I don't tell him about Pearl or why I'm really volunteering at the VA office. I want to, but even he won't understand why I'm spending time on a gamble with such long odds. The closer Ethan and I get to each other, the more committed we become, the more anxious I feel. My boyfriend might be convinced of the existence of immortal souls and multiple lives, but he is too much of an optimist to believe in tragic fate. He sees the future unwinding before us; I see a brick wall, one whose distance I can't judge because I can't tell how fast we're moving toward it.

"I love you," he said to me, the night of my birthday. We lay tangled together in the sheets, my head on his chest. I felt his words shift the weight of him beneath me.

I kissed his shoulder. I wanted to cry. "I've never grown up. I've never been married or had kids or been old."

"Me neither."

"Yes, you have," I insisted. "You just don't remember."

"Then we might as well be even."

I was annoyed at him. "You don't understand. I have a short expiry date."

"That's ridiculous. I admit I don't understand it, but I don't think you do either. Maybe you only remember lives that ended badly and you've had plenty of others that were just fine. Also, people died younger back then, from war and disease and accidents. You shouldn't assume—" He pushed out from under me and propped himself up on one elbow. "Wait, is this why you take those street fighting lessons? And why you carry a switchblade and hand sanitizer with you *everywhere*? And don't drive a car? Because you're afraid death is waiting for you around every corner?"

I lay still and silent, hands fisted close to my body. I wanted to tell Ethan he would be more afraid of violent death if he'd been through more of them. *Did you know that when you burn to death, you actually bleed? You bleed a lot. You would think the blood would steam off or something, but it doesn't. It drips and hisses in the flames.*

I didn't say that. I said, "Let's not talk about this right now."

I turned over and pulled up the covers. After a while, he sighed and put his arms around me. He fell asleep as I lay awake. But he hasn't said it again. He hasn't said he loves me.

MY VOLUNTEER WORK IN the VA office starts out as filing and photocopying, but a week later I catch a break. The receptionist is diagnosed with mono and doesn't know how long she'll be out sick. I offer myself as a fill-in, and soon, I'm sitting at the front desk, greeting everyone who comes in. I see plenty of soldiers and their family members when they come in to apply for benefits. I read each of them as carefully as I can, shaking everyone's hand to get a stronger impression, taking my time, making small talk as I check them in. They think I'm friendly and always willing to chat. A few of the younger vets get flirty and ask for my number. I feel awkward having to disappoint them.

If I was looking to score a date, I'd consider this time well spent, but for my purposes and Pearl's, it's a bust so far. Several of the people I meet have a pattern of military service in their prior incarnations, but I don't find anyone who matches the description Pearl gave me. I've never actively tried to search people's pasts the way I'm trying now, and after my shifts I leave the office with a dull headache. I take the bus home in the spitting rain, only to crack open my textbooks; the dense paragraphs swim before my eyes as I struggle to study for midterms.

One night, as I am about to fall asleep in the middle of a page about Islamic relations with the Byzantine Empire, I think: *This is so useless*. Both the searching and the studying.

I look at my phone; it's almost midnight. I pull up the number Pearl gave me. "Call me when you find him," she'd said, "but only when you find him." I consider phoning now to tell her I'm giving up. She ought to give up too, stop longing for someone who's gone on to another life. Maybe it's not such a great idea for me to string her hope out like this anyway. Even if I find this person, Pearl probably can't be a part of his or her life anymore, just like I can't go back to Jeanne or any of my past families. My finger hovers over the phone screen. *Move on*, I'll say when she picks up.

Then I think about how ridiculous that sounds, coming from me. I need her help. I need answers. If I were oblivious of my pattern, I could live each day in blissful ignorance, up until the final, shocking end. *Would that be better?* Instead, I'm as burdened by and captive to my memories as she is. She's not going to give up. Neither will I.

I close my book and rest my head on top of my arms, sniffing back tears of fatigue and hopelessness. Kelly is up late too, working on a lab report that's due. "Claire bear?" she says. "Are you okay?"

"Yeah," I say unconvincingly. My roommate's pattern is enviably simple. She can't stay away from the ocean. She's been a Micronesian sailor, a Venetian naval officer, a U-boat engineer, and a Makah whale hunter. Now she's studying to be a marine biologist. She's drowned twice, but she doesn't remember it, and it doesn't deter her. Drowning isn't the worst way to go, relatively speaking.

She comes over and gives me a hug. "Is something wrong? Is it Ethan?"

"No," I say, "Well, not exactly." Maybe something *is* wrong. I wonder if he's pulling away from me a little. Last week, he asked me to come with him to visit his family over Thanksgiving, and when I hemmed and hawed, I think he took it as a rejection. He can sense there's something I'm not telling him.

"You should go," says Kelly. "I think he really wants you to meet his family. He's mad about you, can't you tell? Unless— you're not really into him?"

I try to nod and shake my head at the same time. "It's not that. I mean, yes, I am into him. I'm just, I don't know—worried."

"You should do it," she says again. "You've got to take a chance on this really working out. Live a little, you know?"

∞

ETHAN'S PARENTS LIVE IN Tacoma, but his dad is a travel writer and they spend months in exotic places like Morocco and Tibet. "Claire has studied Buddhism," Ethan volunteers while setting the table, which sets me up for a long period of listening to Ethan's dad talk about the devotion of the Tibetan monks and how their harmonious culture is being destroyed.

It's true, there was a time I devoured everything I could read about reincarnation. I wondered whether, if I quit school, became a vegan, and took up a life of austerity and meditation, I could achieve nirvana. But I don't want to *stop* being reborn, and I'm not seeking enlightenment. I just want to stop having horrible deaths at a young age, which seems like a modest goal in comparison. I considered the possibility that I have some karmic debt to pay, but *what?* I don't believe I've been a bad person in any of my lives, not bad enough to deserve what I've gotten. I mean, I donate to the Salvation Army. I give my seat to old people on the bus. I recycle.

Ethan's mom lights up when I ask for a tour of her garden. She isn't the first person I've met who's been a farmer several times: twice in China, once in Russia, and once in Ireland, from what I can see. Ethan's dad has been a Mongolian nomad, a Bedouin shepherd, and a Southeast Asian trader whose geography and ethnicity I can't quite place at first glance, so it doesn't surprise me when his wife laments they haven't been home enough to finish raising the vegetable beds. Ethan's older brother, Kegan, shows up just before dinner. He's as handsome as Ethan, but he's quieter and smiles less. He seems to be five or six years older than Ethan, instead of only three. When Ethan introduces us, I say, "I'm really glad to finally meet you," because it's obvious Ethan looks up to his brother. "Kegan's the go-getter," I've heard him say before.

"Nice to meet you, Claire." Kegan shakes my hand.

A general sits atop his war stallion in flared helmet and crimson armor, watching the flames below.

A guerrilla fighter rests his rifle atop his knees as he empties water from his boots.

A woman in a dark suit walks into the room and sits down across from a man handcuffed to his chair.

"Kegan just got back from Egypt," Ethan's mom says proudly. "He was on a six-week exchange program with the State Department."

We sit down for dinner. My heart races. I barely hear the conversation around me.

Ethan's mom passes me the mashed potatoes and asks Kegan, "How's your Arabic, sweetheart?"

"Good enough." Kegan is matter-of-fact; there's no pride or modesty in his voice. He is too old to be twenty-three.

Ethan's father leans toward me. "Kegan wants to work for the CIA," he explains. "I think he would've joined the military if it hadn't been for his asthma. Michelle and I are staunch Democrats; we don't even own any guns!" He shakes his head. "I don't know where he gets it from."

AFTER DINNER, I STEP outside onto the back porch under the pretense of phoning my parents. My fingers shake as I call the number. After three rings, I hear Pearl's voice.

"You've found him?"

"Yes," I whisper breathlessly. "You won't believe this. He's my boyfriend's brother!" I want to laugh hysterically. I've been searching for months, and he's been one degree away from me this whole time.

There is a long pause. "Tell me about him."

"He's twenty-three. Really handsome. Single, I think." There hadn't been any mention of a girlfriend over dinner. "He hasn't been around lately because he was on an exchange trip, but it shouldn't be hard to find a way to meet him now."

I try to picture how it will go. Will he be drawn to her, the way she is to him? She *is* over five hundred years old—will that matter?

I promise to invite him to visit us and find a chance to introduce them.

"Thank you, Claire." She sighs in relief. Then she hangs up.

CONVINCING KEGAN TO VISIT is easy. He hasn't seen his brother's place and is happy to spend the last day of the long weekend in the city with us. We drive up together on Saturday afternoon and arrive right around dinnertime at the small house Ethan shares with two roommates. They are all out of town, so we have the place to ourselves. Ethan orders in pizza. *We're here,* I text Pearl. *Would you like to meet him tomorrow?*

We sit on the sofa, watching the Seahawks game and eating pizza. I sit next to Ethan on one side of the sofa. Kegan takes the armchair. I study him. I am not completely comfortable with Kegan. He looks like Ethan, but he is not like him. Ethan searches for answers to the unknown; Kegan knows the answers. He sees the world in black and white, and there is a coldness, a ruthlessness that I sense in his prior selves. They are resolute people, but they are not nice.

It's tempting to judge people based on who they were before, even though I often remind myself it's unfair. My sweet roommate Kelly set enemy ships ablaze and ordered men hung. Ethan once stabbed another man in a drunken knife fight in the South American jungle. When I was Hassad, I owned so many slaves that it makes me squirm a little to think about it now. Our lives are shaped by circumstances; we have patterns, but we do change. I haven't known Kegan long enough to see many details of his past, but I'm not sure I want to. He's Ethan's brother, and it's better I try to get to know him for who he is in this life.

I wonder again what his reaction will be to meeting Pearl. What if he doesn't feel any connection to her at all? Will she move on, or pine after him? I try to think of how to bring up my idea to invite her over. *So, I have a friend who would really like to meet you. Who is she? Oh, uh, she's a TA in one of my classes . . .*

Before I can formulate my suggestion, Kegan takes another slice of pizza and says, "So, how did you two get together?"

I glance at Ethan. "We met during freshman orientation," I say. "But we didn't start dating until after that camping trip."

Ethan picks up the thread. "I'd had my eye on Claire for weeks, and then I spied her sitting at the very back of the campfire crowd, practically in the woods, all by herself."

"I'm scared of fire," I explain, embarrassed.

"So I moved my chair to sit next to her, and we stayed up talking after everyone else had gone to sleep and the fire had burned out."

Kegan nods. He pops open a can of soda and says, dead sober, "I'm terrified of fire."

Ethan laughs. "You're not terrified of anything."

"I had nightmares as a kid," Kegan says. "You were too young to remember. I still have them sometimes—nightmares about burning to death."

I pull my legs up to my chest and hug them. "Me too."

"Claire says she's scared of fire because it's how she died in a past life. You think that's what happened to you too, macho man?" Ethan's voice is just a notch past teasing. He sounds a little hurt that we are commiserating over a deep phobia his brother never bothered to share with him.

Kegan looks at Ethan, then looks at me. He mutes the volume on the television. "Yes," he says. "I could believe that. In my dream, there's a woman who's chasing me. It's always the same woman. I don't know why I'm trying to get away from her, but I am. I'm running or driving or riding a horse, always trying to get away, and in the end, I'm trapped by a fire. And I burn to death. And she watches me burn."

We are both silent for a minute. Ethan is stunned, but not for the same reason I am. "That is so screwy, bro. Maybe it means you're afraid of women." He has a half-teasing smirk on his face, but neither Kegan nor I am smiling.

Kegan shakes his head, his left eye squinting in annoyance at his little brother. "No, dipstick. It's just *one* woman."

"Oh my God," I whisper. An iciness bathes me from head to toe. *What have I done?*

The living room window shatters inward.

I SCREAM. ALL THREE of us leap off the sofa, scattering pizza and soda. A hulking figure steps through the window frame. Cold air sweeps into the room around his menacing shape. His combat boots crunch the broken glass against the hardwood floor. I can't see his face; he's wearing a black ski mask. All I can see is the barrel of the gun he is pointing at us.

"*Jesus,*" Ethan breathes. We are both too stunned to move, but Kegan scans the room for the nearest weapon. There's nothing. He grabs the wooden chip bowl off the coffee table and hurls it at the intruder. The man ducks, raising his arm to avoid the flying object. Tortilla chips and salsa spray the wall. Kegan shoves his brother, and together, we run for the front door.

Ethan pulls the door open. A second masked man stands on the doorstep. He starts to bring up his own gun, but before he can aim it, Kegan tackles him. They slam into the doorframe together. The man who came through the window shoves his bulk in front of me and Ethan, his pistol raised, his mouth open in a snarl.

"On your knees!" he shouts at us.

Ethan pulls me roughly behind him. "What do you want?" he shouts back. "You want money? The TV? Just take them!" His voice shakes. He is standing with his arms spread in front of me. I am terrified the man will shoot him.

Kegan struggles with the shorter intruder. He has his hands clamped over the frame of the pistol, pushing the muzzle down toward the floor. The man's right hand is trapped against his weapon, but he cocks his left fist and punches Kegan in the face. Kegan's grip slides. The man yanks his gun free; he swings it up and cracks Kegan across the head. Kegan staggers and falls sideways, barely managing to put a hand out to catch himself. He tries to surge up; his eyes are wild and desperate. The butt of the pistol comes down on the back of his skull, and he collapses like a sack.

"*No!*" Ethan jerks toward his brother, but the hulking man shifts his gun to my temple.

"I said, on your knees!" he yells at Ethan. "Or you pick which one we shoot first."

Ethan goes colorless. His hand on my arm, he lowers himself to the floor. I kneel next to him. I can feel the pulse in his hand beating in rapid tempo against my own.

"What do you want?" he asks again, his voice low so it hides his fear. He looks at his prone brother and swallows hard.

"Dumb prick," the short man exclaims. He shoves Kegan's figure with his boot, then reaches his gloved fingers awkwardly into the eyehole of his mask, wiping his brow.

My heart is pounding so hard I think it might escape my body. This is it. This is the brutal end I've been expecting for years. I wonder how they will kill us and whether it will be fast. Though I am scared out of my mind, I'm more worried about Ethan and Kegan than I am about myself. I'm not surprised that I'm going to die. But they shouldn't have to; they shouldn't be sucked into the merciless magnetism of my pattern, ancillary tragedies to my own.

I have a switchblade in my pocket. Can I reach it? What can I possibly do against two men with guns?

"Which one of them is he?" the big man asks.

The two of them look from Ethan to Kegan and back again. Their eyes are like black pits in the slits of their masks. "I'm not sure," the short one replies. "Put them in the bedroom closet. She'll know when she gets here."

She'll know. These men work for Pearl. My insides turn over.

"What about the girl?"

"The girl too."

"Let her go," Ethan says. "Please, don't hurt her." I cringe at the pleading in his voice, though I know he is only trying to protect me. I want to berate him for ever having doubted my fatalism.

The big man pulls a roll of silver duct tape from his jacket and bends over Kegan, pulling his wrists together behind his back and taping them together tightly. When he's done, he winds duct tape around Kegan's ankles. Then he drags Kegan down the hallway, pulling him backward by his armpits. Kegan's head lolls limply on his neck, the left side of his face swollen a reddish-purple.

Ethan trembles, enraged and helpless.

"Hands where I can see them, punk," the short man says.

His accomplice returns. More duct tape for Ethan and me. My wrist bones rub together painfully as they're bound. When the big man touches me, I get past-life glimpses: a mercenary soldier, a prison guard, an elephant poacher. I choke back a whimper. Suffering isn't going to move him.

"Get up," he orders.

They march the two of us into Ethan's bedroom. The room is dark, and the shades are drawn. Ethan's clothes and books have been thrown willy-nilly from the closet, which is now bare, except for Kegan, who is lying on its floor. Our captors back us into the closet beside him. "Sit down," the big man orders. We do as he says.

They tape our ankles together and then stand back, looking down at us. Behind them, I can see the outlines of Ethan's unmade bed, his duffel bag lying open on the floor, his stereo. The big man lights a cigarette. It dangles from fat, chapped lips set in the mouth hole of the ski mask. He checks his wristwatch.

The short one licks his lips nervously. "Who do you think these kids are? What would anyone want with them?"

"The hell should I know?" says the big man. "Maybe daddy pissed off the Mob? We're being paid is all I care."

Ethan tries to speak up. "There's been a mistake," he says. "You've got the wrong people. We're not mixed up with the mafia. We don't have any enemies. We're just students. I'm telling you, you have the wrong people."

The men ignore him. They close the closet, shutting us in the dark. Their footsteps move around, then leave the room. In the silence that follows, I pray for the sound of sirens, for the police to surround the house and rescue us. It's possible one of the neighbors called 911, but I am not optimistic. The houses here are spaced far apart and full of student renters, all of them gone for the Thanksgiving break. No one knows what's happening to us.

"This is all my fault." I choke back silent tears. "Ethan, I'm sorry."

His shape slumps against the wall. "What for?"

"I should have told you, but I didn't think—I didn't imagine—" My throat is too small; the words come out in a squeaky rush, like water through a small spigot. I tell him about meeting Pearl, about agreeing to help her find someone she knew centuries ago. "I led her to us. To Kegan."

"To Kegan?" Ethan stiffens. "Why would anyone want to hurt Kegan?"

His brother stirs on the floor. A soft groan escapes him.

Ethan tries to shuffle closer to him. "Hey, it's me. You okay?"

Kegan lifts his head off the ground, realizes he's tied up, and starts to freak out. "Let us out of here!" he screams, kicking at the door. "LET US OUT!"

The closet door opens. A silhouette stands over us. Even before the small desk lamp clicks on, I know who it is, and so, apparently, does Kegan. He jerks against the wall, a sheen of sweat breaking on his forehead.

"You." His voice is a rattle.

Pearl's bottomless eyes pass over me, then Ethan, before stopping on Kegan. "Hello, General Zhang." Her voice is silky soft, almost affectionate. "We meet again."

The big man beside her grumbles, "You promised us a lot of cash—"

"Finish the job," she replies shortly, "and you will be paid as we agreed."

The men depart. We are alone in the room with Pearl.

"I have no idea who you are, or what you want with me," Kegan says. Though he's scared, his voice is surprisingly strong. "But let my brother and his girlfriend go. If it's me you want, just let them go."

"Ahhh," Pearl sighs. "So there is justice in the universe after all. I pleaded for my family too. I pleaded for their lives. Then I pleaded for quick deaths. But you granted them neither." Her face is a pitiless pale mask. Her voice takes on a slow, musing quality. "The Red Butcher, the Emperor's most feared warlord. You were determined to make an example of Three Gates Valley, one so terrifying that no other prefectures would ever again consider rebellion."

"We don't know what you're talking about, lady," Ethan says. "You're crazy."

"Am I?" Pearl looks directly at me.

I shudder. How could I not have seen it before, her cold cruelty? "This is wrong. You can't punish him for what happened to you hundreds of years ago. He doesn't remember any of it. He's not even the same person."

"Isn't he? How can you, of all people, say that?" She turns away from me and back to Kegan. "This young, handsome incarnation flatters you, General. But I can see you. Inside, you are still the monster who had my husband and his brothers torn apart by horses and their flesh fed to the dogs. You ordered my children to be thrown from the walls. And you lit fires that burned for five days and nights, until nothing was left of the town." She crouches down smoothly to face him, her long white coat pooling around her. "No one survived. No one but me."

The room chills from the ice of her whispered words. "There are consequences to making an enemy of an Ageless one. I swore to Heaven, to Zhurong, god of fire and vengeance, that I would hunt you down; I would make you pay back with your lives the ones you took from me."

Kegan is shaking his head emphatically. "I didn't—I wouldn't—"

Pearl stands up. The door opens and the big man walks in with a six-gallon jug. He bangs it impatiently against the wall, and it makes a hollow sound. That's when I notice the smell drifting in from the hallway. Kerosene.

Terror floods in. I shake in its grip like a marionette.

Kegan is no better. In his saucer-wide eyes, I see that he knows this has happened before. How many times? Over how many lives has Pearl been exacting her vengeance? "Please," he begs, "please let them go."

Pearl gestures to me. "Take her outside." The big man picks me up, dumping me over his shoulder like a bag of potatoes. I can't resist. I can't do anything. Except start to sob.

Ethan loses his mind. He thrashes against his bonds. "What are you going to do? WHAT ARE YOU GOING TO DO TO HER? You can't leave us like this!" He tries to throw himself in the man's path, but the hulk steps over him. My vision blurs, bobs upside-down as I'm taken from the room.

"Goodbye, General," Pearl says. "We will meet again soon."

The man carries me outside and dumps me on the driveway. Ethan's howls are cut off as Pearl follows the men outside and slams the door behind her. I struggle to my knees, snot and tears smeared across my cheeks. Pearl has a gun in her hand. She rests it against my forehead.

"You tricked me," I scream. Rage boils up through my fear. "I thought you were searching for someone you loved. You said that love never dies!"

"I loved my poor, mortal family. Love *doesn't* die." She cocks the hammer. "Neither does hate."

I stare up at her. She is going to kill me, but in this instant, I pity her. She is the proof that people *need* to forget, to start over, to be given second, third, eighth chances. Or we might become like her. Frozen by the worst of our memories. Imprisoned by histories we can't change and can't leave behind.

"You promised to help me." My voice is a cracked whisper now. "All this time, you were just using me."

"I *am* going to help you, Claire. I'm going to tell you how to break the pattern."

She pulls the trigger.

Click. The hammer falls on an empty chamber.

I blink, confused as to how I am still alive. "Untie her," Pearl orders. A minute later, the duct tape around my wrists and ankles rips loose, peeling a layer of skin off with it. Pearl lowers the gun.

"You were meant to die tonight, but I spared you. Now I will tell you what the secret of the pattern is." She leans forward and whispers. "Choice."

Behind her, the short masked man lights a match and drops it. Fire encircles the house in an enormous whoosh of red heat.

My bladder gives out. Warmth spreads down the legs of my jeans.

"There is always a choice." The black chasms of her eyes are two pinpricks of reflected firelight. "Now run, Claire."

I scramble to my feet. And I run.

I RUN WITHOUT REGARD for direction. I run over lawns, through shrubbery and around trees. My foot catches on a curb, and I gasp as I pitch forward into a garden bed. Whimpers clog my throat as I struggle to my feet and look over my shoulder.

The men are small figures now, climbing into a black van with tinted windows and a missing license plate. One of them rolls down the passenger side window and yells at Pearl, who remains standing in front of the burning house. For a long moment, she doesn't move. The glow of the fire lights up the street and casts leaping shadows like hellish dancing puppets. Pearl takes two slow steps forward, a spot of white against a curtain of red, as if she intends to walk into the flames, to join everything she's lost.

Then she turns and walks calmly to the van. When she's inside, the van turns sharply and peels away.

I dig my hands into the dirt, so wet and cool. I remember what it was like in the fire. The intensity of the pain. Marie—*I*—screamed until my throat burned from the inside out.

I get up. And I run back toward the house.

My body wants to rebel. It cannot believe I am doing this; it wants to shut down in response to terror. *But Ethan is in there. And Kegan. How can I let them suffer the death I most fear?*

When I reach the house, I freeze in a final, stomach-churning moment of cowardice. Then I run to the door. I try to push it open, but it's stuck. Then I remember the broken window and run around to the side of the house. Smoke pours from the living room. I take a deep breath and clamber inside. There's glass on the floor; a shard of it jabs into my palm, but I barely feel it. I pull my sleeves over my hands and keep crawling. I can hear, through the crackle and roar of flames, the sound of screaming. Perhaps I'm imagining it or perhaps I'm screaming in my head.

I make it to the hallway and army crawl forward, elbow over elbow, my nose pressed close to the floor, sucking in short bursts of ashy air. The heat on my skin is like a hundred sunburns. I'm crying and ninety-nine percent sure I'm going to die, but I keep scrambling forward until I reach the closed bedroom door. The knob scalds my hand when I reach up to twist it. I shove the door open and drop back down, coughing. "Ethan," I try to call, but the smoke is too thick. Then I bump into a moving shape. A leg. I follow it up to a torso. Ethan twists in place. His frightened, blood-shot eyes meet mine and grow wide with relief and horror.

"Claire! What are you doing?" he gasps.

I pull the switchblade from my pocket and fumble it open. I start sawing at the duct tape around his wrists. My eyes and nose sting. Adrenaline pours through my system, and I fight to keep my hands steady. Ethan lies still, trying to help me as I keep cutting, inch by inch, until the tape tears free. He grabs the knife from me and hacks frantically at the tape binding his feet until he frees them. He scrambles away toward Kegan.

I am light-headed now. It is hard to breathe. The skin of my hands sizzle and blister. The world swims black and red. *Choice,* I think. And I remember.

I REMEMBER I GRABBED the spade, the only weapon I could find, and followed Donnan.

I ran toward the wounded leopard, drawing it away from Jamal.

I pressed the satchel of herbs into Estelle's desperate hands.

I saw the storm clouds, but I took the boat out; little Asuka was so hungry.

I dribbled water onto the pustule-speckled lips of Owhi, the chief's son, as he lay dying.

I pushed Jeanne down to the ground as the bullets began to fly.

THERE IS A CRACKING, splintering sound from somewhere overhead. Ethan is shouting my name, but it seems to be coming from very far away. A strange calm overtakes me.

My lives make sense now. Tragic death is not my pattern.

Sacrifice is my pattern.

The secret is choice, Pearl had said. She's right. Our patterns are the ones we choose, over and over again. I've never broken my pattern because I've always chosen as I'm choosing now.

Kegan's face appears an inch in front of mine, distorted by the smoke. *"Get up."* His voice is barely his own. He hauls hard on my arms. Ethan grabs me from the other side, urging my body across the ground. My hands and knees scrabble across the burning floor-boards of the hall. Then the two of them are lifting and thrusting me toward the window. It appears, a narrow portal ringed by fire, beckoning urgently.

And then I'm through it, staggering out of the flames. Cold air rushes into my scalded lungs. I stumble several more steps and drop to the ground, coughing, gasping, trembling. The cool grass presses against my raw skin; everything is a tear-stained blur. Kegan and Ethan collapse next to me, heaving for breath. Behind us, the house continues to burn, sending plumes of smoke into the night sky. The blare of sirens and the strobing of lights surround us as we cling to each other. Kegan's swollen eyes are haunted, and Ethan shakes uncontrollably. Their clothes and hair are blackened, their skin red and blistered, but they're alive. I'm alive.

All of us, alive. *We've been given another chance.*

There's always another chance.

∞

Le Guin, more than another other author, taught me that speculative fiction is the genre of ideas. She destroyed any notion that writing and reading science fiction and fantasy were trivial or escapist activities, proving instead that only by expanding our imaginations to their utmost could we fully explore the human condition at its most intimate, nuanced, and real. Le Guin broke down the wall between genre and literary fiction because she never saw it, and so she sailed effortlessly, it seems, into writing some of the most simultaneously fantastical and truthful works of our time. I had the pleasure of hearing her speak at an event two short years before her passing. She was still writing poetry, still fearlessly expounding on her views, still inspiring and encouraging younger authors like myself. She was, and still is, a role model to me personally, and her impact on the field remains immeasurable.

The Ones Who Don't Walk Away

RENE DENFELD

WHEN THE WINDS BLOW to the south of Omelas, you can hear the wailing.

I am number 10024, and this is my testimony.

I came to Omelas when I was five. We came on a bus, from the border between Omelas and my homeland. Worlds have nations, I have discovered, and nations have borders. These you may not see with your eyes, but you can feel them with your heart. They are places of menace.

I don't remember much from before, because all the hurt since has wiped it out, like a hand wipes away the morning blood on your face, or the dust from the window that looks into a solitary sky. I see images instead. My mother, the warmth of her thick skirts. Carrying me across a desert. Realizing she wore pants under the skirts, and had soaked them with urine in fright during our arrest. Them pulling her away from me in clouds of dust that never ended.

Waking up here.

The older kids tried to care for the younger. At first. The guards who came were okay. At first. Reporters clamored to see us. At first.

There were big stories about what happened here, like one called "The Ones Who Walk Away from Omelas," by a woman named Ursula K. Le Guin, about how terribly they treated us children.

But after a year or so, the visitors stopped coming. In the three years since, I have grown a little, not much, because there is something in this concrete prison that keeps the children small. The guards have gotten progressively worse. One of the older kids whispered they passed a law, in this nation that is supposed to stand for freedom, that anyone can work the centers, no background check needed. You can imagine where that leads.

The newspapers no longer talk about us, the forgotten kids of Omelas.

Outside, in the faraway distance, you can see the domed city. It looks perfect. The people there live wonderful lives, I have heard. They have homes with prayer flags fluttering outside, and signs on their lawns that say lives like mine matter. They play in parks and send their kids to schools with names like flowers. Omelas is everything Earth wanted to be, and maybe it was, before the splintering of nations and the taking of resources. The people of Omelas say they care, and maybe they do, but their care is as thin as the wind that comes keening over the sand, and about as cold.

Life is hypocrisy, I have found, and if you think I am too young to know this, you have not led a life like mine. That was true on Earth, and it is true here, on this world, in places like Omelas.

Sometimes I look out the dusty windows—there are dozens of us to each cyclone cage, and the only time we leave is for terrors I don't want to tell—at the distant city. If worlds have borders, then citizens know, someplace in the dark corners of their hearts, what that means.

The food here has grown worse. Greenhouse lettuce slimed with rot. Rotted synthetic meat. Food that leaves us crippled in pain for days, the younger ones dying of cramps the guards cannot unfold.

When we turn eighteen, we are sent back to the border between Omelas and my homeland, and only the three suns can see what happens next. We are unchained and released back into the desert. I imagine a vast generation of us, hobbled with pain, our insides weeping blood from the assaults, wandering into a red, dusty world where no one wants us.

We are the talismans, the curses the people of Omelas believe ward off greater harm. There is no other reason for places like this to exist. In this new world, just like the old, cruelty has become virtue, and silence is the soft whisper in the dark that says, it's okay.

10024 HERE. I AM twelve now. I knew it was my birthday because the doctor came. He examines us every birthday and pronounces us fit as fiddles—whatever that means—even if we are not.

He saw I got my first bleeding, the kind women usually get, and, as usual, said nothing for the chafing on my legs, the darkness that lingers. He shook his head and made a mark on his sheet.

The next week I got the operation. Now, the guards smirk, no one will ever know.

A POLITICIAN FROM OMELAS came, right after my seventeenth birthday. He had a convoy of notetakers and social workers. We hadn't seen a reporter in forever, and some of the children pressed against the cyclone of the cages, but what good have reporters ever done us?

My next birthday I will be gone, to walk the dusty desert. Most the kids I came in with are dead now, of abuse, sorrow, or neglect. You learn to think of people as numbers, just like the guards refer to us. I am 10024. For a long time I remembered my real name, but over the years it slipped away.

Omelas was a lie. I wish my mother could have seen that.

I count her birthdays, along with my own. I think she was in her thirties when they took me, so would be close to fifty now. I feel she is dead. There was a cord there, across the deserts, and it collapsed, sometime over the last few years. It just feels different.

Anyhow, the man from the city came, with his people, who smelled raw with cologne. They walked the cages and saw us with our filthy blankets, and they asked questions of the younger kids they keep bringing, more refugees from the desert, and the younger kids could not answer except with their eyes. No one cries here anymore. The wailing is the sound of the wind outside, over the sculpted hills between us and the city.

In the city, people sit over pretty plates and they put dollops of tasty food on those plates, always watching their weight because they live in a land of plenty, and they know it is children like us that harvest the food in their fields, and I will tell you the truth right now: I would do anything to be one of those children, and not locked up here. That is how far I have fallen, in my own dreams of Omelas. I would rather be a slave than dead.

But here we sit, proof of their own virtue.

FINALLY, THE DAY CAME. I turned eighteen.

10024, they called me, and I rose from our cage for the last time, to be taken down a hall not for more pain but for the door they opened, to the outdoors. The faces of the guards shifted and changed. I could no longer remember how many of them had pressed against me in the dark.

The bus was waiting, and a guard with chains.

In the distance, as clear as a bell, the city of Omelas.

I wished I could go there and ask them, are you happy now? Did I serve my purpose?

The bus was old and clanked with heat. Twice we had to stop while they put water in the radiator. They gave us no food.

But after thirteen years, I was outside, and it felt like a miracle. There was the sky, and the wide-open space of it all, so much it hurt the eyes. My legs were bowed from the atrophy of not getting exercise, the doctor had said, on my final exam, as if he was not part of the cause. My heart was shrunken, and he said I have something called failure to thrive.

But I was on the bus, riding to a new place, called freedom.

After many hours, the bus clanked to a stop, and the driver released the level, and told us to get off.

There were only a few of us, survivors of a group that once numbered hundreds. Armed men came out of the dust to unchain our legs. I saw we were standing in the same place I was taken. My mother was out there, somewhere, in the desert hills. A ghost to find.

"Well, be off with you," one of the men said, with a self-serving grin.

The others and I looked at each other. We were given no water, no food, no clothing against the cold desert nights. There was darkness in those hills, and the yipping of wild beasts. I remembered, long ago, hearing that survivors like us had formed communities in the desert hills, the nomad tribes of the desert nations, gathering strength against the day we could hurt those who hurt us.

Maybe that was just an imagination. Or maybe not.

"You shouldn't have come to Omelas," the guard with the chains said, and they retreated back into darkness.

My new friends and I turned to face the hills.

When I was homeless as a teenager, I spent much of my time in the downtown Portland library, where I became intimately familiar with Ursula Le Guin's work, relating to the themes of disenfranchisement, otherness, and hope. The sense of intellectualism granted to even the downtrodden in Le Guin's books gave me the inspiration that someday I, too, could become a writer, and help others.

The Polar Explorer

LENI ZUMAS

IN THE SUMMER OF 1875, Eivør Mínervudottír lied her way onto a steamship leaving Copenhagen for the Polar North. Not until *Oreius* had rounded the Jutland Peninsula did the captain understand a woman was aboard. He told the explorer, "We have no choice but to bear you."

The odds of her standing on that deck, given who she was—poor, female, and Faroese—were long. Her uncle had taught her arithmetic and Danish; she had taught herself everything else.

In the Arctic Ocean north of Siberia, pack ice closed around *Oreius* and locked it fast for eight months. Mínervudottír spent the besetment recording temperature, salinity, atmospheric pressure, chlorides in the ice. She mapped and measured.

By the time the ship could move again, she had suffered acute frostbite in two fingers.

The captain discharged her in Copenhagen, and upon her

release from the hospital where the fingers were amputated, Mínervudottír found work cleaning a church. She rode the church bicycle to the university library, which had a good collection on hydrology and the polar climes.

When she wasn't writing up her data from *Oreius* or oiling the church pews, she spoke to her notebook: *A pack is beasts who hunt. Wild dogs, wolves, sea ice. To be chased by ice, and torn apart. I want to go to sea again and be torn.*

Only a month after she mailed her paper, "On the Contours and Tendencies of Arctic Sea Ice," to the Royal Society of London, she received a rejection. The Society's board members believed Mínervudottír had either invented the data or stolen it from a man.

Upon reading the terse letter, she held a lit match to the healing stump of her pinky until the skin bubbled.

That week the pews were not oiled. Dust furred the curlicues of the oak pulpit.

LIFE SCRAPED OUT ITS routines. Rag and broom, cheese on buttered rye, her shoulders fluttery from mopping. At night, the polar explorer drank pale beer and read the newspaper, where she began to follow with particular interest the plight of the Greely expedition.

In August of 1881, the American explorer Lieutenant Adolphus Greely and his team of twenty-five men and forty-two dogs had arrived at Lady Franklin Bay, north of Greenland. They were to gather astronomical and magnetic data from the Arctic Circle and meant to attain a new Farthest North record.

The second summer, a ship carrying food and letters for the expedition was blocked by ice and forced to turn back. The third summer, another supply ship was trapped in ice and crushed.

Rescue missions were being mounted.

Mínervudottír said to her notebook: *I would give two more fingers to go back to sea. Each hand would still have three, if we count the thumbs.*

Khione was a steam-powered icebreaker, its bow reinforced with iron. Its crew included a polar hydrologist who specialized in pack ice behavior. The Canadian captain did not wish to be defeated by a few chilled chunks of ocean, and the hydrologist had written a most persuasive letter about his expertise. The hydrologist came aboard at St. John's, Newfoundland, with his face wrapped in red flannel.

When *Khione* sailed from St. John's in May of 1884, the officers started a betting pool: how many of Greely's men would still be alive when they found them? Eivør Mínervudottír stood on deck, feeling the salt wind, the slapping waves, the pull of north, smiling behind her scarf.

Le Guin resisted categories. Her work was omnifarious, polymorphic. She's a North Star for all explorers who aren't willing to stay where others have put them.

Birds

BENJAMIN PARZYBOK

I LIKE SECRETS, DON'T you?

Better, I like secret pockets, secret boxes. Niches and coves and crannies. I like hideaways, which is why I built mine. Here, are you comfortable? I like hot things in cold places. I like small flashlights in inside jacket pockets, anything on a ledge.

I like you, how under your skin is your secret heart pumping, making you run. I like the glimmer in your dark eye. I like how, secretly, you like to be taken advantage of, if the circumstance permits it just so. I like you here, in my nest, my city perch, eye glass in your hand, spying out the passersby below.

It has rained for a week straight, the week in which you stumbled a refugee into my camp.

It's been a honeymoon. Behind the billboard advertising an island getaway, atop the odd little building owned by the bead seller, above the city. We sit and talk—even better, we sit and don't talk.

Here, let me show you this. I have a paperback, it's a book of magic tricks and here is my small flashlight, let's pull the tarp close. We'll learn a trick or two and tell secrets.

APRIL 19TH

I'd always wanted to take a closer look at the gargoyles on the edge of the old Stadtler building. Around back there was a metal-rung ladder built into the side of the building I could reach from the dumpster. I was completely unprepared for what I saw atop the building: a live gargoyle of a man, bearded with a dirty sleeping bag wrapped around his middle. On one shoulder a pigeon was perched, and he had hair like a motorcycle collided with a porcupine. A small campfire burned on the roof—I don't want to know what kind of meat on a stick burned in the middle of it. "Welcome," he said, and "Come on in." As if it were some kind of restaurant, or some kind of "in" to go into.

The intelligent thing to do would have been to turn and climb back down. He asked if I'd seen the sunset from up there—it made a descent into the hole between two buildings, he said.

We got to discussing the weather. He pointed to a cloud and said something like: "When that touches down, we will become engulfed in its insides. It will digest us. When it leaves, we will not be the people we were, fluid for fluid from foreign lands. Part of you will go airborne, off to change the water chemistry of others." I haven't heard weather discussed like this before.

I KNOW THE CITY in a way you do not, and you know the city in a way I don't. How much steel is in that building? I'd never thought to ask that of myself. What's in the bowels of that tower there, its great cement pillars rooting deep into the earth, you know this stuff, you stood on the ground underneath the ground where that was built, with your paper and rulers and love of sharpened pencils and straight lines.

But you seem most hungry for my knowledge. I know where the pigeons roost—I have held their chicks in my hand. Tomorrow I will take you to where there are strawberries like chickenpox under an overpass. They are the sweetest you will ever taste, seasoned with exhaust dust. Am I your guide now? Is it a Virgil you want?

You know how to live in a world other people created. Of course you do. For the last ten years I've stopped trying to figure this out. And those ten have been the happiest—no, the only happy ones of my life.

I live in a world that I create. In my world—you've noticed, don't say you haven't—a passing crow might stop and have a conversation about a change in schedule at the city trash pickup, or, for example, the pigeons. It's a world I want to live in, all the rules are mine. Don't argue yet.

May 7th

I can't stop thinking about him. It's idiotic and I'm not sure who to tell. Franny's got a death wish, Mom would say. I found a book on clouds and brought it by and stayed, and then every damn day I somehow end up there. It's hard to imagine how anyone could honestly live like that, how you could live on top of a building all winter, burning fires on the roof. Doesn't anyone notice? In the studio I spent the day sketching portable shelters, makeshift inhabitances. Nests, really. But then I thought: Why accommodate a problem rather than try to fix it? No one should be living like that. And yet, that's where I'm going now.

I'M SO GLAD YOU'RE here, can I touch your hair? You remind me of a brown mouse, or perhaps a frightened otter. It can get awfully lonely in a world you make by yourself. There are times I'm unsure. Yesterday a cockroach came and spent the night in my sleeping bag and told me about what had been put in the dumpster at the bakery. You cannot say I am not a good host. Here, take another donut. Take this loaf. It will make you remember me, a slice of me in your home. Be not afraid.

You've had some kind of trouble in your past—I see this in how you hold your hands—perhaps you thought this was a secret, but those are things that are easily apparent in my made-up world. Perhaps that's why you like it here with me—you feel in danger. Are you waiting for me to hurt you? Perhaps you're trying to re-create a situation that haunts you, so that you may act how you've always wished you would have. That's all right. I'd like to show you how if you stand in the square at lunchtime, just stand still and watch, the comings and goings of the people are like rain, each of them a tiny drop. And soon, if you prove an apt student, I will take you to where the birds have been teaching me how to fly.

MAY 9TH

Every day I cycle a new set of books through the "perch," as I've taken to calling it. Things that I think he'll be interested in. I pick them up at the library: *Migration Habits of Birds*, *Urban Structures*, and one that I was particularly excited about: *Bats in the Belfry: A Joyous Evocation of Architectural Eccentricity*. I smoke and he talks. Sometimes I bring food, but he picks through it like I'm the one culling through dumpsters. I tell him I want to see what he looks like with his beard shaved and he tells me it's fake. That behind the fake beard there is no face, and behind that is only air.

YOU DO NOT UNDERSTAND at first and we must have a long talk about why you are here, my forger, Hephaestus of skyscrapers, we talk about death, and briefly, curled in my blankets, you talk about how you'd like to save me, clean me, dress and formalize and re-create me into an actual citizen. It's fun to listen to you talk and I let you talk because I know it makes you feel tall and righteous, like an anthropologist among the savages. You are beginning to make up your own world. It takes practice.

MAY 19TH

Every time I walk into my apartment, I see it through his eyes. I look at the refrigerator and think of him reaching for the ketchup or the potato salad. Would he eat potato salad? If I were to cook him dinner, what would I cook? Something rich and heavy. Something that would ground him. The cat sits on my back and I'm reminded of how animals react differently to him. They fly down from the sky or scale up the building and linger there. *I* linger there. I escape to there. He's like another, more fascinating world I disappear to. One in which someone has peeled all the bullshit veneer up and left only a structure of wonder. And yet, he's repulsive. Climbing that ladder, you hit a wave of stench, of dried shit and death and rot, the sour smell of his clothes. Every time I crest that building I reconsider. There are spots on his teeth that consume me with anxiety. Each of them a little timer ticking away the remaining seconds until the tooth rots its way out of his mouth. What crossed wire has disabled his ability to see these things? Something in him is broken. Except.

THANK YOU FOR VISITING today but I wish you'd go. From the moment you walked onto the roof I could see your doubt. I'd like to fold my wings in and turn to stone, like that gargoyle, there, on that building that one of your predecessors installed.

I've been drinking for—I'm not exactly sure how long. A few days. I have gotten up for nothing and the stench of it all is here. You wish to flee? Go.

Instead you stay and pretend you are here to rescue me; I find it irritating and I'm rude. I decide to end our relationship and that I will tell you nothing more. You cry and when you are gone, I feel how something else has ended. Check, there's one more thing I've ticked off on the long list before I die. It is done.

If you really wanted to know, I would have told you. There was a family of cats on the rooftop there, making their home in the ventilation shaft. They don't understand the mechanisms of buildings, not like you or even I. When I found them, they were as if made of rawhide and feathers. This is what happens to what I love, the life-juice sucked out; it was best you fled. I guess everyone wants to save something. Even me.

MAY 22ND

Fuck. Him. I'm relieved, really. The experiment is over. I need to focus on work and see my friends and etc., etc. He's an asshole and a drunkard and I had begun to think of him as someone he obviously is not. Franny's experiment in homeless men! I feel an autobiography being written. Perhaps for company I ought to seek out someone decent and interesting and not those who spend their day in sleeping bags on rooftops refusing to contribute to society.

May 25th

Yes. This is where I'm supposed to write what I'm working on. Or what I did over the weekend. Thoughts on design, a sketch or two, remember those? Or how annoying my mother is.

But every day I wonder if he's dead. I go out of my way to walk by the building, listening for sounds, smelling the air for rot. I can't bring myself to climb that ladder.

I feel partly at fault for our last meeting. He was sad and I didn't want to address it. I had a plan. I was practiced. It seemed so ridiculous to be where he was—by choice—and to be sad. That probably doesn't make any sense. He was such a wreck and had obviously been drunk for days.

YOU CAME BACK. WHY? I'm not sure how much time has passed. You would know this. I suspect you've come to see if I, too, had turned to rawhide, my face open and drunk and inhaling rain. But I have not.

You dressed for me, or you think you did. I'd already decided that if you came, I would show you my secret, so hello then.

I can tell by your eyes that you feel self-destructive, that if you cannot defile yourself somehow with me, you'd consider hurdling the ledge as a substitute. Or perhaps that's what you're here for already, what you've always been here for—is this what drew you? To attempt flight? I have a secret for that.

But I decide I'm not interested in meeting your expectations. Your thighs grip when we hug and you're speaking some kind of new language of personal agenda. But I'm busy. I've got a plan and alcohol has wiped the lust from me. See these boards, this hammer that I've stolen that vibrates in my palm like Thor's own tool?

I'm building a sky walk. I'm remodeling, expanding, I will span rooftops, be the lord over the city. The animals will travel with me above you all.

Despite your initial disappointment, I've distracted you into working with me and of course you're apt—this is how your mind is built. Together we could build a whole city atop this one. We could re-fabricate the rules into our own social tendencies. It would be a simple thing to lay to rest the world that lies below our feet, sixty feet under, RIP. We could love each other and be like king and queen.

But the more I talk, the more I can see you are leaving. Your transformations amaze me—let me catalog them.

You came with suicide on your mind, then you wanted to fuck the dregs, that's me, reluctantly you were coaxed into my project, applied yourself with growing enthusiasm, grew bored and nervous with my chatter, felt you were on a charity mission, and finally relieved of your self-destructiveness and your charity, you look for the first opportunity to flee. Well, fucking go, then.

WE RAN INTO EACH other on the street. Down below, in my underworld, the lower level, dirty and scrounging about. I didn't know what to expect after our last argument went mean. I saw you coming from a block away, but I was burdened by a pain in my leg, and the number of things I'd collected that morning. I tried my best to pretend I had not noticed you—you were with comrades, men, coming back from lunch. All of them with that greasy, well-fed healthiness, licking their lips, wiping their palms on their hips, each eager to out-best the other's speech with his own invective—and I felt nervous. I turned and lifted the lid of a garbage can.

Then when you were obviously going to approach me, I considered making a scene—surely you couldn't want this interaction with me, here. In our lair I understand. But you walked up to me, put your hand on my back—I thought then that you were showing off, and I wanted to shout, stomp, bare my wings. But you waved your people on, leaned in close, whispered "Hi" in my ear. I was touched, even if I'd much preferred you had passed me by.

Afterward, I wandered the streets for a long time with no thought to where I was going, only replaying the moment over and over.

May 30th

I'm going to bring him to my place. He's going to live with me. There's nobody I can tell, not for a few months. But in a few months we'll be different, we'll have stabilized. He'll clean up a little, and I'll clean down. We'll look not wholly different from each other. In a few months his lips won't crack, the blood and bruises and grime will be gone. It's fucking stupid! But I can't help it. I want him here. I want him off of the building where I can't imagine him living another week. It's gotten so I'm obsessed. I pass by there constantly. I don't know what he'll do here, I worry about that. But I am an architect. Humans were meant to be protected by the shell. This is something I can do for him. Just a little stability and warmth might . . . oh. I can't even say it. I don't want to even think it.

YOU ARE SO EARNEST, telling me you love me like that's something that can just be said. You came to see what I've done to my grand plan—I've torn the boardwalk apart. Our grand plan, the plank we were going to walk together. The pieces of it everywhere as if a man three times my size had crushed it with his girth. This dream is meaningless now, I am learning to fly. And you want me to come to your house?

I'm not sure what I'm supposed to do here. What can I touch? Is all this really yours? After the shower I feel like getting drunk and I grab a bottle of your wine and open it and then another and together we get drunk and spill wine on your floor and you break your coffee table. Were you showing off? Are you not well? I feel as if it were my fault and wonder where your wood glue is.

Your cat comes and talks to me and I get disoriented. He is dumb and barely cognizant, like the life he lives has lulled him into the state of some inanimate object. He is needy and redundant and it sickens me and I wonder if I should put him out of his misery and I wonder if this is how I will end up, if the fate you had in mind for me was of a rescued and hypnotized lump of comfort flesh.

At some point in the night watching you sleep next to me, smelling like you do, I realize how wrong this all is. I have my own world and I don't want you in it for the amount of falling you would have to do to get there. Look what you have—you can't live there. And yet, I despise your world, I hate your carpet and your refrigerator. I hate your car, I hate your cat and your Tupperware and cutlery and your Starry Night-rendered wastebasket and I hate your mantel with the remains of some holiday all over it like some god had eaten an oracle and puked it all up. I think about what I might do to myself with a knife from your kitchen just to feel a little.

I fill with rage and I want to destroy that wastebasket, I want to clap that plastic night sky over your head and the only way to properly end this debacle between us is to hurt you, hurt you so that you might have a story to tell office mates and your mother and whoever else is holding you to whatever it is you no longer wish you were. I'd let you fall with me and I suppose there's a part of me that wants you to fall and wants you to fall into me, but I cannot bear being that cushion at the bottom of the well, your impetus for the jump.

I realize I must stab you. How else am I going to cut the tendon binding our worlds together? But I can't find a knife I like to hold. I can't find anything I want to touch at all. I need to hurt you to stay away, like one must hurt a dog that wants to follow you home to let it know your real intentions, but I cannot, and so I clothe myself and leave.

YOU READ ABOUT ME in the paper and you cry. Or perhaps you'd been crying already and read the paper and saw what had become of me. I was late getting here, I soared down from above to your windowsill to have a look in. My feet teetered there, I'm new to this and am not so strong yet.

I WATCH YOUR CAT from my perch and he natters desultory remarks at me from his chair and I realize we could have gotten along. He is lazy and dull but not so dumb. He has learned his lines. He's playing his part. He's doing what I never could.

The body? Oh, what is a body but a rest stop for clouds. The papers talk about how I was drunk, how I'd found my way onto a building and had drunk myself over the ledge one rainy evening. They do not talk about how I rose up from that discarded body, shook my feathers and flew.

Now that I'm here on the outside, talons gripping at this cold wet stone, looking in at you circling about your kitchen, fork gripped in one hand and crumpled newspaper in the other, I realize with immense regret that I've forgotten to teach you how to fly.

The Earthsea trilogy was an enormous pillar of my childhood. My political philosophy—as well as the desire to imbue my own work with political issues and to explore anthropological angles—was influenced by The Dispossessed *and later* The Left Hand of Darkness.

Homeless Gary Busey

TIMOTHY O'LEARY

IAN DAVIS WAS AN orderly man. His closets, length and style-organized on color-coded hangers with pleasing symmetry. His refrigerator, logically structured by height and food type, anything with pending expiration dates moved to the front. His workday uniform rotated between identical Banana Republic chinos and blue denim shirts.

Monday through Friday at 7:15 a.m., he commenced the twenty-minute walk to work, first filling his NPR thermos, then buckling up the shoulder bag that housed his laptop, water bottle, and two Granny Smith apples. He kept a tiny copy of *The Twelve Steps* buried in the front flap, but hadn't needed to pull it out for several months. He navigated the steep stairs from his apartment onto Cardinal Lane, traversed the freeway bridge, and dropped into the park that wound through Portland State University, finally arriving at the downtown home of Jazz Technology.

Ian was well acquainted with the homeless population there, navigating the collision of have and have-nots with few issues. He ascribed to the city's recommendation not to give change to panhandlers, and instead donated one hundred dollars per year to a shelter. He avoided the weed-whiffing punks on skateboards across the street from the art museum, and stayed clear of anyone consuming drugs or alcohol, or engaged in angry conversations with fictional friends.

However, on a July morning, as he passed a vacant lot bordering the bridge that spanned the 405, an enormous form sprang from the chest-high grass, jolting Ian off the curb. Wrapped in a tatty gray blanket, the man was wearing faded red swimming trunks and a Steely Dan concert T-shirt promoting their 1980 Gaucho tour. His feet, dirt-stained, were encased in bright pink flip-flops.

"Where's my Egg McMuffin?" he screamed.

It appeared the man had slept in the field, his blanket mud-caked, hay protruding like knitting needles from his long blond hair.

"I don't know anything about that," Ian responded calmly, to avoid exciting him, before hustling across the street.

"Wait," the man hollered, giving chase. Ian didn't want to embarrass himself by breaking into a sprint, and instead accelerated to a loping speed-walk. The man, flip-flops flapping, stayed on his heels, yelling, "Give me my Egg McMuffin, you selfish dick."

Ian breathed a sigh of relief when he spied a group of construction workers. The man's threats were growing more volatile. "You give me my Egg McMuffin," he said, "or I will shit down your pie hole."

"Gary," a burly, hard-hatted man yelled, "leave the guy alone."

Ian sidled up to the workers, and the homeless man stopped ten feet back. "He owes the toll. One Egg McMuffin."

"I was walking down the street and he started hassling me," Ian countered.

"You crossed my bridge, and I charge a toll. One Egg McMuffin," the man screamed, arms waving in windmill. "Give me my breakfast, you pathetic little Nordstrom yuppie, or you will face my wrath."

"Gary, get out of here." The construction worker made an exaggerated burst forward. Gary jumped back, and then tried to save face by pantomiming an old-timey boxing stance.

"Okay, but tomorrow you will owe two Egg McMuffins, you chiseling mini-man." Gary shook a fist at Ian. "I know where you live, you human skid mark," he yelled, before hustling back the way he'd come.

"Thanks for your help," Ian mumbled.

"No problem," the construction worker said. "We call him Homeless Gary Busey, 'cause he looks so much like that actor. Maybe it is him. Haven't seen him in a movie lately." The man smiled. "Don't know his real name, but he's been hanging out a few weeks. He's harmless."

"Thanks again." Ian started down the sidewalk.

"No problem, little fella," one of the other workers yelled with a laugh. "Come see us if any nasty men bother you."

Ian winced. At five-foot-three and 125 pounds, he was sensitive about his size, and his fear was replaced with anger. Anger at being hassled for no reason. Anger at being ridiculed by men wearing steel-toed boots. He stopped and took a deep breath. *God grant me the serenity to accept the things I cannot change.* He needed to keep "Bad Ian" in check.

That night he Ubered home. He had a strong craving for alcohol, but he'd been sober for the last four years and opted for cranberry and club soda. He was sitting on his tiny deck firing up his Hibachi when he heard the commotion.

"I see you," Homeless Gary yelled from the street. "I told you, I know where you live. I hope you plan to bring me my Egg McMuffin tomorrow, or there will be hell to pay."

"Get out of here," Ian screamed. "I'll call the police."

"The police," Gary said sarcastically. "You think that scares me?" He lifted his arms into a monster pose. "The cops have no power over me. I own this neighborhood, you Starbucks-loving anal wart. Tomorrow I want two Egg McMuffins. Otherwise, I will drag you into my cave, chain you to a wall, and skin you alive.

Skull-fuck your tiny head." Gary dropped his hands to his crotch and made an obscene gesture. "You understand?"

Ian rushed into his apartment and slammed the patio door. He called 911, and a few minutes later met the police car, but there was no sign of Gary.

"Not much we can do," one of the officers told him. "Some of these guys are whacked out, but they're usually harmless."

The next morning Ian took an Uber to work, which put him in a foul mood for the day. *It's ridiculous I can't walk the city streets for fear of an insane homeless man.* During lunch, he went to the police station and met with a detective. The official position was no position.

"A crazy guy yelling threats would be impossible to prosecute," the detective told him. "We'd have to put half of Portland in jail."

"A guy threatens to drag me to a cave, remove my skin, and have sex with my skull," Ian said, "and the police can't do anything about it?"

The detective shrugged. "Let me know if he actually does any of those things. That would make for a good case."

That night Ian Ubered home again. Just after 7:00 p.m., he heard a loud thump on the patio door, a jagged crack spiraling up from the bottom. Assuming a wayward bird had slammed into the glass, he rushed out onto the patio. A stone whizzed above his head. "Where the fuck are my Egg McMuffins?"

Gary was standing fifteen feet below, a bright fuchsia women's bathrobe pulled tight around his shoulders. He was wearing sweatpants, a T-shirt promoting the 1983 ZZ Top "Sharp Dressed Man" tour, and a filthy cream fedora with an eagle feather sprouting from the top. His flip-flops had been replaced by massive unlaced work boots, and his fists bulged with rocks. "I warned you, you half-pint J.Crew scumbag. Now you will pay the price. Tomorrow I want three Egg McMuffins, and two Big Macs. Breakfast and lunch. If I don't get them, I will cut off your dick and feed it to you." Ian dove as more rocks struck the door. When he peeked over the side, Gary had disappeared.

Terrified, Ian slumped into the apartment, carefully double

locking the patio slider, dropping the shade, and then rushing to the front door to make sure it was secure. He combed through his medicine chest until the found the Xanax he'd squirrelled away several years earlier. Ignoring the long-past expiration date, he threw two in his mouth and bent down to drink from the faucet. Returning to the kitchen, he reached into a corner cabinet to retrieve a bottle of Merlot, dubbed "Jazz Wine" on the label, a company Christmas gift he'd hidden after the holiday party—just in case he made a friend. Hands shaking as he uncorked the bottle, he hesitated for a second to consider his hard-fought years of sobriety, but decided this was a dire situation requiring medication. Grabbing an aluminum softball bat, he sat at the kitchen table for the next hour and consumed the entire bottle, waiting for Homeless Gary's next move.

The next morning, he awoke on his couch to the chirping of his iPhone alarm. Head throbbing, with serious Mojave-mouth, Ian was racked with guilt as the previous evening came into focus. *How could I have thrown away all those years of progress?* Dread washed over him as he recalled many mornings like this: waking up sick, sometimes in a pool of his own spew, attempting to piece together the previous night. The awful realizations of drunken antics that cost him jobs and alienated friends or family. He'd been sure those days were over, his fresh start in Portland a way to exorcise himself. But Bad Ian was back.

For the first time since he'd started at Jazz, he called in late. He showered and dressed slowly, considering his next steps. Four years earlier, if Ian hadn't found the courage to leave Minneapolis, he might have ended up on the street too. So he needed to have some compassion. However, he couldn't allow Gary to destroy all he'd built. The program had taught him that to survive, people sometimes needed to be extricated from your life.

Feeling better, he considered that this might be some kind of sign, an opportunity to redeem himself while building character. He would attempt to help Gary. Head pounding, Ian pocketed the pepper spray he kept in the bedside table—just in case.

He walked at half-speed, head swiveling as he approached the bridge. He was halfway past the vacant lot when he heard bellowing from underneath the bridge. "I hope you brought my food."

Gary crawled up the incline, grasping at the thick weeds to hoist himself. He'd abandoned the woman's robe for his blanket, and the fedora had been replaced with an ancient steel army helmet with a ripped Bob Marley sticker on the front. He was carrying a plastic lightsaber. "You look like a man, only smaller," he chortled, then grew serious. "Now show me my fucking Egg McMuffins or face the consequences. I can decapitate you with this thing." He nodded at the Star Wars sword.

Standing on the edge of the sidewalk, Ian couldn't decide whether to laugh or run. "Listen, Gary, or whatever your name is. Let's stop this. I'll get you food, and do more. I can help you find a safe place to stay, and someone to help you. There are a couple clinics downtown. I'll take you to McDonald's, and then we'll find someone you can talk to."

"Are you insane?" Gary puffed large, eyes rolling. "I'm the 405 troll, you ignorant crackhead, and I live in my palace." He motioned underneath the bridge. "The most luxurious home in the world: hot tub and premium cable, a king-sized Serta Perfect Sleeper." He waved his arms. "You just want to lure me out so evil Balthazar can take over. Is that it?" Gary plunged forward, poking at Ian with the toy. "Are you Balthazar's agent?"

Ian jumped back but misjudged Gary's speed, and on his second swing, the plastic sword caught him squarely in the jaw with a stinging blow. "Goddamn it. Knock it off."

Gary swung the toy with a backhanded flip, striking Ian hard on the opposite cheek and splitting his lip. The taste of blood both terrified and enraged him. He crouched, protected his head with his left arm, reached into his pocket with his right, pulled out the pepper spray, then sprayed blindly in Gary's direction. He raised his eyes when he heard a scream. He'd hit Gary squarely in the face with the spray. The big man was clawing at his eyes.

"Aagh, you fuck! I'll remove your midget head and put it on a stick." Gary stumbled backwards. "I'm going to . . ." Then, with an even more sickening yelp, he backed hard into the bridge railing, catapulting in a reverse flip over the side.

"No! Ian yelled, cringing as Gary disappeared, then at the accompanying thud, followed by the sounds of horns and locked brakes. Ian rushed to the bridge railing. On the freeway forty feet below, a Volkswagen had skidded sideways across two lanes when Gary crash-landed on the hood. Another car clipped the rear quarter panel jutting into their lane, sending the Volkswagen spiraling. Gary's unconscious body flew into oncoming traffic, first pinned to the grill of a Dodge Ram, then thrown ten feet in the air into the windshield of a speeding Audi, which crashed into a Toyota Tercel, Gary ricocheting between vehicles like a bloody pinball.

"Holy shit."

Ian looked to his left at two college students. One of them was filming the entire spectacle with his phone.

"Dude," the wide-eyed kid blurted. "What did you spray him with?"

Ian raised his arms in panic. "I was protecting myself. He'd been after me, and I . . ." He flung the pepper spray over the bridge as he collapsed to his knees. "Jesus. He fell."

"Dude, the guy had a toy sword. He couldn't hurt you. We saw it all. You just blew him away."

"I didn't," Ian pleaded. "You don't understand. He'd been threatening me. He said he was going to . . ." Ian swiveled his head when he heard sirens. The kid was holding the camera at arm's length, recording Ian as if he were some kind of science experiment. "I didn't mean to hurt him. I was going to help," he protested, and then sprinted across the bridge. By the time he crossed, flashing lights were coming from both sides of the freeway.

Ian ran two blocks to his apartment, bolted the door behind him, and rushed into the bathroom to down the remaining Xanax. *This has to be some kind of bad dream. I must still be drunk and having nightmares.* He sat on the edge of his bed, gulping deep breaths and waiting for the drugs to kick in, as he listened to more sirens in the distance. Thirty minutes later, he turned on the television. A reporter was on the bridge near the spot where Ian had stood. At least a dozen police wandered behind her stringing crime-scene tape.

"This is the spot where a homeless man was thrown to his death," the intensely coiffed woman said. "And in fact, this is also the bridge where KGW News has a traffic cam, so we have the entire incident on video. I must warn you. This is disturbing and not appropriate for young children."

Ian watched as Gary's body flew by the camera mounted on the lip of the bridge, one flailing hand striking the lens. The footage had the grainy sepia hue of a low-budget horror film and had been slowed down so you could see Gary flipping in midair before slamming onto the car hood and bouncing between lanes.

"According to police, two college students filmed the altercation that led to the man's death, and authorities are currently interviewing witnesses. Back to you, Sheila and Ed," the reporter signed off.

"What a horrible thing." Sheila turned to her sidekick.

"Unbelievable," Ed said, shaking his puffy, Botox-enhanced head. "And now, Les McCord reports on KGW's search for the best barista in Portland."

Ian flipped off the television and began to sob.

Twenty minutes later, he opened the door to a gaggle of police officers, many with drawn weapons, led by the detective he'd consulted the previous day. "I guess you decided to take care of the homeless guy on your own," he said. "Ian Davis, you're under arrest."

♟♟♟

IAN FLOATED IN A Xanax high for the next few hours as he was transported to the station and led into an interrogation room. He did have the presence of mind to request an attorney, and as he was sipping bad coffee and emerging from his drug haze, a gray-haired man in a decades-old seersucker suit sat down in front of him. "I'm Jeff Merrick, your lawyer," he said holding out an age-spotted hand.

"You look like Matlock," Ian muttered.

"Let's just hope I'm as good as him." The man smiled. "You've got a big mess here. You've been charged with second-degree murder. They have video clearly showing you dousing the homeless man with pepper spray, forcing him over the bridge. They found the container with your fingerprints. They have testimony from a detective that you complained of altercations with the deceased. They also have testimony from a group of construction workers that witnessed you arguing with him."

Ian, suddenly feeling very sober, interrupted to explain the last few days. His attorney listened thoughtfully. "Listen, I don't doubt a word of what you're saying," Merrick said. "I'm sure you were afraid and that it was self-defense. Our problem is perception. The videos have gone viral. And the victim, the guy you call Homeless Gary Busey; it turns out his name is Brian Parker. Former Marine. Some kind of hero in the first Gulf War. He suffered from PTSD, and was in treatment, but then his wife was killed in the World Trade Center. He spiraled out of control. He's been living on the streets for years, just moving around, getting crazier. People have a lot of empathy, and they want your head. The DA can see in those videos that Gary was swinging at you, but he can't let you off easy. Too much political pressure. There are protesters outside right now, like some kind of lynch mob. You're the national bogeyman in the homeless debate. Things are going to get ugly."

IAN LEARNED *UGLY* WAS an understatement. For the next few months, he watched his life be degraded, debated, distorted, dissected, and ridiculed. The videos were edited, played, and replayed to make him appear even more the monster. For weeks, until he was knocked off the charts by a man who attacked a school bus with a Glock G37, he was the most hated man in America, as various homeless organizations, veterans groups, human rights advocates, liberal politicians—and even Oprah—vilified him. His rare supporters were a sketchy group: noisy right-wingers, white supremacists, Ted Nugent, and a Southern senator best known for calling women "baby vessels."

His alcohol- and drug-abusing past was detailed in the press. People he didn't remember came forward to relate confrontations with Bad Ian. Jazz Technology terminated his employment via voice mail. He was evicted from his apartment, and his sister, who'd disowned him seven years earlier, after he'd backed over her cat in a Budweiser-haze, sent him a concise email: *I'm embarrassed we share the same blood. Rot in hell.*

Ian observed his decline from a cell in the Multnomah County Jail, then watched his final destruction from the shabby confines of a series of cheap motel rooms, most of them located behind truck stops or in crime-infested neighborhoods. It was dangerous to be Ian Davis—death threats were a daily occurrence—and given his dismal financial situation after the legal fees, he could only afford to rotate between budget accommodations where tenants tended to keep low profiles.

Before his trial, Jeff Merrick strongly recommended he take a plea agreement for manslaughter. "But it was self-defense," Ian protested. "An accident."

Jeff assured Ian he understood, but feared public opinion would prevail. "The DA understands too, but he needs his pound of flesh. Take the deal. You'll do eighteen months in a low-security facility. People will forget about all this, and some other poor sap who was in the wrong place at the wrong time will take your place. It will be a cakewalk, and when you get out, you can start your life over."

👕👕👕

IAN WOULDN'T DESCRIBE THE two years he spent in jail as a cakewalk. Many of his fellow inmates had been homeless at one time or another, and his crime elicited a certain fury from them. Plus, a man his size, with such delicate features, drew the wrong kind of attention in prison. Eventually he was filed away in a wing reserved for those found guilty of similarly nonthreatening crimes, assigned to be cellmates with a check forger and a man who was incarcerated because he'd flipped out and attempted to defecate on an airline serving cart.

It was true that Ian was largely forgotten when he was released. When he'd arrived in Portland from Minneapolis six years earlier, he'd been filled with determination and enthusiasm to build a new life. But now, stepping off a bus, with all his possessions hanging off his shoulder in a cheap duffle bag, optimism was a foreign concept. He'd spent many nights lying in his cell, conversing in his head with Bad Ian, angrily lamenting that his attempt to lead a good life had led to this. *I was better off when I was a stoned asshole,* he'd think in disgust. And once again he'd arrived in Portland devoid of family or friends. *Bad Ian is the only one who stuck with me.*

He'd been assigned to live in a release center for the next few weeks, but after walking the four blocks from the bus station into Chinatown, Ian realized his new home, the Golden Arms, was a tenement hotel that had been rebranded by the state into a bedbug-infested halfway house. He recalled walking by the place when it was a haven for hookers and meth heads, and it appeared little changed. Twitchy drug dealers flanked both corners, and the perimeter of the parking lot was ringed with shopping carts. Two heavily inked men, one with *Cabron* in elegant Latin cursive across his chest and the other with a vicious-looking dog tethered to his wrist, watched over the area.

Ian found there were few professional opportunities for people with felony records, even for a man with his coding skills. He soon found himself wrapped in a hairnet, cleaning deep-fat fryers in the back of a Chick-fil-A. For the first week, he attempted to stay focused and concentrate on logical steps to improve his situation, but Bad Ian was increasingly intervening in his psyche, convincing him there was no upside to the straight and narrow. One night, at Bad Ian's urging, he stopped for a beer after work. Tiny's Tavern served a hopeless clientele, dishing up cheap liquor to patrons who purchased their cigarettes one at a time and frequently bathed in the bathroom sink. Ian got very drunk, snorted some kind of marching powder he bought for ten dollars, and he and Bad Ian decided they'd had enough of hairnets and halfway houses. After retrieving his few belongings, he never returned to the Golden Arms, or the Chick-fil-A.

♟♟♟

SIX MONTHS LATER, HE was camped in the doorway of an abandoned building in the Pearl District when he heard someone repeating his name.

"Ian, is that you?"

Ian blinked awake, suddenly aware of a sharp pain around his kidneys. He had a faint recollection of a fight. *Two men, yes . . . two big, muscular men, fireplugs, slathered with tattoos, laughing as they beat me, and they had a pit bull . . .* He recalled being thrown across a cement garbage can in the park, face smashed into the aggregate, as one of them rifled his pockets while the other pummeled his ribs, the dog clamping onto his ankle, chewing his leg like a chicken bone. Ian's hand moved to a pocket on his skinny ass, and he realized with despair that they had taken his last few dollars and a packet of crystal. He'd worked hard for that little bit of heaven. Five hundred aluminum cans, plucked from filthy trash bins and hauled to the recycling center, all for nothing. He pulled his hand from his backside, suddenly noticing he'd pissed himself. Not unusual, but for a moment he worried it was because of the beating. *Maybe they broke something important.* It wasn't safe to be wounded on the street. His mind went to the next pain point, his ankle. *The dog.* He thought about rabies, or at least not being able to walk, which could be equally deadly.

"Ian, do you remember me?"

Ian looked through liquid eyes at the man leaning over him. *Andy Griffith. I love Andy Griffith. No, wait, not Sheriff Andy. The other one. Matlock.* Matlock was standing in front of him in a rumpled suit. Smiling, with the rosy cheeks of an Irish drunk.

"Ian, its Jeff Merrick. Remember me? I was your lawyer."

"Yeah. Hi." Ian felt momentarily happy, but then fear washed over him. The last time he'd seen this man, they'd taken him to prison. He didn't want to go back there. Had he done something wrong that he didn't remember? He tried to rise to his feet, but his left ankle, the chicken bone, gave in, and he fell back to the pavement. His shoe was gone, and a bloody sock appeared grafted to his skin. He fell back into a peaceful black.

He awoke in the emergency room on a clean white gurney. Matlock . . . no, that wasn't his real name. Merrick. Merrick was standing next to the doctor.

"How are you feeling, Ian?" Merrick's was the only friendly face Ian had seen in a long while.

"We sewed up your leg. Nasty bite," the doctor said. "You might need surgery on that one. Pumped you full of antibiotics. You took a hell of a beating, and there doesn't appear to be any serious damage, but we need to check you out again in a day or two to make sure there's no internal bleeding. The stitches need to come out in about a week. Also, you're malnourished, and half your teeth are ready to fall out."

"Ian," Merrick interjected, "we need to get you some help. I'm going to look into finding you a place . . ."

"I don't need help. I have a place," Ian lied as he rose from the gurney. "But thanks." He stumbled when his feet hit the ground. The doctor grabbed his shoulder.

"No, Ian . . . you're hurt. You need to stay in bed." Merrick came around the gurney.

"Mr. Merrick," the doctor said, "I'm sorry, but unless you're going to foot the bill, Mr. Davis needs to be released. We've handled the critical issues, and I don't have authorization to keep him here any longer. I have a cane we can give him. And he does need to come back. But I'm not allowed to overnight him."

"Well, no, we can't just . . ." Merrick said.

"It's okay, I'm fine. I want to leave." Ian took the cane and hobbled towards the door. Thanks to whatever painkiller they'd pumped into him, he felt the best he had in weeks. Merrick continued to protest as they moved to the hospital entry, but Ian refused any additional assistance. Finally, he allowed Merrick to drive him to a shelter, gladly accepting the sixty dollars the lawyer gave him as they parted.

Normally he got little sleep in a shelter, concerned with protecting himself and his few possessions. But reeling from pain-killers, he slept soundly. The next morning, he showered for the first time in weeks, noticing too late that he'd gotten the bandages on his leg wet, then stopped in a basement storeroom full of donated clothing to pick out a new outfit. Digging through the stacks, he was delighted to find a Hootie & the Blowfish T-shirt promoting their 1994 Cracked Rear View tour. He had a recollection of seeing them in Minneapolis that year, cheering hysterically as he downed beers and snorted coke. He also discovered a pair of Jordache jeans in a child's size that fit, albeit a little loose in the seat, and a Portland Beavers baseball jacket. He completed his outfit with a worn pair of screaming-yellow Nikes, and a child's stocking cap, emblazoned with a Hello Kitty logo.

Ian wandered the downtown corridor, careful to avoid Chinatown, where he might encounter his attackers. Around noon, leg aching, he was able to buy a baggy of heroin for twenty dollars from another homeless man everyone called Slim Pickens. The two crawled between Slim's shopping cart and a wide maple tree, and, sharing a needle, shot up while watching a busload of grade schoolers file off a bus and into the Oregon Historical Society.

His pain now obliterated, Ian traipsed through the Portland State campus, moving like a new man. Peering at his reflection in a Starbucks' window, he thought he looked spiffy in his new clothes. The cane not only minimized his limp, it made him powerful, like carrying a pirate's sword. He waved it in mock menace at students walking near him. "Aye, matey, stay clear or I'll have yer head," he yelled in a bad Cockney accent. He was unaware the stitches in his leg had loosened, and everyone gave wide berth to the crazy man waving a stick, blood dripping over his shoes. Ian realized he didn't need to walk; he could actually levitate like some kind of human hovercraft.

At the edge of campus, he approached the 405 bridge,

suddenly feeling a strong sense of déjà vu. He'd been here before. There was something important about this place. He entered the vacant lot, high, dry weeds poking his chest. He felt strong and clear, the heroin running like warm milk through his body. He fell back on his ass as a pleasure-wave knocked him over.

"Do you have the toll?" a deep voice bellowed. Through the weeds, Ian could see an immense man in a trench coat, pulled back to reveal a ripped Van Halen T-shirt covering a fat-rippled gut. He was wearing sweatpants tucked into cowboy boots, and for some reason, spurs.

"The toll?"

"For you, not much." The big man smiled. "You were very helpful in handling Gary. Got my kingdom back." He spread his arms. "I would take just a touch of what's left in your plastic bag. And later, maybe you can treat me to an Egg McMuffin." The shimmering form extended an arm. "I'm Balthazar," he said. "I've been waiting for you. My palace is just over there, under the bridge. The finest palace you have ever seen. There's room for you there."

Ian flailed for the man's arm, which suddenly disappeared, and he tripped backwards. Balthazar was gone, but through the weeds he could see the door to the palace, wedged into a corner below the bridge, right above the freeway. Balthazar appeared again, standing just inside the entrance, motioning Ian in with a smile. Ian pushed up on his cane and stumbled forward, anxious to finally get home.

👕👕👕

I'm sure most Portland-based writers are more than happy to exist in Ursula Le Guin's impressive shadow. It is one thing to be a great story-teller or wordsmith, but quite another to combine those talents with a brain big enough to construct alternative universes, while also gently nudging the reader towards equality and justice. Le Guin did this better than anyone, and I hope she would have approved of my little story, in which I explore the invisible around us, and the worlds they may inhabit.

Finding Joan

DAVID D. LEVINE

JOAN PUT A HAND into the beam of her headlamp, carefully inspecting the white LED light on her pale, pale palm. Was it fading already? She checked her fanny pack to be sure she had a spare battery.

Sometimes she thought it would be easier to do her foraging during the day. But going out by night not only avoided the need for heavy protective clothing, it was less disturbing. At night she couldn't see the roiling brown sky, or the blackened shells of burned-out buildings, or the bleached and crumbling remains of billboards and road signs.

What little she *could* see in the circle of her headlamp's light was bad enough. The asphalt beneath her bicycle's wheels was cracked and uneven, slumping here and there into potholes. The wrecked cars that lay in her path looked decades old, their paint faded and their trim shredded like old silk. And, of course, there were the corpses. They were all desiccated now, dried-out skeletal mummies, but some of them lay with necks and backs bent backward and mouths stretched wide in silent screams, tendons drawn tight by the baking sun.

She'd found a path to the gas station that avoided most of

those. As long as they didn't enter the light, she could pretend they weren't there.

But as she pedaled along this night, she found that a huge pothole now gaped all the way across the road on the near end of the bridge over I-405. It had just been a large crack the last time she'd made a fuel run, but there had been a couple nights of freezing weather since then and frost heave must have opened it up. She swore and backed awkwardly up, the empty jerry-cans clanging in her trailer.

New potholes drove her four blocks out of her way, forcing her off her comfortable path, making her confront things she'd been able to ignore for so long. A pile of glittering glass lay at the base of a window that must have been smashed in the first hours after the event. A faded, tattered plastic banner flapped in the breeze, promising IF YE HAVE FAITH, YE SHALL BE SAVED. A whole family of mummies sheltered in a doorway, two adult skeletons draped protectively over two children.

But the thing that made Joan lose it was a Subaru Forester.

The car sat waiting patiently in a curbside parking space for an owner who would never return. The tires were flat, of course, the windows yellowed and frosted, and the green paint of the hood and roof bleached nearly to white. In these aspects the car was no different from dozens Joan had seen this very night.

But in the fading light of her headlamp a bumper sticker on the car's back window was still legible, barely: KEEP PORTLAND WEIRD.

Dan's car had been a green Forester. And he'd had one of those stickers on it.

Joan sat still, feeling her lower lip tremble, for a good solid minute before she gave in, put her head down on the handlebars, and bawled like a baby.

THE SILENCE HAD BEEN her first clue, though she hadn't realized it at the time. Even before they'd emerged from the cave in which they'd spent a long weekend meditating and eating vacuum-packed seitan curry, Joan had noticed that the birdsong that had echoed off the cave walls on the way down was strangely absent on the return trip. This struck her as odd, but—trying to hang on for a little while longer to the quiet mind she'd just spent so many hours cultivating—she'd resolved to notice it and then let it go, rather than allowing her monkey-mind to grab onto it and try to find a reason.

The four of them hiked without speaking along the last gravelly stretch of cave floor before the entrance. Joan was dead tired from the long clamber back out of the cave, and her left foot squished in its shoe on every step from the deeper-than-expected underground rivulet she'd stepped in a few hundred yards back. Although she'd had a relaxing three-day holiday from her everyday life, right then she couldn't wait to get to the car, to sunlight and warmth and dry clothes. She planned to sleep through the drive home, then ask Dan to take her to Old Wives' Tales for a proper sit-down dinner.

Then Roger, who was in the lead, took in a short sharp breath. Joan nearly bumped into his skinny back before realizing he'd stopped dead. "What?" she said. Roger only pointed forward and up. Annoyed, Joan stepped up next to him and sighted along his pointing arm at the sky outside the cave mouth.

The sky was a mass of roiling brown clouds. "Is that a storm brewing?" she asked.

"Doesn't look like any storm I've ever seen," Roger replied, stroking his raggedy moustache.

Coral and Bethanie joined them a moment later. Coral was Joan's friend—they'd met when they were both volunteering at Friends of Trees—three years younger than Joan at fifty-five, though thinner and with more of a fashion sense. She was just as much a novice at caving as Joan. Bethanie was Roger's wife, and like him she was an experienced caver, thirty-something, blond, lean, and fit. Neither of them had ever seen a sky like that either, but at least it didn't seem to be raining.

This whole expedition had been Coral's idea. She'd been the

one to introduce Joan to Roger and Bethanie, who lived in her apartment complex, and it had been she who'd thought that a long weekend in a cave would be a perfect way for her and Joan to get away from their daily lives and find some inner peace. In exchange for Roger and Bethanie's caving expertise and the loan of some equipment, they'd do all the cooking and provide instruction in meditation.

The cave had been quiet and peaceful, and the company pleasant enough, but still Joan felt . . . obligated. Apologetic for her heavy, awkward body and for the way she felt she was holding the others back. Concerned that Roger and Bethanie might not enjoy the vegetarian meals she'd prepared. Afraid that Coral would regret bringing her along. Still, she did feel a bit calmer, and counted the weekend as a qualified success.

But as soon as Joan squeezed herself through the narrow cave mouth—she was the only one of the four for whom it was much of a squeeze—she realized that something was seriously wrong.

Every tree in the vicinity looked sick. Leaves drooped limp, with many lying on the ground as though it were late fall instead of early spring. Small branches sagged. Even the conifers were shedding needles like a month-old Christmas tree. The undergrowth looked no better.

"Something's wrong with the trees," she said.

"Not just the trees," Roger said. Joan followed his gaze.

A dead squirrel lay in the path.

They all looked at it in silence. It lay on its back, white belly exposed and little paws curled, eyes open. There were no visible marks, no swelling, no bleeding, no sign of what had killed it.

"Squirrels die all the time," Bethanie said, prodding it with a stick. But she didn't sound very sure of herself.

"Birds," Coral said, pointing to one side of the path.

Joan didn't understand what she'd meant until she realized the brush held dozens of little brown birds, blending in with the undergrowth, difficult to see because they weren't moving. At all.

Nor were there any flies or insects crawling on them.

Joan poked at the loose mulch with the toe of her boot, gray with cave mud. Nothing scrabbled away from the disturbance, but a pill bug rolled down the path and lay still. She poked it gently with a fingernail. Dead.

Suddenly Joan's throat felt tight. "We've got to get out of here."

Coral was staring in all directions, as though expecting something to leap on her. "What's happening here?" Her voice trembled with near panic.

"I dunno," Roger said, "but I'm leaving right now." He started down the hill with deliberate haste, crashing through hanging branches and sending gravel rattling down the trail ahead of him.

"Be careful," Bethanie said from behind. But when Joan turned back, she saw Bethanie coming on nearly as fast as Roger was departing. Joan picked up her own pace to match.

As she hurried down the trail, minding her footing on the loose gravel, Joan's anxiety grew. The lowering sky was a sick yellow-brown color, churning and seething like a pot of dirty poison on a low boil. A dead crow lay atop a patch of wilted fiddlehead ferns like some ghastly entree. And there was no birdsong, no grasshoppers or crickets, no rumble of traffic. Interstate 84 was miles away, but when they'd entered the cave on Friday, the traffic had been clearly audible.

What the hell could have caused this?

Joan wasn't in the best of shape, and after half an hour of rapid descent her heart was hammering in her ears and her breath was ragged. "Hold on a minute," she gasped, and leaned against a tree for a moment.

"You don't look good," Coral said. "You're flushed."

"You too," Joan replied. Coral's skin was bright pink, shiny and taut like a balloon.

Coral looked down at her arms with alarm. "What the hell?"

Roger, hearing the exchange, turned back and climbed up the hill toward them. He was as pink as Coral but didn't seem to have noticed it. "Give me your hand." He pressed Coral's forearm with his thumb. The thumbprint turned white and took several seconds to return to its previous color. "Aw, you're just sunburned, is all."

Coral shook her head. "Roger, we've just spent three days in a *cave*. We've been out here for less than an hour and it's *cloudy*. How could I possibly get *sunburned*?"

Roger put on his smug I'm-an-outdoorsman-and-you-aren't expression. "You can get a nasty burn even on a cloudy day."

But Joan was thinking about the dead squirrel. "I don't think it's just sunburn."

They all looked at her.

"I think it's radiation."

"Can't be," said Roger.

"Why not? You know anything about radiation?"

None of them did. "So, what are we going to do about it?" Coral asked.

"Get the hell out of this place. Where's the nearest hospital?"

"Hood River," Roger said without hesitation.

"Maybe it's nothing," Joan said. "But if it is radiation . . . or, I don't know, toxic chemicals or something, we need to get ourselves to a doctor as soon as possible."

The car was another hour's hike away even at the best speed they could manage. The whole way, Joan worried that invisible particles were sleeting through her body, damaging her chromosomes, twisting her cells. What did radiation feel like? What symptoms should she be alert for? Was she really seeing bright flashes when she closed her eyes, or was it just her imagination? Could anything else have caused the animal deaths and sunburn-like symptoms?

And was there any treatment?

They arrived at the car, flung their packs in the trunk, and peeled out. Joan dug her cell phone out of her purse, but though she had one or two bars of signal here, trying to call out just produced a fast repeating tone. Everyone else's phone had the same problem, and there was nothing on the radio but static.

So much for retaining the quiet mind she'd achieved in the

cave. She tried closing her eyes and thinking the syllable "so" on the inhale, "hum" on the exhale, but between the noisy jostling car and the constant fear of what they might have been exposed to, her meditations went nowhere.

Joan had been seeking peace for most of her fifty-eight years. She'd worked as an accountant during her twenties and thirties, but when just one of Dan's Intel stock options had brought in three times her annual salary, they'd both realized they didn't really need her to work. So she'd become a "kept woman," gardening and volunteering and keeping their two-person household running. But even with "nothing to do," she still found her mind constantly running like a hamster in a wheel.

Meditation helped. But like the yoga and art classes and acupuncture, it didn't help enough or for long enough. Of all the things she'd tried, she still liked gardening best. Alone in her own back yard, humming Crosby, Stills & Nash as she dug and pruned and weeded, the hours seemed to fly by. But with Portland's climate, she couldn't do that all year round.

They crossed the Columbia at the Bridge of the Gods. The tollgate stood open and there was no one in the booth. "Where *is* everybody?" Joan asked, voicing what they'd all been thinking.

"Maybe it's the Rapture," Bethanie said. Her voice was level and Joan didn't know enough about Bethanie's faith to know how seriously she meant it. Joan's own spirituality was much less conventional.

"Isn't the Rapture supposed to take only God's chosen?" Coral said. "And we haven't seen a single car on the road." They'd seen a few pulled over on the shoulder, but they hadn't wanted to stop and see if there was anyone in them. "Why would God take everyone but *us*?"

"Look at that sky!" Bethanie gestured through the windshield. "That's no natural sky. That's an angry-God sky."

Coral didn't have an answer to that one. Neither did Joan.

Roger just kept driving.

There was no one in Hood River, either, though the place didn't look evacuated . . . plenty of cars sat in street parking as though it were an ordinary day. Here and there a car had smashed into a light pole or run up onto the sidewalk. Behind the windshields, Joan thought she could see drivers and passengers slumped in their seat belts. She tried not to look too closely. It helped that it was starting to get dark.

When they arrived at the hospital, they found the parking lot jammed with cars, most of which contained at least one dead body. Large hand-lettered signs directed drivers to park on the street and proceed to triage, but when they walked in the front door . . .

"Oh God," Bethanie said, and threw up on the floor. Roger held her heaving shoulders as she stood, hands on knees, retching.

Bodies lay everywhere: draped across chairs, lying on gurneys parked in the hall, slumped in corners. Their skin was deep red and peeling away in patches; most of them were covered with weeping blisters. Many were dressed as doctors and nurses.

Nothing moved.

The lights were still on.

There was no smell at all, other than disinfectants and bleach.

Joan looked at her own arm. She wasn't nearly as badly burned as the dead people, at least not yet, but she had a few blisters already. She supposed it was only a matter of time before she wound up like the people here.

"I'd stopped worrying about the Bomb," Coral said. Bethanie and Roger were in their thirties and didn't know how it had been. "When I was a kid we had to duck and cover. But I thought . . . after the Soviet Union . . ." She trailed off.

Roger crossed his arms on his chest and shook his head. "Terrorists, maybe," he said. "Dirty bomb. Cobalt 60. Something like that."

"So . . ." Bethanie began, wiped her mouth, tried again. "So what are we gonna *do*?"

Fear rose up from beneath Joan's breastbone, breaking through her shock. Fear for Dan. "We go home," she said.

Roger shook his head again. "No point. Portland's only an

hour away. If there were anyone left alive there, they would have sent someone here by now."

"You don't know that!" said Coral, at the same time Bethanie said, "Unless whatever-it-is is localized here."

Roger planted his hands on his hips. "We need to head for Bend, or Idaho. Away from the big cities."

The other three all started talking at once, but Joan raised her voice. "Take. Me. *Home*," she said, seizing the conversation back. "I need to find my husband."

"Oh Jesus," Coral said. "Oh Joan, I'm so sorry, I didn't think . . ." Coral was thrice-divorced and alternated between insisting she was completely done with men and dating two or three of them at once. Of course she would have forgotten about Dan.

Joan brushed Coral's comforting hand from her shoulder. "Maybe he's okay." But even as the words emerged from her mouth, she realized she didn't believe them.

Bethanie took Roger's hand, her expression pinched. "Let's take her home."

"Crazy," Roger said, and started to turn away.

But Bethanie put two fingers on his chin and turned his head to face her. "C'mon, honey . . . Coral's single, you and I have each other . . . we need to take Joan to her husband."

Roger shook his head, but dug in his pocket for the car keys.

Joan followed him to the car, feeling hollow even though she'd gotten her way.

Darkness had fallen while they were in the hospital, but the streetlights and some of the commercial signage had come on. Automated, Joan supposed, and wondered how long that would last without maintenance. No one in the car spoke as they drove through silent streets back to the freeway.

The trip to Portland took almost three hours. Roger drove cautiously, but they didn't encounter any roadblocks, or indeed, any sign of anyone alive. For all they could tell, everyone was dead except them.

Dan's a smart, resourceful guy, Joan told herself, *and he works in a big high-tech office complex full of smart, resourceful people*. If anyone had survived this . . . this whatever-it-was, it would be him.

She bit her knuckle, staring out the window at a car that had come to rest against the median barrier. It didn't seem to have been moving too fast when it hit, but as they passed the head-lights revealed two bodies in the front seats. She wondered how long it would be until she joined them. At least her skin didn't hurt much—it itched, like a bad sunburn, but it didn't seem to be getting any worse. Maybe they were moving away from the source of the radiation, whatever it was, and Portland would be okay?

But even as they approached the city, her phone still gave her nothing but a fast busy signal.

They stopped at the top of the Marquam Bridge. The city below looked much as it had, with lights glowing in most of the buildings and traffic signals blinking their steady progression from green to yellow to red and back. But even from up here, they could see that nothing moved in the streets. Portland was pretty small for a big city, but even on a Sunday evening it shouldn't be this . . . dead. They didn't stop downtown but continued on to the west-side suburbs.

The Intel parking lot was three-quarters full, cars sitting neatly in their parking places. "Whatever it was," Roger said as he pulled into an open space, "it must have hit on Friday."

Joan didn't reply. She was thinking of all the times Dan had worked weekends, sometimes not returning home until 2:00 or 3:00 a.m. and then heading right back to work in the morning. Perhaps he and his co-workers were gathered around a table in some conference room right now, eating pizza and helping the mayor or the governor with some technical aspect of this crisis . . .

But inside the building they found only silence. The security guard at the front desk lay facedown, unmoving. Acres of gray cubicles stood empty beneath the cold fluorescent light, colorful screen savers spinning on some of the computer screens.

The people were all gathered in the huge cafeteria. Most of them lay on chairs and tables near a temporary aid station, but a few dozen were bunched around a big-screen television in one corner. That's where Joan found Dan. He was slumped in a plastic cafeteria chair, skin red and peeling away, his glasses askew and reflecting sixty inches, diagonally measured, of high-definition solid blue.

"Oh, Dan . . ." she said. She reached out and straightened his glasses, but though she longed to hug and kiss him, the seeping blisters made that unpalatable.

He was where he'd have wanted to be, she thought, *surrounded by the co-workers he respected*. People he'd survived many a crisis with.

But not this one.

"I'm so sorry," Coral said, sniffling, and gathered Joan into an embrace.

Joan pressed her lips together and took a long breath through her nose. Tears pinched behind her eyes, but they didn't seem ready to come out yet. "Thanks."

"It's . . . it's okay, Joan . . ." Coral sobbed, "you'll be seeing him again soon anyway . . . "

Bethanie came over and hugged both of them, patting Coral's back, but not saying anything other than "hush, hush."

Roger just stared at Joan. "Yeah," he said at last. "I'm, uh, I'm sorry too." He turned and started walking toward the cafeteria line. "I'll see if I can find us something to eat."

Joan extracted herself from Coral and Bethanie and looked at Dan one more time. But although the red and blistered corpse had Dan's glasses and thinning hair, it wasn't really Dan. The real Dan was somewhere else, and Joan's hand-assembled New Age spirituality didn't have any reassuring answers about where that might be or whether Joan was likely to join him there.

And she didn't know how she felt about that.

She and Dan had been married for almost three decades. They'd grown together over that time, like two old trees leaning on each other for support, and had expected to remain together for the rest of their lives. But somehow, in all those years of being Dan-and-Joan, she wondered what had become of . . . Joan.

She'd depended on men all her life, she thought. First her

father, then her teachers, and then Dan. Now, suddenly, they were all gone.

In the last few years, she realized now, she'd been looking for something more. She'd thought it was peace she sought, but now that everything in the world had gone quiet, she wondered if what she'd really been seeking was . . . herself. She'd just been too comfortable where she was to go out and look for it.

And maybe she'd found it now.

Just as she was about to die.

She turned away from Dan's corpse. "Let's get out of here," she said to the others. "There's nothing here for us."

Coral raised her head from her arms, folded on the table where she'd been sitting. "And go where?" Her eyes streamed with tears. "Why bother? We might as well die here as anywhere else. Everyone else is dead . . ."

"Maybe not," said Roger.

They all looked at him. He was standing next to a table on which several computers hummed, an untidy pile with cables running everywhere.

He pointed to one of the screens. "This one lit up when I walked past. Must've jostled the mouse. And, well . . . take a look at this."

Joan walked over and looked at the screen.

It was the CNN home page. *GAMMA RAY BURST THREATENS LIFE ON EARTH*, read the headline, accompanied by a photo of a man in surgical scrubs. His face was buried in his hands, the visible skin of his forehead blistered and peeling.

"See?" Roger said. "We aren't the only ones left alive."

Joan peered more closely at the screen. "This is from Friday." She clicked the Refresh icon in the toolbar. "Let's see the latest news." The page blanked, the cursor spun . . . and kept on spinning for half a minute before the page was replaced by an error message.

"Shit," said Roger.

Bethanie reached for the keyboard. "Try another website."

CNN, the *New York Times*, the BBC, and every other English-language news site they could think of were all down. But Google was up, even though most of the links it found were dead. After a while they left the cafeteria and its corpses and moved to the computers in a nearby group of cubicles.

They finally found what they were looking for on a site called jp.wikipedia.org. A Google search on "gamma ray burst" found a page there in English, though the navigation links on the left and top were all in Japanese. The modification date at the bottom of the page was today. "Well, at least someone's alive somewhere," Coral said.

A gamma ray burst, they read, was one of the most energetic events in the universe, a star suddenly releasing a supernova's worth of energy in a focused beam over just a few seconds. They had been observed since the 1960s and were thought to result from the collapse of a giant star into a black hole, or from the merger of two neutron stars. It had long been speculated that if a gamma ray burst occurred nearby, it could mean the end of life on Earth, but the chance of that happening had been considered remote.

Until Friday at 2:39 in the afternoon, just two hours after they'd entered the cave.

Links on that page led to other pages that were still up, mostly in Japan, Australia, and India. Many of them were in English, or something like it. The story they told wasn't pretty.

Half of the Earth, including all of North America and Europe, most of South America, and a good chunk of Africa, had been bombarded by a beam of radiation from a previously unremarkable star four hundred light-years away. The burst had not only been unexpected, it had been far more powerful than any theory had projected. Just about every person, animal, plant, and microbe in that hemisphere was killed by a massive dose of gamma rays, X-rays, cosmic rays, and ultraviolet radiation. Most people had lived for about four hours, but fatalities had approached 100 percent after eight hours. The only known survivors had been those who were deep underground or underwater.

But even those who had survived were in trouble, and that included residents of the initially untouched continents of

Australia, Asia, and sub-Saharan Africa. The gamma ray burst had only lasted thirteen seconds, but in that time it had destroyed half of the Earth's ozone, basically turning it into smog. That was why Joan and the rest had gotten second-degree sunburns in only an hour after leaving the cave, but the damage had stopped as soon as the sun went down: the roiling yellow-brown clouds above were letting through almost three times as much ultraviolet radiation per hour as before the event.

Staying indoors during the day would keep them from getting burned any further. But with the ozone layer half-gone, even those parts of the Earth that had escaped destruction by the burst itself were being sterilized by UV radiation. The death toll in Australia was already above 30 percent, three days after the event, and the ongoing UV burn was killing every crop on land, as well as the photosynthetic phytoplankton on which all life in the sea depended. Natural processes would eventually restore the ozone, but it was expected to take five years or more.

Roger stood up and rubbed his eyes. It was nearly three in the morning. "Bottom line," he said, "we're screwed. Even if we could get to Japan or Australia, by the time we did we'd find everyone starved to death. Just like here, but slower and nastier."

But Coral was waving them all over to look at her computer. "Wait, wait," she said. "Look what I found!"

It was another Japanese Wikipedia page: "List of Survivors in North America." At the top were instructions on how to add yourself. It seemed like quite a long list, thousands of names, until Joan realized what a tiny percentage of the original population it was. "Mostly men," she commented.

"Yeah," said Coral. "Look at where they are."

Most of them were in places like Washington DC, Colorado Springs, and San Diego—military towns. A lot of the rest were in big cities with deep subway systems. There wasn't one name in Portland; the largest concentration of names in the Northwest was Bremerton, Washington. "Bremerton?" Joan asked.

"Submarines!" Roger shouted, pumping his fist. "Bremerton's

a big naval base. Even bigger than San Diego." Any subs that had been submerged at the time of the event, he explained, would have been shielded from the radiation by the sea water above them, and they would have returned to base as soon as they found out what happened.

A Google search quickly found the home page of the Bremerton sub base. The page was dominated by a large, amateurish-looking box, yellow with a red border: "Naval Base Kitsap is open for business! We have food, weapons, and supplies and welcome all US Citizens! UNITED WE STAND!" There was an email link, and a map with the location of the base indicated by a red arrow.

Roger tapped the arrow on the screen with his finger. "That's where we gotta go," he said. "We'll hole up here during the day, then hit the road right after sunset tomorrow."

Roger, Bethanie, and Coral began chattering excitedly—where to find supplies, what to bring, whether they'd be able to get gas— but Joan just sat, a sick sensation settling in her stomach.

"Joan?" Coral said after a while. "You're awful quiet. How are you doing?"

Joan considered the question seriously. "I . . . I'm fine. I just don't want to go."

Roger looked baffled. "What? Why not?"

It was a gut feeling, but after a while Joan realized where it had come from. "Look . . . I like men. I've been surrounded by, supported by, and loved by men, for my whole life. But when I think about living the rest of my life on a submarine base . . . all those young, horny sailors who'll look at me like I'm the last woman in the world . . . because I am, or close to it . . . and all that 'Go USA' crap . . ." She closed her eyes and shook her head. "No. Just no. I'm not going to be the nursemaid for the next generation of patriots."

The others tried to persuade her. They cajoled, argued, and screamed until the sick yellow-brown clouds began to lighten in the east. They moved into the windowless kitchen area and kept arguing. But Joan could not be budged. Finally, they left her alone and went off to discuss the matter among the three of them.

Then Coral returned. She squatted down in front of Joan and took her hands in her own. "Joan . . . we've made up our minds. We're going to Bremerton, with you or without you."

"That's fine," Joan said. "Go, with my blessings."

"So . . . so are you just gonna stay here all alone for the rest of your life?"

Joan squeezed Coral's hands and looked into her eyes. "I don't know what I'm going to do yet, Coral. But I'm going to do it for myself, and no one else."

SHE'D SETTLED AT POWELL'S bookstore, having found her own house too full of memories and the library too cold and drafty. Sleeping through the day, foraging by night, surrounded by all the books she'd never had time to read before, it wasn't a bad life. There was more canned and packaged organic food at the Whole Foods next door than she'd ever be able to eat, and since everything in the world had been irradiated, it would never spoil. And when the power finally failed, she found a big generator and ran strings of Christmas lights down every aisle. Her cheery little book-lined cave.

Sometimes she wondered what was happening in the rest of the world, and how Coral, Bethanie, and Roger were getting along. But her generator couldn't power the whole Internet, and her short-wave radio got only static and a few garbled syllables in what sounded like Japanese. Even if the Japanese decided to come to America, she thought, Portland would not be their first stop.

She'd never added her name to the Wikipedia page.

The night she'd found the green Subaru Forester, almost a year after the event, became a turning point for her. After she'd dried her eyes, blown her nose, and returned to her cave, she realized three things: she'd finally found herself, and achieved the peace she'd sought for so many years, but it wasn't enough.

Two nights later, after a serious bout of research in the Gardening, Agriculture, and Science sections—one of the advantages of living in the world's largest bookstore—she went out with a crowbar and a trowel. Prying the manhole cover off was harder than it looked, but a year of self-sufficiency had made her strong. And finally, at the bottom of four rusty metal ladders, in a dank and drippy vault lined with pipes and cables, she found what she was looking for.

Soil. Soil that smelled like *soil*. Soil teeming with bacteria, not like the sterilized dirt at the surface.

It took her the whole night to drag up enough of the stuff to fill three small planters. The next night, aching though she was, she went out and hauled back every seed packet she could find at every garden store in Northwest Portland that hadn't completely collapsed.

She planted them all. Every single seed. She'd read a lot about food irradiation and knew that *some* of them would have to be viable. It took two weeks and many trips to the sewer for more soil.

She found some grow-lights—keenly aware of the irony of bringing UV lamps into a dark basement when UV outside was her biggest problem—and positioned them over the planters. She filtered rainwater and rigged up a gentle drip system.

She waited.

Five weeks later a few sprouts, a handful of hardy survivors, poked their tender green heads above the soil.

She tended them, and watered them with tears.

This story connects with Ursula K. Le Guin by being very explicitly set in her hometown of Portland, Oregon (also my hometown), by having a middle-aged woman as a protagonist, and by dealing with questions of peaceful coexistence rather than grim survivalism in the aftermath of disaster. It's kind of a Buddhist story in that, in the end, the protagonist's main struggle is to make peace with herself and to figure out who she is in the absence of the society (and men!) who have defined her.

Becoming Human

GIGI LITTLE

THE DAY AFTER THE apocalypse, the ants, being the only survivors, decided to become human.

They'd been watching the humans for generations and they liked many things about them. They liked their kitchen tiles and their picnic baskets and their tallness and their music. They liked their books, which, through these many generations, the ants had taught themselves to read.

Most of all, they loved their cakes and cookies. It was one thing to burrow into a sugar bag. It was an entirely different pleasure to dip into the exquisite dream that was fluffy golden vanilla buttercream.

If the ants became human, they could learn to bake.

They had a town hall meeting in the Jacksons' kitchen. The apocalypse had left the house mostly intact, and shelter was a big plus as far as avoiding baking in the rain. Also, the Jacksons had many books. One of the Jacksons in particular loved science fiction and fantasy, and all ants love science fiction and fantasy.

Hidden along the edges of framed pictures and at the rims of bedside tables, worker ants had long read alongside the humans and used their pheromones and antly energies to broadcast the stories to the rest of the group. They had learned many truths about the world this way. They were especially captivated by Bernard Werber's *Empire of the Ants*, A.J. Colucci's *The Colony*, and Ursula K. Le Guin's *The Compass Rose*, which included their favorite short story, "The Author of 'The Acacia Seeds' and Other Extracts from the Journal of the Association of Therolinguistics." Admittedly, in these books and stories, the writers tended to focus on the more combative aspects of ant life, but the ants forgave them, knowing all humans harbor a bias toward conflict.

Another reason the ants chose the Jackson home was that it was the only all-solar house in the neighborhood, which meant the oven and appliances would still work. The couple also had the latest hologram TVs (although there were no stations broadcasting anymore) and a Milkmaker3000, which would come in handy with all the cows gone.

On the afternoon of the town hall meeting, ants came from yards and yards around, spreading across the floor and up the cabinets and all along the counters until the entire kitchen was carpeted a sparkling, teeming black.

One might think the spigot in the sink would be the perfect perch from which a leader could address the masses. But they did not have a king or a president or a dictator (the queen was revered, but she did not rule), so they left the spigot alone.

Communication was a wave of sound and chemical that flowed across and through the gathered sea of the ants.

"^~^~``~`^"*""*~~'```"^~*," they said. "~^`"`'~~*~`~`*`'`*` '^*`*^`'`~~*~"'`'`'`'*^^^~``~`^`'~~*~`~`*`'^*~"'`'`'******`~`~"'`' *^`^'*~~^```*"*''`'~*~^^^~``~*""*~~'```"^~*~^`'`'~*~~^```*"''`'~ *~^*~~*^```*""*`'`~*~^'~`*'~`*'~*^*^*^^^~~^```~````*'**^`'`'*`'^* `*^``^`'~`~`*~''`'*`'*^^^~``~`^`'"*~'~'```"^~*``~^`'`'~*~'~^` `'`*""`'`~~^*~~''*^```"*~~^```*'*''`'~`*~^''^^~``~'*""*~^~''```"^~* ^`'"`'~*~."

And they all, of course, agreed.

Becoming human would allow the ants to expand their ambitions far beyond the anthill. They could live in houses and bake in kitchens. They could build new cities. They could master aerospace technology and construct their own rocket ships to explore the planets (ants, being very small, were quite enamored of things as large as planets). They had heard tell about a planet called Gethen that was very cold but very beautiful. Many stories had been told among the ants of this planet, and they all wanted to visit.

But for now, this would have to remain a future aspiration.

The first goal would be to create the human form. They would do this by combining their bodies, climbing one on another on another, and hooking their tarsal claws together, to create the needed shapes of head, leg, hand. The second goal would be to learn to coordinate this form so that leg and foot could walk, so that hand could reach out and hold spoon and whisk. The third goal would be to bake their very first cake.

One might think that it would behoove the new humans to start small, with cookies, but the ants, hidden in dark corners, had watched many baking shows, and it seemed to the group that the hand-eye coordination needed to use a spatula to extract an entire batch of cookies from a dangerously hot baking sheet was better left for subsequent baking endeavors.

It would be bad enough to have to figure out how to crack and (dear god) maybe even separate the eggs.

But first things first.

It did not take long for the ants to perfect their pyramiding skills, piling on top of each other and creating different shapes. A simple orb morphed into a skull with jawline and maxilla, morphed into a face with nose and lips. A chin cleft. The elegant topography of the human ear. Hooking ant after ant after ant, they created a head of teeming black hair, squiggling Medusa-like along the tiled kitchen floor.

Heads need bodies. More ants swarmed in to raise the head

into the air. A crossbar of shoulders, a thick torso, the gleaming sprouts of elongating limbs. The body rose toward the ceiling, higher than the ant eye could see.

But the ants did not need to see the whole in order to be a part of it. Communication washed across the surface of the body. "`***`~`/**``*`~`~//`~/`/*`^/*`~~^```/*//*`/`/`~*`~^^^~``~*///*`~~/``^`^," they said.

And the body walked.

Well. It must be admitted that, at that early date, they could not master the coordination of leg and foot, leg and foot, to actually walk without the rest of the body collapsing. Instead, the towering, stately form glided across the kitchen—its limbs immobile, only the individuality of the ants in motion across its surface—like a twinkling black ghost.

But they still considered it a victory. Had they had one, they would have celebrated with cake.

"^~^`/`~/^*``````~`~*?" ant asked.

"*///**``/`~*`~~^``````*~~/```," ant answered.

Which meant, *Shall we have some sugar instead?* And, *Yes, I think sugar would be nice.* And they all agreed.

The ants needed to remain in motion in order to maintain the integrity of the form, lest the ants making up the contours of the feet get flattened by the weight of so many ants above them. It was this constant redistribution that kept the body alive.

The ants decided to create two distinct humans, because this was the number of humans who had lived in this particular house. Anyway, humans always seemed to be broken up into twos. Husband and wife, mother and father, boss and worker. Lucy and Ricky. Bugs and Elmer.

Even in war and politics, which the ants had seen plenty of on TV, things came in twos. Two sides. Always against each other. The ants didn't understand this. They preferred when two was more like one. Like when the Jacksons were in bed together. Or when they laughed.

As the ants perfected their skills in corporeal architecture and operational synchronization, they realized that to truly ready themselves for the next step, they needed more understanding of what it was to be fully human. So, dissolving once again into a mass, they set out to do some research.

From the kitchen, they trekked in a line through living room and dining room and marched along the walls into the bedroom. They journeyed sideways across vast bookcases. Over dunes and past dreams of electric sheep. Past Earthsea and the tombs of Atuan. To the farthest shore. A few of the ants knew that one of the two former inhabitants of the Jackson house had kept a diary hidden under a well-worn paperback of *The Left Hand of Darkness* in a drawer in the bedside table.

The ants had to work fastidiously to use their new skills to pull open the drawer. And form themselves into a hand to haul the diary out. And place it on the bed. And draw it open.

March 23

I'm having some wine. Hard day at the office, and the evening news is full of nothing good. Talks between our ambassador and theirs seem to have fallen apart. Again. They refuse to destroy their arsenal of nuclear nanos, and we've told them that refusal is essentially a declaration of war. Washington's been talking like this for months, but this seems more serious somehow. Sometimes I wonder why it is that we feel like it's okay for us to try to force other countries to get rid of their weapons of mass destruction when we still have ours.

Working as a line, the ants burrowed under pages and advanced the days. They read the words that were written there, yes, but also delicately licked the paper, detecting the chemicals in the smudges left by the human's fingers, and in this way, learned many things.

APRIL 4

We stayed in tonight. Watched a little TV. I wanted to watch the news, but he said let's find one of the old movies. It's true, there's no reason to spend all evening horrifying ourselves over this constant threat of war and destruction. We used the new instant nachos machine, and that was kind of fun.

APRIL 8

Talks have resumed overseas. I don't hold out much hope, frankly. All these guys seem to do is puff up their chests and strut around, talking about who has scarier weapons. I'll never understand why people can't just learn to get along.

We were supposed to go out with Sofia and Eladia tonight but he begged off at the last minute. He's in such a mood. I thought I'd be nice and do the laundry, which is his job, and all he could say was why didn't I pay closer attention to his green shirt. I swear, sometimes I could just kill him.

"**`~*~~^`/*//****~*~**`*~``~//`^^*`^*~~^`````"^~'^`*
~," ant said.

"**`~*~~^*~~~*~^*~~*^```/*//*`~*~^'^//*~~," ant replied.

Which meant, *I think the problem with corporeal humans is that they want too much for themselves.* And, *I think they would do better if they baked more.* And they agreed.

The day to begin was almost at hand. The Jacksons' kitchen was fully equipped with the most up-to-date Milkmaker and other appliances from Synthlicious Industries (*The Latest in Snacknology*™), but natural always tastes best, and so an expedition was organized to go out into the neighborhood and bring back supplies from any of the houses that remained at all intact—cartons of eggs, containers of flour, highly coveted jars of rainbow sprinkles.

The ants were eager to get started on the cake. They glided across the kitchen, two elegant, towering figures working in beautifully coordinated cooperation, ants glimmering across the contours of shoulder and knee and wrist. A poised, ant-black hand held the silver end of a whisk, sending it ringing against the smooth interior of a metal bowl and churning through a vast lake of whipped egg and sugar.

Because the ants were constantly in motion across the surfaces of the human forms, no ant got stuck in an armpit or on a rear end; all ants had the privilege of playing every part in this grand adventure.

Their new life truly was a utopia.

"**`˘ʹ∧*∧ʹ~~`,**`˘ʹ∧*∧ʹ~~`!" ant said.

"∧ʹ~ʹ∧∧*```~~``*∧ʹ``˘ʹ∧`˘*~~~``*`∧∧,**∧ʹ~ʹ∧∧*`~~~∧ʹ**`~*ʹ~ ∧˘ʹ∧ʹ," ant said.

Which meant, *I can't wait, I can't wait!* And, *It is good to have an end to journey toward, but it is the journey that matters in the end.* And they agreed.

Soon the oven glowed and the triumphant scent of warm golden cake filled the kitchen.

But across the house, there was a sound. A click followed by the *shoosh*ing of the front door opening.

The ants turned their feelers toward the noise in horror.

A silence.

Then the slow, even rhythm of footsteps.

A shadow fell across the kitchen. The figure filled the open doorway. It was massive, at least seven feet tall. A hulking human form, broad-shouldered, barrel-chested. Along the writhing surfaces of the new human slipped and skittered the thick satiny brown bodies of cockroaches.

The ants had been wrong. They were not the only survivors.

For a moment, no ant in the room could move.

An ominous sound issued from the figure of the cockroach human, a sick and slithery reverberation formed of the many individual clicks and chirps of the many individual roaches.

"<+</>>+/-/</++\\>>->+>\\//-//+\/+++-><>\<\+\\\-
>>?" they asked.

Which meant, *Hello, might we use your kitchen?*

A WEEK LATER, DEEP into the night, after all baking had ceased
for the day, ants lay sleeping in the crevices of the house. The
kitchen was sweet with the lingering scent of snickerdoodle. Still,
my antennae twitched with unease.

Things had felt a little . . . different since the cockroaches came.
I didn't want to be selfish, but the more they kept coming over to
use our kitchen, the more I felt, well, a little put out, if I had to be
honest. Oh, it was fine. I was fully capable of sharing; I mean, it
was my lot in life, after all. I just wished they were better about
wiping down the counter.

I tried to go back to sleep. The tiled floor was cold. High above
me, moonlight gleamed on the silver of the spigot hanging over
the sink. Someone was standing there. On the edge of the spigot,
looking down across the kitchen. I squinted my compound eyes.
It was ant.

Quietly, so as not to disturb ant and ant, sleeping together
nearby, I tiptoed across the floor and slanted my way up and
across the dishwasher to the counter. Standing out on the spigot
perch, ant didn't notice me approaching, seeming lost in thought.

I stepped along the moonlit silver of the spigot. As I neared,
ant's head turned.

I said, *Is that you, ant?*

Yes, but I'm calling myself Black Ant, now.

My antennae twitched. *What?*

It's a name, Black Ant said. *Like humans have.*

I said, *I'm black, too.*

I couldn't think of anything else, Black Ant said. *I'm new at names.*

The vista of the kitchen spread out below us, a vast tiled floor
with slumbering ants lined all along the dips between the tiles. The
ants slept happy, their bellies filled with cookies.

I don't like this new development, Black Ant said.

Snickerdoodles? I asked.

The roaches, Black Ant said. *They're taking what's rightfully ours.*

No one can bake all the time, I said.

They're using our supplies.

It was true. They were using a lot of flour. Still, this talk made me uncomfortable. I said, *They let us use their Eggmaker3000.*

Like that's the only one in the world. If they're going to hold our kitchen hostage over one lousy machine, we'll go find one of our own. Black Ant was getting worked up, mandibles clicking, antennae waving. *They're here all hours of the day! Why should we have to wait to try out a recipe for a trifle so those selfish bastards can massacre some stupid pie?*

Keep your voice down, I said.

Screw that! The roaches are all holed up in that shack of theirs down the street.

More ants were starting to stir along the countertop and down below. One stepped cautiously out onto the spigot. It was ant.

Black Ant's voice was sounding more oratory than commentary, now. *We have to stop this! Before it gets totally out of control. What if the beetles survived too? What about the worms? Did anyone think to check under the lawn?*

Oh my god, ant said. *I never thought about that.*

Black Ant took a step to the very edge of the spigot, calling out to the gathering masses, who rumbled below us, craning their pronota to hear. Black Ant sent pheromones out across the kitchen so those too far away to hear would receive the message. *My friends, they're trying to take what's ours! What we discovered! What we worked for! We are the owners of this house!*

Shouts rose up from below. Standing there on hind legs like a human, Black Ant looked more handsome, somehow. Powerful. Maybe I could have a name too. Something that was uniquely me. I tried to think about what I was. I was an ant. I was black. Wait. That was already taken.

You think the roaches'll just share? Black Ant shouted. *You think they won't try to steal our sugar for themselves?*

Hell no! someone shouted back.

The air tasted different. Electric and new.

It may not be easy, Black Ant bellowed, *but we can take them! There are way more of us than there are of them!*

It was true. Below us, moving in from all directions, a shimmering black multitude poured across the tiles.

We were legion.

But we were also individuals, and we knew what we wanted. We could fight for it.

We could be fierce.

We could be superior.

We could be human.

Unlike many other, obviously wiser readers, I didn't know Ursula K. Le Guin's work until I was thirty-five years old and was taking a fiction-writing class at Portland State University, where I was fortunate to be assigned Le Guin's fabulous writing book Steering the Craft. *Even before I'd ever read a lick of her science fiction and fantasy, I was moved by her smarts, her wit, and her spirit. My story "Becoming Human" was inspired by Le Guin's exploration of animals, particularly in her short story "The Author of 'The Acacia Seeds' and Other Extracts from the Journal of the Association of Therolinguistics," and I hope it captures just a little of her wonderful ability to take wild inventiveness and use it to say meaningful things.*

Bee, Keeper

JASON LaPIER

KA'S CUP WAS EMPTY. He left his branch and flew to the bush where the other drones buzzed.

There was a queue to the hollow crotch between two branches where the mead fermented. He shoved past the other drones. They flinched and danced angrily in reaction, then saw him and settled into a sulk, giving him space. He bumped up to the lip of the bark and dipped his cup, then settled in, forcing the others to go around his bulk. He ignored the smells of their complaints.

They were all of different hives. All rejected, of course. None of them had been lucky enough to mate before the end of their short lives, else their lives would have been even shorter. Left to their own devices, most drones drifted off to expire in peace. But there had been something in the air, a sign, a hint: *Come to the Dark Woods.*

There were no hives in the Dark Woods, as the presence of black bears discouraged it. But a drone wasn't one for questioning, and many came to follow the scent left only for them. Left by some kind of charity. Someone who brought honey to the Dark Woods, tending to the wayward drones.

The drones didn't know why, and didn't much care. A few of the more industrious among them pooled honey and water together with bits of pear skins, and soon there was mead, and then they cared even less.

Their benefactors appeared periodically, dancing blessings. Like most drones, Ka wasn't much for philosophy. A drone had a part in the Purpose of Bees, but it was not lifelong. These beefolk that brought honey and extracted gratitude were an odd bunch. The sisters in his hive had called them Boxheads. A subclassification of Boxers. Words that had no meaning to Ka.

"So what?" Ka mumbled into his mead. He eyed the Boxheads as they buzzed closer. Most days he ignored them, but then again, most days he took his cup deeper into the Dark Woods and nodded off. This time was different. They were circling, buzzing and dancing. Through the encroaching mead haze, he saw them seeking him out.

"What?" he said when they came near.

"Greetings, fellow beekind," their leader said. Ka peered at her with his oversized eyes. She was young and looked strong, near her peak. Still, she was a third his size. "My name is Hanannahah," she said, settling in close to him.

He leaned away from her slightly, steadying himself on the lip of the bark. "And?"

"I understand your bitterness," she said softly. By way of response, he drank noisily. "You are still a brother, even if your hive expelled you."

Ka looked at her. "Doesn't your hive beat out your drones?"

She dropped her head, as though a sadness overtook her. "It is the way; drones cannot stay in the hive. But we still care. That's why we come here." She gestured at the bush, or maybe all of the Dark Woods. "That's why we bring you honey. Does the honey not nurture?"

"Aye, but it's better when it rots a bit. Ha!" Ka shot a look at a nearby cluster of drones, who pretended to join in his mirth.

Hanannahah nodded at her companions. "We have come

here sunrise after sunrise. You alone are always here. You've lived longer than most brothers."

"So what?" He pulled the mead up as though he would drink, then lowered it, disgusted with himself. With their observation. "I don't know why. I have no Purpose."

"We can give you a Purpose," she said.

He frowned. "My sisters warned me about your kind. Boxheads."

"Mankind saves us with those boxes." She leaned a little closer. "They are Power. They are Shelter. They truly save us."

"I got no interest in your religion, miss. Or any religion."

She looked away, then looked back at him. "Have you interest in Justice?"

"I don't even know what that means."

"You were cast out. Unable to serve your part in the Purpose." She touched him, causing him to flinch. None dared touch him, and yet she had. "What if you could use your last days to right that wrong?"

Ka glared at this brave worker, his abdomen twitching, waving a phantom stinger. "How."

"Take vengeance on those that cast you out."

"What? Attack my hive? My queen?"

"You're the strongest drone any of us has ever seen. Your colony—your queen—saw to that."

"Miss, you might not have noticed this, but drones don't get the Weapon." Again his abdomen twitched impotently.

"We can give you a Weapon. You are strong enough."

Ka shook his head. "I dunno what you mean. But it don't matter. I can fly fast, but I can't fly far. I don't know how to get back to my hive. And if I did, they would smell me."

"We can take care of that. We have strong workers who will lift you together. And you don't need to go to your hive. We know where you can find the heretical queens. Unsheltered."

He drained his cup and pushed away from the mead well. "Enough of this talk, Boxheads. I'm going to sleep."

They backed away from him. "We'll be back," Hanannahah said firmly. "Sleep well. Tomorrow you must decide."

Ka shook his head. "Whatever." With a grunt he took flight, swarming dizzily in search of the tiny hole in the rotten tree he called home.

It was Villivinall's first attendance at the Congregation of Queens, but she had been well prepped. Her mentor, Yursillinianna, was a queen in her eighth season, as strong as ever; not a miracle, but an achievement of the work of colonies like hers that had put their minds toward bettering their species incrementally, one generation at a time.

Ironically, their improved lifespans reduced the number of genetic permutations their colonies could achieve, but her mentor had made up for such depth by increasing the breadth of her influence. Though the Congregation had no official leader, Yursillinianna was considered to be the wax that bound them, the scent that united the hives. And she had chosen Villivinall to be her successor in this effort.

Which meant she was nearing the end of her brooding potential. It was possible that Villivinall's mentor had just completed her last laying.

But the key to everything Yursillinianna had taught Villivinall was that while individual lives were short, collective lives—that of the family, the colony, the species—were long.

Villivinall's attendants buzzed around her busily. "I don't know why they do this," one said, cleaning up the space around her. "Queens leaving their hives for this meeting. It's dangerous."

"Sannsanna, you don't need to clean the whole time we're here," Villivinall said, partly annoyed at her fussing, partly amused at her absurd commitment to her role.

"Well, what am I supposed to do?" The cleaner flapped her wings in a shudder. "This place is filthy!"

The Congregation was being held in a massive old oak tree

that stood alone in the Yellow Fields of the North. Every year the location changed, though it really just rotated between four or five spots. Large old trees such at this were ideal—this one had a great gaping hollow in the center with abandoned burrows worming out from it, providing safe havens for arriving queens.

A guard buzzed in and alighted next to Villivinall. "Queen," she said shortly, "we've established patrols throughout the fields. We're taking shifts, using the nectar we brought for fuel."

"I'm sure we'll be fine," Villivinall said, feeling uncertainty flitter through her response.

The guard ignored her and left. Though she was of Villivinall's hive, Villivinall, as queen, had little say in how the feeders, cleaners, guards, and the rest went about their business. All were driven by their own contributions to the Purpose.

Never resent their diligence, her mentor had told her on several occasions. *We queens do not rule by command. We rule by science. We rule by progress.*

"It's time," Villivinall said to the attendants buzzing around her.

They proceeded into the vast chamber of the hollow. The light was dim, but she could see and smell the other queens emerging from their respective burrows.

Twelve had come. They each represented not only their own hives, but sister-hives in their respective geographies. More had been invited, but Villivinall had been warned that not all queens saw the point of the Congregation. A few even directly opposed it. To some, intercolony cooperation was unnecessary at best, and highly suspect at worst, and Yursillinianna had earned nearly as much criticism as she had respect. Some box-homed bees even called the work of the Congregation *unnatural*—as if slicing a tree into rectangles and squaring it into a hive with walls was any kind of natural.

The queens assembled and introductions were made. Then began some small talk, mainly sharing information about which areas had seen more or less food versus more or less predators or other dangers. Throughout these purely data-based discussions, Villivinall could already see divisions—some queens were content to report and return to prepare for the winter season, others were thinking beyond the coming winter, and the next.

Inevitably, the discussion turned to humans. Villivinall again had been prepared by her mentor on this topic. Her hive was free, suspended in a great cedar, oblong and natural, but so many of the others built combs in convenient crates left by humans. Most free bees were content to keep their distance from those curious creatures, but bees raised in boxes were more likely to extol the virtues of symbiosis with them.

And then there was the other view: that the humans were not keeping their end of any such mutual relationship. That they brought more death and poison than shelter and food. Over the years, Yursillinianna had postulated that the humans' constructions and machinations were damaging the Queen of Queens herself.

"There's no denying the humans have helped us," one of the box-homed queens said. She seemed to be arguing internally as well as externally, and Villivinall could not stop herself from staring at the blue dot on her back whenever she turned and it became visible. A human marking, though its function was not clear. "Some have the best intentions—they recognize our Purpose, and they help us propagate. Though the relationship is always transactional for them."

"Exactly." Rillixintraxil was another free-hive queen whose dances and scents were both sharp. "They cannot give without receiving, and *taking*. They receive bountiful crops by our Work, and then, still unsatisfied, they loot the honeycombs. Because fools like *you* are tricked into building within their boxes."

The blue-dotted queen shrank, unwilling to offer a rebuttal. But another box-homed queen stepped up to take her side. This one was specked with a bright red dot on her back. "Hyperbolic nonsense! The honey they take is excess—an excess achieved only thanks to the abundance of flowering crops they've planted nearby. It is a mutual relationship that these humans cultivate."

"Mutual!" Rillixintraxil spat. "You are livestock!"

"We are bees that fulfill our Purpose!"

"And what of the others? The ones that poison us? They cloud the skies with their death machines that spray toxins like rain. Their fat crops attract the hungry bellies of other insects, and their solution is to pollute their own flora, destroying everything with antennae."

"We need to think defensively," Villivinall said. She had been trying not to be drawn into the argument, but her mentor was looking on in silence, expectant. Villivinall felt compelled to prove that she could carry on as the guiding voice in the coming years. "We have made great progress on our immunities."

"The Free Hives have, yes," Rillixintraxil said. "But those Boxers refuse. And crossbreeding is unavoidable. When we breed in new immunities, the Boxers breed them right back out. It only works when the species is aligned."

"Be careful with that word," Red Dot said. "Some of us accept the mutual relationship, but that does not mean we *worship* the humans."

This statement brought the discussion to a standstill, as all thought of the recent emergence of the fanatics. Hives that saw the humans as *more* than symbiotic, as protectors, creators, as gods.

Villivinall's mentor broke her silence. "Let us be prepared for any danger that these zealots might pose. But let us not allow preparedness to replace our compassion for those who do not share our vision, for they are beekind."

"REALLY NEED SOME MEAD right now," Ka said as the four Boxhead workers lowered him onto the thin branch of a low blackberry bush.

"Accept this mission and we will take you back to the Dark Woods and you can have all the mead you can drink," one of them said.

"Mission, bah."

One of them shoved bread in his face while the other three huddled around some object. He ate and they came around behind him; two of them grabbed him, as if to hold him down. He was much larger than all of them together, but he didn't resist. They buzzed among themselves as they worked.

He finished the food and they backed away from him. "The Weapon is affixed."

He flinched at those words. All his life, he'd been impotent, feeling a shadow stinger at the end of his abdomen, and now he looked down and saw it. He flexed slowly and felt its power.

"This Weapon does not have a barb, so you will be able to use it many times," another one said. "Remember, this is the scent of Yursillinianna. She poisons the mind of all the others with her blasphemous notions. She is your target. Understood?"

Ka shook his stinger and then shook his head. "That's not the mark of the one who refused to mate with me. Not the mark of the hive that beat me out, either."

They looked at each other uncomfortably, buzzing lightly. "Yursillinianna first. The rest . . . they will be there. You do what you will."

"How do we know this will work?" the one who had fed him said.

Ka flexed his abdomen, the tip of the Weapon rising erect. "Let's give it a try, eh?" With a shudder he buzzed his wings and lifted up, then his body spasmed, spiking the questioning worker in the left eye.

As the victim twitched and slowly twisted, falling from the branch, the other three leapt into the air and backed away, squirting a clamor of warning scents.

"I'm not one of your lot," Ka said, the force of his glare buffeting them further. "I'm not some worker-born drone. I'm queen-brood. I'm royalty. One queen denied me my mate-right. And my queen-mother denied me the shelter of my hive. Now tell me where they are."

"MY HIVE HAS INFLUENCED the development of the Weapon," Rillixintraxil said. "We have seen how it affects some of the humans—sickens them, even kills them. Our studies have shown through generations that it can be strengthened, that it can be effective against more and more of them."

Villivinall bristled. "The Weapon is for defense only! It should not be used to make war!"

Rillixintraxil rose, hovering above the Congregation. "We are Keepers of the Queen of Queens! We are part of *her* system, the cycle of nurture and production and birth and death and rebirth! Those creatures, the humans, are not. What system do they serve? They spread like mites, choking out Her children wherever they infest. We," she said as she landed once again. "We have our Purpose."

There were murmurings among the other free queens and Villivinall shook with anxiety. She wanted to speak, to denounce such plans of violence, to pronounce plans of *progress* instead, but she felt her confidence wavering as a few queens agreed with Rillixintraxil's outburst.

Yursillinianna puffed a scent into the room and the murmurs died, and all turned to her. "Aggression leads to destruction, and destruction directly opposes creation. All that we do, our Purpose, is to serve creation.

"What is the Purpose of the humans? We cannot fathom. They create and destroy on scales beyond our comprehension. Maybe they were supposed to protect this world. Maybe some of them *do* serve that Purpose. But some do not. Why? We cannot know. All we can know is that it is not our Purpose to war. It is our Purpose to flourish.

"Evolution is natural to us. Our Purpose applies to our species as well as the flora of the world. Evolution works best when seeds are spread. Diversity begets improvement. Our Purpose, our job, for the plants, is to carry their seeds across the lands, as they cannot. What the Queen of Queens does with the seeds after that is her business.

"But nothing says we should not apply these methods to ourselves. I believe it is our *duty* as servants to the Queen of Queens to follow her example, to aid our own evolution. The more resilient we become, the better we can serve her and the rest of life in this world."

"Your words are wise, as always, Yursillinianna," Rillixintraxil said, bowing. "But we are facing a crisis!"

"Yes," Yursillinianna said. "As we in this Congregation understand this, we must hope that some of the humans understand this. But we will not wager our species on this. We must continue to pursue science and progress. We must strengthen our future broods so that they may *endure*. If we go to war, we cannot serve our Purpose."

KA, WELL-RESTED AND WELL-FED, unleashed the full stretch of his long wings. He flew fast and hard, spying the guards from a great distance with his oversized drone eyes. He let his route curve to split the nearest ones. They would smell him, but not until he was shooting past them.

He flexed his body in midflight, slowing for only a second to once again verify that his stinger was no longer a ghost limb. It carried no venom and no barb, but it was sharp. He didn't know where the Boxheads got it, and he didn't care.

The singular oak rose in the field before him. He shot toward it. The alarm scent was in the air. Let them shout out, he thought. He had his own Purpose.

He flew into the massive hollow of the tree. A few guards buzzed around, disoriented by his speed, flying to intercept him and missing badly. Twelve queens ringed a circle before him. They each took flight at his entrance.

All but one.

He quickly identified his queen-mother, Rillixintraxil, rising to his right, and the young queen that had spurned his mating attempt, Villivinall, rising to his left. For a moment he could not choose which to attack first, but the scent of a queen that remained on the ground caught his attention. The mark of the Boxheads' target. One of the oldest living queens. Who could say why they hated her so—but sitting on the floor of the rotting oak, she was too easy a target. She would be his first kill.

He dove. She rose just before he reached her, and as he slammed into her, she gripped him as hard as he gripped her. They tumbled together, bounding across the floor until they hit the side wall in a puff of rotwood dust. He shook his head, momentarily disoriented, then felt her stinger jab him. As a queen, her Weapon was not barbed either, and she pulled it back to jab again.

But he was strong and fast, and excited by the presence of so many queens. He spasmed, stabbing viciously with his new Weapon. She gripped him as he lanced her over and over.

The air began to darken and the buzzing that was in his frenzied mind faded into a real buzzing, all around him. The old queen's legs fell limp and her body twitched. He looked up to see dozens of guards, some of them his own sisters, closing in on him.

They blacked out the light and pushed against him, buzzing and vibrating.

"No!" he screamed. "Get away from me!"

He could feel the heat building from their bodies. The air getting thicker and harder to breath. The darkness becoming fuzzier. The smothering. Smothering.

VILLIVINALL WATCHED THE BALL of guards slowly expand, drifting away from the attacker and landing about the hollow, exhausted. The drone lay immobile on the floor, without so much as a twitch. The odd Weapon protruding from his abdomen made him look like some kind of mistake, half queen and half drone.

She drifted down next to him, joined by Rillixintraxil. "Queen of Queens," Villivinall said, "he was so big. I thought he was a hornet or a wasp."

Rillixintraxil lowered her head. "He was one of mine. My hive has been breeding them this way."

Villivinall looked up at her. "Why? For war?"

She fluttered a sigh. "A side effect of making the Weapon more powerful for our daughters. Our sons are getting bigger."

"More aggressive," Villivinall said with a glare. A memory came to her then as she caught the expired drone's scent. She had seen him on her mating flight. That aggression had unnerved her; she had avoided him.

Rillixintraxil shot her a look, then looked at the fallen Yursillinianna. "She was right. This is not the way I want." She tapped at the unnatural attachment. "It was those Boxheads. They sent him in. Sent him as an assassin. But it was me . . . I bred him to be truculent."

Villivinall left her to stand over her monstrous son and hovered over to the still form of her mentor. "I'm so sorry," she said, then realized that's not what she wanted to say most. "Thank you."

The other queens joined her, releasing a scent of mourning. Villivinall thought she should feel broken with the loss of her closest friend, but everything she had learned told her there was no need. So she faced the others, and spoke.

"We know this meeting of queens is a risk, which is why we choose to hold it after laying season. There are many who don't have our long-term view. They see only the pollen-bearing stamen before them, they see not the horizon and the way it ever rolls. Those who sent this assassin think this is a statement, perhaps even a strategic one. But Yursillinianna will live on in her brood. And her hive will produce a new queen that will carry her vision.

"As will I, and those of you who wish to join me. She once told me, every drop of water in a river moves downstream, and the next day is replaced by another drop. But when we fly high, we don't see the drops of water, we see the river as a whole. Yursillinianna's vision is one of progress. Of respect to the Mother of Mothers. And of serving our Purpose: to see *all* life flourish, in *every* generation."

Le Guin took exception to the notion that her fiction was purely 'message' motivated; and yet we find mind-expanding messages throughout her works. She wrote with depth, through intricate world-building and integrity, through complex, multidimensional characters. By putting immersive storytelling first and foremost, she was able to introduce concepts that if stated outright may seem absurd, and yet in the context of her worlds, felt as real as history. She will forever remain a guide for the rest of us who aspire to use story to communicate even the most challenging ideas.

KwaZulu-Natal

JUHEA KIM

WHEN IT'S BLIMMIN HOT like this in August, during dry season when it's supposed to be cool but the sun makes the yellow earth go poppoppop as it cracks, I always think on my elephant. It was just this kinda day when I was eight when my Da brought him home in the back of his bakkie. Da pulled over and went round and lowered the ramp for him to walk down on, but he didn't want to move. Da said Jezus it's bladdy hot I'm going inside, and just like so he disappeared. And I got so worried leaving the elephant by itself in the bakkie with the sun beating down on his back, but I ran inside chop-chop and got a bucket of water and an umbrella. I climbed on the bakkie and the elephant still didn't move or make any sound like it was dead. It was a few inches shorter than me and its trunk was the size of my own arm, a baby probably born in the last wet season.

Come on, little oke, I said, setting down the bucket in the front of him, be a good elephant and drink some. He stood still there unmoving even tho there were goggas buzzing round allasudden attacking him. He didn't even try to flap his ears to get the blad-suckers off and cool down a little. I sat down next to him shooing at the flies with one hand and holding the umbrella over us with the other until the sun went down and the stars came up.

Da came back out and said, What are you doing there and not making the dinner hey, and I said, If I go away he'll die. It was by now freezing cold and I was throwing my body over the elephant like a blanket. He started coming to, only cos he was shivering and not cos he was done being bladdy stubborn. We were both shivering like so and Da said you better check yourself for the ticks when you come in, I'm ganna beat you raw if you don't. But then Da threw me a blanket and a vetkoek before going back inside. I put the blanket on Rocky—Stallone was the tops back in day, bru—and I was scarfing down the vetkoek with both my hands when I noticed a plunking sound and realized it was Rocky dipping his trunk in the water bucket.

Ever since that moment me and Rocky did everything together. When I ate he ate, when I sat he sat right down on his arse, and I slept cuddling him in the kraal Da made next to our house so I could feed him his bottle in the middle of the nights. While he sucked on it he liked to snuggle his trunk in my armpit, it made him feel comfy like being with his Ma. We both didn't have Mas, Rocky and me. My Ma I have no recollection of cos she ran away when I was a baby, but I know she was Zulu. My Da was Afrikaner and he was a hard, hard man, hey. He drank also, but he was just a bladdy mean kind of oke. Even his chommies, other rangers at the park, were kinda spooked by Da sumtimes. Nobody bothered him for having a bruin ou for a son hidden away on the fringe of the park, far from the other rangers' houses, cos they all knew Da would kill them and their families if they so much as laughed the wrong kinda laugh at him.

That's why they put Da in charge when they had any kinda culling mission to do. That year it was the elephants and the park decided it had more than five thousands elephants in excess of. They were ganna kill two hundred a year until they got the numbers down to where they wanted. So that's how Da and these other okes tracked down one herd of thirty or so which was picked out of some bad luck. They snuck up in their Jeep, and Da aimed and shot the matriarch right between the eyes like he's supposed to, killed it instantly. Then all the other elephants were confused and standing still, so aggrieved they were at losing her, and Da and his mates went and shot them all down cos if you leave even one alive it's ganna be trouble later on.

Afterwards they were having a pack of smokes back at the Jeep all quiet cos they were in that special zone of having done something they don't like only out of a sense of a force bigger than them, hey. The smokes was that camp of unsaid acknowledging between them that they did something terrible but necessary that okes sumtimes had to do to keep the world turning like so. Once they were finished Da said I'm ganna go make sure they're all dead and got off with his rifle. He walked round where the thirsty yellow earth was drinking in their red blad and their bodies were already giving off the sick, shitty smell of death. There was nothing moving except huge black goggas tearing into the wounds, laying their eggs already. But then there was summin slightly off, Da saw the leg of a large cow shudder a bit. Hidden beneath there was Rocky hiding his face in his Ma's haunches, his ears stuck flat to the side of his head.

Da put his rifle up, aimed at Rocky, and then—I reckon this is why you never know what kinda oke anyone is, hey—he put it away. It was against the rules to keep the babies alive, it made them grow up to be bad elephants. All Da needed to do was leave him there and let the nature take its courses, the lions or the hyenas would have eaten Rocky like a sarmie before dinnertime. I don't know why to this day, but Da brought the Jeep round and got his chommies to help him put Rocky in the back.

After bringing Rocky home Da wanted nothing to do with helping me raise him. It was all up to me to feed Rocky every few hours and play with him. Da taught me how to read and write but I never gone to school—he didn't want to send his son to a school for blacks. So I never had any mates or anyone to talk to except Da, until Rocky came. I was his Ma, boet, and chommie all at once, hey. After I came back to sleep inside the house, this was how our day was. I woke up before sunrise cos Rocky came round and stuck his trunk inside my window, sniffing for me. We went for a walk in the bush staying pretty close to the house like Da warned but getting a bit farther out each day, Rocky being curious to see what was out there. He liked to chase warthogs or impalas that come in our path but when he see a cheetah he hide behind me. Rocky knew exactly what to eat even without his Ma, he went right up to the umbrella acacia and munched on the finger-long thorns like cendy. Back home we played football or tug-o-war with a stick he found. At night I had to tuck him in, putting my hand in the soft snug place behind his ear or he couldn't fall asleep. In the morning it would begin all over again. I can still feel our walks, my hand on the spiky skin of his back and the calm flapping of his ears shaped like Africa, the rustling of the gruss, the sweet smell of acacias weaving through the icy dawn air. That was the best ever, my bru—I can't ever forget. It was like we were one and each knew what the other was feeling. He knew right away what was wrong with me, even sumtimes when I was sick he got all worried for me.

One night—this was about five years after Rocky came—Da drank too much and got all mean. He said, You care about that elephant more than you care about your own Da, izit? I shook my head. You bladdy liar, he kept going. I should've killed him when I was supposed to. This made me mad and I shouted, You have to kill me first before you kill Rocky. Da looked at me like he couldn't believe what he was hearing and said quietly, Come here. I didn't budge and then next thing you know his fists were flying at me left and right, right and left, sort of like Sly Stallone blikseming his punching bag. I stumbled backward out of his reach, which usually stopped him, but this time he kept coming after me shouting, You bladdy liar, I'll kill you and then I'll kill that fucken elephant too.

Summin came over me and I just burst out the door and ran into the pitch-black bush, hey. I ran and ran, not realizing how my skin was being torn to shreds from the acacia thorns. When I finally stopped I saw in the moonlight that blad was soaking through my clothes like I stood outside in a downpour. It was silent all round me. I realized allasudden that Da didn't follow me—and that instead he mighta gone to the kraal to shoot Rocky. I was about to turn and run back, make my feet fly, when I saw these bright glowing eyes in the bushes to my right.

If you're ever unlucky enough to run straight into a pride of lionesses, my bru, just know that the worst thing you can do is run cos then they know for sure you don't have a rifle or anything. So I backed slowly away from them, and they just as slowly came closer to me. There was a noise like the ground being torn up, trees breaking, and I thought, Here they come. But it was coming from behind me. The earth was boomboomming now. And through the trees behind Rocky came bursting out, raising his trunk high over his head and trumpeting as loud as he never done before. That drew the lionesses out into the moonlight and there were three of them—I knew them by reputation. Three sisters with three little cubs each that needed to be fed, and a baby elephant that Rocky still was then would have made a lekker meal. But Rocky—you should've seen him. He charged at them, stopping and making sure I was still behind him, rumbling, then charging again, until they gave up and slinked back into the bush. Rocky just knew I was in danger, and he came to save me, hey, he and I had that kinda bond where we were in each other's skins.

NOT LONG AFTER, DA said Rocky had to join one of the herds in the park. I knew it was the right thing to do, for him to be with his own kind eventually. Da told me where to lead him on our morning walks so he could get to know these elephants. When we saw them drinking and bathing in the watering hole, I said to Rocky, Go on, little oke, go make new chommies. If you get scared then you come right back to me. Rocky wrapped his trunk around my shoulder like he wanted to stay and I peeled him off me, saying, Come on. He was curious too, so he shuffled forward swaying his trunk all shy. When he poked out of the bush all the elephants looked at the matriarch, trying to see what she do to Rocky. She took one look at him, turned round and went back to grazing. Seeing that, the other elephants went right back to doing what they were, ignoring Rocky. He walked a little closer to a calf about his size, trying to say howzit. But that calf's Ma rushed forward and whacked Rocky with her trunk so he slipped and fell in the mud. She rumbled and kept pushing him this way and that until he got his legs beneath him and ran back toward me, shaking. We kept trying for months to get Rocky accepted by a herd but nobody wanted him. If he kept wandering round the bush by himself the other elephants mighta killed him.

Rocky kept growing and needing hundreds of kilos of food every day. Da told me he got his boss to arrange for a transfer to a private reserve nearby—it was a place that didn't cull so he be safe. I slept with Rocky that night in the kraal, putting my arm in the soft place behind his ear as we lay. The next day, I got on the back of the special bakkie for elephant transport. He didn't budge until I said, Come on, Rocky, don't be scared, I'm going with you. We drove for maybe an hour and a half south in the soft, misty rain that glows off the trees like halos. When we got off I read a sign that said *U__ Sanctuary* and then another one saying *Elephant Interaction Tour*. I said to Da, I hope Rocky gets to make lots of chommies here, and he said, There's only one other elephant here. I said, in the whole place there's just one other elephant? It turned out that the sanctuary was separate from the reserve, it was only a closed-off place for animals that got raised by humans and couldn't go back to being wild animals. Cos Rocky was so tame they were ganna put him in an exhibit from morning until late afternoon, seven days a week. Fully knowing this and how much Rocky was ganna hate it, I led him to his new kraal and fed him his favorite dried corn one last time. Rocky my boet, this isn't the end, I whispered to him, I'm ganna come get you as soon as I can. Rocky snorted up the kernels through his trunk and waved his ears at me like he thought I was just going to the toilet and was coming right back.

After that, I couldn't stand being with my Da anymore so I

begged him to let me get a job. I was not quite fifteen when I started working at a coal mine near Richards Bay. For the next fifteen years my life was complete darkness, I got just one day off each month. Buried beneath the rocks I kept thinking of how, in the bush, Rocky and I used to race up to the top of the red ridge like Stallone running up the steps. At first I could remember so real how lekker it was to look down on the world with Rocky by my side, but after a while my lungs forgot whatzit like to breathe free. There comes a point when only the shape of being a human is what's keeping you walking and working and eating instead of dissolving like air, cos you've got nothing inside. The misery becomes comfortable like tattered old pyjamas you prefer to lekker new clothes.

If there hadn't been that accident I would have kept on wearing my misery to hide the empty shell I was already. But my bru, this is what happened. As I was working underground one day, I felt my heart go boomboom and those scars I got from the thorns that night started hurting. I looked down and I swear to God, they were bleeding fresh after all these years. I dropped my tools and came running out, not minding the okes asking where I'm going. The second I came up to the surface I felt the trembling of the earth and the kukuku sound of rocks crumbling like a piece of stale bread. I was the only one out of hundreds of okes who got out alive.

AS SOON AS I could, I went to see Rocky. The scaly look on the director's face showed me something was wrong before he even said anything. Rocky hurt a visitor, he said. He picked up a boy with his trunk and threw him down. Fortunately, the boy only broke his leg.

There must be some kinda misunderstanding—Rocky would never hurt anyone, I said. Let me see him.

Rocky was standing alone in his kraal, chained in place by each of his ankles. He become massive, his head was the size of a sofa and his tusks were like the masts of a sailboat. He become an elephant that could touch the sky, if only he were outside. I went up to him and he rumbled low, moving side to side. It's me Rocky, my little boet, I said to him, slowly getting closer. I told you I'll come get you. Slowly I got near him until I was close enough to lay my hand behind his ear, just where he liked being pet. He sighed and shuddered, he put his trunk around my shoulder. That's when I saw the bladdy crack on his trunk and a nail sticking out of it. What they do to you, I cried. My tears fell into his wound as I dug the nail out with my fingers.

Even when I showed him the nail, the director said he had no choice but to put Rocky down, it was the law against human-hurting animals. I said, Give me just a week and straight away went to Da, who asked round and told me to go see this manager at P___ National Park.

Driving there, I liked how it was full of trees, much greener than where I grew up. Soft gray clouds were draped over the mountains like laundry out to dry. There was plenty of food for Rocky as far as the eye could see. The manager—a red-faced oke who had a habit of licking his lips—agreed that adding one elephant would trouble his park none, it had enough hectares to feed a thousand elephants and one or two more wouldn't change much. He assured me that culling wasn't going to be done and besides, he would be sure not to eliminate Rocky as Da's special china and all. Rocky would probably get to sire his own calves and help diversify the park's gene pool. The only thing was that the translocation fee was expensive, 40,000 Rand—as he said this he had this look on his face like I wouldn't have that kinda moola. I pulled out an envelope, counted out exactly 40,000 Rand in cash, and pushed it across his desk. It was all the money I got from the mining company after fifteen years' work plus the accident, my bru. On the way out I was feeling how Stallone must've felt at the end of fifteen rounds with Creed, beat up but happy like I done everything I could.

Just before the park exit, I stopped to go to the toilet and have a sarmie at the picnic table. By now the clouds had disappeared and the sun was shining through, and it had turned into a lekker mild afternoon, all green and gold. There was just another person there, a ranger, and I offered him half my sarmie cos I was feeling thankful. He took the sarmie and said, Thanks, bru, and we got talking. I asked if he liked working at the park and he said, Ja, it pains me tho that so many animals get poached now, my bru. What do you mean? I asked. I have to be working all the time, bru, like I can't take a single day off. It's been six weeks since I seen my kids, he said. If it's a full moon, we lose one. If I'm off-duty, we lose one. The truth is, bru, it's an inside job. The manager opens the gates to whoever pays him enough.

I went back to the sanctuary and told them what happened. An under-the-table elephant like Rocky, with those huge tusks of his, would be killed off no problem on the next full moon, likely sooner. I had no more money to offer them, could they please keep Rocky alive sumhow? The director shook his head, saying even if it weren't against the law, they be forced to shut the whole place down if Rocky hurt another visitor.

THE LAST TIME I saw Rocky, he was still in his chains. He vacuumed up the corn kernels I held out, then sniffed me all over my face, neck, and hands looking for more. The wound on his trunk had all healed up like his body was determined to keep going and that made me angry too—why do we even bother if it's all going to end the same way no matter what? What the point? I just couldn't lie to him and say, This isn't the end—I'll come get you. He saw me crying and he knew what it was, he just gently wrapped me up in his trunk and pulled me close to him. My bru, that elephant wanted to console me even while knowing he was ganna die.

AFTERWARDS, I WENT TO Durban and got on a fishing boat. I wanted to go far far away from the bush. So I went all over the world for a long time—Indonesia, Australia, Japan, Ecuador. I never known that there be so much blue, it flooded and covered all the dry earth inside me so I forget.

Just once there was a call for me when I was at the sea, on a clear, windy night. A lawyer saying Da drove his Jeep into the bush and was found days later, picked clean to the bone. No rifle or pistol on him. The house was the park's, the lawyer said. He could sell whatever's inside and send me the money. I said, Burn everything—but then I looked up and saw these same stars I seen that first night with Rocky. We were crossing over the equator just then, thousands of miles of black sea allaround, black sky up above. I said, No—bury them. Before I heard him reply, the wind picked up again and the signal died.

On the boat the okes kept to themselves, it was the kinda place where you didn't ask alotta questions. Only the wind and the waves talked to me until I could understand them. It was in Alaska while watching out for the icebergs that I heard a voice say, I want to go home. *Home!* It gave a little shout. I heard it as clear as you can hear my voice right now.

It took me months to come back to KwaZulu-Natal, to the park where I grew up. Eventually the sea ended and the smells changed, all that heat and dust and sky dry and high like it's about to shatter. The closer I got the more my heart swelled up inside, making my bones ache to hold it in. The sun was scorching the earth, and the trees had mostly gone brown in the heat except for the acacias. I saw that they grown stronger from drinking in the blad that they drew. The house with its kraal came into view, and I couldn't help myself—I stopped the car and jumped out. I fell knee first into the red earth and curled into a ball, rolling around and gathering up the dust in my hands.

I knew then why everything was. The voice I heard wasn't mine, it was Rocky's. Some part of him had been inside my body all along, that's why I never jumped off the ship even tho the thought crossed my mind about a thousand times. When you really love someone, a little piece of you goes inside them and a little piece of them goes inside you—it's most often your Ma and Da but it doesn't have to be your family or even human, my bru. They won't ever die as long as you live, understand. And if I had to say one truth about my life bru, it's this. Out of everything and everyone on earth, I loved that elephant the most.

A gentle rumble came from up above just then. I looked to the top of the ridge and saw him holding up the blue sky on his shoulders, waving his ears at me like a butterfly.

As a writer, I've been inspired by Ursula Le Guin's unmatched power of world-building. Her commanding voice turns the strange and imagined into the palpable and real—and in the process, holds up a mirror to our humanity.

Mr. Uncle's Favor

KESHA AJỌSẸ-FISHER

I HAD NOT SEEN the woman standing behind the door when I barged into Mr. Uncle's room shouting about my brother. The door hit her. The woman sucked air through her teeth. I turned to face her.

"Get out. *Omo esu,*" she hissed as she shoved me out of his room. She slammed the door.

I sat on the floor in the corridor, crying with my headless doll cradled in my lap. She came out minutes later. When she saw me, she gasped and clutched the cross on her necklace.

"Child of Lucifer," she said.

Frozen in my spot, I stated, "I am not *omo esu.*"

"But you want blind man to beat your brother or kill *am,* which one?"

I shook my head.

She ran her eyes along my body. "You be that *omo akata* from flat number one—no?"

I snarled at her. "Mommy said you shouldn't call us that."

She rolled her eyes. "*Nah,* Americana you want, *ehn?*"

Stiff-eyed, I shrugged.

"Where your mama? I go tell am *wetin* you say."

I sprang up. "No!"

She scoffed. "Oh. You want make I keep secret?"

I dropped my gaze. "No, mah. Please."

"How many years you get, *seff*?" She tilted my head by my chin.

I stared confidently at her. "Seven."

She chuckled. "You better pray say make God forgive you." Then she walked head down through the hall and out the building.

The next morning, on my way to the latrine, I pressed my ear to the old man's door. When I heard rustling, I knocked. The same woman opened the door.

"*Esu*. You have returned?"

"Please—*ejo*, mah. Can I see Mr. Uncle?"

She shut the door behind her and pointed at me. "If I catch you here again, you go pray say you never enter *dis* Nigeria." She twisted the doorknob after locking it and glared at me. "Leave that man alone. So *gbo*?"

I dropped my head and nodded. "Yes, mah."

She slipped the key inside her purse and veered around me into the hall. I followed behind her. She glanced back at me then quickened her steps. As she raced out of the building the clapping of her sandals echoed off the walls. I stopped at the bench on the stoop. She had crossed the road and stood with an umbrella stretched over her head.

A rickety bus rolled in on the mud-sloshed road, coughing smoke into the sodden air. The conductor shouted, "Obalende. Obalende, *propah*."

The woman climbed in and took a seat. She stared at me blankly through the window until the conductor whistled to the driver to whisk them away.

For ten days after that, I did not hear the scraping sound of Mr. Uncle's wooden cane moving through the corridor. I did not hear his knock at our door. I did not see him sitting on his wobbly stool to wait with me for the school bus. He vanished, as seamlessly as he had entered my life the year before.

I had been sitting on the stoop that day, playing with my doll, Polly, when his voice first floated near: "*Omo akata?*"

He took a seat on his stool and perched both hands atop his wooden cane.

I turned to him and spoke English. "No. My name is Kofo."

"Your mama *nah akata*—from the *ilu oyinbo?*"

"*Ilu oyinbo?*"

"White man country—America?"

I nodded.

He added in more broken English, "*Shay* you *sabi* Yoruba?"

I nodded again.

He chuckled. "You see I am blind, now. Use words."

I smiled. "*Mo gbo* Yoruba. Small-small."

"*Omo odun melo nie?*"

I answered in my shoddy mix of Yoruba and English, "I am *mefa* years old."

"Six?"

"Yes."

"So you say, *omo odun mefa ni mi.*"

I replied, "*Om-o-oh-doon mefa nee mee.*"

"Excellent," he said. "We meeting here. I will teash you Yoruba, and you teash me Heengleesh, *so gbo?*"

I smiled and spoke with enthusiasm to my doll, Polly, "We're gonna learn to speak Yoruba."

"From where inside America you come?"

"Brooklyn."

"Where *dat?*"

"Do you know New York—where the Statue of Liberty lives?"

He shook his head. "*Shay wa ko mi*—you will teash me then?"

"Yes."

"Say, *ma ko yin.*"

"*Ma a ko yeen.*"

"Good, good."

Mommy came out of our flat amid my conversation with the old man.

"Sound like you making friends already, Kofo."

Mr. Uncle stuck out his hand. "You are welcome to Nigeria."

With my hands funneled over my lips, I mouthed to her, "He's blind."

She took his hand and said, "My name is Denise. Nice to meet you."

"I am Diekoolaoluwatimojogun Obaoluwa Oyelowo."

She smiled. "I don't know if I can say all that."

"You look like a grandpa and an uncle," I said.

Mommy said, "How about we call you Mr. Uncle. That okay *witchu*?"

He nodded. "Yes. It is okay."

"Mommy, Mr. Uncle said we are *akata*."

Her eyes broadened and she shook her head with a finger to her lips. She chuckled nervously and said, "Say goodbye, now. We got plenty unpackin' to do."

"Bye, Mr. Uncle."

"*Odabo*, Kofo. Bye, Madam."

In the hall, Mommy said, "*Akata* ain't a nice word. Don't let nobody call you that, okay?"

"Yes, Mommy."

WITHOUT INTERRUPTION, MR. UNCLE and I had begun this routine of give and take, meeting in the mornings and again after supper. He planted Yoruba inside my words and taught me to count in the language too. I shared as much English as I knew. He introduced me to *agbalumo*, a leathery fruit with a milky orange pulp and black seeds that chipped my front tooth the first time I tried it.

Mommy was not happy about my broken tooth. I showed her the *agbalumo*. "Mr. Uncle said to give you this."

She twirled the small bruised fruit in her hand. "This li'l' thang cracked your tooth?"

I nodded then showed her where to bite it, but she sliced it in two.

"I like my teeth."

She scooped out the seeds and dropped the flesh onto her tongue. Her eyes squinted at the taste then widened with pleasure as the juice moved from bitter to sweet.

"Ooh, that is good," she crooned.

I told her it was my favorite thing about Nigeria.

"Second to meetin' Mr. Uncle?"

"Yes, Mommy."

"Just be careful," she had said.

I took Mr. Uncle on a tour around the life I missed in New York—from eating hot dogs at Coney Island to watching *Sesame Street* to the family on *Good Times* to the Saturday evening parties where Mommy and Daddy barbecued ribs and burgers, and all the neighbors came to eat, drink, and dance.

He liked to say, "I can picture it."

Mommy brought him a plate with a hamburger and French fries one evening.

"It is too wet," he said, after she pressed it between his hands. He bit into it. "The meat is too soft."

"Try the French fries then," she said, after steering his hand on the plate.

He nibbled on a handful of the fried potatoes. "*Mmm,* these are chips."

Mommy and I laughed.

He devoured every chip on his plate and left the soggy bun and its filling along with an apology for me to take back to Mommy.

"He a nice man," Mommy had said.

"He is my best friend."

She paused and glared at me.

"And Polly."

"All right. Just be careful," she warned again.

Now, a year later, I had lost both. I wondered if Mr. Uncle was angry with me. Then I thought he was sick. Then I thought the woman had killed him and taken his room. Each morning she came with swollen nylon bags and left empty handed, wearing a different wrapper and blouse. After she got back on the bus to Obalende, I waited for the swept-up mud to settle, then I dashed toward his room and leaned my head against the door and listened for breathing. I heard nothing.

On day ten, I was finished by worry. I ran back to our flat and interrupted my parents' card game with my fist against their table, startling them both.

They paused and glared at me. Mommy said, "What?"

"A woman killed Mr. Uncle."

Daddy spat the paste from his chewed kola nut into a cup. "I am sure you are mistaken, Kofo."

They resumed their game.

"I saw her," I insisted.

Mommy tilted her head at me. "Say what now?"

"Mr. Uncle has not come out of his room, and I saw a woman coming and going, and I think she killed him."

Mommy dropped her cards and turned her chair to face me. "All right, baby. Speak slowly. What happened?"

"A-woman-killed-Mr.-Uncle."

My parents laughed.

Mommy said, "Ain't nobody killed that man."

"It's true, mah. Ten days ago."

She palmed my face, covered it in kisses and said, "Baby, that woman is his caretaker. The sun is settin' on Mr. Uncle's days. He is just pulling away—naturally."

"Naturally?" I asked.

She wrapped her fingers around mine. "Some people wanna be by theyself when they die."

"Why is Mr. Uncle going to die?"

"Baby, he is really old."

"Why should he die by himself?"

"It seem sad to you, but look at it like this: he got to live to be a old man. That's what everybody want—to grow old and die."

I pictured his gray head atop that limp pillow and his empty slippers and his lifeless cane adjacent to his listless body. My mother's words unraveled inside of me. I clenched my breath.

"I'mma need you to breathe, li'l' girl," she said.

I pulled on air, but it would not come.

She fanned me with a magazine and pressed her cup of water to my lips. I gulped it and steadied my breaths.

"I have to help him," I said. "Mommy, please. Daddy?"

My mother turned her eyes over to my father. He winked at me.

She sat back in her chair. "Nigeria got this girl losin' her damn mind."

He chuckled. "Reminds me of someone."

She tilted her head at him. "Who? Ain't me."

"You remember all the stray dogs when you first landed in Lagos. You tried to adopt every single one."

"That's different. They was all in the streets being hit by cars, eatin' outta gutters—now that was sad."

He stared at her and smirked.

She laughed. "You just eat your damn kola seeds and catch this whoopin'."

"These seeds, as you say"—and he spread his eyelids apart—"have never failed me."

"Well, I hope they help you see these then. Read 'em and weep," she sang before laying down her cards.

I stepped closer to my mother and tugged on her sleeve. "Can I go to see him?"

She shrugged.

Daddy said, "That man lost his only brother years ago. It's probably nice to have someone paying him some attention."

I looked over at Daddy. "What happened to his brother?"

He shook his head. "It's nobody's business."

My mother turned to her game. "Up to you. I don't care."

My father nodded and said to me, "Go on then."

I leapt from my seat, kissed his cheek, and bolted out the door. I raced down the hall, stopped in front of Mr. Uncle's room, and double tapped his door.

The same woman opened it. "Blood of Jesus!" she cried.

"Mr.-uh-Uncle-p-p-lease?"

She glared at me. "He is gone."

A bomb went off inside my chest. I shut my eyes. The swirling in my head dropped me. The woman fell to her knees and her lips rained spittle onto my face while she attempted to rouse me.

Mommy's watery eyes appeared before me as slaps to my wrist pulled me from the draw.

"What happened?" I whispered.

Mommy cradled my head to her chest. "You fainted."

"I mean what happened to Mr. Uncle?"

She looked up at the woman. The woman looked down at me, clutching her chest.

"Please, just tell me. Please."

"Him *dey* hospital," the woman said. "I go bring *am* come home today."

"See?" Mommy spoke, with a kiss to my forehead. "He's fine."

Later that night I moved through a haze of sleep as my parents' jumbled voices sifted through the walls from the parlor. "Enough is enough," I heard her say. "I don't care if he *is* blind."

After supper the next day, I asked my mother, "Please can I go and visit him?"

She scratched at her temple. "Baby, I just don't want you to—"

"Please?"

A shrug of her shoulders released me.

I knocked on Mr. Uncle's door and awaited permission to enter.

"*E wole*," he sang.

"Where were you?" I asked as I took a seat on his bed.

He sighed. "Resting. Rainy season gives me catarrh."

"You did not go to die alone?"

"*Ah ahn*, you see me here now."

I wrapped my arms around him. His frame quaked through an unruly cough and he pleaded, "I am fine. I am fine."

I placed three kola nut pods I had taken from Daddy's drawer inside his palm.

He twirled them between his fingers. "*Ki re?*"

"Kola nut. My daddy uses it to feel strong. He said it opens his eyes."

He laughed and patted my knee. "Thank you, dear. Any new thing happening? Any new friends?"

"Mr. Uncle, did you forget?"

"Forget what?"

I stared at his drooping jowls. They hung loosely like the dewlap on the cows at the market. "Did you forget that—*ehm*, you are my only friend."

He scratched his head. "Polly, *nko?*"

"Polly is a doll. On top of that, she died."

"My apologies. *Ki lo pa?*"

"Enitan threw her head inside the gutter and the flood took her away."

"Sad one. *Pele*. Why did he do that?"

I whispered to him, "My brother is *omo esu*."

He grunted. His head grew heavy and slowly tilted forward as if he was falling asleep midresponse.

I broke the silence with a clap. "Mr. Uncle, did you hear what I said?"

"Yes. You said Polly fell inside *guttah*."

My shoulders slackened. I knew then he did not want to help me with my brother.

He cracked the shell of the kola nut with his teeth and bit the rubbery seed and chewed it quietly. "*Shay o fe?*"

I accepted it and scraped the skin of the seed with my front teeth. The bitterness twisted my tongue and I spat it out. "I don't like the taste, sah."

"I don't blame you. So, tell me about your friends."

I scoured my thoughts. "I don't have any," I began. "I think my sister used to be my friend, but ever since she turned twelve, she only talks about Gbenga from across the road."

"Is that right?"

I stood up. "My sister sprays my mum's perfume and walks like *si-si* woman when we go to his house to buy foodstuffs. Gbenga's eyes grow big like pawpaw when he sees her moving her waist like so."

He laughed. "You know I cannot see what you are doing."

I returned to sit next to him. "And then the two of them laugh about nonsense things, but I know Gbenga only likes her because of her skin."

"Her skin?"

"She is fair."

"*Bi oyinbo?*"

"Not white, but her hair is the color of sand and you can see the lines of blood under her skin. Everywhere we go, people point, and children sing *oyinbo pepper* to her, but Mommy told her to say she is not a white person."

"Oh, *bi afin?*"

"No. She is not albino. People are afraid of *afin*. With my sister, people smile at her and they ask to touch her hair. If she says I am her sister, they look at me as if she pointed to shit."

"So you are *du du* and your sister is *fun fun?*"

"Yes."

"You never told me."

I shrugged. "Hmm."

He reached for the mug at his feet and drew sips from it.

"Can I look at you?"

"But you can't see, Mr. Uncle."

"Don't fear, *ehn?* Stand for me."

"Okay."

He turned to me and raised both hands to my face. He ran his fingers across my forehead and pressed them around my temple down to my ears and under my jawline before stopping at my chin. He traced my lips, nose, and eyes. Next, he moved his hands atop my head and followed the two braids hanging from my scalp down to my shoulders, and said, "I can see you are very beautiful."

"Thank you, Mr. Uncle."

He faced forward. "If your sister is not a friend, what of your brother?"

I tensed up. "I knew you remembered what I said."

"Remembered what, Kofo?" His brows furrowed.

I gave up.

"Before we lived in this house, my mom bought us two chickens."

"*Adiye*?"

"Yes. But not to eat. To keep as pets."

"Americans keep *adiye* as pets?"

"Yes. It is what she wanted for her first birthday in America."

I told him about how my mother had carried the chicks around like babies, talking to them and washing them and digging up worms to feed them until they went from chirping yellow dust balls to one feisty cock and a temperamental hen.

His head went back as he guffawed. "I like the way you tell story."

"But someone stole them, *sha*, and probably ate them. Now Mommy wants something no one can steal and eat: a dog."

"*Ah ahn*. People will steal and eat dog too, now. What you are talking?"

"People don't eat dogs here!"

"Oh yes. With onions, hot pepper—*seff*."

"That's disgusting."

He went on about how dog meat was sweet and no different from cows and chickens and goats. I countered with how Mommy would never allow it in our house.

I whispered in his ear, "I hope Mommy forgets. The rain pains her body and beer is her medicine. Then she sleeps and forgets things."

He shivered from my breath along his skin.

I told him that when my mother drinks, she forgets she loves

Daddy and fights with him, and he forgets it is the medicine's fault and they shout at each other until the noise bounces off the walls.

The old man said, "Even blind man can see when somebody carries heavy load."

I raised my hand and touched his face. He flinched. I pulled back.

"What are you doing?" he asked.

"Could you see?"

"Your hand?"

"No, sah. I mean when you were a boy."

"I think so."

"You don't remember?"

"I do not, *ehm*, talk about it."

I threw my head back. "None of my business; I know."

His voice lightened. "Finish telling me about your brother."

I returned my hands to my lap and grunted. "Enitan. Mommy said fourteen is too old to be playing with a seven-year-old."

"Why?"

I rose suddenly, wringing my fingers as I paced the small space of his room.

"Mr. Uncle, Enitan used to like only lizards. Now he says he likes dogs too."

"And so?"

I returned to the day Enitan brought home a lizard the vibrant color of banana leaves. It had black around its eyes like someone had traced them in with char.

I said, "Enitan called the lizard Tutt. 'Like the Egyptian king.' Tutt crawled up and down his arm and sat on his head and Enitan was smiling. When he let me play with Tutt, I laughed at the way the lizard tickled my face, and then it jumped from my shoulder to my head and his—how do you say 'nail' in Yoruba?"

"*Enkono*."

"His *enkono* caught my hair and Enitan pulled Tutt so hard, I thought the lizard's arm fell off."

He gasped.

"Enitan then kissed Tutt on the lips and said sorry to him and he placed him inside a biscuit tin."

Mr. Uncle's head shook in disbelief.

"Don't worry, sah. I saw the holes in the lid before he closed it. Enitan then asked me, 'How long do you think Tutt can live without air?' I begged him to free Tutt. He said, 'What if I shake it, *nko*?'"

Mr. Uncle said, "*Jesu.*"

"I shouted at Enitan, 'Don't do it', then Enitan said, 'Do you want to see a magic trick instead?'"

I paused to compose myself with a breath.

"My brother then twirled the wand up and down and around the tin. He said, '*Abracadabra*,' then blew into his hands. When he opened the tin, my knees were shaking, but the lizard climbed up and looked at us. I was so happy, *sha*. Then Enitan said, 'Here is the real magic, Kofo. Look closely.' Suddenly, the wand became a knife and disappeared the lizard's head."

Mr. Uncle's hand went up to seal in another gasp. "*Fada*, God."

I sat down. His black marble eyes danced back and forth.

"I told Enitan I would tell Mommy, but he snatched off Polly's head and ran outside. I chased him but he threw it inside the gutter. Now I think if we buy a dog, Enitan will kill it too. That is why I asked you to help me—"

He held up his hand. "I had a brother once too."

"No, Mr. Uncle. My parents said I cannot know about your brother."

"They did?"

I nodded. "Yes. It's none of my business."

"Well, if I tell you, can you keep a secret?"

I shook my head vigorously. "No, Mr. Uncle. My mother says no keeping secrets."

"Then let me tell you first and *you* can decide what to do."

I sat up straight, nodded and released my breath. "Tell me."

He began, using the sort of broken English that required my attentive ear.

"After church, me, and my brother, Ganiu, was walking home. A man come shouting on us near road. I thirteen, fourteen, not more than your brother, Enitan, *sha*. Ganiu older than for me. The man ask, 'Which one you is Ganiu?' We do not know, we say. He again, shouting, shouting, hand inside his pocket. He can bring out knife, or stone, *anyting*, so I run. I look to see if Ganiu running, but the man on top him, beating my brother. I going back, push man to leave Ganiu. The man saying Ganiu looking at his wife at the river. Ganiu saying no, never! Then Ganiu pointing at me.'"

Mr. Uncle pressed his palms to his eyelids as if preventing the memory's escape. He also appeared to be crying, but his cheeks were dry.

"Did the man blind you, sah?"

"No."

"Did your brother?"

"No."

"Who blinded you?"

"Myself."

"How?"

He chuckled and said in Yoruba, "Kofo, I am happy to know you, but I am sad it is inside this kind of world. When I went blind as you say, it was as if somebody dropped me inside darkness. But then one day, a forever light took its place."

"Forever light?"

"Yes. You, my dear, are the one who still cannot see, but one day, someone will show you how to open your eyes and it will be dark when you do, but you will then only want the light."

He reverted to his choppy English. "When Ganiu putting trouble on me, I tell the man say, 'No, I not Ganiu.' The man bringing him wife and say to her, 'Tell me who look at you.' She shaking her head."

Mr. Uncle paused. "Your Yoruba is better than my English, let me go back, *so gbo*?"

"All right, sah."

"When the man showed us his wife, Ganiu ran away. The sky

opened to sing, *sha*, and my heart fell from my chest and I said, 'I have never seen this woman in my life, *o*.' I looked at her and I said, 'But now that I have seen you, nothing in this entire world will ever pass your beauty. *Abeg* make God *kuku* remove my eyes.'"

I slapped his knee. "Mr. Uncle, you said that?"

He chuckled. "Oh, yes. And I remember her smiling before—"

"Before the man blinded you?"

"*Ah ahn*, I just told you, I blinded myself."

Until I sniffled, I did not know I had been crying. "I am sorry you lost your eyes and your brother on the same day, Mr. Uncle."

He placed his right arm around my shoulder and drew me close. When we split, he gave me his handkerchief and said, "Go to your mama, Kofo. She will open your eyes. *So gbo?*"

I nodded and answered, "Yes, sah."

When I returned from Mr. Uncle's room, Mommy was standing in the doorway to our flat with hands on her hips, shaking her head. She pushed out the mosquito screen and said, "*Gitchyo* ass in this house."

Mr. Uncle's caretaker was sitting on the couch with a twisted face. *Had she been chewing on kola nut pods too?*

"Madam, I *dey* go," she said when I walked in. She avoided my eyes as she left.

"What do y'all be doin' in his room?" Mommy asked.

"We talk, Mommy."

"About favors?"

"No, mah."

She knelt to meet my eyes and cupped my shoulders. "Baby, has that man ever asked you to keep a secret?"

I searched my mind and nodded. "Yes, mah."

She sprang up. "Jesus."

"What, Mommy?"

She paced the room for a moment then returned to me. She brought her eyes to mine. "Has-he-ever-touched-you-any-where?"

"He wanted to see me."

She shut her eyes and screamed at the ceiling, "Oh my God!"

I thought of the way he held me to his chest and added. "And when I was crying."

She clenched her fists.

"What's wrong, Mommy?"

She wagged her finger. "Don't go back in his room no mo'."

"Why?"

She slapped the dining table. "Because I said so, goddamnit."

Through breakfast, she sat beside me and petted my head and shoulders and smiled at me with watery eyes as if I were dying. She followed me to and from the latrine and snatched my head forward when I turned to look at Mr. Uncle's door. She played back-to-back recordings of *The Cosby Show* to keep me indoors.

After lunch, Mr. Uncle's cane tapped on our door and his voice played with warm liberation, "Good afternoon, Kofo."

My mother opened it. She snatched him by the collar, and his cane fell. She screamed into his face, "Stay the fuck away from my kid." Then she slammed the door and said to Enitan, "You see him 'round here again, you fuck him up."

Enitan smiled.

I went out to the front stoop the following day. Mr. Uncle's stool was not there. After supper, I left two kola nuts wrapped in his handkerchief at his door and tapped on the wood twice. When I returned in the morning, the nuts were gone, and the handkerchief was tied to the handle.

LONG AFTER THE RAINY season ravaged our neighborhood and finally died, whispers still carried on in our building about me and Mr. Uncle. I sat on the bench out front and let my eyes wander about, sopping up glimpses of the ruin left by the floods. Dried mud encrusted the concrete grounds of our courtyard. The road had become a cemetery of fallen trees and planks and tarpaulin roofs that once housed families and their stories. Across the road, where the bus to Obalende stopped ten times a day, flies swarmed a ballooned dog with taut legs.

I stared at the glaring sun and shut my eyes. Inside the dark came that endless glow Mr. Uncle had spoken of. Thinking of him still saddened me, so I swelled my lungs with midday air and felt calmed by its release. When I opened my eyes to a creaking sound in the doorway, Mr. Uncle was standing there.

"How now, my dear?"

"Hello, Mr. Uncle."

Enitan came out and said, "Kofo, go inside the house."

"No," I yelled.

He gritted his teeth and grabbed my arm. "Get back in there, now."

"Leave her," said Mr. Uncle.

My brother released me and went to stand next to him. Enitan's hand went up.

Mr. Uncle said, "Behave yourself, my friend."

Enitan slapped the old man.

I buried my face between my knees. I heard shuffling and then Enitan screamed, *Mom*! When I raised my head, Mr. Uncle's cane swiped my brother's legs and he landed with his head on the concrete floor. Mr. Uncle then turned to me and winked, and smiled, and I could have sworn I saw a blind man see.

I was first introduced to the writings of Ursula K. Le Guin by my high school English teacher, Mrs. Mori, during the early nineties. I was relatively new to America and when I wrote for that class, it was often stories about Nigeria and many of our superstitious beliefs—witches and spirits and juju (voodoo)—used to control the world around us. "What you want to do with storytelling is possible," she told me, "and here is someone who does it well." Mrs. Mori steered me toward Le Guin's work with a copy of The Left Hand of Darkness, *and it changed what I believed was still possible when telling realistic stories with unconventional bounds. To be included in this tribute is a full-circle moment for me in my writing career, and I only wish Mrs. Mori were still here with us to see it.*

Interlude

Ib & Nib
and the Golden Ring

STEVAN ALLRED

In this "Ib & Nib" tale, the two cousins are portrayed as children, although in other tales they are adults. Habben plays based on this and other Ib & Nib tales are popular diversions throughout Karhide.

THE HEARTH WHERE LIVED Ib and Nib was built over an ancient well, and to get water from the well one put on one's shoulders a yoke that held two buckets. Then one went down into the cellar, where all sorts of dusty things were stored, and then through a trapdoor in the floor of the cellar, and down and down and down a stairwell until one came to the bottom of the stairs. There was no door at the bottom of the stairs, only a room, and there was no floor in this room, only water, and the bottom of the stairs was not really the bottom of the stairs because the steps went right down into the water.

Now it so happened that Ib had found a golden ring on the ground while playing outside the Hearth. Ib put the ring on their finger, and it fit perfectly! *What a pretty ring,* Ib thought. They turned to show the ring to Nib, but Nib was busy climbing a tree. The ring had scales carved into it, like a fish, and when Ib turned it on their finger, they saw that the ring was indeed carved in the shape of a fish, a fish that was swallowing its own tail. *How clever,* thought Ib, *a clever ring for a clever child like me. I shall keep it hidden in my pocket, and I shall only take it out when I fetch water, for that is the only time I am completely alone.*

The next time it was Ib's turn to fetch water, they put on the yoke with the two buckets and went down the steps to the cellar, where they stopped and set the yoke down while they took the golden ring from their pocket and put it on their finger. Then they put the yoke back on their shoulders and opened the trapdoor in the cellar and went down and down and down the steps to the well, and on down three more steps as they always did until the cold, cold water was up to their knees. Ib dipped the first bucket into the well, and they set that bucket of water on the first step above the floor that wasn't a floor but only water. They took the ring off their finger to admire it, and they saw that it was especially golden in the lamplight. But then the ring sprang from Ib's hand, and fell into the water, and sank down and down and down into the water until it disappeared from sight.

"Oh no!" cried Ib, "I have lost my ring!" Oh how Ib wept to lose that ring! Their tears fell like rain into the depths of the well.

Then Ib saw something moving deep down in the waters of the well, a dark shape swimming down there, circling, swimming up and up and up to the surface of the water that was the floor of the room at the bottom of the stairs. Closer and closer and closer the dark shape came until Ib could see that it was a fish, and when the fish's head broke the surface of the water, there, on the tip of one fin, the fish had Ib's ring!

"Oh thank you!" said Ib, taking the ring and putting it back on his finger.

The fish bowed its head at Ib, and said, "You are most welcome."

What does one say to a fish in the well? thought Ib. The hearth-mothers were always telling Ib and Nib to mind their manners, so Ib said, "May I ask you a question?"

"Of course," said the fish.

"What is your name?" said Ib.

"Oh," said the fish, "I am older than names. Call me whatever you like."

Strange, thought Ib. *Someone older than names—what does that mean?* "Why have I never seen you before, Fish?" asked Ib.

"Oh," said the fish, "I live in the darkness at the bottom of the well, where the water is sweetest and clearest and coolest. 'Twas the ring that brought me to you. Such a pretty ring—you are lucky to have it."

"Yes," said Ib, "I found it on the ground outside the Hearth, on the bank of the river Arre."

"How interesting," said the fish. "Now, may I ask you a question?"

"Of course," said Ib.

"Alive without breath and as cold as death, clad in mail never clinking, never thirsty, ever drinking—what am I?"

"A riddle!" said Ib. "Let me think a moment." And so Ib thought and thought, and while they thought, the fish, who was as big as Ib, rose upright, halfway out of the water and spread its fins, and then winked at Ib.

"A fish!" laughed Ib. "A fish is alive without breath, and cold as death. A fish has scales like mail, but never clinking, and is never thirsty yet ever drinking!"

"Just so, Ib!" said the fish, "clever fellow. I shall see you anon." And the fish began to sink into the water so as to swim away, but Ib called out, "Wait, Fish! How did you know my name?"

But the fish did not answer. It only raised a fin in farewell, and then swam away.

And so their friendship began, Ib and the fish. Every few days, when it was Ib's turn to fetch water from the well, the fish rose up and up and up to the surface, and they would talk a bit, and always the fish would ask Ib a riddle.

"Glittering points that downward thrust, sparkling spears that never rust," riddled the fish.

Ib was quick with the answer to this one. "An icicle!"

"The more you take, the more you leave behind—what am I?" riddled the fish.

This one took Ib some time. The answer came when they were outside, crossing a patch of snow, and they happened to turn around to look back at the Hearth. The next time Ib went to fetch water they were ready with the answer: "Footsteps!"

"What do people love more than life, fear more than death or mortal strife? I am what the poor have, and the rich require, I am what the miser spends, and the spendthrift saves, and what all people carry to their graves—what am I?" riddled the fish.

This one Ib pondered for days until the answer came: "Nothing!"

"Just so!" said the fish. "So tell me Ib, did someone help you find the answer?"

"Oh no," said Ib. "No one helped me. No one knows about you, Fish."

"And why have you kept me a secret?" said the fish.

"Because the hearth-mothers would not like you," said Ib.

"Wouldn't like me! And why not?" said the fish.

"The hearth-mothers have rules for everything. Be quiet, they are always saying. No jumping off the second balcony—you'll break a leg. No running, no yelling, take that kind of play outside the Hearth. They don't believe in snowghouls, nor kobolds, nor talking fish I'm sure—they say that's all a bunch of nonsense."

"But you," the fish said, "you don't think it's all nonsense?"

"Of course I don't," said Ib. "You're here! I'm not imagining all this, am I?"

"Indeed not," said the fish. "For here we are, a fish talking to a person, and a person talking back. And what about your ring? Have you kept your ring a secret?"

"Oh yes," said Ib. They held their hand out and admired the ring. "I don't want anyone taking this away from me and saying it's not mine."

"Yes," said the fish, "that ring is meant for whomsoever has found it."

Ib felt quite special now, having both a secret ring and a secret friend who was a fish. The next time it was their turn to fetch water, they had dipped the first bucket into the well when the fish swam up and up and up from the depths.

"Good day, Ib," said the fish. "I have a riddle for you, and if you answer it correctly, I will bring you something special."

"Yes?" said Ib. "Something special?"

"First the riddle," said the fish. "What always runs but never walks, often murmurs, never talks, has a bed but never sleeps, has a mouth but never eats?"

Ib thought for a moment. The well had a mouth that never ate, but not a bed. The eldest of the elders murmured but never really talked. Who had a bed but never slept in it? Who ran, but never walked?

"A river!" said Ib. And at this, the fish nodded, it's fishy lips turned up at the corners in a smile.

"Dump that water back into the well," said the fish. "You are such a clever child—let me take your buckets to the deepest part of the well. The water there is sweeter and colder and cleaner than the water up here at the surface."

So Ib dumped the first bucket of water back into the well and gave the buckets to the fish, and the fish did as promised, swimming the buckets all the way to the bottom of the well, and bringing them back up full of the sweetest, coolest, cleanest water Ib had ever tasted.

"Thank you, Fish!" said Ib, and again the fish bowed its head and said, "You are most welcome."

The next day was Nib's turn to fetch water, and when they brought the two buckets back to the kitchen all the cooks said, "What is wrong with this water? The water Ib brought yesterday was so much sweeter, and so much cooler, and so much cleaner than this."

So Nib decided to follow Ib the next time they went to fetch water. He crept along behind Ib, hiding in the shadows, keeping their footfalls soft on the stone steps. Then Nib saw Ib talking to the fish in the well, and they saw the fish take the buckets down deep into the water, and come back up with two buckets from the very bottom of the well.

So Nib crept back up the stairs and told all the hearth-mothers in the kitchen what they had seen.

"Oh, this is bad," the hearth-mothers said. Such sour looks they now had on their faces! "That fish is an evil spirit," the hearth-mothers said, "and no good can come of this." They swore Nib to secrecy, upon pain of no breadapple pudding for the rest of their entire life if they told Ib the hearth-mothers were planning something. They did not like this business of Ib thinking they were friends with a talking fish, no they did not!

The next day, they sent Ib off to help the weavers for the day. Then the hearth-mothers went down to the well, and they called for the fish, and when the fish rose up from the depths of the well, they threw a rope around it, and dragged it out of the water, where they killed it.

When Ib came back from helping the weavers there was a great feast laid out on the table, and in the center of the table was the fish from the well, gutted and cleaned and cooked. Ib burst into tears and ran outside into the cold, where they sat on a bare patch of ground and refused to come back inside the Hearth. *My heart is broken*, thought Ib, *for they have killed my friend the fish.*

Nib went outside and begged Ib to come back inside, but Ib only cried and cried, their tears falling from their face and sinking into the earth. And Nib noticed a strange thing, which was that Ib was sinking into the ground. Their feet were covered to the ankles, and their bottom was sinking into the ground too. Nib went back inside to tell the hearth-mothers that Ib was SINKING INTO THE GROUND, but they would not listen, saying, "Oh Nib, you must be imagining things, for the ground out there is frozen solid this time of year." They were just carving the fish, and they sent Nib back out to see if Ib would come in and have a nice piece of fish from the tail, where the meat is flakey and light.

So Nib went back outside to see if he had been imagining things, and now Ib was sunk into the ground all the way to the waist.

"I feel strange," said Ib, for they felt as if their legs had scales on them, scraping against the earth, "and no, I will never eat any of that fish, for that fish was my friend."

Nib went back inside to tell the hearth-mothers that Ib was SUNK INTO THE GROUND TO THEIR WAIST, but they would not listen, saying, "Oh Nib, you are still imagining things, for the ground out there is still frozen solid this time of year." Now they were carving the middle of the fish, and they sent Nib back out to see if Ib wouldn't come in and have a nice piece of fish from the fish's belly, where the fat is so delicious.

So Nib went back outside, and now Ib was sunk into the ground almost up to their shoulders, with their arms sticking out, and now Ib had what seemed to be a fin growing out of the back of their neck.

"I feel even stranger," said Ib, for now they felt as if their whole body had scales. "And no, I will never eat any of that fish, not even the belly meat where the fat is so delicious."

Nib went back inside to tell the hearth-mothers that Ib was SUNK INTO THE GROUND UP TO THEIR NECK, and now the hearth-mothers did listen, and they ran outside to see the top of Ib's head disappearing into the ground, and only their arms and hands sticking up. The hearth-mothers grabbed Ib's hands, but Ib sank and sank and sank, past their scaly armpits and their scaly elbows and their scaly wrists, and though the hearth-mothers tried to pull Ib out of the ground, they could not. The last thing they saw of Ib was the tips of their scaly fingers sinking into the earth.

Nib was very sad that their cousin had disappeared, but what could they do about it? The following spring, as soon as the world had thawed enough that they could play outside again, Nib left the Hearth to stand under the open sky, and to escape the harsh faces of the hearth-mothers, who seemed to be angry at everything, even spring itself. Then Nib found a golden ring on the ground in the very spot where Ib had sunk into the ground, and they put the ring on their finger.

"Oh, what a pretty ring this is!" said Nib. And then they ran inside, because it was their turn to fetch water from the well.

III. On Time and Darkness

That moment of his life when he saw all things clearly came when he had lived on Earth thirty years, and after it he lived on Earth again thirty years, so that the Seeing befell in the center of his life. And all the ages up until the Seeing were as long as the ages will be after the Seeing, which befell in the Center of Time. And in the Center there is no time past and no time to come. In all time past it is. In all time to come it is. It has not been nor yet will be. It is. It is all.

—The Sayings of Tuhulme the High Priest,
a book of the Yomesh Canon,
from *The Left Hand of Darkness*

Neuron

LIDIA YUKNAVITCH

THE DAY LUCINDA GOT spit out of her universe, she'd been holding a large piece of ginger—its fat thumbs bulging out in all directions—in front of her face at the grocery store. She thought about rhizomes from dendrology and botany in her science class, how they sent out roots and shoots from their nodes. She thought about vegetative reproduction, how the separated pieces can be used to reproduce new plants. Her mother said, *no, not that one, a smaller one*. Her mother said, *smell it*. But as Lucinda brought the pungent rhizome toward her face and inhaled deeply, what she smelled was not the dirt-born root, but the carcass of a maggot-in-fested corpse. She could see the corpse. Standing in the produce aisle, her mother next to her, hovering over and palming beets, Lucinda saw not rows of tubers and rhizomes, but a snowy field, dirtied with mud and blood.

The corpse was a girl's about her age, and Lucinda could make out every detail, including the half-eaten eyeball lolling from its socket, the silver cross on a chain hanging about its blue-gray neck, even the gold stitching of what was once a white uniform—a nurse's aide uniform perhaps, Lucinda could see it clearly now, a training nurse's cap strewn slightly to the side of the rotting head.

Lucinda dropped the ginger on the floor.

The corpse-girl's skin smell wafted up like the smell of dirt and leaves do, and so of course the smell became Chloe, the girl at school—the one she loved more than her own life, the one she was forbidden to ever see again, the one she'd written love letter upon love letter to and from whom she'd received countless in return, hidden behind her headboard, the one who'd caused her mother to turn their house into a prison and Lucinda's life into a dead series of woman-errands chained to her mother, the one whose body left a longing in her that threaded through her entire nervous system.

Chloe.

Standing there in the grocery store, Lucinda felt a shot of high voltage through her body. Closed her eyes. Inhaled the smell of the word *Chloe* as deeply as possible: Her body vibrated.

Somewhere far away: *What have you done?* From her mother. Her mother rescuing the ginger and returning it to the bin. *You can't just throw food on the floor!* Her mother calling and calling her name. Her mother shaking her shoulders. The sounds of her mother receding. Then a falling. External stimuli leaving.

A girl, gone into an otherwhere, some realm where she could not be cut down for existing.

First it seemed she'd blacked out. Meaning all she saw was something like space, and her body lost its bearings enough that she thought she might lose her balance and fall. But then there was a whooshing sound, and the black sort of sucked out and away, and she seemed to be in a kind of lilac-colored light. Not like the light of a light bulb or the sun, but more of a tinted-ness. She reached her hand out in front of her face and looked at it. Her hand crackled with sparks, but there was no pain of any sort. She checked her own body up and down. Everything seemed fine except for the fact that she clearly was not with her mother at the grocery store. No mother, no ginger. Her breathing normal, though her pulse flickered erratically at her neck. And her hair seemed to be carrying some kind of static electricity; the sand-colored strands lifted a little off of her shoulders as if they were trying to fly.

THE LAST TIME HER hair had lifted and her hand had crackled with sparks had been in her high school chemistry class, with Chloe. They'd been assigned the task of making batteries. Some students made lemon batteries. Others made batteries from vinegar. Chloe and Ludmila used tubers—however, their potato batteries had failed. After they'd inserted a copper penny into the potatoes, after they'd driven in the galvanized steel nails, voltage occurred, but when they put several potatoes with pennies and nails in them next to each other, when they connected anodes to cathodes, instead of producing a voltage circuit, they had inadvertently zapped each other's hands with electricity that made a *POP* sound and sparks. Both of them felt it. It may have had something to do with the fact that Chloe wore rings on every finger, or not. Neither of them knew enough about chemistry to be sure. Both of them stared at their hands. In that moment it seemed the electricity in each of their bodies had threaded into the other's.

In biology, they sat so close together Lucinda could feel Chloe's skin breathing. When they learned about neurons her mouth watered, the images of all those connections making her dizzy with the word, the sound, the smell: *Chloe*. The smell of Chloe's skin—something between dirt and leaves.

The day their batteries failed, the electrical jolt sent Chloe to the floor, passed out cold. Before any other thought could enter Lucinda's head, she thought that Chloe was dead. Even after the school nurses came and carried Chloe away on a stretcher.

The longing and pulse of what had been threaded between Lucinda and Chloe had been unthreaded by Lucinda's mother when she found the love letters. She took her daughter to a psychiatrist and asked for brain tests. She believed her daughter to be ill. Being ill was safer than being a daughter too close to another girl. Outside the house, murderers killed queer girls and boys like human threshers. Clearing the fields.

INSIDE THE WEIRD LILAC light, Lucinda felt a buzzing around her body.

Then plain as day, an old crone of a woman came walking up to her through the haze. The crone's hand gnarled itself upon a walking stick. Her teeth looked like barnacles. Her eyes deep-set and black like vortexes. Lucinda stared at the crone.

The crone's voice had a strange echo-effect and jerkiness to it . . . like sticks clicking between words. "You want to know what you are?"

Lucinda considered the question. She put her hand to her neck. Her hair floated around her head.

The crone sighed heavily, the sound like rocks being washed over by an ocean surf. "Wonderful. We've got a moron. I said, WOULD YOU LIKE TO KNOW WHAT YOU ARE, GIRL-THING?" The crone waited, bent over and draped with some kind of cape-type garment, or just blankets, or just folds of something.

Lucinda squinted and tried to make out a landscape or environment. All she saw was something like a purple fog. "I want to know *where* I am," she finally responded. If this was a dream, she felt answering in dream-form might do the trick. You know, the kind of puzzles that appear from strange figures in dreams like tests on a journey.

"Same question, stupid," the crone snapped back. "Molecules moving from a grounded state to an excited state don't ask stupid questions."

Lucinda's head made a little circle atop her neck. This crone was not like any old woman she'd ever met before. If this was not a dream, what was it? Had she passed out? Was she hallucinating? Was she dead?

The crone stepped too close to her, eyed her up and down. The crone had chin hairs. Long ones.

"You're a neuron. Face facts." She slapped Lucinda across the face—not hard, but not not-hard either. The crone turned to walk away.

Lucinda lunged. "Wait! Are you a neuron too? In this place? Are we neurons?" So far, the crone was the only thing Lucinda had going for her.

The crone swung back around, nearly hitting Lucinda with her stick. "Don't be an idiot, girl. I'm a pulsar. Obviously! That's completely different. Things back home must be getting stupider and stupider," she muttered, and walked away.

Lucinda followed. Sort of. The crone kept blinking in and out of focus. Is that what she'd meant by pulsar? And was Lucinda really a neuron? What in the world did that mean? To the best of her memory, from Biology and Psych, neurons were nerve cells. Electrically excitable cells that received, processed, and transmitted information, the primary components of the central nervous system. Lucinda pictured a brain and a spinal cord, the autonomic nervous system and the somatic nervous system, in a kind of chart in her head. Then a question jerked her head up. "Hey! Am I a sensory neuron or a motor neuron? Crone?" The crone was only barely visible. But at Lucinda's question she went high beam.

"Did you just call me a goddamn crone? This ain't some goddamn fairytale, girl!" The crone suddenly looked larger in size, so big her body threatened to envelop Lucinda. Her voice became an echo chamber. "I said I'm a pulsar! I'm a white dwarf that emits electromagnetic radiation, you mental cretin! I keep time better than . . . TIME for chrissakes! WAKE UP!" The crone clenched her barnacle teeth. Then spit all of them out at Lucinda like bullets. In a toothless mumble, the crone yelled, "Get on with it, then! We're not just dead matter sitting around inside some moronic regular meat-sack life! This is it. This is the big time! Though how *you* were chosen is a complete mystery to me . . ."

"Please," Lucinda begged, tugging at her own brain to try to find information that might help in this situation. "Can you just tell me if I'm sensory or motor?" It was all she knew to ask.

The crone shrank back down to normal human size. "Put your hand out."

Lucinda did.

The crone whacked Lucinda's hand with her walking stick so hard it shot Lucinda's arm back behind her. "Got it?! Now leave me alone. I'm busy! I'm emitting pulse better than a goddamn lighthouse. I'm on a roll!" And with that, the crone dissipated.

Lucinda's hand went red like meat. Fear and pain make a body come to. Sensory, then. Touch, sound, light, and other stimuli impacting cells of the sensory organs. Convert stimuli into electrical signals via transduction and send to the spinal cord or brain.

Was this a kind of deranged heaven? Or eerie dream? Or unfortunate brain injury? Or what? The fog seemed to become less fog-like and her environment shifted to a kind of vast field of shivering tendrils that made a web or a map. Was she looking at the universe or the inside of a brain or both? Everyone who mattered to Lucinda, meaning Chloe and no one else, knew that we are all made of everything around us. Matter and energy. Starjunk.

Then Lucinda noticed a tree with the most intricate, beautiful patterns and layers of bark that she had ever seen in her life. Like eucalyptus tree bark only even more complex. She put her hand against the layers of peeling bark—gray and red and green and even blue. She looked up: the tree had hundreds of branches that she could not see the ends of. She looked down: the tree's roots were visible and seemed to go on and on. The tree's skin on her hand felt so comforting and grounding, Lucinda put her cheek, her chest, her leg against the tree. She closed her eyes. She breathed.

"Check your dendrites, dearest," the tree said in a voice exactly like a worded wind-whisper. "Neurons can lack dendrites here, or be absent an axon, and you definitely want both a dendritic tree and an axon . . ."

The sound of the tree's voice made Lucinda look around. She felt compelled to agree.

"Put your arms out in front of you and spread your fingers as wide as you can," the gentle tree murmured.

Lucinda did.

"Feel anything? I just worry for you if you have no dendritic tree . . . no axon . . ."

But Lucinda *did* feel something. It started at the base of her skull, but it also started in her kneecaps and her outstretched fingers and maybe her feet—anyhow, her feet felt tingly and hot and weird. She looked at her hands and fingers and each finger shot out and multiplied, extending and branching multiple times.

"Excellent! There's your dendritic tree, dear!" the tree softly cooed. "And look: an axon hillock. That axon process will travel for a distance, you know. As far as one meter in humans and even more in other species. Especially trees . . . but we can't all be trees."

Lucinda's arms and fingers did feel a little like branches. She felt vaguely vegetal.

"Now go find her," the tree said.

That's all it took, the word *her*. Wherever she was, Lucinda felt lit up with the possibility that Chloe might exist here. "How do I find her?"

"Sensory whispering," the tree said. "The passing of chemical signals directly through your dendrites."

Lucinda's mind tracked back briefly to the failed battery . . . maybe they'd been sensory whispering. "Should I hold still? Or move?"

The tree, Lucinda now saw, was not a tree at all, but a vast network of knobby neurons and dendrites reaching out in all directions.

"Listen carefully, child. This is a very big choice you must make."

Lucinda put her shoulders back and lifted her head.

"If you choose to leave this place, you will re-enter the dimension you came from, your mother will take you to many doctors and even a place where they will try to treat your existence as something to be cured. You will be loveless in life—that is, if you survive the threshers—and will eventually care for small animals.

The animals will be grateful. You will eventually be impregnated by a male of your species and bear an extremely unhappy child."

Lucinda held her breath.

"If you choose to stay, you will never return to the realm you came from, but you will thread together with something . . . is it called a Chloe, dear?"

Lucinda shook her head yes vigorously.

"You will thread through forever with a Chloe, and become a great and unending electrical impulse, passing between all living things on earth and everywhere, plants, animals, humans, the ocean, mountains, rain, dirt, even the music of the universe that hums all matter and energy into being."

In her mind's eye, Lucinda saw a successful battery coming to life. The little potatoes glowing with voltage.

She closed her eyes. Without moving a muscle, she moved through the fog. Soon she could see thousands of strands all around her, webs of filaments like an entire realm made from spider webs. Terror locked her throat for a moment as she worried that it would be too difficult to locate Chloe, but then things all around her became a deeper shade of purple, and in that darkening light a soft, glowing gray pulse in the distance drew her attention. She focused her attention as hard as she could. Soon she was right next to the throbbing soft gray. Her body rang like a tuning fork. It had to be Chloe. Or "a" Chloe or "the" Chloe, as things seemed to be in this place. She risked reaching her hand out and yep, her hand instantly crackled with sparks. Just like in science class.

AN UNTOLD STORY MADE from the bodies of girls—that has nothing to do with their being on the cusp of sexual reproduction—exists under the skin of the world. There is a storymaking moment that has to do with matter and energy, language and imagination, a narrative path that could have emerged were it not for metaphysics, philosophy, power. The agency is about threading. Like those oldest forms of women's work: stitching, mending, weaving, storymaking. That love was stolen from this untold story made from the bodies of girls is another way to think about why they bleed.

LUCINDA RECOGNIZED THE EXCITED molecules of Chloe in her hands. She rethreaded every moment of her body into the energy before her. Their names transmitting across dendrites like electrical whisper: Chloe, of Demeter. Chloe, the blooming, the young green shoot of the world. Lucinda: light. For language, like electrical currents, might yet find different pathways.

The pulse of their first kiss, an energy signature shooting across the night sky—although only some girls can see it.

A PROFOUNDLY CONFUSED MOTHER grates ginger in a kitchen. Sometimes she accidentally shreds her own knuckle on the grater, and a little blood appears. The mother mourns the disappearance of her daughter every time she shreds ginger for a meal, and later at dinner, each daughterless mouthful of violence, something she must swallow.

This story is a direct result of a dinner meeting during which I was seated next to Ursula and we were talking about pee. Yes, pee. I was saying something like 'Ever since I went menopausal I have to pee ten thousand times a night,' and she said something like 'At my age, keeping the pee in is like holding back the sea,' and then she told me a microstory about a time she was at an awards ceremony where she experienced an electrical shock at the podium and it almost made her leak. My story is an homage to a micromoment in time—an electrical flash altering a girl's reality forever, pitching her toward a space of free-floating and fluid desire for the girl she loves. The body of Ursula Le Guin's work has influenced me mightily all of my life, because she was willing to write across realities into an otherwhere where everything is still possible.

Laddie Come Home

CURTIS C. CHEN

LAD WOKE FROM STANDBY in an unknown location (searching, please wait). The Local Administrator Device's GPS coordinates had not been updated in more than three hours (elapsed time 03:10:21). Internal battery meter hovered at 20 percent (not charging). LAD forked a self-diagnostic background job and checked the bodyNet event log for errors and warnings. It was LAD's responsibility to maintain proper functioning of the entire system.

The initial findings were discouraging. LAD's last known-good cloud sync had been at Soekarno-Hatta International Airport (Java Island, Indonesia) after LAD's user, Willam Mundine, had arrived from Sydney and his bodyNet had connected to the first accessible Wi-Fi network (SSID starbucks-CGK-962102, unsecured). There had been no wireless coverage after Mundine's taxicab left the airport (4G/LTE roaming denied, no WiMAX footprint, TDMA handshake failed). Mundine had lost consciousness 00:12:10 after the sync completed, and all his personal electronics, including LAD, had automatically gone to sleep with him, as designed.

Mundine's bodyNet had awoken now only because battery power was low (estimated remaining runtime 00:09:59), and all the bodytechs needed to save state to nonvolatile storage before shutdown. LAD attempted to dump a memory image to Mundine's bioDrive but received device errors from every triglyceride cluster before timing out.

The self-diagnostic job finished and confirmed what LAD had suspected: the battery had run down because LAD's hardware housing, a teardrop-shaped graphene pendant attached to a fiber-optic necklace, was not in contact with Mundine's skin. The necklace drew power from the wearer's body via epidermal interface. LAD was not designed to function without that organic power supply.

"Mr. Mundine," LAD said. "Can you hear me, Mr. Mundine? Please wake up."

It was possible that the diagnostic had returned a false negative due to corrupted data. LAD triggered the voice command prompt fifteen more times before breaking the loop.

In the absence of direct commands from Mundine, LAD depended on stochastic behavior guidelines to assign and perform tasks. The current situation was not something LAD had been programmed to recognize. LAD needed information to select a course of action.

GPS was still unavailable. The antenna built into LAD's necklace could transmit and receive on many different radio frequencies, but the only other bodytechs in range—Mundine's PebbleX wristwatch, MetaboScan belt, and MateMatch ring—supplied no useful data. No other compatible devices responded to outbound pings.

The complete lack of broadband wireless reception suggested that LAD was inside a building. Mundine had installed an offline travel guide before departing Australia, and according to that data source, regular monsoon rains and frequent geological events (current surveys listed 130 active volcanoes in Indonesia) led many in this region to use poured concrete for construction. Those locally composited materials often included dielectric insulators which interfered with radio transmissions. Weatherproofed glass windows would also have metallic coatings that deflected any wavelengths shorter than ultraviolet or longer than infrared. And the absence of satellite beacons like GPS implied a corrugated metal roof that scattered incoming signals. Perhaps without realizing it, the builders of this structure had made it a perfect cage for wireless Internet devices like LAD.

After 3,600 milliseconds of fruitless pinging, LAD reprioritized the voice command UI and began processing input signals from boundary effect pickups in the necklace's outer coating. It was sometimes possible to determine location characteristics from ambient sounds. The audio analysis software indicated human voices intermingled with music, and the stream included a digital watermark, indicating a television broadcast, but without Internet connectivity, LAD couldn't look up the station identifier. However, the offline travel guide included Bahasa language translation software, so LAD was able to understand the words being spoken.

"See Indo-pop singing sensations Java Starship in their international cinema debut!" an announcer's voice said over a bouncy pop-music soundtrack. "When a diplomat's daughter is abducted from a charity concert, and corrupt local authorities do nothing to find her, the boys of Java Starship take matters into their own hands. . ."

New voices overlapped the recorded audio stream. Audio analysis indicated live human speakers in the room, and LAD adjusted audio filters to emphasize the humans over the television. Based on pitch and rhythm, there were four separate voiceprints, speaking a pidgin of Bahasa and English.

"What are you showing us? What is all this?" said an adult female (Javanese accent, approximate age thirty-five–forty years, label as H1: human voice, first distinct in new database). "Where did you get these things?"

"They're from work," said an adult male (Javanese, age forty–forty-five years, label H2). "A little bonus. You know."

"*(Untranslatable)*," said the woman (H1). "You haven't had a job for months. I know what you do, drinking with those gangsters—"

"You don't know!" said the man (H2). "And you don't complain when I pay for our food, our clothes—"

"Hey!" said a female child (thirteen–fifteen years old, label H3). "That looks like graphene superconductor material. Can I see?"

"Which one?" asked the man (H2). "What are you pointing at?"

LAD took a chance and switched on the pendant's external status lights. If the girl recognized graphene by sight, she might also know about other technologies—like the Internet.

"The necklace, there. Look, it's blinking green!" said the girl (H3).

"You like that, Febby?" asked the man (H2). "Okay, here you go."

LAD's motion sensors spiked. Two thousand five hundred milliseconds later, the entire sensor panel lit up as its galvanic skin response (GSR) signal went positive. The girl must have put on the necklace. LAD's battery began charging again.

"Cool," said the girl (H3, assign username Febby).

"How about you, Jaya?" asked the man (H2). "You want something?"

"The wristwatch!" said a male child (fourteen–seventeen years old, label H4, assign username Jaya). With all the voices cataloged, LAD decided this was likely a family: mother, father, daughter, and son.

"It's too big for you, Jaya," said the mother (H1).

"No way!" said the father (H2). LAD heard a clinking noise, metal on metal, likely the PebbleX watch strap being buckled. "Look at that. So fancy!"

"Pa, they have schoolwork to do."

"It's Friday, Nindya! They can have a little fun—"

"Arman!" said the mother (H1, assign username Nindya). "I want to talk to you. Children, go upstairs."

"Yes, Ma," Jaya and Febby replied in unison.

LAD's motion sensors registered bouncing. The adults' voices faded into the background as Febby's feet slapped against a series of homogeneous hard surfaces (solid concrete, likely stairs). LAD was able to catch another 4,580 milliseconds of conversation before Febby moved too far away.

". . . going to get us all killed," Nindya said. "I can't believe you brought him *here*!"

Arman muttered something, then said out loud, "They'll pay, Nindya. I know what I'm doing. . ."

LAD KEPT HOPING FEBBY would go outside the house to play, thus providing an opportunity to scan for nearby wireless networks, but she stayed in her room all day with the window closed. Incoming audio indicated writing (graphite/clay material in lateral contact with cellulose surface), which LAD guessed was the aforementioned schoolwork. There seemed to be an inordinately large amount of it for a thirteen-to-fifteen-year-old child.

The good news was that Febby's high GSR made for efficient charging, and LAD was back to 100 percent battery in less than an hour. With power to spare, LAD accelerated main CPU clock speed to maximum and unlocked the pendant's onboard GPU for digital signal processing. Sound was the only currently available external signal, and LAD had to squeeze as much information out of that limited datastream as possible. The voice command UI package included a passive-sonar module that could be used for rangefinding. LAD loaded that into memory and began building a crude map of the house from echo patterns.

After the family ate a meal—likely dinner, based on the internal clock and local sunset time—LAD heard footsteps heading from the ground floor down a different set of concrete steps, likely into a basement or storm cellar. Febby stayed upstairs in her room. There was no way to adjust the directionality of the necklace microphones, but LAD increased the gain on the incoming audio and utilized all available noise reduction and bandpass filters.

When LAD isolated Willam Mundine's voiceprint (91-percent confidence), system behavior overrides kicked in, and the Bluetooth radio drivers shot up in priority. As implied by earlier data, and now confirmed, Arman was holding Mundine captive in the basement of this house. But Mundine was too far away, and there was too much interference from the building structure, for a Bluetooth signal to reach Mundine's bodyNet. The only thing LAD could do was listen.

If Mundine said any words, they were unintelligible. Mostly, he screamed. Those noises were interspersed with shouting from Arman, also unintelligible, and sounds that the analysis software identified as rigid objects striking bare human skin.

System rules kept demanding that LAD activate Mundine's implanted rescue locator beacon—more commonly known as a kidnap-and-ransom (K&R) stripe—but LAD couldn't control any devices while disconnected from the bodyNet. The fall-through rules recommended requesting user intervention from other nearby humans. After careful consideration, LAD decided to risk making contact.

LAD waited until Febby was alone in the bathroom to speak to her.

"Hello, Febby," LAD said. "Don't be afraid."

Sonar indicated that Febby was sitting on the toilet. LAD's motion sensors measured her neck muscles moving, likely turning her head to look around. "Who's talking?" she asked quietly. "Where are you?"

"I'm hanging around your neck," LAD said. "Look down. I'll flash a light. Three times each in red, green, and blue."

LAD gave her one thousand milliseconds to move her eyes, then activated the pendant's status lights. The three-way OLEDs burned a lot of power, but LAD believed this was an emergency.

"A talking necklace?" Febby said. "Cool."

"Listen, Febby," LAD said, "I need your help."

FEBBY SNUCK OUT OF her room shortly after midnight, when LAD had 95-percent confidence based on breathing patterns that Arman, Nindya, and Jaya were all fast asleep. Febby padded silently down the stairs to the ground floor, then down the steps at the end of the back hallway behind the kitchen. LAD's Bluetooth discovery panel lit up as soon as Febby rounded the corner at the bottom of the steps and entered the basement.

LAD immediately tried to activate Mundine's K&R stripe, but there was no response. LAD queried all available inputs for Mundine's physical condition. Medical monitors reported that Mundine's back and both legs were bruised. The fourth and fifth fingers on his left hand were broken. His left eighth rib was cracked—that was why the K&R stripe wasn't working.

"Who's that man?" Febby whispered. "Why is he in our basement? He looks like he's been hurt."

"This man is Mr. Willam Mundine," LAD said. "He's my friend. I believe your father brought him here, and they've been"—LAD spent 250 milliseconds searching for an appropriate verbal euphemism—"arguing, I'm afraid."

"Ma and Pa argue a lot too," Febby said, "but he never hits her. Your friend must have made Pa really angry."

"I don't know what happened," LAD said, "but I need to speak to Mr. Mundine. Is there anything tied around his mouth?"

"Yeah," Febby said. "You want me to take it off?"

"Yes, please."

Febby knelt down and moved her arms. "Okay, it's untied."

"Thank you, Febby," LAD said. "Now, would you please remove my necklace and give it to Mr. Mundine?"

"Don't you want to be friends anymore?" Febby asked. Voice-stress analysis indicated unhappiness, likely trending toward sorrow.

LAD consulted actuarial tables and determined that greater mobility provided a higher probability of successful user recovery. It would be difficult to once again be separated from the bodyNet, but LAD's current primary objective was Mundine's safe return to his employer.

"Of course I want to be friends, Febby," LAD said. "I just need to talk to Mr. Mundine, and I can't do that unless I'm touching him."

"I can talk to him," Febby said. "Just tell me what to say."

LAD had not considered that option, but it seemed feasible. "Okay, Febby. Please repeat exactly what I say."

Febby listened, nodded, and leaned forward. "Mr. Willam Mundine, this is your wake-up call!"

LAD heard rustling, groaning, and then a sharp intake of breath. "Who—what?" Mundine's voice was a hoarse rattle.

Mundine's eyes struggled open, and LAD received video from his retinal feeds. A young girl sat cross-legged on the bare concrete floor under a single dim fluorescent light panel. She wore a white tank top and orange shorts. Long, straight black hair tumbled over her shoulders and framed a round face with large brown eyes. She spoke, and LAD heard Febby's voice.

"Mr. Willam Mundine, L-A-D says: 'Your K-and-R stripe is inoperable, and there is no broadband wireless coverage at all in this location.'"

"Ah," Mundine coughed. He struggled up to a kneeling position. His wrists and ankles appeared to be tied together. "That's unfortunate. And who are you?"

"I'm Febby."

"Pleasure to meet you, Febby. I suppose you already know who I am."

"Well," Febby said, "the necklace says you're his friend. And he's my friend now. So maybe that makes you and me friends too?"

"I'll go along with that," Mundine said. "So tell me, friend Febby, where am I?"

"In my basement."

Mundine coughed again. "I mean, what city?"

"Oh. We live in Depok," Febby said.

"Did you get that, Laddie?" Mundine said.

LAD had never considered asking Febby for this information. Most of LAD's programming focused on retrieving data from automated systems to fulfill user requests. LAD updated local guidelines to note that humans were also valid data sources, even when the data might be more efficiently provided by tech.

"Febby, please tell Mr. Mundine I have recorded our location data," LAD said, searching for information about Depok in the travel guide.

"He says yes," Febby said. "So his name is Laddie?"

"That's what I call him," Mundine said. "He's very helpful to me."

"Why were you arguing with my Pa?" Febby asked. "Why did he hurt you?"

Mundine inhaled and exhaled. "These are all very good questions, Febby. But whatever disagreements I might have with your father, I hope they won't affect our friendship."

"Okay," Febby said. "What are you doing in Depok? Did you come to visit my Pa?"

"Not precisely," Mundine said. "I work for a company called Bantipor Commercial, and we build many different kinds of electronics. Like computers. Do you know anything about computers, Febby?"

"A little," Febby said. "We're learning about them in school. My brother has one in his room, but he only uses it for shooters. He plays online with his friends."

"Thank heaven for video games," Mundine said. "Febby. Your brother's computer, do you know what kind it is?"

"Okay, I think I got it," Febby said. "Yes! What do you think, Laddie?"

LAD waited for the pendant lights to finish the cycle Febby had encoded. Unlike Mundine, who wanted fast replies, LAD found that if he responded too quickly, Febby would get upset, because she felt LAD hadn't taken enough time to consider what she was saying.

"It's very colorful," LAD said after eight hundred milliseconds.

"It's a secret code," Febby said. "In base three counting. Red is zero, green is one, and blue is two. Can you tell what it says?"

LAD knew exactly what it said, because LAD could see the

actual lines of computer code that Febby was transmitting from Jaya's previous-generation gaming PC into LAD's necklace over a Bluetooth 2.0 link. There was more computing power in Mundine's left big toe—literally, since he kept a copy of his health care records in an NFC node implanted there—but the big metal box on Jaya's desk had a wired Internet connection, which LAD needed to call in a recovery team for Mundine.

"If I interpret the colors as numeric values in base three," LAD said, "and then translate those into letters of the alphabet, I believe the message is *Febby and Laddie are super friends*."

It had taken Febby less than an hour to write this test module. LAD noted that she worked more efficiently than many of the engineers who performed periodic maintenance services on LAD and Mundine's other bodytechs.

"You got it!" Febby clapped her hands. "Okay, the programming link works. Now we need to set up the—what did you call it?"

"A wired-to-wireless network bridge," LAD said, "so I can connect to the Internet."

"Right." Febby started typing again. "You know, I could just look things up for you. Would that be faster?"

LAD had considered asking her to make an emergency call, but LAD couldn't trust that local police would take a child's complaint seriously. LAD also didn't want Febby's father to catch her trying to help Mundine. LAD estimated that Mundine's best chance of a safe rescue lay with his employer, Bantipor Commercial, which would dispatch a professional search team as soon as they knew Mundine's precise location. And only LAD could upload a properly encrypted emergency message to Bantipor's secure servers.

"I have a lot of different things to look up," LAD said to Febby. "I wouldn't want to waste your time."

"It's not a waste," Febby said. "This is fun! I can't wait until Hani gets back next week. She's going to freak out when she sees you!"

"Hani is your friend?" LAD asked. Requesting data from

Febby was an interesting experience. She always returned more than the expected information.

"Yeah," Febby said. "We sit together in computer lab. She showed me how to—"

A clanging noise came from downstairs, followed by loud male and female voices. Febby sighed, got up, and closed the door to the bedroom.

"What was that transport proto-something you said I should look at?" Febby asked.

"Transport protocol," LAD said. "Look for TCP/IP libraries. They may also be labeled 'Transmission Control Protocol' or 'Internet Protocol.'"

"Okay, I found them," Febby said. "Wow, there's a lot of stuff here." She was silent for 1,100 milliseconds, then made a flapping sound with her lips. "Are you sure there's not an easier way to do your Internet searches?"

"I'm afraid not," LAD said. "I actually need to send a message to Mr. Mundine's company in a very specific way."

"You can't just do it through their website?" Febby asked. LAD heard typing and mouse clicks. "Here they are. Bantipor Commercial. There's a contact form right . . . here! I can just send the message for you."

This procedure was not documented anywhere in LAD's behavior or system guidelines, but the logic appeared valid. LAD forked several new processes to calculate the most effective and concise human-readable message to send. "That's a great idea, Febby. Is there an option to direct the message to Bantipor Commercial's security services?"

"Let me check the menu," Febby said. Then, 5,500 milliseconds later: "No, I don't see anything that says 'security'. How about 'support and troubleshooting'?"

"That's not quite right." LAD was at a loss until the new behavior guidelines from last night kicked in. "Can I get your opinion, Febby? I'll tell you what I'm trying to do, and you tell me what you think is the best way to do it."

"Like a test? Sure. I'm good at tests."

"Cool," LAD said. The voice command UI had started prioritizing that word based on recent user interactions. "I need to tell Bantipor Commercial's security services that Mr. Mundine is here in Depok. Normally I would upload the message directly to their servers myself, but I can't do that without an Internet connection."

"Security," Febby said thoughtfully. "Do they monitor this website too? Like for strange activity? I remember last year the BritAma Arena had trouble with hackers, and the police caught them because their software bot was making too many unusual requests to the ticketing site."

LAD couldn't research those details online, but Mundine's bodyNet also had standard protections against denial-of-service attacks. If the same client made too many similar requests within a specified time period, that client was flagged for investigation. "Yes. That is very likely. And the server will automatically record your IP address, which can be geolocated to this neighborhood. This is a very good idea, Febby."

"I'll write a script to send the same message over and over," Febby said, starting to type again. "How long should I let it run?"

"As long as you can," LAD said.

"Okay. I'll make the message . . . *Dear Bantipor security, Mr. Mundine is in Depok. From Laddie.*"

LAD's behavior guidelines could not find an appropriate response to these circumstances, so they degraded gracefully to the default. "Thank you, Febby."

"Here it goes."

Someone pushed open the door and walked into the room. LAD had been so busy evaluating Febby's proposals, the incoming audio analysis had been buffered, and the sound of footsteps coming up the stairs had not been processed.

"What are you doing?" Jaya shouted at Febby. "That's my computer!"

"I'm just borrowing it," Febby said. "I'm almost done."

"Don't touch my stuff, you'll mess it up!"

LAD detected vibrations, as if Febby's body were being shaken. There was more shouting, and Febby fell and hit the floor. Someone else banged on the computer keyboard.

"What is all this garbage?" Jaya said. "You better not have lost my saved games!"

"Don't do that!" Febby said. "No, don't erase it!"

"Don't mess with my stuff!" Jaya hit some more keys, and LAD heard the unmistakable sound of a desktop trash folder being emptied.

Febby's body collided with something, and Jaya screeched. The fighting continued for several minutes until Arman and Nindya came upstairs to separate the children.

AFTER BREAKING UP THE fight in Jaya's room, Arman dragged Febby back to her own bedroom and scolded her for nearly half an hour, then left her alone to cry. It was now nearly noon, local time, according to LAD's internal system clock.

LAD noted that Arman wasn't angry because Febby hadn't asked permission to use the computer; he was angry because he didn't think his daughter needed to know anything about technology. That was what he said when Febby tried to explain what she had been doing. Arman wasn't interested when she told him the LAD necklace was actually a piece of sophisticated bodytech, and he wasn't impressed when Febby showed him the blinking lights she had programmed.

There was a knock on the door, followed by Nindya's voice asking if Febby was hungry.

"No," Febby replied. "I was *doing* something, Ma."

Nindya walked into the room and closed the door. "You don't need to know all that computer stuff."

"Why can't I learn about computers?"

"You *can* learn anything you want, Febby," Nindya said. "But you have to think what people will think of you. Boys don't want a girl who knows computers."

"Boys are stupid," Febby said. "Can I go to the library?"

"Maybe tomorrow," Nindya said. "Pa doesn't want us to go outside. He thinks some men might be watching the house." She sighed. "Don't worry, Febby. . ."

The rest of her sentence lost priority as system behavior overrides kicked in. LAD modulated the necklace antenna to seek for spread-spectrum radio signals, which a recovery team would use for secure communications, and ultrawideband pulses, which they would use to create precise radar images of the building structure.

Nindya left the room while LAD was still scanning. The radio analysis jobs took so many clock cycles, it was nearly 1,200 milliseconds before LAD checked the audio buffer again and heard Febby talking.

"Did you hear that noise?" she asked. "What was that? Laddie, can you hear me?"

"I'm analyzing the sound," LAD said, switching priority back to the audio software and analyzing the sound spike just before Febby's question. The matching algorithms came back in 50 milliseconds: .22-caliber rimfire cartridge, double-action revolver, likely Smith & Wesson. From the basement.

LAD increased the audio job priority for the noise immediately following. The gunshot had attenuated the microphone, so LAD also had to amplify the input and run noise reduction filters on it. The result came back in 470 milliseconds: hard impact, metal projectile against concrete surface. Not flesh and bone.

LAD flipped job priority back to the voice command UI. "That was a gunshot. Febby, I need you to go downstairs, please."

"A gun?" Febby ran to her bedroom door, then stopped. "Who has a gun?"

LAD heard Arman's muffled voice echoing in the basement, but couldn't make out the words. On the ground floor, Jaya and Nindya shouted at each other.

"It's your father," LAD said. "He's in the basement. Please,

Febby, I need you to go downstairs so I can hear better. I need to know if Mr. Mundine is hurt again."

"That was really loud," Febby said, her voice trembling. "I'm scared."

"I'm afraid too, Febby," LAD said. "But Mr. Mundine is in trouble. Please, Febby. I need to help my friend."

Febby sobbed once, then rubbed some kind of cloth against her face. "Okay."

"Thank you, Febby."

"YOU STAY HERE! STAY here!" Nindya shouted.

"I have to go back!" Jaya said. "Pa said to get him—"

"I don't care what he said! You're not going down there while he's shooting a gun!"

Their voices grew louder as Febby approached the kitchen. She stopped at the bottom of the stairs and whispered, "I don't think I can sneak past them. Can you hear better now?"

LAD filtered the incoming audio, passed it to the translation process, then refiltered the sample using a different algorithm and tried again. No good. The translator still couldn't understand what Arman was saying.

"I'm sorry, Febby, we're still not close enough," LAD said. "But your mother and brother are on the other side of the kitchen. Your mother's facing away from you. If you crawl along the floor, the table should hide you from your brother's line of sight."

Febby dropped to the floor and started moving. "I thought you couldn't see."

"I can't. I'm analyzing the sound frequencies of their voices and extrapolating propagation paths using a three-dimensional spectrograph."

"Cool. Is that a software plug-in?"

"It's a dynamically loaded shared library. Let's talk about it later, okay?"

LAD could tell when Febby reached the end of the hall by the echoes of Nindya's and Jaya's voices. Febby sat up and put her ear against the door leading to the basement. The translator software began producing valid output.

"You want to talk now?" Arman shouted. "Are you ready to talk?"

LAD heard rustling noises, and then Mundine's voice. "Sorry, friend, it doesn't work like that."

"You came here to make a deal," Arman said. "I know how it works. You don't bring cash, but there's a bank. Tell me which bank! Tell me your access codes!"

"It doesn't work like that," Mundine repeated.

LAD was just about to ask Febby to open the door—hoping her presence would distract Arman long enough for LAD to do something, anything—when the radio monitoring job started spewing result codes into the system register. Twenty milliseconds passed while LAD examined the data: multiple ultrawideband signals, overlapping and repeating, likely point sources in the front and back of the house, approximately one meter above ground level.

"Febby," LAD said, raising output volume above the shouting from the kitchen and the basement, "Febby, please lie down on the ground now."

"Why?" Febby turned her head away from the basement door. "What's happening?"

LAD turned output volume up to maximum. "Down on the ground! Get down on the ground *now*, Febby, *please!*"

Febby dropped and flattened herself against the floorboards 150 milliseconds before the first projectile hit the wall above her. That was enough time for LAD to analyze the background audio and estimate there were two squads advancing on the house, four men each, walking on thermoplastic outsoles and wearing ballistic nylon body armor, likely carrying assault rifles.

Three hundred and forty milliseconds after the first team broke down the back door, the second team charged the front door, and another spray of tiny missiles tore into the kitchen. Something thumped to the ground, and Jaya cried out. He ran three steps before a burst of rounds caught him in the back. He crashed against the wall and slid to the floor.

Febby was still screaming when the first team reached her.

"I've got a girl here! Young girl, on the floor!" called a male voice (H5).

"Where's the IFF?" asked another male voice (H6). LAD checked to verify that Mundine's identification-friend-or-foe signal was broadcasting from the necklace.

"It's right here," H5 said. "I'm reading the signal right here!"

"Febby," LAD said. "Febby, please listen to me. This is very important."

Febby stopped screaming. LAD took that as an acknowledgement.

"Please roll over, slowly, so these men can see me," LAD said.

Febby rolled onto her back. LAD drove 125 percent power to the OLEDs on either side of the pendant, flashing Bantipor Commercial's distress code in brilliant green lights.

"It's her!" H5 said. "The girl's wearing the admin key."

"Damn," H6 said. "Target's probably dead. Search the house, weapons free—"

"Febby," LAD said, "please repeat *exactly* what I say."

Four thousand five hundred sixty milliseconds later, Febby proclaimed in a loud voice: "Willam Mundine is alive, I repeat, Willam Mundine is alive!"

After 940 milliseconds of silence, H6 asked, "How do you know his name?"

"Willam Mundine is being held in the basement," Febby said, pointing to the door. "His K&R stripe number is bravo-charlie-9-7-1-3-1-0-4-1-5. Challenge code SHADOW MURMUR. Please authenticate!"

"What the hell?" said another man (H7).

"It's gotta be the admin software," H5 said. "She can hear it.

The necklace induces audio by conducting a piezoelectric—"

"Save the science lesson, Branagan," H6 said. "Response code ELBOW SKYHOOK. Comms on alfa-2-6. Transmit."

LAD passed the code to the secure hardware processor, and thirty milliseconds later received a valid authentication token with a passphrase payload. LAD used the token to unlock all system logs from the past twenty-four hours, used the passphrase to encrypt the data, and posted the entire archive on the recovery team's communications channel.

"I've got a sonar map," Branagan said. "One hostile downstairs with the target."

"Ward, you're in front. Anderson, cover. Team Two, right behind them," H6 said. "Branagan and I will stay with the girl."

Febby sat up. "What are you going to do?"

"They're just going to go downstairs and have a talk with the man," H6 said.

"No!" Febby started moving forward, then was jerked backward. "Don't hurt my Pa!"

"Febby, it's okay," LAD said. "They're using nonlethal rounds."

LAD kept talking, but she wasn't listening. Something rustled at H6's side. A metal object—based on conductivity profile, likely a hypodermic syringe—touched Febby's left shoulder, and LAD went to sleep.

LAD WOKE FROM STANDBY in an unknown location (searching, please wait). GPS lock occurred thirty milliseconds later, identifying LAD's current location as Depok (city, West Java province, south-southeast of Jakarta). LAD's internal battery reported 99 percent power (charging), and LAD's network panel automatically connected to Willam Mundine's bodyNet and the public Internet. A network time sync confirmed that 11:04:38 elapsed time had passed since Febby lost consciousness.

"Good morning, Mr. Mundine," LAD said. "How are you feeling?"

Mundine groaned. "I've been better." He opened his eyes and looked around. LAD saw a hospital bed with a translucent white curtain drawn around it.

LAD lowered the priority on the wake-up script. The entire routine had to run to completion unless Mundine overrode it, but LAD could multitask. While giving Mundine the local weather forecast, LAD simultaneously ran a web search for news about a kidnapping in or around Jakarta and also started a VPN tunnel to Bantipor Commercial's private intranet.

LAD found Mundine's K&R insurance claim quickly, but there was nothing in the file about the family of the suspect, Arman (no surname given). LAD's web search returned several brief news items about a disturbance in Depok late last night, but none of the reports mentioned a girl named Febby.

LAD continued searching while a doctor came to talk to Mundine. After the wake-up script finished, LAD started scanning Depok's local school enrollment records for a thirteen-to-fifteen-year-old student named Febby, or Feby, or February, who had a brother named Jaya, or Jay, or Jayan, in the same or a nearby school. But much of the data was not public, and LAD could not obtain research authorization using Bantipor Commercial's trade certificate.

Fifteen minutes later, a Bantipor Commercial representative named Steigleder arrived at the hospital to debrief Mundine. LAD suspended the grey-hat password-cracking program that was running against the Depok city records site and waited until Steigleder finished talking.

"Mr. Mundine, this is your admin speaking," LAD said.

"Excuse me," Mundine said to Steigleder, then turned away slightly. "What's up, Laddie?"

"Apologies for the interruption, but I would like to ask a question," LAD said.

"Absolutely," Mundine said. "Steigleder tells me I've you to thank for surviving my hostage experience. Didn't know you were programmed to be a hero, Laddie."

"Febby helped me, Mr. Mundine."

"The girl?" Mundine scratched his head. "Good Lord. Is she the one who caused that—what did you call it, Steigleder? The web problem?"

"A DoS attack on Bantipor's public website," Steigleder said. "Wait a minute. Are you telling me a thirteen-year-old kid made us scramble an entire tech team?"

"She was only helping me," LAD said.

Mundine chuckled. "Come on, Steigleder. Didn't you tell me this web problem helped security services pinpoint my location? I really should thank Febby in person. She wasn't harmed in the raid, was she? Or the others?"

"She's fine, Mr. Mundine," Steigleder said. "The recovery team used stun darts. The mother and the boy were knocked out. They'll be a little bruised. The father has a fractured right arm from resisting arrest. And Bantipor is going to prosecute him to the full extent of the law."

"As we should," Mundine grumbled, "but the family shouldn't have to suffer for the sins of the father. Couldn't we offer them some sort of aid?"

"Sorry, Mr. Mundine," Steigleder said, his voice's stress patterns indicating indifference. "The Bantipor Foundation won't be up and running locally for another couple of years. Until then, our charity packages will be extremely limited. Marketing could send them some T-shirts. Maybe a tote bag."

"That seems rather insulting," Mundine said. "Surely we can do more for the person who very likely saved my life."

"Look, Mr. Mundine—"

"An internship," LAD said.

"Excuse me," Mundine said to Steigleder. "What was that, Laddie?"

"I've reviewed Bantipor Commercial's company guidelines for student internships," LAD said. "There's no lower age limit specified. An intern only needs to be a full-time student, fluent in

English, and eligible to work for the hours and employment period specified."

"It's a lovely idea, Laddie, but we can't take her away from her family after all that's happened."

"She can work remotely. Bantipor already supports over five thousand international telepresence employees," LAD said. "Indonesia's Manpower Act allows children thirteen years of age or older to work up to three hours per day, with parental consent."

"Won't the mother be suspicious of such an offer from the corporation which is also prosecuting her husband?"

"Bantipor Commercial owns three subsidiary companies on the island of Java." LAD was already drafting an interoffice memorandum.

"All right, fair enough," Mundine said. His voice pattern suggested he was smiling. "And I suppose I already know what kind of work Febby can do for us."

"Yes, Mr. Mundine." LAD blinked the OLEDs on Mundine's necklace: red, green, and blue. "Febby is a computer programmer."

My first formal writing critique circle was a seminar class taught by Pat Murphy and Ursula K. Le Guin. It was amazing. The two of them basically set the tone for the rest of my writing life, and despite knowing that I'll never achieve what they did in terms of body of work, I continue to do my best to pay forward their lessons about the importance of stories in shaping our lives and our futures.

The Way Things Were

JONAH BARRETT

JANIS LEFT HER PHONE with me while she ran up to the counter to order drinks. I hadn't been inside a café in years, and the cleanliness of the place unnerved me—not to mention the Downtown Guides who'd carded us on our way in. They'd looked me over with suspicious eyes (probably because they didn't often see brown folks around here), and I knew I was only here because I was Janis's plus one. A localized branch of the nation's Safety Alliance forces, members of the Portland Safety Alliance always sported orange helmets and riot gear. The City of Portland had tried to put a fun spin on the concept, announcing that Downtown Guides were mostly there to help inform visitors about the fun and "weird" opportunities of downtown Portland with a little "Ask Me!" button pinned to each bulletproof vest. Janis assured me they were friendly, but I had heard otherwise. Now they'd shifted their attention to a homeless man outside. I looked away as they quietly escorted him from the neighborhood and tried to focus on the video Janis wanted me to watch. Though she graduated college years ago, Janis's family still paid for her Premium

Teal Package—a plan that included 15 GB of Google and Facebook services. The video on her phone took over a minute to buffer; after five commercials the video started.

Upload title: Aliens in Texas??
YouTube user: Kealakai Rice (Teal Subscription)
Run-time: 1:20
The video opens in the center of a picketing crowd, part of a demon-stration to protest the detention camps in Canada and Mexico. People cry out as an orb of blue appears in the center of the crowd—it's massive, the size of a small house. Some take pictures with their phones.

Everyone gasps as three figures step out of the orb. They are bipedal, taller than any human, and shine brightly. The figures of blue light tower over the humans like great pillars. It is hard to tell if they're confused; they have no faces. There's a sequence of sounds, but it's jumbled and incomprehensible. It's as if the first figure is trying to speak.

"What's happening?!" someone cries, and the noise stops. A hush sweeps over the crowd, then the figure begins again.

"We would like to extend an invitation," a voice says, but it's drowned out by screams off camera. A truck speeds toward the three figures, but light has no physical form, so the truck just runs through and into the crowd. The audio blows out, and the camera flies to the ground.

The clip ends.

Janis came forward with our coffees. "Pretty wild, right?"

"Holy shit," I said, taking my drink. "That guy ran into all those people."

Janis sighed. "We don't know that yet. For all we know it could be deepfake."

But something told me computers hadn't made the video. "If it *was* real, that was horrific."

She took a sip of her latte, shaking her head. "But those aliens, right?"

"What makes you think they're aliens?"

"It's all over the Internet—haven't you seen?"

"I don't have a package, remember? And those things . . . people got hurt because they arrived. What if they come *here*?" I asked.

Janis laughed. "Nick, I don't think any aliens are coming to Portland. We have enough weirdos here."

Shouting rang out from outside. We turned to see the homeless man running past the window, the Guides following suit. One Guide lifted her gun and shot the man with a stream of electricity. He hit the pavement, shouting every curse word he could think of while the other Guide handcuffed him.

"Oh geez," Janis said. "Like that guy." She chuckled and took a sip of her drink. I looked down at my lap, trying to ignore both what was happening outside and across the table from me.

MY OTHER PARTNER, DAL, worked at the welding shop on Hawthorne with a bunch of white cishet men—which made it a bit awkward for Dal, who was agender and used "they" and "them" pronouns. Inside the shop I found Dal alone amidst a light show of orange sparks. They saw me approach and immediately stopped, shoving their helmet up.

"You shouldn't be watching without eye protection," they said. Dal's welding mask hung over their forehead like a space helmet. If there were aliens in Texas, I figured, Dal could be their astronaut. "How was your trip to Janet-town?"

I made a face. "It's Janis, and she's fine."

"Hey, whoever you play heterosexual house with is fine by me," they chuckled. We smiled at each other for seconds that felt like eons.

"Hey, so did you hear about the uh . . . aliens?" I asked.

Dal's playful attitude dropped. "D'you mean the Texas shit? Saw it this morning. Neighbor's got YouTube so we rigged her phone up to the TV. That was so fucked up."

"So you think the video's real?"

"I have no clue, but I think the truck part is," they said. "If you pause the video there's a white moth on the side of the car. Seems like the people in it were gonna run into that crowd with or without the aliens, Nazi shitheads."

"Oh, yeah. Probably." I didn't want to encourage Dal on one of their Nazi rants.

"But, hey. You still up for pizza tonight?" They winked. We both knew what they meant by "pizza." I smiled at them, thankful the terrors of the world could just melt away with one safe person.

"Sure."

Upload title: BREAKING: Ouliponites in the UN
YouTube user: United Nations (Lavender Subscription)
Run-time: 2:45
Within the newly appointed United Nations headquarters in Dubai, a blue orb appears in the center of the Third Committee. One tall figure of light steps out this time. The General Assembly members gasp and jump from their chairs.

"In the beginning," it says, "there was but one thought: the a priori of consciousness. This would not be the last, for the nature of thoughts is duplicative, and thoughts give rise to ideas, and ideas give rise to form. Soon forms began to differentiate from one another, and the phenomenal surface came into being. On every surface, there are junctions—forks in the paths of realities that lead into the vast multiplicities of the Manifold Aether. Some planes descend into darkness, while others rise into enlightenment; many do both.

"We are the Ouliponites, and we hail from such an intelligible surface. We come in peace. Our kind transcended our phenomenal forms eons ago in the age of posteriori cognitions, and we learned to ride the threads between surfaces. This plane of yours spirals exponentially into darkness, and we have heard the cries of your suffering.

"The Ouliponites offer salvation for the Used onto the next surface over, the surface of our noumenal world. Wickedness had spread throughout your reality. Our own realm knows no such suffering, only sublime existence and eternal life. On the next full moon, we shall descend once more unto this darkening surface, and those willing may transcend

the threads with our own kind. The constraints of this place are but atoms to the Aether."

The clip ends.

Janis giggled when she drank. We were sprawled out on her living room floor with her friends, wine drunk with large bowls of blue dye and gloves.

"I can't believe the aliens are *real!*" Janis said. She leaned back, spilling a glass of merlot on the white carpet. Keisha and Hadley, childhood friends of hers, went rushing for paper towels.

"Oh, don't worry about it!" Janis said. "By the time we're done dyeing our pussy hats, this whole rug will be blue. A little wine will only add more color!"

"Why are we dyeing these, anyway?" I asked. Janis had asked me to come over with my vintage pink pussy hat. We were soaking them in dye while watching the news.

"It's for solidarity," Keisha explained. "So the Oulipo know we're on their side."

"Get it?" Hadley said. "'Cause they're blue. Everyone's doing it. This is gonna be so fun! I haven't been to a protest for years."

"You know what's *not* fun, though? Buying dye for synthetic fibers. So expensive! Had to get a rush-drone to drop this stuff off this morning. No lattes for *me* next week!" Janis joked.

I shook my head. "'On their side' for what? You didn't tell me anything about this."

Janis rolled her eyes. "Sorry, I would've told you sooner, but you're always off with that guy, Dal."

"They're not a guy," I said.

"Anyway," she said, and then put on her deep, mock-serious voice: "It's for *Traverse Day.* When we storm the capital and let the people of Oregon leave if they wish."

I shook my head, unwilling to believe that Janis and her liberal friends would actually break the law. "Guys, the Safety Alliance's guarding the gateway, and all the capitals are already on lockdown."

"That's why it's important that we resist this." Janis leaned over, slapping her gloves onto my cheeks and dyeing my face, giggling.

"It's all over the web!" Keisha said.

"Again." I smiled. "I don't have a package."

"Oh my gosh! Here, lemme look it up for you." Hadley pulled out her iPhone XXIII and browsed the *HuffPost*. Under the headline "Why We Need #TraverseDay Now More Than Ever" was the thumbnail of a video, revealing a group of white men standing on a capital building's steps. An update in bold was below.

"Hold on, that's new," Hadley said.

Upload title: Saints of M Leaders at Capitol Building (Olympia, WA)
YouTube user: LazyEyesInc (Scarlet Subscription)
Run-time: 4:03

Six members of the Saints of Muspelheim stand upon the steps of the Washington State Capitol in Olympia, holding a press conference with a local TV station. Slicked-back undercuts, suave gray peacoats, and white, chiseled features: these men look more like the cover models of an H&M catalog than a hate group. Each man has a white moth around his neck, trapped in resin. One of them speaks into the microphone.

"We, the Saints of Muspelheim, address the people of our nation with concern. Creatures from another world have crossed our borders and have called for mass immigration at an unprecedented scale, while also describing our country as 'wicked.' They have disrespected our nation, accusing us of 'spiraling' into a so-called 'darkness.' But 'darkness' for who, exactly? Why isn't everyone invited to become enlightened? These so-called Ouliponites, illegal aliens in the most literal sense, have self-identified as enemies of the State and of Western culture. Their political agenda is not for us; it is for themselves and their affiliates, the 'suffering.' These free helicopter rides to another world are meant to distract us from the threats that may lie on the other side of their portal.

"These creatures have proved themselves more than technologically advanced, and a human extinction event looms before us. If we choose

to stay behind as Earthlings, are we not doomed for decimation at their hands? To abandon your fellow humans is cowardice. The Saints of Muspelheim, the 'wicked deplorables,' support the President's ban on gateway immigration, to and from this reality, and any realities we may encounter in the future. We must make a stand. The Saints of Muspelheim will not give in. Come Traverse Day, the aliens will be met with confrontation against this radical form of mind-policing."

The room was quiet after that. It was difficult to process the jargon, but I remembered what Dal had told me about these men. The Saints of Muspelheim were not idealists. They were Nazis.

"It'll be fine," Janis said. She no longer slurred, as if the Nazis had sobered her up. "Remember what we vowed all those years ago? We're here to resist. Democracy dies in darkness."

Keisha chuckled. "It's already pretty dead. I haven't gone a day without some Downtown Guide IDing me while I was minding my own business."

"Oh my gosh," Hadley said, "I keep telling you not to worry. Those guys are just there to help. They're freakin' called the Portland Safety Alliance!"

"Easy for you to say, you're white. Personally, I don't feel safe," Keisha said. She pointed to the phone. "And I don't know if I want to fight one of those Saint guys."

"They're called Nazis," I added.

"They're actually just idiots." Janis downed the rest of her wine. "And we don't have to fight them. Violence doesn't solve anything. We'll challenge them and let them realize how stupid they sound. The Oulipo are a beacon of hope. Do you guys remember when 'hope' was our slogan?"

Hadley snorted a laugh. "I'm sorry, but how are these aliens a beacon of hope? They're literally offering us a way to run away."

"This isn't about us," Janis said. "It's about the people who are suffering, who want to leave, who have no other option." She looked over at Keisha. "Who feel unsafe from our Downtown Guides."

"Thanks, I guess," Keisha said.

I spoke up. "But, babe, it's . . . dangerous."

Janis scoffed. "So? That anarchist you're fucking would go."

"That is just so cool, by the way," Hadley interjected. "I *love* poly people." She nodded in a sign of approval that made my skin crawl.

"What do *you* want to do, Nick?" Janis asked. They all stared at me, blue dye on their gloved hands. I looked around the room. Being the center of attention was not my forte.

"I don't know. I hate Nazis, but I don't know what to do about them. Maybe we shouldn't go. I'm not like Dal—and Janis, I'm sorry you hate them. I just don't want anyone to get hurt. Please."

Janis shook her head. "That's sweet Nick, but I can't sit back. And I don't *hate* Dal, I just think he's one of those dogmatic punk-communist assholes. It's not my fault your boyfriend thinks I'm too privileged or whatever."

I tried not to show my discomfort. "I told you babe, Dal uses they/them pronouns, and they just come from a different world than you."

Hadley giggled. "Is Dal one of the aliens?"

"Hadley, can you not?" Janis snapped.

Keisha pulled Hadley away, whispering, "Stay out of this."

My girlfriend sighed, losing steam. "And you're right. Me misgendering Dal is problematic, and I'm sorry. I just . . . it feels as if you like Dal more than me sometimes." She looked around the room, at each of us, at the blue stains and one red stain on the ground. "This world is so fucked up. I think I'll go to bed." Janis dragged her feet on her way to the bedroom. She turned back. "Nick, will you come to bed with me?"

I winced. "Maybe I should go home."

DAL AND I LAY naked in bed, listening to the news on their FM transistor, staring at the water-stained ceiling of their studio apartment. I hid my face in the crook of their neck, breathed in their scent. No shooting. No violence. No burning world. Just Dal.

They drew back. "You're not going to this Traverse thing, right?"

"Janis is set on going, on 'resisting hate,'" I said.

"Huh, didn't think she had it in her." They turned and looked at me. "Don't go, though. Or at least, I'm asking you not to. You do know there'll be a shit-ton of Nazis there, don't you?"

"I . . . yeah, I do."

"These people get violent fast, Nick. We've been following them for a few months, and—" Dal stopped themself.

I blinked. "Who's *we*?"

"Fuck," Dal muttered. "Just . . . some people I've been working with."

"The welders?"

"God no." They laughed. "They're all idiots."

Dal's laughter died down. Some strange wall came down between us right there on that mattress. Dal and I shared everything with one another, or at least I thought we did. "C'mon," they said. "It can't be *that* surprising."

I cleared my throat, not sure what to ask: If Dal was in danger, if they were involved with any violent groups, or what exactly Dal was planning to do at Traverse Day.

"Dal, do you . . . hunt Nazis?" I asked.

They coughed. "I mean, *hunt*'s a strong word. We just . . . track them down. Dox them. Infiltrate their ranks and turn them against each other. It's important that they don't get a platform."

"Well, you obviously fucking failed at *that!*" I said. "What are you even gonna do tomorrow at the gateway?"

They sighed, looked over at me, and shot some queer arrow through my heart. "There will be so many people there. People who are looking for a way out of this shitty world. And those motherfuckers, those Nazis, fully intend to stop them so they can . . . what? Put everybody *left* in those camps in Canada? We're not letting them show any strength. If people wanna get through, then they're fuckin' gonna get through. Fascists don't get to decide what's right and what's wrong."

"And you do?" I asked.

Dal scoffed. "Listen to yourself. Are you really gonna be on the side of *pure fucking evil?*"

"Dal, you're running around with a group that goes around *punching people.*"

Dal got up and started to wrangle on a pair of jeans. They sighed. "Nick, I love you, but that was some naïve shit right there."

I swallowed down a bubbling argument. "I don't want you to get hurt. You know how I feel about violence."

Dal slid their pants over their ass and zipped them up. "I won't get hurt, and I don't want you to get hurt either."

"Why do *you* have to fight the stupid Nazis? Can't you let others take care of that?"

"Others aren't doing jack shit, and it's up to us to work together. Don't you think everyone should help as much as we can?"

Little tears of frustration formed in my eyes. "What can *I* do?" I yelled. "I'm just a stupid kid. I miss not being stressed out all the time about rising oceans and Internet Packages and the fucking Safety Alliance! I miss the way things were! I miss not knowing you *hunt* people!"

I started crying, for real, right there and then. Dal and I didn't do this sort of shit. But they wrapped their arms around me, and I didn't push away. I just cried into their chest, mourning the death of the world I once knew.

I calmed down a little after a few minutes, and Dal took a deep breath.

"Listen, don't tell the other punks this—I'll lose my street cred—but I actually don't *like* hurting people," they said.

I looked up, and there they were, staring into me.

"You have to understand that it's necessary, though. We can't let them get away with their shit. When the system wants you dead, the only option is to fight back."

I DID NOT KNOW Salem's capitol could harbor this many people, and it took me awhile to realize they had come from all over

Oregon. Keisha and Hadley never showed up, so it was just Janis and me. Over half the crowd sported blue pussy hats, blue particles swarming about within the whole, contrasted by the orange helmets of the Safety Alliance. A line of armed troops had formed around the orb, warning people to stay back. The orb itself towered over the people like a great gray beast, threatening to swallow up the capitol if it expanded any further, but the people flocked to it like it was their friend. I hadn't seen any Nazis yet.

People squished and fumbled over one another everywhere, some carrying signs and wearing blue hats, others carrying children and stuffed suitcases, and some apparently just there to watch what would happen. Janis and I held hands and tried to make our way into the crowd.

We walked past a group of people with crosses, who shouted and spat at us and said we were willingly walking toward the realm of false gods, and that Jesus was the only way to Heaven. We kept pushing through, Janis's hand painfully squeezing mine. Thousands upon thousands swarmed the capitol, looking up into this swirling, colorless, limitless sphere of light.

And then it turned blue.

The people screamed in delight, ecstasy, terror, joy, hatred. Two Ouliponites stepped out from the gateway, Safety Alliance troops scrambling to get out of their way. We could see them clearly, even as far back as we stood; the aliens loomed over the crowd like awesome redwoods. The Ouliponites looked around, as if assessing how many people—the "Used" as they called them—had actually showed up. One waved its arm, and the orange troops were gently moved to the side, screaming in protest. The great beings turned to one another and nodded. They raised their hands to the sky. Our ears almost blew out as the masses screamed. And to everyone's joy, to everyone's horror, they spoke:

"The full moon has arrived. As promised, the Ouliponites invite the Used of this realm to escape. Darkness and authority rule this surface. As one wicked thought breeds another, thoughts gather to attract demons of all varieties. We invite the Used to ascend to the next surface over. We

provide refuge from the grave, the monstrous, and the ravenous. There is room for all who wish to ascend."

The people screamed praise and damnation and everything in between. I saw people sobbing all around. After all this time, after all their suffering, someone had heard them and was offering help.

I saw a small dark object fly through the sky.

Screams. As the explosion hit, I felt the pressure hit me in the chest, pushing Janis and me back even as I heard agonized, painful cries. Shrapnel and body parts flew away from the gateway's base, but the beings stood untouched. In the heart of the crowd, dozens of people had just been wiped out. People screeched inhuman cries as they fled for their lives, half of them heading away, the other for the gateway.

The Ouliponites ushered in those who ran toward it.

"Come, children of darkness. Come into the light. Your physical forms, no matter how wretched, will be transcended and forgotten."

I could see people running in, disappearing forever behind that utopian wall of blue, including some orange-helmeted Alliance troops. Janis and I held each other's hands tightly as we tried not to get trampled.

"Come on!" Janis yelled. "We have to help those people!" Others were dragging the wounded and dead into the orb with them, heeding the alien's words about "physical forms."

I stopped in my tracks, pulling her to a halt and shook my head. "There are others that can fix this! They'll make the fascists go away!"

"We're here, aren't we? We can help too," she told me.

"I thought you just wanted to make a statement!" I yelled. "Dal was right. It was the Nazis. They said they'd stop us from leaving and we didn't listen!"

A gigantic truck with a white moth emblazoned on the side ran through the crowd, crushing screaming people underneath it. A few Safety Alliance troops cheered. Others trampled one another in a mad dash to flee.

Janis pulled us out of the way just as the truck sped past. A number of white men with white moths printed on their shirts, some I recognized from the welding shop, jeered at us from the back as it sped to the gateway. Two more Nazi trucks followed and circled the gateway.

The first truck sat idly, as the people it had bulldozed over crawled away or were helped by others. A Nazi in a gray peacoat climbed onto the truck's roof and shouted into a megaphone.

"Do not listen to these aliens' false Zionism! They are enemies of the State and their promises of multicultural utopia will only lead to our destruction! Any attempts to approach the portal will be met with force!"

The Nazi turned to the Ouliponites, shouting up at them. "And *you!* Blue cuck fuckers, you are an enemy of the United States and the white race! We will take back this country, and we will find ways to disassemble your pretentious bodies atom by fucking atom!"

The Ouliponites slowly shook their heads. *"We can do no harm, and harm may not be done to us. Your dark efforts are fruitless compared to the likes of noumena."*

The Nazi spat in their direction. "We'll see about that, faggot aliens!" He climbed back into the truck as it sped off to join the others in their testosterone-filled patrol of the orb.

I pulled Janis's sleeve. "I made a promise that I wouldn't get hurt today."

She shot me a glare. "Then go home, I'm staying."

A car honked behind us, and people moved out of the way as it drove forward. I recognized that car. It stopped next to us, packed full of people in black hoodies with bandanas hiding their faces. The driver rolled down the window and pulled off their hood.

"You okay?" Dal asked. My heart sank and swelled at the same time.

They looked over to my girlfriend and nodded. "Janis."

"Dal," Janis said.

"The Nazis are here!" I cried.

"We know," Dal said. "We didn't know about the missile, but

we came prepared for the trucks." More honking, and a dozen more cars filled with punk fighters wove carefully through the crowd.

"We gotta go fight the white supremacists. Tell whoever's still here to help carry injured people into the gateway if they want to go. Physical injuries disappear on the other side, right? Some lives could be saved," Dal said, and then they drove off with the others toward the Nazis. Janis yelled for help, and a dozen or so fellow blue hats ran toward the injured.

"Do you still want to go home?" she asked. I paused, looking back at the partner I loved heading toward danger, and the partner I had been so apathetic toward about to do the same.

"No."

One of the punk cars swerved into the path of a truck. Two more cars followed, forming a blockade. Nazis started to pour out of the truck.

Janis and I found a trampled woman, barely conscious, amongst the still bodies. She moaned as we shook her awake.

"Help me get her up," Janis said.

I looked around. Small white specks danced in the air—actual moths, as if this were some cruel joke. I watched as one fluttered to the ground over trampled limbs and crushed skulls. It began feeding among blue hats and orange helmets soaked in red. Red! So many hues and shades of red upon red upon red. The white moth was eating the red.

"*Help* me, Nick!" Janis yelled.

Shit.

More punk cars formed a barrier between the wounded and trucks, and I could see people fighting hand-to-hand in the distance. Gunfire rang throughout the campus. Other punk volunteers helped the blue hats escort the wounded and Used who wished to go through the gateway, while more punks kept the Nazis and Alliance troops at bay, and the Ouliponites watched over everything from above. I helped Janis get the poor woman up, supporting her shoulders, and began walking her to the gateway.

We made it behind the line of cars and quickly rushed the injured woman toward the light.

The gateway hurt to look at. Behind the walls of the orb I could see masses of energy swimming around, off into the next plane. The assortment of cyan shades and swirling lights seemed like that of the northern lights, and I found myself tearing up.

Janis held out the injured woman's hand out to the light. The woman cried out in pain from the movement, and Janis soothed her as we slowly pushed her into the gateway and she dissolved into energy—becoming, presumably, one with another universe.

"You are true light," a voice said.

We looked up to see one of the Ouliponites watching over us, translucent blue. I felt like a child once more, looking up into the towering wonder of the celestial world. I saw no chaos within its astral form. Only an aura of ethereal compassion as stars and nebula drifted about within. I dropped to my knees.

"You stupid fucking cucks!" someone called out.

A Nazi, the one in the gray peacoat, ran at us with a gun in his hand. Before either of us could make a move, the sound of gunfire coincided with an explosion of red from Janis's stomach. She yelled out.

"No! Fuck, Janis! No!" I screamed. We dropped to the ground, and I tried pressing down on the bullet wound. Tears flowed down Janis's face. She clutched my arm so tight it broke the skin.

"Fuck," she said through gritted teeth.

A figure ran toward us. Dal.

Dal charged the Nazi and threw him to the ground, the gun flying off into the gateway. The Nazi looked up in surprise, just in time for Dal to punch him in the mouth. Teeth flew into the air.

The Nazi cried out in pain, his mouth and nose dripping with blood.

"Please don't hurt me!" he begged.

"Too fucking late!" Dal screamed in his face.

They jumped off the Nazi and kicked him in the chin. The

Nazi kept crying as Dal dragged him by the peacoat toward the gateway. The Saints of Muspelheim leader squirmed and pleaded, trying to wriggle out of his coat.

"No! No, stop! I can't go there! The aliens are going to kill Western culture! We are the majority minority!" he screamed.

Dal swung the Nazi inches from the portal, placing their foot on his side.

"The *actual* minorities want you to fuck off," they said.

Dal pushed forward with their foot and sent the writhing fascist through the gateway, where he dissolved into something inhuman like the rest.

"Darkness cannot survive the forces of Intelligence. His being will change into something better, something brighter," the figure of light said above.

Dal ran up to Janis and me. They helped press down on Janis's wound, and she winced in agony as Dal checked her pulse.

"Her pulse is fading," they said.

I cried, nose full of snot and tears dripping down onto Janis herself.

"Please don't go. Please, please, *please* don't go. I'm really, *really* sorry, Janis. For everything."

Janis smiled and touched my wet cheek. "It's too late," she said, faintly. "But that's okay."

"Fuck!" I held onto her hand and kissed it.

Dal nudged me. "I need to get her up," they said. I wasn't much help as Dal carried her. I just kept crying.

"Didn't think I'd . . . actually be going," she muttered. Janis was getting weaker by the second. I sobbed, holding her hand.

She smiled at me. "I loved you, y'know . . . a lot." She turned to Dal. "Do it."

Dal sent her through the gateway, and she disappeared forever, off to become a peaceful being of divine intelligence.

"She will live on as pure light," the Ouliponite said.

Through my tears I saw the Nazis and Safety Alliance troops

driving away in their trucks, the punks and blue hats cheering and helping the Used enter the next realm, and the Ouliponites looking on. Moths swirled around in the blue light. I breathed in.

"It's not too late. You could leave this world for something better." Dal smiled.

I took their hand and kissed it.

"I think I'd like to fix this one."

When I first started writing this story in 2017, that video of Richard Spencer getting punched was circling the Internet. I got into a number of discussions with the neoliberal folks in my life on whether or not it's ethical to punch Nazis. At the same time I read The Word for World is Forest, *which illustrates violence against oppressors but never glorifies it. I tried writing that into my story, but I must admit writing the punching scene at the end was a little cathartic. Maybe I can't truly be neutral and unbiased in this situation. I think Ursula still has a lot to teach me.*

Valuable

MO DAVIAU

WHEN I WAS A kid, maybe nine or ten, a woman named Jennifer Thurman would squat in the yard beside my family's house in Seattle and drink from our garden hose. She and my mother were the same age, but her hair had already turned gray, and was held in a greasy ponytail that always looked like it needed to be redone. Jennifer used to come around in the afternoons, before my parents came home from work, when I was outside with my babysitter. I once offered this woman the string cheese my babysitter gave me as a snack, and she took it.

I asked my mother if the woman who drank from our hose was homeless, and so one afternoon when she was home early from work, my mother asked Jennifer if she needed anything. When Jennifer began to twitch and pull at her hair, my mother told me to go inside the house.

My parents were physics professors at U-Dub, the developers of the first system of time dilation—rudimentary time travel via the Einstein-Rosen Bridge. My parents explained it as a series of unseen pulleys and weights that tugged your body across space-time into the past, controlled with a wristlet app called GloWorm,

which my parents named after me, Glory, and the term *wormhole*.
I never knew if Jennifer Thurman had chosen the Time Traveling
Family's house on purpose, but that day, when my mom asked
her if she needed anything, Jennifer said, "Go back in time and
kill my father."

JENNIFER RECOUNTED THE STORY of her childhood undoing
this way: she was sitting in the backseat of her father's Lincoln
Town Car as it fishtailed along Highway 26 toward Portland. She
was nine. She knew that her father was the one who had murdered
her mother, though he had told her that a buddy of his had accidentally done it when she tried to step in and stop a fight. He told her
that her mother was a stupid bitch and she was better off without
her. Jennifer tried not to cry when he told her not to be scared. She
tried to put it all together in her mind when he told her where she
was going, and what to do when the men came in her room, how it
didn't matter if she liked it or not, to just say she did.

WHY MY MOTHER TOOK me along on a high-risk time travel
reconnaissance mission, I did not understand, but I came with her
to July 29, 1987. Hoping to look like good prospects for robbery,
we borrowed, or stole—this was easy as travelers, because we had
no identification, and what were the cops going to do to people
who could escape custody by just disappearing?—a brand-new
Mercedes sedan. Gleaming gold, it seemed unlikely that this
brand-new vehicle could actually break down, but my mother
would just let Jennifer's dad think she was another idiot woman
who'd forgotten to fill her gas tank.

My parents are remembered not only as scientific pioneers but
as feminist heroes. The number one use of the wormhole, before
the government commandeered it for military combat and intelligence—before my father cut a clean, inch-long incision into my
upper arm and installed one of three magnetic wormhole tethers

that functioned independent of the now-monitored GloWorm control system—was to delete past sexual assaults from the lives of women. My mother taught them to go back and edit that part out, so that everything after that would be different.

Randall Wayne Thurman slowed the Town Car as he eyeballed my mother and her little girl and the gold Mercedes with the hood up along an isolated stretch of highway. Maybe he thought to himself that he could at least make off with that idiot woman's purse, if not with the child.

My mother, scientific genius, had brought me along as *bait*.

Mom stood arms akimbo as Randall Thurman pulled over and swaggered towards her, leaving the drivers' side door of his Town Car wide open. Jennifer's father was a thick man with a red face, plucking a cigarette from his lips and tossing it into the road.

"Excuse me, ma'am, can I help—"

The gun lay atop all the other items in her purse. Out it came, silver and shiny. The bullet hit him right between the eyes, and he fell backwards onto the pavement.

"Get in the car!" my mother yelled at me, pushing me towards the Mercedes. Her plan was to pull nine-year-old Jennifer out of the car and drive her to safety. As I opened the door to the backseat of that Mercedes, I turned and saw that there was one detail of the story Jennifer had left out.

A woman had been riding in the passenger seat of the Town Car. This woman burst out, screaming and coming at my mother with a raised fist. She wore her reddish hair in a curly ponytail, and her pale yellow T-shirt, which exposed her belly, said *Good Samaritan Community Church*.

"What the fuck did you just do? Who the fuck are you?"

My mother fingered the gun. Should she kill this woman too, whom she didn't know? Instead, she went for the release button on her watch. She could reverse the charge and have us suctioned back to the year 2023.

"You're taking a young girl to be sold into sexual slavery?" my mother yelled. "What the hell is wrong with you?"

The woman stopped to consider this. For about three seconds. Then she wound her fist back. Mom panicked and hit the button. We were in the wormhole tunnel before that woman's fist could connect to my mother's face.

IT WOULD BE YEARS until I figured out the flaw in my mother's plan, which was that the iteration of my mother who made the trip to avert Jennifer Thurman's cruel fate didn't know what the more experienced version of her did: that some women aid and abet the evil of men. Some for their own safety. Some to satisfy their own cravings for power. My mother did not know this until her bungled attempt at saving Jennifer.

Patricia Stoddard, 26, of Prineville, was arrested at the scene for the murder of Randall Wayne Thurman, 31, also of Prineville.

Over the years, my mother and I would debate if it was right for Patricia Stoddard to serve time in prison for a murder she did not commit. My mother argued it was, because she was aiding a man in kidnapping and selling a child into prostitution. I argued that we didn't know for sure that she was his accomplice. She could have been a victim, too. Bad men have a way of changing good women. I told her we should go back and fix it, but she refused, and Jennifer Thurman never drank from our garden hose ever again.

MY MOTHER DIED IN the Last Great Extinction. Before she went up in flames, quite literally, she gave me her spot in the Survival Pod. As a distinguished astrophysicist, she was elected a Valuable—someone who could help if things went wrong—and given a room in the floating city the filthy rich had built as their escape. Trillions of dollars that could have been spent to save the many would save the few. The very few. The best and brightest would live out their days in a climate-controlled bubble on the coast of Antarctica in a floating utopia. There would be fresh food and water, luxury accommodations, and medical care. The Pod habitat was built for 600, plus 300 "essential workers"—doctors, police, dentists, janitorial staff. In the end, only 423 of the Valuable entered the Pod. When news of who was deemed as Valuable and who was not circulated, many of the Valuables were hunted down and killed. Televised competitions for the last few Pod spots aired on television—with beatings and beheadings and the spectacle of the undeserving fighting for their lives as Planet Earth gave up the ghost. I felt sick about the whole thing.

The last time we spoke, my mother said, "You don't even need the Pod, Glory. You've been time traveling since you were a little girl. You could just, I guess, be like a tetherball, bouncing across time but situated in a fixed point, forever."

I could travel at will thanks to my father's surgical implant—which had flown under the notice of the government. GloWorm time travel had become a popular plaything of the rich for a time, and when the planet got too hot to grow food and the evacuations and groundswells started, the government put an end to the program because too many people were using it to try to save themselves.

My mother was in her eighties, wanted to die in my stepfather's arms, and didn't see the point in sticking around. My father had left the planet five years earlier and was living with his third wife at the Mars Colony, or so we assumed—there hadn't been any communications from the Mars Colony in three years. So he was essentially gone, too.

My generation wasn't one for marriage, and most of us were so full of chemicals that our reproductive organs didn't work, so few of us had partners or children to consider. I had a beloved, but the heat and the mold had made her ill, and her work with the climate refugees had shown her the mercy in the end of the world. Frieda, her voice reduced to whispers, insisted I take the spot in the Pod.

On Extinction Day, everyone I ever loved burned to death. My mom, my stepfather, and their dog. My Frieda. The outside temperatures in what was once North America were nearly two hundred degrees Fahrenheit. Meanwhile, I was transported by the US government to an enormous plastic bubble in Antarctica, to spend the rest of my days floating in a luxury cruise ship. Somehow, we ate lobster the first night.

ON MY SECOND NIGHT in the Pod, I was trying to sleep in my new bed with the luxury sheets when the light in my quarters clicked on. A heaving, sweating young man had broken the lock and let himself in. His name was Todd Rudd, son of some fat-nosed Southern senator who not only connived to get him onto the Pod but also, at the end of civilization, saw to it that his boy would not be deprived of vodka. The young man's eyes were red and swollen.

I alerted him to the fact that I was a forty-eight-year-old lesbian, and told him get the hell out of my quarters.

"For God's sake, I'm not here to rape you. I'm a Christian. I need to talk."

"I don't want to talk. Get out."

"I left my wife for this," he said, his voice quivering. "I let her die."

"My wife is dead as well," I said as coldly as I could form the words.

The young man steadied himself against the wall. He was in distress, but I couldn't be moved to care. "I can't . . . I can't go back. It's all gone. She's gone. She's really gone."

"Did she let you go to the Pod or did you just say to her, 'Sorry you don't have a rich daddy, enjoy getting toasted with everyone else'?"

My words must have stuck him in the gut. He grabbed his midsection as if I had stabbed him. "I made a mistake," he cried. "A selfish mistake."

Compassion was not my strong suit in the Pod. I was lucky, maybe, to still be alive, but the company I would now have to keep was atrocious and I resented not being with my loved ones. I thought of Frieda, my sweet girl. Her own mother had perished a year earlier when the groundswells started. The groundswells that had also swallowed up our friends.

"You're the woman who can time travel, right?"

"No," I lied.

I swiped at my wristlet and asked for a security officer to come to my quarters immediately.

"I know who you are. Glory Park. I remember you as a kid. With your parents."

I stared straight ahead.

"I was jealous of you. You had the coolest life."

My eyes wandered over to the wall next to his head. Whoever painted this room did a sloppy job.

"Can you get me out of here? I want to go home." Todd Rudd gestured towards my wristlet. "I know your parents gave you an implant."

"We're not friends," I said icily. "You need to go."

"I'll pay you."

I laughed. The man in front of me had learned nothing from all our recent years of loss and pain. "You'll pay me? With what? There's no money anymore."

I kept my mother's gun under the covers with me. Todd did not flinch when I pulled it out and aimed it at him. He pulled a screwdriver out of the pocket of his pants. Where he had found a screwdriver in the Pod, I could not say, but the security men arrived just as the first long, dark red stream of blood shot from his jugular onto my floor. I wasn't sad to see him go.

I reached for my wristlet and hit the release button. I ran. I fumbled into the tunnel. It was my heart's wish to land in Frieda's arms in our college-era bed, naked and giggling, that first moment when I felt the most loved. But my mother had changed the tether setting on my wristlet. When I told her to set it to home, she'd assumed I meant our house in Seattle, and I couldn't bring myself to correct her.

INADVERTENTLY, I HAD CALIBRATED my travel portal to return to the scene of my mother's first time-travel mistake. She was a vigilante for a time, before the government took control of my parents' wormhole technology. Her vigilante-ism didn't always work. Sometimes, it made things worse, so she stopped.

Highway 26 in Oregon. Jennifer Thurman. 1987. Child trafficking. That woman.

Gusts of wind from the passing logging trucks blew across my forty-eight-year-old body as I stood on the side of the road, this time without my mother or the decoy Mercedes. When the familiar Town Car passed, I fired a single bullet from my mother's gun, into the front tire. The Town Car skidded to a stop.

Inside the car, I saw the outline of Patricia Stoddard, accomplice or victim.

As he got out to survey the damage, Jennifer Thurman's father yelled at me, "You got a problem, lady?"

Slowly, I walked to the car. I peered inside the passenger side window to see the woman, Patricia, sitting in a mess of wadded-up tissues and drink cups, smoking a long cigarette. I breezed past her and pulled open the door to the backseat, finding nine-year-old Jennifer wearing nothing but panties, clutching her chest, struggling to breathe.

"You a cop?" the woman yelled at me. I ignored her. "Stay away from my girl," she said, stabbing out her cigarette on the red vinyl dashboard before making an attempt to stop me.

To Jennifer, I said, "Take my hand. Grab it. You have to make contact. I'm getting you out of here."

Jennifer looked at me stunned, but she did what I asked. I jolted us into the wormhole tunnel. My first repair was done.

And when we landed, I found myself back home. Seattle, before and intact, the home where I was once a child of privilege. But Jennifer was crying, running around my childhood yard like an animal. I turned and looked down the street in the direction that my parents would soon appear, walking home after work. I wanted my mom—not that she could help me with this. I just wanted her.

The child Jennifer howled at me. She needed clothes. She came running toward me, heaving and sobbing, asking me where she was and why she was here. I didn't know if it was because she was relieved to be free of the horrid future that awaited her, or because either way, either direction, it was horrid, and like me, she wasn't going home ever again.

I read The Left Hand of Darkness *in a coffee shop in 2010, when I had just started writing* Every Anxious Wave. *I was utterly taken by the sharp, deft prose—cutting and precise, like a diamond, but underpinned by so much raw emotion and empathy. Le Guin was always so wise, and with so much to teach. I look to her as a great instructor, in craft and in life.*

Hard Choices

TINA CONNOLLY

A. YOUR LITTLE SISTER is tired of picnicking and wants to explore a cave. She says if you don't come, she will tell mom what you were doing last Saturday. If you grudgingly accept her blackmail, go to B. If you let her tell mom that you were skinny dipping with Bitsy on the shapeshifter reservation, go to Z.

B. THE CAVE IS dark. You try to scare your sister with tales of carnivorous shapeshifters who eat bad children. She says everyone knows that shapeshifters are cowardly beasts, easily beaten by the first planetary settlers. You ask why she knows so much history when you are flunking. If you vow to stop looking at Bitsy's shirt in history class, go to C. If you tell your sister to be quiet and respect her elders, go to D.

C. YOU THINK ABOUT Bitsy's shirt as you explore the moist dank cave. Stalactites drip on your head. Go to D.

D. A SWARM OF glowbats fly out. They have a wingspan as wide as your chest, and are phosphorescent during mating season. It is suddenly so bright that your sister sees you drop and cower, trying frantically to get the feeling of claws and wings out of your hair. "Let's go back!" you squeal, but she says if you don't press on, she will tell Bitsy you're afraid of mating season. If you grab your sister and march her out of the cave, go to Z. If you dry your tears and press on, go to E.

E. BY THE LIGHT of three hanging bats, you see cave paintings. One painting shows many differently shaped shapeshifters greeting a rocketship. One painting shows the shapeshifters bringing stalks of grain to humans. One painting shows a yin-yang picture—a shapeshifter eating a human who is killing him with a spear. One painting shows the shapeshifters huddled in a circle, surrounded with lightning bolts. "Graffiti," sniffs your sister. If you think about the struggles inherent in the coming together of two sentient species and how we always seem to flub the hard choices, go to F. If you think about Bitsy's skin in sunlit water, go to F.

F. PAST THE PICTURES, the cave forks in two. One tunnel smells like rotten eggs. One tunnel smells like the strawberry shampoo in Bitsy's hair. Your sister goes down the eggy path. If you follow her, go to H. If you follow the memory of Bitsy's hair, go to G.

G. YOUR CAVE ADVENTURE was a funny prank by Bitsy, who paid your sister ten bucks to bring you to her. Bitsy is waiting for you, arrayed only in long locks of strawberry-shampooed hair. Unfortunately, Bitsy is a carnivorous shapeshifter and you die.

H. AT THE END of the eggy tunnel is a bear. Since there are no bears on this planet, it is likely a carnivorous shapeshifter. If you proffer a handshake and recite the Human-Shapeshifter Protocol, go to I. If you throw your sister to the bear to buy time, go to J.

I. THE BEAR'S PAW becomes a maw and bites off your hand. It

chews it up while it recites some manifesto about how it rejects the Human-Shapeshifter protocol. You throw your sister to the bear to buy time. Go to K.

J. YOU FEEL A little regret and try to save your sister. The bear bites off your hand. It spits the fingers on the floor. You feel ashamed that your fingers aren't worth eating. Go to K.

K. FAINT FROM BLOOD and sister loss, you wrap your wrist in your shirt and run for the entrance. You lose some time when the bats fly over your head in a triumphal finish to their mating flight. Suddenly Bitsy is there to save you. She helps you stand and dries your tears. She takes off her shirt and uses it to bandage your wrist. You feel a lot better. Then she eats you.

Z. YOUR MOTHER GROUNDS you from the prom. Bitsy finds a new date. When you are thirty-one, the great Shapeshifter Revolt comes to fruition, the human settlement is overthrown, and the electric fencing destroyed for good. Bitsy finds you cowering in a bathroom, weeping that you will die a virgin. She makes love to you, tenderly, sweetly, and you remember a day of sunlit water and glorious splashing. There is no fumbling, there is no miscommunication, there are no tears. Then she eats you.

Le Guin's work has long been important to me for the close look it shines on complex characters and their difficult choices as they try to find truthful ways to exist in the world. Her stories often explore the nuances of cultures coming together and the problems that can result. This story takes a look at those same topics, but with a bit of a twist.

When Strangers Meet

SONIA ORIN LYRIS

"THE VOICES FROM THE sky have called again, Great One," said the One's Second.

"When strangers meet," said the One, "all benefit."

"Are they strangers," asked her Second, who happened to be an older sister, and pale green, "these new ones from the sky?"

The One sat back on her soft throne, stretching all her top limbs out to the side in a motion that said that she could wait until tomorrow to worry about tomorrow.

The Second hesitated, unsure if this meant a dismissal from the throne room or not. The One laughed, a hissing sound that relaxed the Second. The sound of the One content was always a good sound.

"I think these new ones may be strangers," the One said. "We have sent them our language books, and they have sent us theirs. They wish to come, to meet us. To understand us."

"As strangers?"

"They say they are friends, but they must study our language and then understand. I don't think they mean to be familiar."

"I am sure you are right, Great One. Shall we give them permission to join us?"

The One considered.

"Tell them to ask again, after the festival. The new year brings clarity, and strangers bring benefits."

TODAY THE GREAT ONE'S Second was younger, and nearly pink in shade, and her soft movements around the room soothed the One.

"I do not recognize you," the One said to her sister. The Second pressed her limbs to her stomach, uncertain.

"Thank you, Great One," she murmured. "I only hope to please."

"You do please. Your smell is unfamiliar. You do not distract."

It was a good day, this tenth day before the festival of the cooling time, and the One felt good. Her Second moved around the large room, cleaning away the specks of dust and dirt, replacing a few of the long sheets of odor-absorbing textile, and touching the deep sound bells so that they spun and their low hum might better soothe the One.

And it was a good day because the voices from the sky had called to say that they were happy to be strangers. Strangers always brought benefit.

The One drifted sleepily, daydreaming of the coming festival, her pastel-colored younger sisters who would soon be adults, the flower tastes her sisters would bring to tempt her to delight, and the spin dance the silks would perform. And then, later, of the days and nights she would have, secluded with the many males who had matured since last year.

She drifted, the One, filled with the calm that the bells brought, hearing only the unanticipated sounds of her Second as she moved around the room, tidying and adjusting and turning.

"THE SILKS HAVE COME again, Great One," the green Second said.

The One had felt herself grow euphoric and relaxed lately, and though it happened every year, she found herself surprised at how complete the change was, so complete that those who came day after day to consult with her about festival plans did not irritate her even though they were, by now, quite familiar.

"The silks," her Second said again, quite softly. Barely a breeze to remind the One that her attentions were asked.

"Yes, of course," said the One. "They want—what they always want."

"Yes, Great One."

"Then I will see them. Him. Is it a him?"

"Yes, Great One, their leaders are usually male." The Second's tone was a mild echo of the One's own amusement.

So hard to remember, the One thought. But then, so many things were hard to remember in this season before the festival. Male leaders? She shook her head.

In it came, the long, slender, warm silk, walking in on two long legs, its arms hanging down like long leaves at her—his, the One corrected—side. Every inch coated with the lush, fine cream strands that gave them their names.

Clumsy it seemed, for a silk, walking in as though uncertain, hesitant, not using the grace that his kind could so easily bring to every movement. And yet, she reminded herself, not all of them were equally talented.

But they would dance for the spin dance—how they would dance. Whirling like snow crystals in sculpted storms, this was how they would dance.

And when they had danced with every last bit of life that was in them, spurred on and on by the delight of the One and her many sisters, when blood squeezed from their poor bodies, lovely but too fragile to hold the passions poured into them, then would they be truly lovely indeed.

He stood before her, large pale blue eyes raised shyly. He did not smell bad, but musky, like the grain they were fed.

It was good that he visited now, when she was not so irritable. Another season and he would have so disturbed her that she would not be able to talk with him at all. He looked down to show his respect.

It was well that they gave respect. The One and her sisters kept the silks alive all year round, gave them shelter, planted their food, saw to the health of their young, and let them alone to live their lives as they saw fit.

The One felt deliciously relaxed. She wanted to drowse again. Just as soon as she was done with the silk. She tilted her head at the silk.

"You are strange to me," she said.

"You honor me, Great One."

"Speak."

"Great One, I fear to disturb you—"

"If you have concerns, you must speak. We care for you. You are dear to us."

The silk looked down, his large eyes sparkling.

"Great One, it is the festival. All of us were young last year, and did not see it, but—"

He glanced up at her, then away.

"Yes?" The One prompted.

"We have been told, about the dance in the cold, on the warm arena floor. Of how many hours it will go—so many hours! Great One, we were young last year, and our parents did not return to us from the dance. We owe you everything, of course; our food and water—you are so very kind to us, but—"

"But you want to know whether you will die in the dance."

He looked to the side of the room, then to the other, and then down again.

"Yes."

The Great One stretched a little, moving two of her limbs to another soft place on her throne where they might be even more comforted. The soft throne called to her to rest, to sleep, to dream.

"Yes," the One answered. "Of course you will die. All of you who dance will die."

The silk's eyes were very large now, and they sparkled quite like ice in the sun. His lovely eyes cut through the One's easy calm, and she was filled with the sharp delight of anticipation. She had seen twenty silk dances in her lifetime, and they never ceased to give her awe of the loveliness the silks could create out of their own bodies.

"But, Great One," the silk stammered, "surely you don't mean—surely I do not understand."

He was breathing heavily, so upset that she could nearly taste it. He would upset the others if she left him unchanged, and then they would fear before they danced, and there was no need for that.

She pressed the scent out of herself, pressed it into the air and toward him, along with her reassurances, which she breathed onto him, into his large, wet eyes.

The pale blue, frightened eyes closed a little, and his breathing slowed.

"You didn't understand before, it's true," said the One. "But you do now."

Slowly he blinked, staring at her, and a crease came to his mouth, one that meant pleasure.

"What else, then, silk? Have I answered your concerns?"

The silk considered, brushing his long nails through his arm hair.

"Yes, Great One. You are kind and gracious. I regret having disturbed you over this small thing."

"We care for you. Your needs do not disturb us."

"Thank you, Great One."

"Go now and rest with your sisters and brothers, and antici-pate with us the festival of the cooling time."

"It is cold," said the One's newest Second, just after dawn on the morning of the festival.

"Is it too cold?" asked the One, feeling pleasure as the ritual of the cooling time began.

"It is not too cold," said the Second, shaking leaves around the room, their sweet, sharp odor clinging to the One's throne. For the moment, in her tranquil state, the smell was simply a contrast to the calm odor that she had lived in all year.

"Is it not cold enough?" she asked her Second.

"It is cold enough," answered the Second, crumbling the leaves between her many limbs, scattering the pieces all around in a ranging disarray that would have been an outrage to the One on any other day of the year.

"When it is cold enough, but not too cold, then we must leave this place, as we leave all that we know from the year past, and go to make new life in a new place," said the One.

The odor of the leaves was becoming disturbing. The One knew she could not stay in her room much longer. Knowing this, and remembering that it happened every year this way, did not prevent her from beginning to feel irritated.

She stretched her limbs and slowly pressed herself up and out of the soft throne. How long had it been since she had last left this room? Or even her throne? The cold was a heavy blanket on her thoughts, and she could not remember.

Two Seconds were at her side, ones she did not recognize, which was good. At half her size, she could hurt them if she thought them too familiar. And the way she felt now, she might have hit them just because of the smell of the leaves, which was now so thick in the room that she wondered if she might become sick from it.

"We go," the Seconds chorused, encouraging her. She managed to step down from the throne and walk, leaning on her Seconds.

Out they went, from the room in which the One had lain comfortably all year, to the long, tented hall that led to the arena. As they stepped out into the bright sunlight, the world seemed a simple, white place, every rock and plant covered in snow and ice. The One saw rainbows in the cracks of white, and deep red in the few spots of shadow.

They escorted the One to her winter throne, which was not

at all soft, and this did not improve her mood. Knowing that the throne was hard for the purpose of keeping her awake through the long festival did not help.

Around her in a large circle, above the arena floor, sat all her many sisters, most of whom she would recognize if she looked closely at them, so she did not. On the ground below, at the edges of the floor, huddled the silks.

At that moment, the One did not care about the silks, did not care about the snow and ice, did not even care about the males who now would be waking and beginning to call to her from inside their soft nests. What she felt more than anything was an overwhelming sense of outrage that she should have been forced out of her soft room with terrible odors, forced into the bright sun and for what? To discover that it was winter?

The One clicked her throat in anger and turned side to side, looking for the Seconds who had escorted her here. She had decided to kill them.

Instead, others were there now, though she did not remember them coming; they were older Seconds, ones she recognized. She was about to squeeze scent at them, to command them to die, and to bring others so that she could kill them all for having done this to her. She would breathe on them so that their bodies would decide to die; their eyes would darken and grow black and they would fall to the ground, their limbs twisting together tightly in death.

Then a scent grew from plates that her sisters held. Flower scents. The One felt sudden hunger, and she reached to take and taste the array of treats they had made for her. As she put each delightful edible in her mouth, her anger melted.

She tasted each of the flower foods, and wriggled at the ones she liked best. Other Seconds ran off and brought back more of her favorites. She tasted and ate, tasted and ate, as she did her stomach grew full and her mood calm. After what must have been a very long time, she sat back on the hard throne.

"Let the festival of cooling begin."

ONE BY ONE THE many silks stepped into the ring, moving their feet slowly across the dark gray, heated floor. Some looked afraid, but the One and her sisters sent their reassurances to the silks, and the silks smiled and began to turn. Soon they were all turning, arms spread, turning and turning, cream silk fur flowing in the breeze, blurring their shapes as danced.

As every sister watched, their heartbeats came into alignment with the One's heartbeat, their breath with her breath. Below, the silks twisted and whirled, their eyes wide, their breath steaming out into the cold air.

They met and separated in intricate patterns, held each other and released, pushing far away and coming back again. Every move was as graceful as if it had been planned and practiced for years.

The One found herself forgetting who and where she was, so entranced was she with the dance. It should go on, this dance; it should go on for many days.

When a silk fell, the others helped it to its feet, pulling it back into the dance. More fell. Each was helped to stand, to continue the dance.

When daylight failed and night came, the sisters kept breathing their delight down upon the dancers, who often faltered but never stopped. The cool white shapes moved with every bit of strength and passion they had. Those who were unable to stand lay on the heated floor, writhing, no less lovely for all their exhaustion.

The One and her sisters watched all night long as the silks danced, always breathing their reassurances and pleasures down upon the silks.

When dawn came, only two of the silks were still moving. All the silks had dark stains on their bodies—at their eyes, mouths—and dark smears across their fur. The two who moved lay on the ground, staring up at the lightening sky, their limbs trying to keep rhythm with the heartbeat of the One and her sisters. At last, these two were still as well.

The One felt a great joy. The new year had begun.

THE ONE WENT TO the males' nests, and there she stayed in darkness for a good number of days, until she was well-satisfied, and all the males were dead.

The old throne room had been burned to the ground, as it was every year, the smell of crushed leaves having made it uninhabitable. In place of the old throne room another one had been built. She sat there now, on the new throne, which seemed softer than the old one, and smelled most reassuringly of nothing.

The Second who came to her today was very young, having only just reached adulthood at the new year with all of last year's children.

"You are strange to me," she told the Second.

"I am honored," said the Second, twitching with the awkwardness of her youth, which the One found charming.

But best was that the One felt her own clarity again. With the festival and mating over, she found she could think again, could reason, and did not feel the need to constantly drowse.

"Are the young silks healthy?" the One asked her Second.

"Yes. Healthy and growing, Great One."

"They mate next season. See to it that it is a fruitful season so that next year's dance is plentiful."

"Yes, Great One. And Great One, the voices from the sky—"

"The strangers."

"Yes. They wish to join us. They have asked again, now that the year is new. They say that they have studied our books, and that they come as strangers."

"When strangers meet, all benefit," the One said thoughtfully.

"Yes, Great One. They say that they have many hopes for mutual understanding between our kind and theirs."

The One clicked her throat. Her Second stepped away.

"Not too much understanding. There should not be too much understanding between strangers."

"No, Great One," the Second said, limbs twitching.

"They have much to learn yet."

The Second watched as the One stretched on her throne.

She was young, this Second, very young. She would learn, in time, what it was to be the One's Second. If she did not first become too familiar.

"I wonder what gifts the strangers will bring," the One said. "I wonder if they will dance."

Ursula Le Guin's worlds and wisdom shaped me from childhood. When I finally met her, I was a published author and Clarion West grad, yet I stumbled over my words and could barely speak. But she did not let me fall; she met me with a gentle graciousness that changed me as surely as any of her stories ever had. Without her, I would not be the writer I am today.

JoyBe's Last Dance

JASON ARIAS

Morning comes whether you set the alarm or not.
—Ursula K. Le Guin

IT WAS THE MOMENT before the auditorium lights dimmed and the stage became illuminated. The faces in the audience beamed brightly with anticipation. The words *The JoyBe Hour* in large lettering were hung on the marquee outside the theater above the smaller tagline *Joy Be Seen from Shore to Shore, Fo' Sho'*. It was already a hit, one of the hottest new theatrical productions in the nation—the newest installment in the JoyBe saga. The JoyBe Team had booked fifty sold-out engagements within the first week in the most populated cities across Crematoria (not the largest of the continents, but the loudest and the newest, and the one JoyBe called "Ho, Ho, Home"). The producer, the writer, his agent, the thirty-six-person team of animatroners it took to bring him to life each night were (all of them) over the three moons with happiness.

JoyBe lay crumpled behind the curtain, preshow, listening to patrons' voices singing drunkenly along with the loud soundtrack coming out of the house speakers. Bottles clinked. Hands slapped.

A man quoted a JoyBe line from the last installment of the JoyBe saga, *Joy Be to Absolve the Masses*, followed by an impromptu donkey bray.

The audience was primed. Loving the preamble, bracing for the moment that the MANionette that they were all there to see would take the stage.

Upon entering the theater they had been greeted by JoyBe's dark face, presented proudly on the poster in the "Now Showing" display case—smiling so big that it appeared to be nearing an explosion point—out in the lobby next to the concession stand where the patrons could purchase fried calcitrons and oversized tonic bottles to step even deeper into the tailored JoyBe experience. For the next sixty minutes the audience would be transported to the place where they believed JoyBe to live. And JoyBe was so . . . "Hap, Hap, Happy to be here, Mister! Yes, sir." And, in the last scenes of *Joy Be Seen from Shore to Shore, Fo' Sho'* JoyBe would be gifted a small bit in an insurance commercial and a thermos full of bullets and say, as sincerely as his animatroners could move his jaw, "Don't forget to buy everything they tell you to, ya hear?" before kneeling with an elbow on a bent knee, his fist smashed adorably against his chin, his eyes shining like the newly discovered 111,111,111,111,111,111,111th named star, Holy Number, his joint ropes pulsating his entire body to create the impression of being on the brink of tears.

JoyBe should have been bursting with smiles bigger than those on his featured posters in the lobby, but inside he wasn't. On the outside JoyBe looked as he always had: his moth-eaten sweater, weathered shoes, ripped tramp pants, and the white-white teeth of his ensemble all fuffered and ruffed to a tee. But on the inside he was off.

It was the stagehand two cities back, in Port of Lands, that had gotten to him.

The stagehand had approached JoyBe backstage, looking both ways quickly before squatting square in front of the preshow, inanimate MANionette.

He looks like me, JoyBe thought of the stagehand. *Same surface tone and build but less enunciated features, dressed differently. And moving all on his own.*

The stagehand didn't have the translucent ropes JoyBe was born with—attached to every body-joint, all 360 of them—like umbilical cords that the animatroners dragged him around with. Danced him with. Made him tremble, in fear or sinner's lust or heartfelt forgiveness (depending on the saga requirements) with. The stagehand gazed back at Joybe not with interest, but disgust. While looking deep into JoyBe's dream-painted eyes he'd whispered, "Just listen to those hungry patrons out there, Joy. Be." Dissecting the MANionette's name into two new names. "What do you suppose they are so hungry for? Why should you have to satiate them?"

And then the stagehand rose and sauntered deeper backstage. And JoyBe never saw him again.

At the stop after Port Of Lands, in the city of Boys See, JoyBe could not fully believe the smile that the animatroners fashioned him with, from their nest high above the stage. But he held the smile throughout the performance, partly because he had no choice and partly because he was still trying to believe in the invisible ropes that kept him trembling on one knee at the end of the show the way everybody expected. And the audience applauded, and some cried out and others jeered and nothing about this felt right anymore. That night JoyBe had leaked face juice for the first time ever and an audience member had yelled out, "Hell, yeah! He bleeding liquor, just like I always wished he'd do." And JoyBe could hear that this patron didn't normally speak like this. He could hear the mimicry and could no longer find the flattery. But that was in Boys See and now they were in Chick And Go, with the same song and dance. A new crowd. A new night. Things could start going right again at any time.

The curtains parted. The audience rose in a sudden wave of applause and fell silently into their seats.

JoyBe began spreading joy.

He pirouetted around a white plasma rope on the floor, fashioning it into the silhouetted shape of a body with his shuffling feet. JoyBe lay down, perfectly still, inside the silhouette on the floor. He stayed motionless for an entire minute. Enough time for some of the audience members to wonder if it was over, if they'd somehow been robbed of their full engagement. Then, at the height of the tension, JoyBe's head cocked sharply towards the audience, a half-questioning smirk on his face, an *"Oh, you sillies"* headshake being orchestrated from above.

JoyBe rose from the floor with the white plasma rope in one hand, making quick work of forming a noose out of it.

He stood facing the audience, holding the noose out in front of him with both hands for a long time, his animatroners cultivating the guise of confusion on JoyBe's face. JoyBe placed the noose on the stage floor and stood inside it.

The audience shouted, "No, you silly!" They knew this recurring bit. It was nice to know bits. It was rewarding to know how to respond to them.

JoyBe picked the noose up and put his whole arm through it, letting it dangle pointlessly from his shoulder like a purse that would never hold anything.

"Warmer!" the audience cried.

Everybody was having a time. But JoyBe's joint attachments had never felt so encumbered. His head felt heavy. His thoughts were thick. His thirty-six animatroners sweated and scurried performing their choreographed chaos, out of view, high above him. They made JoyBe shrug the noose off his arm and hold it by opposite sides of the loop with his arms outstretched in front of him, quizzical, turning slowly to view different sections of the audience through the imperfect circle of the noose. And suddenly it was like JoyBe was looking at a panoramic photograph of old friends that he'd never had, through the bottom of a tonic bottle. Their faces distorted. Their features semifamiliar but frightening.

"Warmer!" the audience prompted.

JoyBe looked through the circle until he saw beyond the ways the audience members were different from him. Saw through their present hopefulness and annoyances. All the way through their workday and night distractions. Through their recently purchased tramp-pants costumes and fears and failures, as if JoyBe were living the entire audiences' lives backward, all the way through their wedding days and first dates and childhood crushes. He saw that on some level they, like him, were only children playing games they couldn't understand. They were expert apers. They were brothers and sisters. There were invisible ropes for all of them. Through the imperfect circle JoyBe saw how fraternity could be used to execute both beautiful and immoral ends.

The animatroners worked frantically above the stage. Pulling and tinkering. JoyBe was not responding the way he should. Six pairs of hands on each of JoyBe's primary elbow ropes. Three pairs of hands on each of his secondary wrist ropes. The rest of the team deployed to rudimentary balance points.

Half of the audience intoning, "Warmer!?!" with less confidence this time, as JoyBe stopped midturn and remained perfectly still. The audience grew silent, watching JoyBe watch them through the circle, just a circle, a meaningless symbol until given a purpose.

"What is it you hunger for?" JoyBe said. Asking, truly asking, but getting no reply.

No animatroners had worked the mandible ropes, but JoyBe's mouth had moved nonetheless. JoyBe wasn't made for his face to leak, and few knew that it even could—later some people would say that those weren't really tears at all, but only the sweat falling down from the animatroners' toil during the MANionette's betrayal, while others would know better. Those in the audience that knew, would leave the theater more somber than they could ever remember being. "What is it you hunger for?" those people would ask themselves, their partners, their children before leaving for work, prior to dinner, at bedtime. "What is it you hunger for?"

Those people would take interest in JoyBe for different reasons after that experience. They would find themselves perplexed by the new meanings they found around them and take to further self-examination and quiet contemplation, always choosing these modes over presumption and pronouncement. The three moons in the sky would look different for these people. They would tell others that the three moons were doing something important if they would only watch closer, if they could only listen deeper.

"What is it you hunger for?" JoyBe said again on the Chick And Go stage. "What is it you hunger for?" Despite the animatroners' efforts. "What is it you hunger for?" JoyBe's jaw hinging on repeat. His elbows wouldn't bend, holding the plasma noose far enough away from his body to never wear as a necklace again. His body remaining frozen, save the words coming out of his mouth, until long after the five stagehands picked him up horizontally, walked him off stage left, and deposited him in his crate with the lid open.

"You could still hear him echoing in there," one of the stagehands told his wife that night. "The saddest thing you could imagine."

And, before the theater emptied, much more silently than it had filled, one man in the audience could be heard shouting, "Why didn't they close the curtains for that?" He could be seen with his hands held to his head asking, "Why the hell did they let us see that?"

☾ ☾ ☾

I came late to much of Ursula K. Le Guin's work. Too late. Like, after she was gone. I'm ashamed of that. But I am thankful that there are so many of her words to continue to know her through. Every Ursula K. Le Guin story, poem, essay, or interview that I've read or listened to has been further insight into her mastery of prose, her incredible heart, and her extraordinary thought processes. She honed the skill of seamlessly infusing social commentary, devastation, beauty, and subversion into her worlds, and ours. You can read it in her words and hear it in her laughter: A beacon calling us home. A reminder not to fall asleep again.

The Taster

TJ ACENA

TWICE A WEEK I took the train into the inner ring of the capital. The Spire rose from its center, a five-cornered silver tower twisted up into a point, creating the impression that the city actually revolved around it. It was one of the nine Hubs, massive structures that served as the administrative points for the system government. A continuous stream of senators, diplomats, and bureaucrats came and went at all hours of the day.

My workplace was far removed from that center of power. It stood just a few blocks from the train station, a small, windowless building surrounded by thick hedges: the Repository of Digital Humanity.

IT WAS TUESDAY. RAVI stood from his large oak desk and greeted me as I entered the lobby. As the public face of the institute, he was the only employee who wore a uniform, a high-collared black kurta with golden lining around the neck (though except for the occasional aimless tourist and the yearly school trip, no one actually visited). He scanned his badge on the wall behind him and we went into the Gray Room. It had no official name, but the room was a light matte gray, as was the table and chair that sat in the middle of it. The air was warmer here than the lobby, just below body temperature, the environment designed to minimize outside stimulus.

I sat and Ravi attached the sensors of the interface to my head and chest. I could attach them myself, but he spent most of his day alone and enjoyed these brief moments of human contact.

Ravi had wanted to be an actor in soap operas but was not selected to attend the repertory after his general education. Acting was in his blood, he told me. His great-great-great-great-great grandmother was one of the most famous soap stars on the Indian subcontinent. While he set up the interface, he explained the latest episode of his current favorite, *Taming the Red Planet*, set on Mars during the early terraforming efforts. I found the show contrived and overemotional, but Ravi loved the melodrama. "It's set pre-immortality. People knew how valuable life was back then," he often told me.

Ravi left and the door clicked twice as the locking mechanism cycled, an obsolete security feature from the first years of the repository when anger over the exclusive nature of the technology was widespread. A white number flashed on the table display: 3.2 million digital citizens were connected to the interface.

In front of me were five mandarin oranges on a gray plate. I had never eaten a mandarin before this job, as they had only recently been reintroduced to the continent, and they were not sold commercially, but the digital citizens had requested I eat them every other session because of my especially strong responses to the fruit.

"Hello, Silas," came the voice over the speaker.

Over the centuries, the digital citizens had formed a gestalt entity in order to speak through the interface. The collective voice was soft and genderless.

"It's an honor to serve," I said.

"Please begin."

I stuck my thumbnail into the dimple at the bottom of a mandarin and peeled the rind away; a fine mist of juice erupted into the air. As I did this, my physical responses were fed into the interface. I placed a wedge in between my teeth and crushed it. The familiar sweet juice flowed into my mouth as the flesh fell apart. A soft sigh escaped the speaker as I closed my eyes.

When I put the last rind down, however, the door did not unlock automatically.

"Are you feeling all right, Silas?" asked the digital citizens.

I stared at the ceiling speakers. There were no cameras for them to watch me through, but I could not talk to them without focusing on something. A sense of unease had followed me to work this morning. I had almost forgotten about it until that moment.

"It's nothing."

"You may speak freely. We wish to know what troubles you."

"I read something in the news."

"What was it?"

"Something about the colonies. A mining colony. Ceres. There was an accident, I think." I looked down at my hands. "A tunnel collapsed. There were fatalities." Our bodies didn't age anymore, but they were still fragile things. And so death still came for us, often in the bloodiest ways imaginable. "It's scary, to think about death. When you were alive, how did—"

"We do not wish to speak about that."

"I'm sorry, I—"

"Thank you for your service, Silas." There was a sharp modulation to their voice I hadn't heard before.

The display went dark, the locking mechanism unsealed, and Ravi entered. My shoulders slumped against the back of the chair. The digital citizens had been humans centuries ago, before the end of natural aging. They had sacrificed their bodies in order to exist forever. I had made a misstep in mentioning death.

"Did something happen?" Ravi asked as he peeled off the electrodes.

I stared down at my hands, brow knitted. "I don't know."

He sighed. Ravi always wanted to speak to the digital citizens, but only sensates were allowed to initiate a conversation with them.

"What did you do during my session?" I asked. Ravi had taken up a lot of hobbies to pass the time at the front desk.

"I'm working on a puzzle."

"What kind of puzzle?"

"A jigsaw puzzle."

"What's that?"

"A long time ago people used to make pictures. On thick paper. They'd cut them up into interlocking pieces, mix them up, and then put them back together."

"And then what?"

"And that's it."

"Seems pretty boring."

He laughed. "It's a good way to pass time. Do you wanna see it?"

The front desk was covered with hundreds of tiny, irregular shapes. He had snapped a few together, forming the corner of the picture. I traced my hand over its surface, feeling the seams. "What is the picture supposed to be?"

He handed me the box top. A small wooden house stood near a dense pine forest. It was dusk and the sky was settling into a deep purple. In a brightly lit doorway stood the silhouette of a woman, and a young girl in a red dress was running up to her from the dark woods.

It had been many centuries since people had stopped living like that, so far away from each other, taking whatever space they could. I wondered what it would be like to travel through a forest.

"It's not really about the picture. It's the act of putting it together," Ravi said.

I picked up a piece and found a partner for it. They snapped together with a satisfying click.

On my way out, I passed Juno, another sensate. Her sessions with the digital citizens were always after mine. She listened to music for them. We often joked that she helped the citizens "digest" their virtual meal.

Outside, the afternoon air was warm. There were no clouds in the sky, but the weather report warned of severe hailstorms later. Last week, huge hailstones had damaged several of the reinforced windows of the Spire. The shadow of the tower stretched over the Repository, a giant needle on which the whole planet balanced.

TASTE SENSATES ARE CHOSEN based on genetic testing. I have a mutation that causes me to have elevated responses to food. When I was at the end of my general education, I was told that I was not qualified for a skilled position, but that if I wanted to, I could work at the Repository. The position came with a small stipend and an apartment in a middle ring of the capitol. Many of my schoolmates still live in communal housing for the nonworking back home. I was not used to so much privacy, and for the first year I lived there, I had the home screen playing sitcoms in the background most of the time. Mostly comedies set in education centers like the one I had just left.

When I got home from work, the apartment felt suffocating. I tried doing a callisthenic workout to relieve my restlessness but couldn't stop thinking about my conversation with the digital citizens.

I opened the news page on my home screen and searched for the article I had read that morning but gave up after an hour. It was as if I had dreamed the disaster.

I clicked my home remote and asked it to show me a forest. The articles disappeared, and moss-covered trees filled up the wall of my living room. During my youth I had been to the city arboretum with my classmates. It was a large area, and you couldn't see the boundaries, but you could still feel them. This view felt endless. I leaned back on my couch and watched the leaves of the undergrowth rustle in the wind. Birdsong twittered over the speakers.

After a few minutes, birds flitted down from the canopy to peck at the forest floor. An orange fox slunk through the undergrowth, projected just a few feet in front of me, and I jolted upright. I'd seen so few wild animals before. The fox turned towards me, a dead mouse in its jaws, before disappearing behind a boulder.

THERE WAS A NEW puzzle on Ravi's desk when I came in on Thursday. A mountain range, covered in snow. I thought the white pieces on the table looked like a blizzard, though I've only seen blizzards in old movies.

I grew up on the Pacific Coast, south, near the old border. It hasn't snowed there in centuries, but scientists think it might again soon.

"Would you like to work on the puzzle with me when you're done?" Ravi asked. "Unless you have something else to do."

I smiled. "I suppose I can spare some time out of my busy schedule."

When Ravi opened the Gray Room, I smelled fresh-baked sourdough bread.

The door shut, and 2.2 million voices said, "Hello, Silas."

"It's an honor to serve." I picked up the serrated knife next to the loaf and paused. The blade hovered in the air.

"Is something wrong, Silas?" asked the voices.

I looked up at the speakers. "I'm sorry about last session. I hope I didn't upset you."

"We're not upset with you. It was just upsetting to experience . . ."

"Fear?"

"Yes. It has been a long time."

"I understand. It won't happen again."

I pressed the knife into the warm bread, feeling the resistance, then pulled it towards me to cut through the thin crust. Gently, I worked the blade back and forth, splitting the loaf in half. The faint fermented smell enveloped me.

Ravi came to get me, and when he and I exited the Gray Room, Juno was standing at the front desk.

"You're over time," she said as she pushed a puzzle piece around with her finger.

"Sorry, I was trying to eat an entire loaf of bread."

She looked up. "Did you?"

"No. And I feel a little bloated now."

"Sometimes I have to listen to hours of music," she said. "Symphonies back to back. Or hours of drumming. I fall asleep sometimes. They always let me. I think they like to feel that. Sleep."

Without waiting for a response, Juno headed into the Gray Room with Ravi. I thought about what it might be like to not have slept in several hundred years. To never feel tired. It saddened me a little.

At Ravi's desk, while we worked on the puzzle, I watched the screen that displayed the Gray Room. Juno was reclined on a small sofa, staring at the ceiling. There was no audio, but I could see her tapping her finger on her thigh.

"I've never seen another sensate in a session," I said.

"It's pretty boring," Ravi said. "Mostly, you all just sit there."

Juno smiled. It felt intimate to see her like that.

Ravi looked back down at the puzzle. "How was your bread?"

"Good."

"It smelled good. I like when you get something baked."

I picked up a puzzle piece that was completely white and turned it over and over in my fingers, trying to figure out which direction was up.

A NOTIFICATION ON MY home screen announced a message from Ganymede station. I opened the video message, and my great-great-maternal grandmother Andrine appeared onscreen. She had been in her sixties when science had ended aging and wore her gray hair with pride because it was so rare.

"I'm just checking in on my favorite great-great-grandson," she cooed.

I smiled. Between my parents and their various other partners over the decades, Andrine has eight great-great-grandchildren. I hadn't met any of them but was irrationally proud of this distinction. I met her once when I was twenty-two. She was on the planet for a conference and came to visit me at the education center. (Besides my parents, no other relative had ever come to visit.) We spent the day together, and she told me about her husband, who had passed away right before the end of aging. She told me about her parents and her grandparents. She showed me pictures—actual photographs—of these people. People my mother had mentioned but never spoken much about.

"I want you to know the people you came from," Andrine had told me. "It's so easy to forget now. Life is so long."

The video message concluded, saying, "I hope work is going all right at the Repository. I'll be around for the next few hours if you want to send a message."

Andrine was a botanist who worked the colonies, monitoring hydroponics gardens and breeding new low-gravity crops. She traveled often and was difficult to reach. It had been several months since we've spoken.

I sat up on the couch and stared at my own face reflected in the screen as I recoded my message, updating her about my job and the jigsaw puzzle I was working on. Satisfied with the playback, I clicked *Send* on the remote and skimmed through the newsfeeds while I waited for a reply.

Forty minutes later, her response arrived.

"I remember jigsaw puzzles," Andrine burst out. "I can't believe someone still makes those! You could never find anything like that out here." She got quiet for a moment, looking down at her hands. "I don't know when I'll make it to Earth again. Things are"—she looked up—"difficult. I don't know if you've heard about . . . what's going on out here. But I'm worried." She looked out of the frame for a moment. "I hope you're all right, Silas. I love you."

I sat up after the message and immediately recorded my reply.

"Is this about what happened on Ceres? I thought I heard about an accident there. But I haven't heard anything since. Were you there recently?"

An hour passed with no reply.

I called the communications service line but got nowhere with the automated help menu. "The system is functioning normally," said a soft voice from the screen.

"YOU ALL RIGHT?" RAVI asked as he started pressing the sensors onto my head.

"Do you know anyone who lives in the colonies?"

"No, but my son sometimes goes out there."

Ravi's son was part of the terraforming project on Mars. He had shown me a picture of him from a visit a few years before I started at the Repository. The two stood in front of a fountain in a plaza. They looked like brothers, having the same thick fuzzy eyebrows and deep-set eyes.

Ravi knelt down while I unbuttoned the top of my shirt.

"And things are fine? On Mars?"

He pressed the sensor to my chest. "As far as I know, yes. Why do you ask?" Behind Ravi the display on the table flashed on. 2.3 million. He put his hand on mine. "Are you sure you're okay?"

Despite the heat of the room I could feel the warmth of Ravi's hand on mine.

The display flashed 2.9 million.

"We can talk more after if you'd like." He gave my hand a squeeze and turned to go.

Ravi was almost out of the room when 2.9 million voices whispered his name. He froze, shoulders hunched, then looked up at the speakers. He also knew the citizens could not see us, but it made me smile to see someone else do it.

"Hello . . . honored citizens."

"No need for formalities. We have a concern about the interface."

Ravi looked at me, and I shrugged.

"Could you check the electrodes again? The connection feels . . . off."

In the ten years I'd been a sensate, we'd never experienced a problem with the electrodes.

Starting with my head, Ravi reapplied each sensor, tracing each adhesive pad with his fingers against my skin. I felt his breath on my neck as he worked. A faint hum came out of the speakers. Finally, he peeled off the sensor on my chest and then pressed it back firmly with his palm.

"How is that?" Ravi asked.

There was silence for a moment.

"The system appears to be operating normally. Thank you, Ravi."

He smiled at the ceiling and made his way out of the room. The door sealed shut behind him.

"You may begin, Silas."

I reached across the table for a mandarin.

ON THE TRAIN HOME, I could not get a seat. That had never happened before. Many commuters bore the patch of the diplomatic core. But there were a few military ones as well. Some huffed at each other quietly while others held the vacant expression of exhaustion.

I found it difficult to enjoy eating after leaving the Repository for the day. At a grocery store, I spent twenty minutes staring at brightly colored boxes of instant soy-based meals before leaving empty-handed.

The streetlights turned on as I made my way home, and I noticed a small shape on the side of the road. A dead pigeon. A bright pool of coagulated blood flowed out of its beak. The street was empty, which wasn't unusual, but made me anxious. I stood there transfixed for a few minutes, unable to walk past it. Then a street-cleaning robot passed by, playing its soft, cheery melody, and swept up the limp, feathered body. The robot sprayed down the sidewalk and glided away. The bird's entire existence had been erased in less than a minute.

THE LIGHTS IN THE Gray Room flickered. I was holding a mandarin in my hand, its rind blossoming off of the fruit, and looked up at the camera Ravi monitored. I wondered if he was paying attention, or if he was lost in another puzzle.

"Silas?" said the citizens. "What's happening?"

The room went dark and the scent of the fruit became stronger. The lights returned a few seconds later, but the speakers crackled with confusion, and I saw the display on the table: 3.1 million. There had been 3.2 when I started.

The lights flickered again, and the display read 3 million. The citrus in my stomach turned to acid.

The room was plunged into red light and the speaker screeched with the sound of 2.9 million people shrieking in terror, *"They are killing us!"* The mandarin exploded as my hand snapped shut around it.

I kicked my chair back and stumbled to the door. It was still locked. I called out to Ravi as I pounded on it. The gestalt broke down and the speakers squealed as they tried to process the millions of voices trying to speak at the same time.

The numbers on the display ticked down: 2.9 million. 2.8 million. 2.7 million. I wanted to turn away, but I couldn't. I could feel tears streaming down my cheeks.

Over and over I heard my name under the screeching, individual citizens trying to reach me, "Silas, Silas, Silas. Calm down, Silas."

Then the speakers popped and there was a ringing silence.

I slumped down on the floor next to the door and curled up. After a few minutes the lights returned to normal, and Ravi rushed into the room.

"Silas," he whispered, "are you okay?"

"What happened?"

He swallowed. "There was an electronic attack on the capitol mainframe. Some kind of data corruption. It was deep. Affecting all lev—"

"An attack?"

"I think it was the colonies. There was a broadcast. A man with a red armband. He said they didn't want to hurt anyone. That they wanted independence—"

I started to shake. Ravi put his arms around me and walked me out into the lobby. The cool air felt hard against my skin.

"I want to go outside," I mumbled.

He took me through the front door and I lay down on the lawn. I had never stretched out on the grass in front of the Repository before. I could feel the tiny blades pressing through my shirt. Ravi sat next to me. People murmured in the street but I couldn't hear any traffic. Above us, the Spire pierced the sky. A twisted knife.

"How many?" I asked.

Ravi looked up at the Spire, "Two million."

"Two million," I whispered. I had never known anyone to die until that moment. And now I knew two million.

"The rest are safe. I think. The corruption was contained."

I touched my chest and felt the sensor still clinging to my skin. I gave it a quick tug and peeled it off. The sting brought tears to my eyes.

They were supposed to live forever. That was the deal they had struck.

Ravi picked up my hand and held it in his. It was still sticky with the juice of the mandarin. We stayed that way for several minutes.

He lifted our hands up to his nose and inhaled the scent.

"I've never tasted a mandarin," he said.

The Left Hand of Darkness *was on my mind when I started writing this story. We tend to think of anthropologists as individuals who exist in, or put themselves outside of, a population to observe it. But I think that destabilizations of our lives make us look hard at the society we inhabit, to become aware of its tides. Like Gethen, the Earth my protagonist inhabits finds itself at a tipping point and he is in a unique position to understand it.*

Let It Die

ARWEN SPICER

IN ALL OF WHITE Bells, there was only one locked door. From a distance, the door looked like slab of eroded rock in the grassy hillside, but as Nera, Esha, and Grandmother made their way up the trail toward it, the black line down the center grew plain.

The place obviously scared Esha; she was only six, a year younger than Nera, and always hung back. But Nera would stand on the flat gravel threshold of the door and crane her neck up so she could make out the letters carved in a swirly script at the top.

"What do the letters say, Grandmother?" she once asked.

Grandmother knelt beside her. "It says, 'Let it die,' as every tech center does."

"Let what die, Grandmother?" Nera asked.

"Everything that lives, little berry cheeks. Everything must be let go when its time comes, just like your mama when she got sick."

Grandmother said the tech center was where the people kept all the thingies that made the spaceships fly. Nera had never seen a spaceship, but she longed to fly in one, to soar like the hawks and even higher, even as high as the stars. But the grown-ups said ships only landed once in ten or twenty years, and then only if they needed fixing. Then tech things could go outside the tech center, but only to mend the ships.

"But why can't we see the spaceship thingies, Grandmother?"

"'Cause they're ugly," said Esha, a little behind them, rubbing curly red bark off a manzanita.

"Because they make life harder," said Grandmother.

"Harder? But they let us fly!"

"Yes. We need those things to keep the spaceships running so people throughout the Kiri planets can visit and share teachings. But that's all we need them for. We have fire and meat and flax, feather beds and leather coats." She squeezed Nera's shoulder. "Come on, let's go crush up the fairleaf and get some salve to the Manzanita Circle homeplace."

There was nothing scary about the door. The same could not be said of the ogre who guarded it. Her name was Otel, and she wasn't really an ogre. Probably. But all the children ran away if they spotted her sitting outside the tech center, blockish and dressed in black, hair iron gray, wearing a frown that said she saw the mischief they were planning. But Otel didn't come out often. Usually, nothing stood between Nera and the door. Yet sometimes it seemed the door stood between Nera and everything.

One day, Nera and Esha got tired of digging roots by the creek, and when Grandmother wasn't looking, they chased each other up the trail. It was Sticker Season, the exhausted grass pale as Grandmother's hair and pushed flat by the deer bedding on it. If they strayed off the trail, stickers caught in their shoes and they slipped on the slick grass. But the evening breezes softened the land, and they ran with the pent-up energy of a bored day spent napping in the heat.

At a sudden movement, they pulled up short. There she sat, Otel, on the long, flat stone just a few feet from the door, a book in her hands.

Esha shrieked and darted back down the trail. Nera whirled to follow but a sharp voice called her back.

"Nera. Where's your grandmother?"

"Just—just there, Keeper Otel." She pointed back down the trail toward the creek.

"And why aren't you girls helping her?"

"She said we could play."

Otel raised an eyebrow. "Would you like to see inside?" She nodded at the door.

Nera wanted to and didn't. She shrugged.

"Not sure, eh? Let's find out." Otel's lips quirked in a smile. She went up to the door and waved her hand. And the door, without being touched at all, made a sound like a reed flute and swung out.

Nera jumped back, and Otel's smile widened. "Come, child." She held out a hand.

Nera did not take the hand but followed her toward the dark cave.

"Lights." At Otel's voice, a pale winter glow filled the cave.

Nera gasped. Shelves towered to the ceiling, piled with books and funny bits like puzzle pieces. Some of them reminded her of the lenses of Grandmother's microscope. When she looked way up, she saw the light came from round spots in the ceiling, like tens of moons all full at once.

"You live here?"

"Nonsense, girl. You see that door? I live through there and up the stairs, in quite a nice room. This here is the research room, where people who have permission come to study. Behind it are the storerooms and, below them, the making rooms, where pieces of tech are used to make other pieces of tech."

Nera tried to imagine people studying these things, spaceship things and glowing moons. "Who studies here, Keeper Otel?"

"Oh, no one from here in White Bells. Traveling teachers, pilots and repair folk, scientists—people I give leave. That's part of my work as keeper."

Nera looked up at Otel, who was almost as tall as Grandmother. "Do you think you could give me leave—"

"Nera!"

She whirled at the sound of Grandmother's voice. Esha's round face poked out behind Grandmother's flaxen tunic.

"What do you mean by running off with half your basket empty?"

Otel barked a laugh. "So she said you could play, did she?"

"I'm sorry for her prying, Otel." Grandmother held out a hand to Nera and quickly led the girls home.

ONE EVENING NOT LONG after, Otel came to their yurt, the homeplace called Behind the Folded Oak. Grandmother sent the girls behind the curtain of the sleeping space with Father. There, in the flickering of the oil lamp, Nera picked at some mending and listened.

"She has the curiosity and the talent," said Keeper Otel. "You've said yourself she knows your microscope better than you do."

"I don't deny the talent," said Grandmother, "but curiosity is a two-edged knife. The idea of tech excites her. What if she gets too excited?"

"Apprenticeship is a proving ground. If she's not suited, time will tell."

A small silence. "I wanted to train her for a healer."

"Oh, pshaw," said Keeper Otel. "You have Esha. But tech keepers are a rare breed."

Nera glanced at Father. He was carving an antler knife handle with slow, deliberate strokes.

"Father," said Nera, "do you think I could be a tech keeper?"

"Ugh, then you'd be scary," said Esha.

Father gave Esha's shoulder a squeeze, even as he spoke to Nera. "You're clever enough, little supple-hands. But is it really what you'd want? To spend most of your life shut up underground with those lifeless things?"

In the end, however, Otel won, and Grandmother let Nera go back to the tech center.

She went once every five days and stayed for several hours. The walls pressed on her and the lamps shone feeble as fog, but the tech itself delighted her. Otel let her play with data crystals that contained microscopic images of genes and viruses. She showed her a screen with moving pictures of fish in amazing bright colors, like flowers of the sea.

"Where do they live?" asked Nera. They were nothing like the dull catfish and minnows she knew.

"Nowhere anymore. They're extinct."

Nera looked at her, uncomprehending.

"Extinct—none left. There was a volcanic explosion under the sea and it poisoned their water. We saved some in a tank for a while, but we couldn't find a suitable habitat to move them into, so they died."

"*You* did? You were there?"

"Yes, me. I was a fish scientist as a girl. But enough of that."

Otel took Nera next to see a giant machine deep under the hillside that waved spider arms and whooshed like the creek in flood.

"What is it doing?" Nera gasped.

"It's building another machine," said Otel, "or rather, parts to replace worn parts on a machine—the machine that drills down into the earth to gather the energy to run the machines."

The words went around in Nera's head. "Why?"

Otel laughed. "Why is a machine making a machine to get the energy to make machines? For the spaceships, mainly. Sometimes that machine there makes parts to keep the spaceships flying, and it needs the energy—called electricity—to do that, too."

Otel taught her that much of tech in the center ran on electricity, even the lights overhead. And there were things called batteries that let you catch and store electricity.

"This is a battery," Otel said one day, holding up a little bead that might have been a necklace pendant. "And this is a battery." She held up a white tube about as long as a catfish. "And this is a battery too." She pointed into a corner where some wires poked out of water jars. "That's a very low-power one. I just made it for fun, and to keep in practice with the basics."

"Can I?" said Nera.

"Certainly. You've come here so I can teach you these things. But—" She bent down and stared till Nera shrunk back. "None of this leaves the tech center, ever. People who take tech outside without a keeper's permission are punished. They are sent away from their homeplace. Forever. Do you understand?"

Nera nodded.

Electricity defined much of what the tech center hid—or "sequestered," as they called it. Grandmother's microscope was a machine too, but its lenses didn't need electricity, so it didn't have to stay in the tech center.

Nera learned a lot from Otel, but she still had to listen with the other children when the young traveling teacher came through White Bells. It was Flower Season, when the manzanita berries swelled hard and green and the ground grew dry. The teacher sat with the children in a circle among the poppies and yellowcups.

"Any city needs self-sufficiency," she said. "It must be able to meet most of its own needs—with a little trade, perhaps, as your city trades for flax. In the same way, a person must be able to make most of her own wares, just like you, Nera, are making that yellowcup chain instead of listening."

Nera froze and set it down.

"Self-sufficiency's important," said the teacher, "because it creates stability. The fewer pieces one relies on, the less there is to break."

Nera piped up. "So as long as you can make something and repair it yourself, it's all right?"

"Generally speaking. As long as you—or people in your city—can make all the parts too. By hand. And as long as it doesn't need a source of electricity."

❖

"ALL RIGHT, GRANDMOTHER, YOU can open your eyes."

Grandmother stared at the odds and ends piled on the manzanita litter. "What are all those wires for? And what do you think you're doing, taking my cups without asking?"

"Just watch, Grandmother."

Nera put on her gloves and carefully connected the electrodes to the water battery. The frail glow of the bulb sharpened the edges of the shadowy litter around it. She looked up, grinning. "It's a lamp. I put together all the pieces myself from odd bits in the center."

Grandmother gaped.

"I know I didn't make all the pieces myself, but I'm pretty sure they're things we *could* make in White Bells: wires and glass and stuff."

"Nera—"

"And I know it *uses* electricity, but I made this really simple battery, see? So it doesn't need a special source of electricity. I need to tinker more, but I'm pretty sure we could use it to see through your microscope at night."

"Nera, turn it off right now." Grandmother took Nera by the wrist and held her hard. "Come along. We're taking that light back."

At the center, Otel grabbed the bulb and set it on a shelf. "Nera, how dare you sneak that out!"

"But it's just a saltwater battery lamp."

"It's electric. Electricity connects things. We can use it to make very complicated machines, and once people start using it, sooner or later something breaks, and the whole system crashes. It happened with our ancestors, who destroyed much of life on the Motherworld long ago. It's happening with our fellow humans in the Sama planets now. They're fighting some plague as we speak that came from using poison space-flight fuel—that all started with using electricity. That's why we sequester it. That's why we punish those who don't."

Nera's heart began to thunder. "Am I—am I being sent away?" She tried to imagine life without Grandmother and Father and Esha, without the Folded Oak and the catfish pond.

Otel sighed. "Be glad you're just a little girl."

"Is she banned from the center?" asked Grandmother.

Otel hesitated. "Next time, if there is one—and banned from the planet too."

IN THE WHITE BELLS of Nera's eleventh year, the sun flickered silvery behind the clouds and hundreds of manzanitas glittered with white bell-shaped flowers, giving the city its name.

With the rains, the root-welt illness came through, spreading its pattern of thin red lines over the faces of the sick. Most fought it off, but some of the elders and children ran a dangerously high fever. Esha was among them. When her fever spiked, she tossed and cried, complaining that her legs hurt too much to lie still; the yurt smelled thick with her sweat.

"We need the antibiotic," said Grandmother, and she took Nera to the hole where the creek ran brown and sluggish. There in the drizzle, they cast nets for catfish. Nera and Grandmother grasped the slippery bodies and used a blunt bone knife of Father's to scrape slime from their skin into a bowl.

"Ugh, it smells worse than Esha!" said Nera, her britches soaked and tunic smeared with fish stink. "Does it hurt them, Grandmother?"

"Probably," Grandmother said, her knotted hand firm on the fish, "but their pain will pass and save people's lives. That's the way we weigh things, supple-hands."

Back home, drying off by the fire, they mixed the reeking stuff with herbs and water and made Esha swallow it. Then, back into the rain they went to make their rounds to the others.

"A couple of days," Grandmother said, "and they'll begin to feel better, but they must take it for a week, until the bacteria is killed off." She hugged Nera. "You've done me proud today, little healer."

The next day, as Esha slept, Grandmother let Nera look at the slime under her microscope. "Do you see those fine little lines? The old books say that's what kills the bacteria."

And it did just that. The root-welt passed and not a single person died. In bed at night, Nera listened to her sister's breathing and thought how close they'd come to Esha ceasing to breathe forever. She'd helped Grandmother save her, and others too. In the tech center, all she did was study and tinker with things she wasn't allowed to actually use. If she became a keeper, maybe two or three times in her life, she'd get to help fix a spaceship, but what was that worth?

"Grandmother," she said the next day. "I would like to be healer, like you."

But when she thought about being shut out from the center, never using the electron microscope again, or fixing gadgets or watching videos of tropical fish, she wasn't quite sure of her decision.

▢▯

For the time being, Nera trained with both Otel and Grandmother. Many children explored two or three vocations, until their thirteenth birthday, when they had to choose.

One day, while using the center's computers, she came across a news report from some planet she had never heard of. The video showed a place of high rectangles pricked with starlight—a kind of building, repeated over and over, no trees or grass or streams. The scene changed to inside a big building with white lights like the tech center. People lay in rows of beds, faces and hands grotesquely swollen and flesh melting with sores. Over the images, someone spoke in a foreign language, calmly. How could he be so calm?

"Turn it off," said Otel.

Nera jumped at her voice. "What is that place?"

"The Sama worlds. It's that plague of theirs from their space-travel tech."

Nera shut the screen off. "Why do they use tech that makes them sick?"

"Because it's faster than conventional FTL, and they need it to transport their food stores fast enough to feed all their worlds."

"But why do they live so far from their food?"

"Because they have ships fast enough to transport it," said Otel crossly.

That night, Nera dreamed she was trapped in a building with people whose faces melted under lights like moons in the ceiling. When she woke, for a panicked moment she was sure she was buried within those lifeless walls. Then she heard Father clinking pots by the fire and smelled the breakfast oats boiling. When she pulled back the canvas from the window, she saw the juncos hopping in the dry grass. Relief rushed through her like a sudden wind. But when she went to the tech center that day, it was hard to close the door and block the sun out.

It stayed hard, though she enjoyed learning science.

One day she said to Keeper Otel, "Why do you keep the lamps so pale? It's like an eternal winter. And why are the walls so gray? Why is it all so ugly?"

"So we remember," Otel said, "that life exists *out there*." She nodded at the door, and Nera imagined the hill, the creek, the deer trail with its deer droppings, and the iris just coming into bloom, white and purple.

ON NERA'S THIRTEENTH BIRTHDAY, the people gathered at the meeting place on the hill above the center. It was Silver Season and the old grass trampled flat. All the city had assembled, some seventy people, and Nera stood in the midst of them, wearing the red robe passed down from girl to girl. The red signified the ancient days when girls began to bleed at puberty, and the blood signaled they were adults. Boys wore travelers' blue, for they were more likely to leave their home cities. Grandmother and Otel stood in front, each facing Nera with lowered eyes and each clasping a scarf: black for Otel, white for Grandmother. The people sang softly,

Living is a wave.
Dying is a wave.
Childhood a wave.
Now the childhood wave is over.

After the song, Grandmother said, "Nera Behind the Folded Oak, I release you from your childhood homeplace. In this circle, you are only Nera."

Nera bowed low to Grandmother. The silver grass shimmered, and her gown fell at her feet like blood. The sun weltered low on the horizon, swollen with summer dust. Now she would walk to Otel and be Nera White Bells Tech Center—but her feet stuck.

She raised a heavy foot and another, and her feet took her not to Otel, but to Grandmother. Tears sprang into Grandmother's eyes as she laid the white scarf on Nera's shoulders.

"Welcome, young healer." Grandmother's voice caught.

The people pressed their hands together. "Welcome, young healer. May you have luck."

The circle broke into smiles and hugs.

Through the press, Nera saw Otel picking her way toward her. "May you have luck, Nera," Otel said. "There's much wisdom in a life in the sunlight."

❮█❯

NERA WAS ASHAMED TO look Otel in the eye after wasting six years on training she would never use. But she missed her, too, for Nera rarely saw her now, sequestered as she was, like the tech in the center. Nera also missed the tech. The spider machine and data crystals, the electron microscope and videos, all seemed to exist in another dimension.

But as the seasons passed, her pangs subsided. She enjoyed her work and the freedom of grown-up life. Like all girls at thirteen, she started taking herbs so she couldn't conceive an unplanned child, not that she was interested in sleeping with boys—or girls. Esha talked about nothing else: who would initiate them and who they'd marry. But Nera found herb lore more worth her while. When she needed a break, she rambled with friends to the surrounding cities, two or three days away, once even as far as Flat Flower Ridge, a metropolis of some two hundred yurts.

At fifteen, she was sexually initiated. The man her family chose was nice to her, but except for feeling she'd passed a milestone, she didn't see the point. Grandmother said not to worry. "Some are content without lovers. Just look at Otel."

⬛

AT TWENTY, NERA HAD become a full healer and saw to most of the city's simpler needs.

Esha worked as a weaver and lived in her own yurt with her husband. But one morning in early Flower Season, she showed up at Behind the Folded Oak with her new baby, Tanser, yowling and hot with fever.

"It's root-welt, isn't it?" She traced a finger over the lines on his cheeks.

"The flax traders must have brought it," said Grandmother.

"But there's the antibiotic, right?" said Esha. "The baby won't die?"

"Of course he won't," said Nera. "We'll make up a catfish tincture right away."

After three days of treatments, the fever broke.

After four days, the dark lines receded. Nera breathed more easily and moved on to other matters.

But on the fifth day, the fever came again, without the characteristic lines, but Tanser's skin burned even hotter than before.

"What is it?" cried Esha. "Why isn't the antibiotic working?"

Grandmother took a little blood and they looked at it under the microscope in the light of the midday sun. "It should be," said Grandmother. "But I still see bacteria, those dots there, see?"

"I want to check the antibiotic," said Nera. She made up a slide and examined it. "I knew it. See? Bacteria. Oh, Grandmother, it did cure the root-welt, it did. But it's contaminated with something else. It's given him something else."

They went back to the pond, scraped the catfish again, and made up a new batch, but it had the same dots. They tried again: the same result. It seemed the catfish themselves had some infection. Bereft of their cure, they could only offer cool cloths and herbs to lessen the fever. The next day, the baby was sicker.

"I'm going to go to the tech center," said Nera, "and find out what that bacteria is."

"Nera," said Grandmother sharply, "you can't bring tech out of the center."

"I'm not going to bring tech out of the center," said Nera, already headed down the deer trail.

At the center, she rang a little clay bell for Otel, who seemed a very long time in coming. When she did, she stood in the open door like a wall of rock herself.

"It's a dangerous thing for healers to use tech. 'Let it die.'" She hooked her thumb at the words overhead. "It's painful for the few but it keeps the world healthy."

You wouldn't say that if you heard my nephew screaming, thought Nera, but she said, "I only want to use tech *inside* the center. All I want is to identify this illness and look at records. Maybe there's a simple herbal cure."

Otel grumbled but let her in.

Nera ran her samples through one of the computers. She didn't even need to look through a microscope. The computer analyzed the microorganisms and classified them on the screen.

"It's an anaerobic bacteria found in ponds," said Nera. "It must be infecting the catfish."

Otel looked over her shoulder. "I remember that one from my studies of fish. But there's no low-tech remedy."

"I'll have to figure out how to make an antibiotic here."

"No," said Otel. "That is not what the tech center's for."

"Then what is it for?" snapped Nera.

"For spaceship maintenance," said Otel tersely.

Nera stormed out.

Overnight, little Tanser's fever climbed. He cried himself hoarse and his lips cracked and bled. Esha sobbed. Grandmother's mouth drew to a grim line. Father slipped out quietly to comfort Esha's husband at their yurt.

How could they purify the medicine? How could Nera remove the bacteria? Not heating—that would neutralize the medicine too. The computer said the bacteria was an obligate anaerobe. Enough oxygen exposure would poison it. She tried vigorously mixing the sample, but as far as she could see, the air bubbles only slightly decreased the anaerobe's concentration. No, she needed to oxidize it, and to oxidize it required electricity.

At dawn, she was back at the center. "Keeper Otel!" She jangled the bell. "I need to use some batteries. I won't bring them out."

At first, Otel ignored her.

But after a quarter hour of shouting, Otel opened the door and said, "No, Nera, no. That is how it begins. You'll tell me it will be an exception, but then everyone wants an exception, and then everyone needs batteries and computer diagnostics and machines to repair the computers—and what if those machines break down and we've forgotten how to live without them? We can lose a spaceport here and there, but what if we lose our life skills?"

"Saving Esha's baby won't destroy the world."

"No, Nera." The door whirred and clanked in her face.

"Keeper Otel!" Nera rattled the bell, but there was no response.

She was just turning to leave, when she heard the door flute open. "Here." Otel handed her a spool of copper and some nails.

"Why?" asked Nera.

Otel shrugged. "For the fish."

"The catfish?" said Nera, uncomprehending.

"The tropical fish, all those years ago." She smiled slightly. "I was too scared to try, and they died in those tanks."

Nera nodded. "Thank you."

Back in the city, she gathered supplies: a bottle and two vials from a friend who collected glass, a bladder with a thin rubbery tube Grandmother used for transferring liquid, several teacups, some soda salt traded from Froth Springs. She'd also need a bowl of saltwater and two empty vials. But how could she suspend the vials above the bowl? A lid? A wooden lid would be hard to cut through. Leather. A jerkin of hers fit over the bowl. She took everything out into a manzanita thicket some distance behind the Folded Oak, where, hopefully, no one would see her.

She cut two holes in the leather for the vials to fit in, suspended with their openings pointing downward.

Now, if she could only remember how to make the batteries. She cut the wire into small pieces and tied them around the nails. Then she filled the teacups with saltwater and connected them with the wire. The apparatus tipped over and spilled several times before she got the battery hooked into the bowl so that the cathode and anode nails sat in the bowl right below the two vials. Lastly, she filled the bowl with soda water.

The sun arced across the sky; the afternoon breeze swelled. She shivered as the shadows lengthened, but her little vials bubbled as gas rose up from and through the water, oxygen in one vial, hydrogen in the other, the oxygen half the volume of the hydrogen. At last when the bubbling had subsided, she gingerly wrestled the leather off, holding the oxygen vial in place, casting the hydrogen vial aside. Then she maneuvered the rubber tube through the water into the vial and used the bladder to suck up as much as oxygen as she could.

She put the antibiotic into the little glass bottle and ejected the oxygen from the bladder into it, then pressed the bladder in place to act as a cork. She shook the bottle vigorously.

IN TWO DAYS, TANSER'S fever broke. He seemed to have lost hearing in one ear, but he burbled happily again.

"You're a genius, Nera." Grandmother beamed. "Show me how you knew which catfish were healthy."

Nera shrugged and looked away. "It was just a guess, Grandmother."

Grandmother's smile slipped. "Well. Sometimes we get lucky."

The rest of the day, Esha chattered merrily but Grandmother was quiet.

She suspects something, thought Nera. *What did I do with those wires anyway?* She'd been so eager to give Tanser the medicine, she'd forgotten.

When no one was looking, she went behind the yurt to clean up the evidence. She plucked a flask and several wires from the gentle young grass. The soil was rain soft. She'd bury the wires—

"Nera, what are you doing with those things?"

Nera froze as Grandmother's white head bent beside her.

"I had a feeling."

"Let it go, Grandmother," Nera pleaded. "Tanser's better. No one has to know."

"I know," said Grandmother. "Nera, let it die. A healer who cannot learn that lesson is nothing."

GRANDMOTHER SENT A RUNNER to Flat Flower Ridge for the teacher, who must render the official judgment. But the day after the runner left, Grandmother and Esha both came down with fever.

It's all right, Nera told herself. *They're strong. They'll come through it.*

And Esha did come through it. Her fever broke within two days and Father carried her home to her husband and baby. But Grandmother's fever continued to climb.

"Can you eat, Mother?" Father was smoking hyrax over the center fire.

She shook her head, her back to him.

Father looked searchingly at Nera.

"I'll purify the medicine again," she said. "After all, I'll be exiled anyway."

"No, you will not," Grandmother croaked. "It stops here."

She turned her sweating face to Nera. "Perhaps the teacher will be lenient if you show restraint this—" A fit of coughing cut her short.

The next day, the teacher arrived, but she postponed her judgment to let Nera care for Grandmother. Soon, Grandmother's mind went muddy; she moaned and called Nera by Mother's name.

Nera gave her fever-reducing herbs, but they had no effect. Her body blazed under Nera's fingers.

Tears slipped down Father's face.

Esha visited and said, "Just give her the medicine!"

Nera put her hands over her ears to drown out Esha's shouting.

In the end, Nera gave Grandmother opiates to soothe her— and then more, as Grandmother had taught her. Death, she had taught, was nothing to fear, but dying could be terrible. Healers existed to heal the living and soften the path of the dying.

They buried her uphill from the stream, near the clumps of fairleaf she had gathered for decades. Bad luck, everybody said, in those sad, sympathetic voices.

Nera hated them—everyone: Otel, Grandmother, but mostly herself.

The judgment was held on the flat above the tech center, the spider machine pounding so deep beneath their feet the hillside didn't even tremble. Half the city came.

Otel stood. "Teacher, I wish to speak on behalf of the violator. I gave her the wire she used to make the battery. I knew what she would use it for. If you exile her, you must exile me too. I have no apprentice and this center will have no keeper. That, however, is your choice." She sat down again on the wet grass.

The teacher stood, eyes soft as her gray robe. "Keeper Otel, thanks for your courageous words." All the rustling in the circle ceased. All eyes held the teacher. "This young woman, Nera, watched her grandmother die rather than violate tech limitation again. That shows she has learned her lesson. She has paid enough. That is my judgment."

The circle released a collective breath. Father and Esha smiled. Then Nera stood. "No, Teacher. You are mistaken. I have not learned my lesson, not the lesson you teach. My grandmother is dead. I could have saved her. She would be here now, with years ahead of her. Never again will I stand by and rob people of their loved ones when I have the power to save them."

The sun peeked out behind a cloud, lighting up the last of the manzanita blossoms.

After a long moment, the teacher said, "In the Sama worlds, they're looking for healers; they don't have tech limitation there."

Nera thought of the tall rectangles and walls and melting sores. "I know," she said. "That's the place where I belong."

The teacher nodded. "Keeper Otel, send for a ship. We're going to send the Sama worlds a healer."

Le Guin once stated she enjoyed writing protagonists who were misfits in their own society, a theme especially rich in the context of an ambiguous utopia. This misfit-in-utopia story is particularly inspired by the Hainish character of Havzhiva in Four Ways to Forgiveness, *though it also echoes Shevek in* The Dispossessed. *It's a story about culture clash, albeit internal to one culture, and follows the format of a person's life history, as Le Guin often used in exploring cultures from an anthropological perspective.*

Each Cool Silver Orb a Gift

NICOLE ROSEVEAR

HELENA HAD NOT YET been born when the long war, the last war, began, but she had been in the Southlake settlement from its beginning, providing her unfocused childhood labor to the construction of communal households, dining and medical facilities, gathering spaces, and gardens. Over decades, she had moved her way through the full set of work cycles, adding her name to the lottery of women eligible to sit on the Council late in her fourth decade, knowing the chances of being drawn were slim. She did not need that particular honor to hold a deep pride in her small part in the building of Southlake, this newly gentled world, made better for all by the ruling hands of women.

When Sasha, the last remaining member of the original Council, added her name to the list of those withdrawing from the work cycles, Helena attended the lottery, excited to witness the drawing of a new member, a rare and momentous event. The afternoon was cool and muggy, the hazy sun unable to break through the clouds. When the name was drawn and called, she did not recognize it as her own, looking around at the women, men, and thirds gathered in the main square for this other Helena. When she realized others were looking back at her rather than past her, that she was that Helena, she cried out in surprise. To step into the shoes of one of the original Council members was an honor she had not dreamed of.

Walking back to her household, the flurry of conversations and introductions already a blur, the metal of her new Council pin cool against her throat, Helena passed a group of three men and two thirds in an alcove near a dining hall. She heard the tail end of a hissed whisper, one of the thirds saying, ". . . their pawns to being yours." When they saw her approaching, the man directly facing her tapped his collarbone twice, near the spot Council members wore their pins. The group turned quickly away from each other, one of the thirds offering her a casual open-handed greeting.

"Afternoon," she said, returning the gesture. It seemed that they did not want her to have heard them, and it was easy enough to imagine she hadn't.

O

WHEN THE MEN RETURNED from the war, or when those left of them did, the settlements had welcomed them. They were fed and clothed and healed, treated as family and lovers and friends. Sometimes they fathered children, the children the settlements so desperately needed to thrive into an unknown future.

The earliest thirds—neither male nor female, but indistinguishable from men at first glance other than their startlingly pale blue eyes—were born in that first year. The settlement's biologists had been unable to explain their emergence, but most believed they had come into being as a result of the horrors the men had inflicted on themselves, on each other, and on the world around them. Incompatible with both men and women, and having no apparent capacity for reproduction among themselves, adult thirds were excluded from family units and child-rearing. They also had a distinct predisposition, emerging in their early teen years, toward delicate constitutions that kept them from the more physically strenuous work of the settlement, but otherwise they were generally average infants and then average children and then average adults, entering the lower-intensity work cycles without difficulty or fanfare. Like men, though, they were not eligible for positions of power, their temperaments still being under study. This study mandated quarterly testing of every third in the settlement, a painless procedure Southlake's doctors took care to ensure they neither feared nor remembered. The thirds were not at fault, of course—had not even existed yet when women quietly stepped into the space left by the men who'd gone to war—but the Council had agreed the precaution was needed.

THE BUILDING THE COUNCIL met in three days a week, from mid-morning until their day's work was complete, was unassuming, a building that had once been either a large shed or a small barn. It sat on the outskirts of Southlake, on a low hill not far from one of the solar fields that powered much of the settlement— the post-war, relentless sun having at least that benefit. Helena had always associated this building with the stories she had been told about the place Southlake used to be, before the war. She imagined the Council building had once been surrounded by meadow. Stumps revealed the former forest just beyond, the kind that left woody cones and fragrant green needles on its floor—descriptions she still heard in the precise lifts and dips of her father's voice, from the stories he had told her in the few years he had survived after the war ended. She was sure the ravine behind the building once held water more regularly than just after a heavy rain, and she wondered sometimes what it would have been like to live in reach of the shade of those trees, the sound of that water, the smells her father had so longingly described of lush grasses and wildflowers in the sun.

The Council building's tall ceilings were the only regal thing about it. A circle of twelve chairs took up the center of the large room. Outside of this circle, a few simple cabinets and one large rectangular table were the only furniture of note. The Council members ate in a nearby dining hall, lived in the communal households. They used this building primarily for planning work and addressing questions or concerns from settlers. This was all in deliberate contrast to the world before the war, where decision-makers had lived apart, in luxury, and were difficult to access.

"Are you with us, Helena?" Sasha's voice was gentle, but Helena flushed with embarrassment at being caught in her own thoughts rather than listening to Council proceedings.

She dipped her head toward her notepad so Sasha wouldn't see her blush. "I'm here," she said. "I'm listening." It was still early in her transition period, and Helena was not fully involved in Council discussions yet, but she took notes, paid attention to how the women spoke, observed the ways each made small compromises to arrive at the most beneficial outcome for the settlement as a whole. It seemed an art form to her, one she hoped she could master.

The Council was considering future developments for Southlake's growing population. It was a relief to be having this discussion after the fears of decades past that the population might not survive the infertility crisis. For years, barely one in ten pregnancies had come to term. Other settlements had never recovered, shrinking until they merged with nearby populations. Southlake itself had taken in the remnants of two communities from the nearby foothills, absorbing the remaining population of Fairview only two summers ago. The miscarriages were determined to be the fault of chemicals of war doing precisely their job: poisoning everything around them. The war was the only response needed when men questioned why they were not in the lottery for Council seats. All other work they were eligible for, but power was something they had proven over and over again they could not safely hold. In listening closely to her new peers, Helena had gained the sense that this cornerstone of Southlake's structure was more in question now than it had been before. Groups of men were petitioning with increasing frequency and insistence that it was not reasonable, was itself a kind of tyranny, for them to be governed by a power structure they were so thoroughly excluded from.

The supplements the Council had approved for development and—after a brief testing period—use by all Southlake women of childbearing age had been nothing short of miraculous. Helena had been in the first work rotation packaging the supplements, each cool silver orb a gift, a promise, as she counted them into small bags for distribution. It was some of the simplest work she had done in her life, yet had felt among the most meaningful. Miscarriage rates had dropped below fifty percent. It was enough for the population of Southlake to stabilize and, slowly, begin to grow rather than shrink. Women, and eventually most men and thirds, took to calling the supplements "pearls," round and glowing and precious.

O

"MAY I?" SASHA SET her lunch bowl down and motioned to the bench next to Helena.

Helena smiled and scooted her own bowl aside, broth sloshing close to the rim.

"You're quiet in Council meetings," Sasha said, twirling noodles around her fork.

"There's so much to learn."

Sasha's laugh was quick and brighter than Helena would have expected. "If I've learned anything in my time on the Council, it's that there is always more to learn." She looked up from her bowl. "It's also important to remember," she said. "If we remember, we will make new mistakes, but not the old ones again."

The truth of this statement was clear to Helena. Despite the air being so bad for so long, the initial uncertainty about the thirds, and the terrifying dip in fertility, despite the isolation between settlements and the challenges of survival, most agreed that this world—for it really seemed like a new world—was better. She knew that it was, could feel it in the communal work, the kindness between neighbors, the prioritization of social structures focused on improving life rather than generating harm, the respect for everyone's contributions. This was certainly better than the world her parents had described, the one she barely remembered. She was glad to have played some role in its current thriving. But in the few short weeks since her name had been drawn, she had become increasingly aware of whispers, of furtive glances when she walked into a room, Council pin gleaming at her collar. More than once, groups similar to the one she encountered on her walk back from the lottery, men and thirds in impassioned discussion, halted their conversations with that double-tap at the collar as she approached. While they had joined the work cycles and communal spaces with ease, many from the Fairview population chose to wear slightly different clothing than other residents of Southlake, making them easy to identify. These discontented groups always included men or thirds from Fairview—thirds who seemed extraordinarily hearty, not prone to the frailty so prevalent among those from Southlake.

Something was twisting its way up out of shadows she hadn't known existed around her, and it filled her dreams with murky shapes she was unable to name. Helena lifted a spoonful of broth to her mouth. "Did you ever wonder—have you ever wondered—whether someone else should have been chosen in your place?"

"Every day I wear this pin," Sasha said, pressing her fingers to the collar beneath her gray ringlets. Her eyes closed, and Helena could see how tired she was, how the years had left her worn.

AFTER FINISHING THEIR MEAL, the two women started down the winding dirt path. The path from the nearest dining hall to the Council building led past a communal household, where a small medical team was collecting a third for testing. The third was pulling away from the team, pale eyes wide with fear.

"You can't force me!" They retreated until they were pressed against the wall of the household, the medical team surrounding them. Moments later, they slumped down the wall, unconscious.

"We shouldn't interfere," Sasha said.

Helena realized she was stopped on the path, openly

staring. The heat of being caught gawking warmed her cheeks. "Of course." She urged her feet again across the hard dirt. But the image of the third and the medics lingered, a twist in her stomach. She wanted to ask the medics if this resistance was unusual, if it had happened before, if it had started recently, since their absorption of the Fairview settlement, since all the whispering began.

They were mere meters away from the Council building when Helena almost tripped over another third. They were crouched low to the ground and hiding, poorly, near an old stump. "Ah!" Her cry came out a tangle of surprise and fear.

"Quiet, please!" The third whispered, the s in their *please* a low hiss. "They can't know I'm here."

"Who can't?" Sasha asked, standing square and tall, a certainty in her stance Helena wished she felt.

"You're Council," the third said, their voice fracturing on the second word. They tensed, glanced at the path back toward the center of Southlake.

"I'm Helena." Helena raised her hand in greeting, but they did not respond in kind, instead looking carefully at the ground. "You're safe with us."

"I'm not giving my name to a Council member."

"Why not?"

The third looked up, their eyes, almost white in this light, meeting hers. "The settlements are not as generous to everyone as they are to Council members."

"We all live by the same rules," Helena said, and the third was laughing, an unpleasant sound, before she had spoken the final word. Something from the whispers and nightmares, something not quite heard or that she'd forgotten, seemed to be bubbling up around her, approaching a boiling point. She felt afraid to look, but she wasn't sure at what. Helena's mother had been gently critical of the Council in her final years, talking sometimes of the inevitable blind spots of those who hold power for any length of time, regardless of gender. Helena had dismissed these statements as paranoia, excused them as part of her mother's age or illness, but now she found herself returning to these memories.

Sasha put her hand on Helena's arm. "We should return to the Council," she said.

"There should be no Council," the third said, "if the rumors are true."

"Without the Council, there would be no settlement," Sasha said, "and no future for our species."

"Without thirds, there would be no future for the species," they said, but there was no fight in their voice, just weariness.

"It's not wise to take rumors at face value," Sasha said, and turned crisply back onto the path. There was something rote about her words, unconvincing.

"What was that?" Helena asked, catching up. "What were they talking about?"

Sasha walked faster than her normal pace. "The peace we live in here is real, but the Council has made mistakes."

"I don't understand. Are the rumors they mentioned true? Has the Council been unfair to them?"

Sasha's pace slowed. "Maybe we have."

INSIDE THE COUNCIL ROOM, the other members were already gathered.

"Here they are," Marie said when Sasha entered the space, Helena close behind. "It's ten past."

"We were waylaid," Sasha said.

Marie had been about to say something else, but seemed to lose her words at this. Sasha removed her jacket and draped it across the back of her chair. "Waylaid?" Marie finally asked.

Sasha glanced at Helena. "Some commotion with a third."

"Two thirds," Helena said, but she could hear the timidity in her voice.

Sasha put a hand on her shoulder. "The Council still has a lot to cover today."

Helena closed her eyes, nodded once, and took her seat in the circle. She hoped she could be strong enough to see these conflicting things but still do the work in front of her.

○

THAT NIGHT, HELENA SAT in the small kitchen of her communal household, eating dried apples and hazelnuts. The day played on a loop in her head, the conversations and decisions, the feeling that she'd made a meaningful connection with Sasha, the moments with the thirds. These difficult moments in particular seemed heightened, elongated, as she considered them at the end of the day. She pressed her fingers into her hair, against her scalp.

"Long day at Council?" Bea, a long-time housemate, sat down across from her at the table.

"I'm not sure I know what an average Council day is yet." Helena pulled her fingers out of her hair and sat up straighter. She had not removed her Council pin for the day and felt a responsibility to set a better example.

Bea took a dried apple ring from Helena's bowl. "I put my name in the lottery bin forty years ago this year," she said. "For a long time, I was sure I would be chosen, wanted it so badly it was hard to watch the drawings—tangled me up in knots for days ahead of time."

"And now?"

"I wish I could pull my name out, wish I'd never put it in there in the first place."

Helena didn't think to compose herself, to look anything other than startled. This was not a sentiment she'd heard before, and certainly not from Bea. "But why would you wish that?"

"If you're part of the Council, everyone's watching. You can't be just a person anymore, minding your own business." She nodded toward Helena's collar and took a bite of the dried fruit, chewing slowly, thoughtfully. "Everyone knows where you are. Everyone sees that pin."

O

Days after her unsettling walk with Sasha, Helena stepped into the Council room before the sun was up. Her dreams had become broken, messy things, sleep increasingly difficult. The Council pin at her collar felt weighted with secrets she was being asked to carry without knowing quite what they were, rather than an extension of the joy and pride she had felt in her other roles at Southlake. The Council was convening that day, and arriving early to make herself useful in some way seemed a better choice than lying awake in bed. The little garden they kept out back could use water, and simple acts like these soothed her.

When she arrived, the door was half open, voices coming from inside.

"It's already out there," she heard Sasha say, "spreading like wildfire."

"We tell them it's just another rumor," Marie said. "You know men's desire for power. It will be easy enough to remind others of it as well."

"It was always going to come back to us in some way."

"Would you have let us die out? Let this settlement go the way of the others?"

It seemed Helena was not the only one wrestling difficult thoughts recently. Unsure whether she belonged in this conversation, but certain she should not be eavesdropping, she pushed the door fully open and stepped inside.

"Helena!" Marie said, the surprise in her voice loud in the large room.

"A trio of early risers," Sasha said.

"Or poor sleepers." Helena joined them inside the circle of chairs. "What are these rumors?" She waited for an explanation, some bit of clarity, but Marie looked at her with her lips pressed together, and Sasha would not meet her eyes at all.

The three of them stood silent long enough that Helena wondered whether she should leave, whether she was being asked to, when there was a scuffing behind her, work boots on worn floorboards. A third—the same third, Helena was sure of it, who had been so afraid of her and Sasha on the path just a few afternoons ago—had stepped inside the open door and stood outside the circle of chairs.

"Hello?" she said.

"Orris," they said, speaking directly to Helena, the pale glaciers of their eyes not wavering from hers. "My name is Orris."

"This visit is outside standard protocol," Marie said, her tone not unkind but formal, stiff. "We hear requests and complaints in four days' time."

Orris wiped a hand down the thigh of one pant leg. "We know what you've tried to hide."

"Hide?" Helena looked to Sasha, who had taken a seat in the circle. "You must know something I don't."

Orris nodded. "Perhaps. Although you would be the only one here who doesn't know."

Helena could see this truth, plain as writing, on the faces of both Marie and Sasha.

"Tell her," Orris said.

"Why come to us?" Sasha asked. "Why not stage your coup? That is what's being planned, isn't it?"

"Some men would use this, would use us, in their own bid for control. I don't want to form alliances in the shadows," Orris said. "I want to see the face of a new Council member as she learns this truth about her peers." They stepped into the circle and took a seat, legs crossed. "Tell Helena the story. Tell her about the children."

Helena felt the shadows unraveling into this moment, into whatever words would come next.

Marie shook her head.

Sasha turned to Helena. "The story," she said. "You remember the years before the pearls, how few children were born."

Helena nodded.

"The Council could see where that would leave them, leave

us all, in thirty years, fifty, a hundred." She turned her palms up, fingers spread. "Gone."

Helena looked from Sasha to Orris, riveted to these threads of a story they clearly already knew, their eyes bright in a way that could have been tears or exhaustion or a trick of the interior lighting.

"When our science teams discovered that thirds held the key, the path to our survival, we had to take it. We had to survive. Do you understand?"

"Pearls?" Helena asked, still watching Orris, who sat perfectly still, shoulders square, hands folded in their lap. "But what do they have to do with thirds?"

"It takes three to create a child now," Orris said. "What do you think is in the supplements? Where do you think they come from?"

"We've been careful to do the least possible harm," Sasha said. "Minimize any adverse effects." Her voice became a disembodied thing in the background as pieces clicked into place.

"The studies," Helena said.

Marie spoke up. "The Council made difficult choices when difficult choices were necessary."

"If the Council felt so certain in their actions, why hide them?" Orris asked. "Why must we be unconscious for these studies? Why do thirds from other settlements not have the weaknesses we do?"

Helena thought of the children in her communal household, many of whom, if this was true, had been born through the anonymous, stolen, contribution of a third. "What would you ask of the Council?" she asked Orris.

"We want our role in the survival of Southlake to be known, public. We want to be parents in the family units, partners in raising the children we've helped create." The brightness in their eyes deepened, pooled at the corners. "None of us benefits from the population failing. You will have willing volunteers for the supplements we all need, but we want to be asked, and our answers respected."

"Of course," Helena said. The request seemed so reasonable, so simple to grant.

Marie tapped her fingers on the back of one of the chairs. "The Council will take this into consideration."

"What is there to consider?" Helena asked.

"There is value in a society having faith that its leaders have made good decisions," Sasha said.

"This will make you look bad." Helena could hear her own voice, dull and strange to her ears.

"Possibly."

"Possibly." Helena grazed her Council pin with a fingertip and paused. The pin had been hers just long enough that sometimes she forgot she was wearing it.

"The others will arrive soon," Marie said. "We will discuss, together, when this conversation might be more appropriate." She turned toward the conference table.

"More appropriate." Helena remained seated, something furling out from inside of her, from the places where the shadows and dreams and whispers had taken root. "It is appropriate to force thirds into sustaining the population? To build a civilization on deception? Coercion?" Her voice was strong, more confident than she had heard herself in Council before.

"Your idealism is a strength," Sasha said, "but things are not so simple."

"It looks simple from here." Helena wiggled the pin at her throat until it released from the fabric. The clatter of it on the wooden floor brought a sharp look from Marie and a soft smile from Orris.

"We can't have a better world without making better choices," Helena said. "Including acknowledging when we were wrong."

On her way to the door, Helena paused to hold a hand out to Orris, which they took. Marie said something behind her, words she did not catch, but Sasha's quiet words—"Let her. It's time."—carried clearly. From the path outside, the low, sprawling buildings of the settlement were silhouetted against the gold of the rising sun as Helena and Orris walked to the center of Southlake with stories to tell.

My earliest memory of Ursula Le Guin's writing is pulling The Tombs of Atuan *from the shelves of the local library. I was seven or eight years old, and an omnivorous reader—sci-fi, nonfiction, YA contemporary realism, I piled it all in my arms and took it home to devour. Most of those books I have no memory of now, but I can still picture this cover, and I remember sitting down to start reading it, tucked between the library stacks, before I'd even checked it out. Something about this protagonist spoke directly to that younger me, which was thrilling to experience and set the stage for my future interactions with her work.*

Wenonah's Gift

MOLLY GLOSS

IN THE SPRING OF the year, in the days that are known as The
Assuaging, the girl Dulce built her house beneath the limbs of a
great cedar, climbing first straddle-legged to hang wind-bells in
the lowest branches so when the air moved against the shards of
glass the delicate unstructured music would speak to her while she
worked. Two rills ran together near there, with the tree standing in
the crotch between. The sound the waters made, sliding, turning,
and rubbing against stones, and the wind stroking the glass bells
and shaking the high boughs of the cedar, seemed to her to weave
a complex song, a finely textured chorus, which was her reason for
choosing this place where her house would stand.

She had already thrown the pottery, all the bowls, pitchers, and
jugs, heavy and brown, speckled with a bright berry color, before she
began the laying of the foundation. She had pieced and tied a quilt,
thick batted and nappy, had braided a sleeping mat from rags dyed
hazelnut brown, all this before she began the building of a place
where they would see use. And she had fashioned a narrow oaken
trunk carved in bears and branches of spruce, made it specially for
Guy, and as soon as it was finished had traded it for one of Guy's

great curving windows made specially for her, a wide arch hung with pendulous glass ropes of wisteria. She had traded to Enid a long stool with knuckled feet so she might have a sun-saver to heat her house and impel her wood-working tools. All this first. And only then, with everything in readiness, did she begin the dwelling itself, setting the stones for the foundation, laying the notched and planed floor boards, raising the squared-log walls from trees she had felled and stacked to dry two seasons earlier.

Often, she did not work alone. One or another of the people would come along the path between the rills and stay to talk and to work, asking, *Shall I do it this way?* or *Is this the place to make the notch?* so that the work and the house remained hers, though shared.

Finally, on the last day, Wenonah came, pushing lean-legged through the pea vines that bloomed beside the water. The old woman did not put her hands to the work. She squatted on the grass in the stippled shade and from her seamed walnut face, from those deeply lidded eyes, simply watched while the girl built the house of her majority.

When Wenonah had been there a long time and Dulce's sweat had darkened her shirt at the neck, the old woman said, "I've brought a cheese," and they sat together on the thin spikey grass and ate cheese and passed a jug of very cold cider. Dulce let the soles of her feet rest on stones in the creek. She looked sideways at her house. She was a little afraid to look at Wenonah.

Finally, carefully, she said, "It's small," so the old woman might say, *No, girl, no, it's a house of good size.*

But Wenonah moved with faint impatience, pushing the palm of one hand through the air. "Yes, it's small." And then, puckering her mouth, shifting her buttocks against the ground, "Who needs more? It's the right size." And after a silence, lifting her chin as if there had been argument, "This is a good place. I like the sound the waters make."

Because it was the last day before the holy days, in the afternoon several people came to work on Dulce's house. Guy's window had not yet been set, the shingling was unfinished, the door had not been hung. So they drifted in one by one and set to work. Sometimes, if there was a small stillness, they could hear hammer blows ringing from other places among the trees—Chloe's house, and Thom's, both unfinished as Dulce's, with other groups of people lending hands there too.

When the sunlight began to fail, someone came with a sodium torch and the house was finished in that false day-brightness, with Dulce, alone, straddling the roof peak to nail the last shingles. Then they extinguished the torch and stood together silently, studying the dark bulk of the house against the trees. Finally the old woman, Wenonah, made a sound that was nearly a sigh, a sound of weariness or of sadness, and patted the girl's arm.

"Good. Good."

In small knots of twos and threes they straggled back through the scattered houses and the trees, moving gently, with the sounds of their voices and the gestures of their hands muted like the dusk. Where the woodland opened out a little, someone had made a fire in a ring of stones, a high yellow blaze, and people gathered in the glare around it, standing or squatting together, and children in bunches too, spurting round and among the adults, sending their thin shouts rising with the firesmoke.

The girl and the grandmother stood together, and while Wenonah spoke to this one or that, Dulce held herself apart, and spoke only the few words that were necessary for courtesy. No child spoke to her, though she was often the focus of their furtive stares. There were already foods passing from hand to hand around the group, flat rounds of bread and bunches of bright red radishes, narrow-neck jugs of beer, steaming ribs of lamb, but Dulce, fasting, only handed them on.

Afterward, there was tale-telling, with first one and then another Teller standing on the hewn stump of a tree with the children sprawled closest and then the others, the adults and the three who would be confirmed as adults, sitting in a wide fan, making audience. Wenonah, who was one of the Tellers, took her turn but did not bother to push through the crowd to take the stump. She only stood where she was among the people and sent her canorous voice out over their heads, with all the faces turned up and toward her as though she were the hub of a wheel. She chose a tale of the ancient Civilized tribes, the people who had called themselves The Mare Comes.

Dulce sat beside the old woman's sandaled feet and looked out past the shoulders and faces crowded there. In the jumping firelight she glimpsed Chloe once, and later, more clearly, Thom, sitting rigid and aloof. He might have felt her watching. His eyes came round and snagged her and then lurched away.

Afterward, Dulce could not remember the tale Wenonah had told—only that it was a story of great passion and souls swollen with blood. The Civilized tales always ended in war.

There was dancing and game playing, and the minstrels brought out their stringed instruments. Dulce stayed with Wenonah, or perhaps Wenonah with her. The old woman listened to this one and that, and sometimes laughed or spoke some light thing herself, and once she shared a pipe with two clansmen, another time gambled with sticks and lost and went off grumping and disgusted. All the while, Dulce was near her, keeping very stiff and silent with her eyes often turning out to the darknesses of the trees.

In time, there were people sleeping on the ground, fallen where they would, and the others stepping over them carefully to go on with their gaming or to find their own path home to bed, until finally more slept than celebrated. Then the old woman plucked Dulce's sleeve.

"I am too old to pillow my head on a stone."

In darkness and weariness and silence, the girl and the old woman climbed the ridge to Wenonah's house. It sat on a high shelf, so the window looked out on the tips of cedars and the far edge of sky, dark as metal against the serrated line of the trees. From there, they could see pillars of pale smoke rising from the valleys, marking other villages, other bonfires celebrating the Vernal Assuaging, where there were, as here, new houses, untrod thresholds, unproven young adults.

Wenonah was a maker of bows, and from the rafters of her house hung sheaves of wild-cherry arrow-woods and half-shaped bows of yew and ash, and raw limbs drying, rubbed shiny with grease. The floor was littered with wood shavings and peeled bark, the dark stains of spilled fat, fragments of feathers and twisted fiber bowstring. Wenonah cleared a space on the floor and unrolled a mat there and she and Dulce lay down together beneath her thin old confirmation quilt. They did not touch.

After a while Wenonah said, "You must wait." She lay on her hip and spoke the words into the darkness. "Find a place and then wait. The others will be anxious, will run to the hunt, and one will come to where you are."

Dulce lay on her back and looked at the long, straight shapes of the unfinished bows. She hugged her own shoulders under the quilt.

For a long time she listened to the old woman sleeping, and later the rain dribbling against the roof. Then she went out and stood at the edge of the bluff with the hood of her shirt thrown back so the rain purled in her hair, and she waited until the beclouded sun made a dark wound against the horizon. Behind her, there was a sound of a bare foot on the grass and when she turned it was Wenonah, holding a long bow and sheaf of arrows with both her hands stretched out flat and wide so the things lay across her palms like a formal offering. The bow was very pale, a smooth double curve with the short straightness of the grip between, and the ends curving back again equally, and the bow string taut and dark. The tips of the arrows were obsidian.

The old woman sucked in the edges of her mouth. There were fine, clear beads of rain in her eyelashes. She thrust the gift toward Dulce, pushing it hard into her hands. They did not speak. The girl made a small sound and the old woman looked away, frowning, ducking her chin. But they did not speak. And the only touch between them was the dry rasp of the old woman's hands against the girl's wrists as she gave over the bow and the arrows.

The priest, Daivid, sat hunched on the crosspaths stone with the hood of his cloak pulled high against the rain. Perhaps he had drunk too much beer or gambled too long: his eyes were faintly swollen, his mouth a thin line. Dulce squatted a little way from him. Chloe was there too, sitting on the wet grass with her knees drawn up under her shirt and her arms lapping round her shins. In the thin daylight she seemed gray faced. Her eyes touched Dulce and slid aside. A bow carved of yew lay on the grass beside her feet. The three waited and in a moment the other priests came—the tall woman named Hannah and the old man, Steev. They waited together, all of them, in silence, until at last Thom came, holding a red-lacquered longbow in the tight fist of his hand. He did not quite look into Chloe's face, and not at all toward Dulce. Perhaps it was their old childhood friendship that kept his eyes hard and narrow and turned from her. Then the priest, Daivid, stood with a little grunting sound and led them all through the rain, away from the houses.

The sky paled a little, hanging ragged in the points of the trees, but there was no hardening into daylight, just a wooly and timeless grayness so that Dulce did not know how far or how long they walked. Often she smelled the salt water of the Sound, but the way was known only to the priests and they did not speak. Dulce's new bow and sheaf rubbed a line where she carried them slung across a shoulder. The hem of her long shirt drew wetness up like a wick, so it slapped stinging cold and gritty against her calves.

The sky began to darken with twilight—they had walked very far—when they came finally to a ruin of Civilization, some ancient wreckage of their many wars. Among the trees there were long hillocks of bricks and broken sheets of paving, hard under the moss. And there had been a gate: part of a stone arch rose into the limbs of the cedars. Daivid stood beneath it and threw back his cowl and then Dulce saw the others who were gathered already at that place, faces she did not know, or knew a little, priests and youths of other villages. They made no sound, they only crouched or stood or lay silently, separately, under the shadows of the trees and among the fine twigs of huckleberry bush and salal. Above their heads there were enigmatic symbols gouged in the granite: U NAV L RESE.

In the darkness under the high stone arch, Dulce found a place for herself and squatted down, bunching her body against the cold. And then she simply waited for day. She could feel the others near her, crouching silent too, waiting too. Only the priests slept. She could hear, sometimes, the sounds of their dreams.

Others came in the night—one thin boy and several girls, following their priests through the darkness. They found places under the arch and made their own bodies small against the cold. Afterward, in the stillness, Dulce heard someone make a faint sound, a sigh.

Through high gaps in the trees, the sky seemed not to lighten but simply to clarify so that everything became easier to see but without brightness. Finally, the old priest whose name was Steev came quietly and bent to touch Dulce's wrist. She followed him into the timber of the Proving Ground. Others had also begun to scatter. She saw Thom, following the priest Hannah, turning to cast Dulce a quick white look.

Steev led her through the darkness under the wet trees, a long walk to a small cave along a bluff with a view of the Sound. It was an old cave, Civilized, with concrete walls and unglassed windows, small and high, looking out over the gray water. They did not go into the cave's mouth.

In toneless weariness, standing beside the dark opening, Steev said, "Wait at this place for the call to start. And afterward, when you have been confirmed, you may go out through the gate where we were." He was an old man, and perhaps he had attended too many confirmations. He did not quite look into Dulce's face.

She stood out of her shirt, stood naked with her hair cold and lank against her neck, and handed the shirt to the priest. She held Wenonah's bow fisted in one hand, the sheaf of arrows across her shoulder, a thin-bladed knife strapped to her calf with a string. She stood watching the priest go back along the path toward the gate, and then she crouched with her hips against the cool flat wall of the cave and she waited. She could see her heartbeat in her breast.

At dawn, above the gray mist rose a clear, distant bell-note from a horn. Irresistibly, she ran. The haft of the knife struck hard little blows against her ankle bone, the sheaf of arrows beat against her spine. She ran until the breath and the first spurt of fear were gone out of her. Then from a high ridge she rested the heels of her hands on her knees and sucked in the frigid air, panting. From this height, she could see behind her the gray finger of the Sound, and ahead between distant hillocks, several priests standing in the drizzle under the arch of the gate. Through the gauze of rain, standing utterly still, they seemed faceless, bodiless, like the phallic stones that stood in small groves at the edges of some of the old ruined villages of the Civilized tribes. And seeing them, Dulce remembered her grandmother's counsel.

When she had chosen a place, she crouched among the leaves and held the bow across the tops of her bent legs and simply waited. Her chest was very tight, so she took air in through her mouth. The rain beaded on the backs of her hands, her shoulders, the crown of her head. She waited a long time, squatting silently, with her naked buttocks resting against her naked heels and the foliage dripping and the wind running cold against her back, tangling the loose strands of her hair.

Finally, in twilight the color of pewter, between the long straps of leaves there was a transient paleness, a shape sliding. She closed her mouth, lips tightening stiffly over teeth, and waited. In a moment, it came toward her through the high leaves, moving soundless on fine, long-boned legs. She waited, crouching still, with the bow in her hands nocked, waiting too, and the straight shaft of the arrow pointing away from her breast. There was only a little shaking and it did not reach her hands.

She waited until she could see the smooth glide of muscle beneath the skin, until even the sharp body smell was in her nostrils, and then she made only one fluid motion rearing above the leaves with the bow lifting in her hands and the bowstring drawn taut and then freed, all of it a single wholeness, complete and seamless, with only the face startling toward her, the widened eyes, seeming separate and disconnected.

She stood afterward with the bow still poised and her heart beating behind her eyes, stood very still, staring, watching the rain puddle in the folds of the body. Then a little sound came out of her on a little breath and she let the bow down and squatted where she was in the wet fronds, hugging hands to elbows, rocking back and forth on her hips, until she was done with shaking and weeping.

It began to be dark. In a while she dipped her thumbs in the small stream of blood and marked her face and her breast with pairs of bright stripes, but in the darkness there would be no seeing the red tokens of her confirmation, so she waited for daylight, sitting alone and still. Her hair was heavy and wet, and the wind brought it into her face. After a long time, she groped in the stems of grass beside the body until her hand closed on the lacquered red bow. Under her fingertips, in the darkness, its touch was cold and hard as bone—the rib of a giant. She freed the bowstring with the edge of her knife so she might tie back her hair with its stiff strand.

When there was a little light, she took the body across her shoulders and went away cautiously toward the gate of the Proving Ground. She held Thom's red bow in one fist, her own bow resting in a pale double curve low against her back.

Later, in all the valleys, there were heavy palls of smoke, and ashes dusting the trees, and where a newly-made house became a funeral pyre, there would be black cinders for a while and then, in the sweetened soil, small blooms, and tall thin trees growing.

"Wenonah's Gift" was written in 1981 during a ten-week science fiction writing workshop Ursula taught at Portland State University. It was the fourth story I had ever written, and the seed for the story came from an exercise Ursula had assigned during one of our early workshop sessions. The story was published in Isaac Asimov's Science Fiction Magazine *in July 1986.*

Postlude

Ib & Nib
and the Hemmens Trees

STEVAN ALLRED

A habben play based on this story is a favorite among the many troupes who perform these plays in Orgoreyn. It is traditional for the audience to join in the humming at the end of the play.

LONG, LONG AGO, WHEN Ib and Nib were yet too young for *kemmer*[2] but still old enough to be useful, they were sent to the forest by the hearth-mothers to gather kindling.

"Go south," the hearth-mothers said, "for there was a great windstorm not two days ago to the south, and there will be many branches blown down."

There were two paths to the south, one on either side of the River Arre. Ib and Nib crossed the bridge over the river and took

---

2 In the Gethenian sex cycle, the specific part of the cycle entered on the 22nd and 23rd day, whereupon a person becomes sexually active.

the west side path because it was prettier, and because they liked having something in their lives that they chose on their own. Along the way, they sang a song of praise to the trees in the forest for letting them take wood home for the Hearth.

Just at the edge of the forest they saw an elder whom they did not know, squatting on a large stump.

"Good day," said the elder. Their clothes were as well-worn as their face, and their face was as lined and creviced as the bark of a tree. "I've been waiting for you."

"For us?" said Ib, astonished.

"Who are you to be waiting for us?" said Nib, rather rudely, for which their cousin Ib elbowed them in the ribs.

"Hush!" said Ib. "Have some manners." Ib put their hands together and made a slight bow to the elder. "I am Ib," they said. But before Ib could continue, the elder said, "And that is your cousin Nib, yes, yes, I know. You may call me Iddru. Pleased to meet you both, I am sure, but we are wasting time here, so let's be off."

"Off?" said Ib. "Off to where? We have to gather kindling."

"*Nusuth*, you can do that later," said Iddru. "We'll be back here in no time."

"But where are we going?" said Nib.

"Into the forest," said Iddru. "Follow me."

Iddru seemed so absolutely certain that they would both follow that they both did. "We'll let the old one get ahead a ways," whispered Nib.

"And then we'll fall back, and disappear," said Ib.

But even though Ib and Nib tried to walk more slowly than the elder, their legs walked faster and faster, and when they looked down, there were vines wrapped around their waists, pulling them forward. The vines ran up the path all the way to Iddru, and up their back, and around their forehead.

"You've been thinking you'll lose me," called out Iddru, "by hanging back." They said this without bothering to turn around, as if they could see where their eyes were not.

And soon enough Ib and Nib were right behind Iddru, and the vines disappeared like so much steam.

Iddru kept walking at a steady pace, but they turned their head and said, "You are not the first to have the idea of hanging back." Ib and Nib had been caught out at their trick, but there was mirth in Iddru's voice.

Ib looked at Nib, and Nib looked back at Ib, and they both shook their heads. This was an elder to be reckoned with.

They walked until they came to a grove of very old *hemmens*[3] trees. Their trunks were thick, and they formed a rough circle, with a clearing in the middle. Now Iddru faced them in the center of that clearing, their eyes full of mischief, their arms wide to take in the grove and all the forest beyond.

"Quiet your minds," said Iddru, who now reached out with both hands, and touched Ib's forehead and Nib's forehead with the tip of a forefinger, so they were all connected by touch. It seemed to Ib and Nib that someone hummed inside their minds, a soothing, empty, wandering sort of sound that was nonetheless melodic and pleasant. After a time—a short time, a long time, who can say?— Iddru pulled back their hands and then slid their palms past one another and made a flinging motion into the air. Ib and Nib felt their minds settle, and grow still.

"Come, sit with me," Iddru said. They all sat in the middle of the clearing with their backs to one another, as Iddru told them to.

"One or another of these *hemmens* will call to you. Let them."

And so they sat, and after a time, first Nib, and then Ib, felt themselves growing taller. They looked down on the clearing and saw themselves sitting there. Saw themselves? No. Smelled themselves? No. They felt the heat coming off their trunks. They breathed in the air that they themselves had breathed out of their human bodies. They were two places at once, here sitting on the

---

3 *hemmens:* The most prevalent tree on Gethen (or Winter, as the planet is called by the Ekumen), a conifer with thick, pale scarlet needles.

ground, trees all around them, and here standing tall, where they knew their fellow *hemmens* as warm shapes nearby, shapes they had stood beside for centuries.

Down below, Ib and Nib were covered in bark, the hair all over their bodies pale scarlet conifer needles, growing right out of the bark. And there, on the ground, Ib and Nib looked up at themselves—that tree there, with its broken crown, that was Iddru, and that tree there, with a burl like a big wooden head, that was Nib, and that tree there, with that pair of branches spreading like arms, that was Ib. They all got up, Iddru and Ib and Nib, and those three of the *hemmens* trees as well, and they walked back to the Hearth. And as they walked Ib and Nib no longer felt themselves to be in two places at once, for now they were merged, bark-skinned and covered in needles, trees that walked, and hummed a quiet, wandering melody as they strode along as humans do. They were blind but not blind, for though they could not see as they once had, they felt everything about them now as heat and shape and living body, whether that body be plant or animal.

Iddru was no longer with them, and neither Ib nor Nib could remember just when Iddru had melted back into the forest, anymore than they knew when day had faded into night. They stood now before the doors to their Hearth, tall trees, Ib and Nib, just the two of them where there had been no trees that morning. Then all the people of the Hearth gathered at the windows to see them, and the hearth-mothers looked at them, and the mothers of their flesh knew them to be Ib and Nib, even though they had no faces, even though their bodies were bark and needles. Ib and Nib swayed in the wind as if they were dancing, and their pale scarlet needles gave off the scent of the forest, sharp and sweet and clean. There was a humming all around them, as if the very stones of the Hearth were singing to them, such a round melody, and all their cousins and hearthsibs joined in, open-mouthed, all of them singing "Oooh" and "Aaah" together, Ib-as-*hemmens* tree and Nib-as-*hemmens* tree joining in, such friendly harmonies in the voices above and below theirs, a sound to fill the long empty night, a chorus that might never end.

In the morning Ib and Nib awoke to find themselves in their human bodies, inside the Hearth, asleep on the floor in front of the fire, covered in hides and blankets to keep them warm, the floor around them littered scarlet with *hemmens* needles.

Contributors' Bios

TJ Acena is a writer living in Portland, Oregon. His writing has appeared in *Somnambulist, Hello Mr., Pacifica Literary Review, The Oregonian*, and *The Portland Mercury*.

Kesha Ajọṣẹ-Fisher is a Nigerian/American author, speaker, and dreamer. She is the recipient of the Oregon Book Award in fiction for her debut collection, *No God Like the Mother*. She was a pilot, a deep-sea diver, a boar wrestler, and once led an army of rescued dogs in her former life. Now, she tells stories in a reincarnated body and people call her an author. She hopes the world becomes a kinder place before she leaves it.

Stevan Allred lives in Portland, Oregon, halfway between Hav and the Isle of the Dead, which is to say he spends as much time burrowed into his imagination as he possibly can. He is the author of a novel, *The Alehouse at the End of the World*, a collection of linked short stories, *A Simplified Map of the Real World*, and a contributor to *City of Weird: 30 Otherwordly Portland Tales*, all from Forest Avenue Press. His alter ego, Pan Demented, is a comics artist, a heartburn survivor, and a wrangler of vintage wooden clowns.

Jason Arias lives on the Oregon coast. His debut short story collection *Momentary Illumination of Objects In Motion* was published in 2018 by Black Bomb Books. Jason's stories and essays have appeared in *NAILED Magazine, The Nashville Review, Oregon Humanities Magazine, Clockhouse, Harpur Palate, Cascadia Magazine, Perceptions Magazine,* Lidia Yuknavitch's TED Book *The Misfit's Manifesto,* and multiple anthologies. For links to more of Jason's work please visit him at JasonAriasAuthor.com.

Stewart C. Baker is an academic librarian, speculative fiction writer, and poet. His fiction has appeared in *Nature, Galaxy's Edge,* and *Flash Fiction Online,* among other places. Stewart was born in England, has spent time in South Carolina, Japan, and California (in that order), and now lives in Oregon with his family—although if anyone asks, he'll usually say he's from the Internet, where you can find him at https://infomancy.net.

Jonah Barrett is a queer filmmaker, writer, and multimedia artist. Their debut book, *Moss Covered Claws,* came out in 2021 from Blue Cactus Press. Jonah has also directed and written three feature films, a dozen-ish short films, and four web series. They usually find themself in old haunted buildings or overgrown swamps. Find all their work at linktr.ee/JonahBarrett.

Once a Silicon Valley software engineer, **Curtis C. Chen** (陳致宇) now writes stories and runs puzzle games near Portland, Oregon. He's the author of the *Kangaroo* series of funny science fiction spy thrillers and has written for the Realm originals *Ninth Step Murders, Machina,* and *Echo Park 2060* (forthcoming). Curtis' short fiction has appeared in *Playboy Magazine, Daily Science Fiction, Oregon Reads Aloud,* and elsewhere. His homebrew cat-feeding robot was displayed in the "Worlds Beyond Here" exhibit at Seattle's Wing Luke Museum. Visit him online: https://CurtisCChen.com.

Tina Connolly is the author of the Ironskin trilogy from Tor Books and the Seriously Wicked series from Tor Teen. Her stories have appeared in *The Magazine of Fantasy & Science Fiction, Tor.com, Analog Science Fiction and Fact, Lightspeed, Strange Horizons, Beneath Ceaseless Skies, Uncanny,* and many more, and are collected in *On the Eyeball Floor and Other Stories* from Fairwood Press. Her stories and novels have been finalists for the Hugo, Nebula, Norton, Locus, and World Fantasy awards.

Mo Daviau is the author of the novel *Every Anxious Wave,* which was a finalist for the Ken Kesey Award for Fiction/Oregon Book Award in 2017. She earned her MFA in fiction from the University of Michigan and lived in Portland, Oregon from 2014 to 2020.

Rene Denfeld is the internationally bestselling author of three novels: *The Enchanted, The Child Finder,* and *The Butterfly Girl.* Her work has won many awards, including a prestigious French Prix, an ALA listing for Excellence in Fiction, a Carnegie listing, an IMPAC listing, and more. In addition to writing, she has worked hundreds of cases as a public defense investigator, including death row exonerations and representing rape trafficking victims. *The New York Times* named her a Hero of the Year in 2017 for her justice work, and she received the national Break The Silence Award for helping abuse victims.

Molly Gloss is lifelong Oregonian. She is a novelist and short-story writer whose work has received, among other honors, a PEN West Fiction Prize, an Oregon Book Award, Pacific Northwest Booksellers Awards, the James Tiptree, Jr. Award, a Theodore Sturgeon Award, and a Whiting Writers Award. She writes both realistic fiction and science fiction. Her work, including some of her science fiction, often concerns the landscape, literature, mythology, and life of the American West.

Rachael K. Jones grew up in various cities across Europe and North America, picked up (and mostly forgot) six languages, and acquired several degrees in the arts and sciences. Now she writes speculative fiction in Portland, Oregon. Her debut novella, *Every River Runs to Salt*, is available now from Fireside Fiction. Contrary to the rumors, she is probably not a secret android. Rachael is a World Fantasy Award nominee and Tiptree Award honoree. Her fiction has appeared in dozens of venues worldwide, including *Lightspeed, Beneath Ceaseless Skies, Strange Horizons,* and *Nature*.

Juhea Kim is a writer, artist, and advocate based in Portland, Oregon. Her novel *Beasts of a Little Land* will be published in fall 2021 (Ecco). Her writing has been published or is forthcoming in *Granta, Slice, Zyzzyva, Catapult, Joyland, Times Literary Supplement, The Independent, Sierra Magazine, Portland Monthly,* and elsewhere. She is the founder and editor of *Peaceful Dumpling*, an online magazine at the intersection of sustainable lifestyle and ecological literature. She has received fellowship support from the Bread Loaf Environmental Writers' Conference, the Regional Arts & Culture Council, and Virginia G. Piper Center for Creative Writing at Arizona State University. She earned her bachelor's degree in Art and Archaeology from Princeton University.

Jessie Kwak has always lived in imaginary lands, from Arrakis and Ankh-Morpork to Earthsea, Tatooine, and now Portland, Oregon. As a writer, she sends readers on their own journeys to immersive worlds filled with fascinating characters, gunfights, fashion, explosions, and dinner parties. She is the author of supernatural thriller *From Earth and Bone*, the Bulari Saga series of gangster sci-fi novels, and productivity guide *From Chaos to Creativity*.

Jason LaPier is originally from Upstate New York and moved to Portland in 2007. In 2015, his debut novel, *Unexpected Rain*, was published by HarperVoyager as the first of a science fiction thriller trilogy, followed by *Unclear Skies* and *Under Shadows*. By day he is a

CTO of a Portland-area startup that aims to promote and empower volunteerism. By night he continues to dabble in science fiction, fantasy, horror, and anything weird.

Fonda Lee is the author of the epic fantasy Green Bone Saga, beginning with *Jade City* and continuing in *Jade War* and *Jade Legacy*. She is also the author of the acclaimed science fiction novels *Zeroboxer*, *Exo* and *Cross Fire*. She has won the World Fantasy Award, the Aurora Award three times, and been a multiple finalist for the Nebula, Locus, and Oregon Book Awards. Born and raised in Canada, she now resides in Portland, Oregon. You find Fonda online at www.fondalee.com and on Twitter @fondajlee.

David D. Levine is the author of Nebula Award winning novel *Arabella of Mars* (Tor 2016), sequels *Arabella and the Battle of Venus* (Tor 2017) and *Arabella the Traitor of Mars* (Tor 2018), and over fifty science fiction and fantasy stories. His story "Tk'Tk'Tk" won the Hugo, and he has been shortlisted for awards including the Hugo, Nebula, Campbell, and Sturgeon. Stories have appeared in *Asimov's Science Fiction*, *Analog Science Fiction and Fact*, *The Magazine of Fantasy & Science Fiction*, *Tor.com*, numerous Year's Best anthologies, and his award-winning collection *Space Magic*.

Gigi Little is a freelance book cover designer and house designer for Forest Avenue Press, as well as the editor of *City of Weird: 30 Otherworldly Portland Tales*. Her fiction and essays have appeared in lit journals and anthologies including *Portland Noir*, *Spent*, and *The Pacific Northwest Reader*.

Sonia Orin Lyris has played many roles. Among them: barista, software engineer, communications director, life coach, dancer, and storyteller. She's worked in artificial intelligence, ecommerce, micro-finance, social justice, and the fine chocolate industry. A lifelong love of animals has led her to various memorable moments: an emu hatchling asleep in her hand, a cougar cub body-slam, and a face-full of llama spit—adventures in interspecies communication. She's the author of the epic fantasy *The Seer*, as well as other published SF&F works, long and short; you'll find more at https://lyris.org. She speaks fluent cat. She likes to chase crumpled-up pieces of paper.

Tracy Manaster has lived in Portland for twelve years now, during which time Tyrus Books/Simon and Schuster published her first (*You Could Be Home by Now*) and second (*The Done Thing*) novels.

James Mapes has had short science fiction published in *Every Day Fiction, Perihelion, Stupefying Stories*, and the *Devilfish Review*.

C.A. McDonald holds a Bachelor of Arts in Comparative Literature and Spanish from the University of California, Davis. Her sci-fi, horror, and fantasy works have appeared in online magazines and print anthologies. Her latest short fiction piece "Flash appears in Eerie River Publishing's horror anthology *It Calls From the Sky*. She lives in Portland with her husband, daughter, and two rescue mutts, where she enjoys the very normal hobbies of long distance running and witchcraft.

David Naimon is the co-author, with Ursula K. Le Guin, of *Ursula K. Le Guin: Conversations on Writing* (Tin House Books), a Hugo Award finalist and winner of the 2019 Locus Award in nonfiction. He is also the host of the literary podcast Between the Covers (tinhouse.com/podcasts) where Ursula joined him for three long-form conversations, one each in fiction, poetry and nonfiction, and where he continues to interview many science fiction and fantasy writers including N.K. Jemisin, Ted Chiang, China Miéville, Nnedi Okorafor, Jeff Vandermeer, Sofia Samatar and William Gibson. His own writing can be found in *Orion, AGNI, Fireside, Boulevard*, and *Black Warrior Review*, has been reprinted in The Best Small Fictions, cited in *Best American Essays* and *Best American Travel Writing*, and garnered a Pushcart prize.

Timothy O'Leary is the author of *Dick Cheney Shot Me in the Face—And Other Tales of Men in Pain*, and *Warriors, Workers, Whiners, & Weasels*. His fiction and essays have appeared in dozens of publications. He won the Aestas Short Story Award, received multiple Pushcart nominations, and has been a finalist for Glimmer Train Emerging Writers, the Mississippi Review Prize, the Mark Twain Award, and The Lascaux Prize.

Benjamin Parzybok is the author of the novels *Couch* (three-time Indie Next pick) and *Sherwood Nation* (chosen for the Silicon Valley Reads program). Among other projects, he founded *Gumball Poetry*, a literary journal published in gumball capsule machines, co-ran Project Hamad, an effort to free a Guantánamo inmate (Adel Hamad is now free), and co-runs Black Magic Insurance Agency, a one-night city-wide alternative reality game. He lives in Portland, Oregon.

Nicole Rosevear lives, writes, and teaches in Portland, Oregon. She is a graduate of the Bennington Writing Seminars and her work has appeared in *Bennington Review*, *VoiceCatcher*, *North American Review*, and the anthology *City of Weird: 30 Otherworldly Portland Tales*.

Michelle Ruiz Keil is a writer and tarot reader with an eye for the enchanted and a way with animals. She is the author of the critically acclaimed novels YA novels *Summer in the City of Roses* and *All of Us With Wings*. Her short fiction has appeared in *Cosmonauts Avenue* and *The Buckman Journal*. A 2021 Tin House Scholar, her work has been supported by The Sitka Center for The Arts, Hedgebrook, and the Community of Writers. Born and raised in the San Francisco Bay Area, Michelle has called Portland, Oregon, home for many years where she curates the fairytale reading series All Kinds of Fur and lives with her family in a cottage where the forest meets the city.

Like Le Guin, **Arwen Spicer** grew up in northern California and migrated north to Portland. She studies utopian science fiction and did doctoral work on Le Guin's "ambiguous utopia," *The Dispossessed*. More recently, she has studied Le Guin's intersections with indigenous science fiction. *Kirkus Indie* called Spicer's social science fiction novel, *The Hour before Morning*, "A carefully paced, rewarding sci-fi debut." She has two bumptious kids and a bumptious, bitey cat.

Lidia Yuknavitch is the national bestselling author of the novels *The Book of Joan* and *The Small Backs of Children*, winner of the 2016 Oregon Book Award's Ken Kesey Award for Fiction as well as the Reader's Choice Award, the novel *Dora: A Headcase*, and a critical book on war and narrative, *Allegories of Violence: Tracing the Writing of War in Late Twentieth-Century Fiction*. Her widely acclaimed memoir *The Chronology of Water* was a finalist for a PEN Center USA award for creative nonfiction and winner of a PNBA Award and the Oregon Book Award Reader's Choice. *The Misfit's Manifesto*, a book based on her recent TED Talk, was published by TED Books. Her new collection of fiction, *Verge*, was released by Riverhead Books in 2020.

Leni Zumas won the 2019 Oregon Book Award for her national bestselling novel *Red Clocks*, which was also shortlisted for the Orwell Prize for Political Fiction and the Neukom Prize for Speculative Fiction. *Red Clocks* was a *New York Times* Book Review Editors' Choice and was named a Best Book of 2018 by *The Atlantic*, the *Washington Post*, *HuffPost*, *Entropy*, and the New York Public Library. *Vulture* called it one of the 100 most important books of the 21st century... so far. Zumas is also the author of *Farewell Navigator: Stories* and the novel *The Listeners*. Her fiction and nonfiction have appeared in *Granta*, *The Times Literary Supplement*, *Guernica*, *BOMB*, *The Cut*, *Portland Monthly*, *Tin House*, and elsewhere.

About the Editor

AN AMERICAN OF INDO-GUYANESE descent, Susan DeFreitas is the author of the novel *Hot Season*, which won a Gold IPPY Award; her work has been featured in the *Writer's Chronicle, Story* magazine, *Daily Science Fiction, Portland Monthly*, and *High Desert Journal*, among other numerous journals and anthologies. As an independent editor and book coach, she specializes in helping writers from historically marginalized backgrounds, and those writing socially engaged fiction, break through into publishing. She divides her time between Santa Fe, New Mexico, and Portland, Oregon.

Forest Avenue Press

Manolo Lualhati, a respected doctor in the Philippine countryside, believes his wife hides a secret. Prior to their marriage, he spied her wearing wings and flying to the stars with her sisters each evening. As Tala tries to keep her dangerous past from her new husband, Manolo begins questioning the gaps in her stories—and his suspicions push him even further from the truth. *The Hour of Daydreams*, a contemporary reimagining of a Filipino folktale, weaves in the perspectives of Tala's siblings, her new in-laws, and the all-seeing housekeeper while exploring trust, identity, and how myths can take root from the seeds of our most difficult truths.

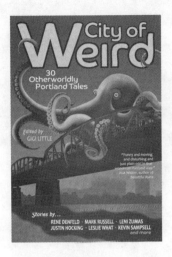

City of Weird conjures what we fear: death, darkness, ghosts. Hungry sea monsters and alien slime molds. Blood drinkers and game show hosts. Set in Portland, Oregon, these thirty stories blend imagination, literary writing, and pop culture into a cohesive weirdness that honors the city's personality, its bookstores and bridges and solo volcano, as well as the tradition of sci-fi pulp magazines. Including such authors as Rene Denfeld, Justin Hocking, Leni Zumas, and Kevin Sampsell, editor Gigi Little has curated a collection that is quirky, chilling, often profound—and always perfectly weird.

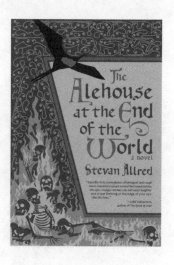

When a fisherman receives a mysterious
letter about his beloved's demise, he sets off
in his skiff to find her on the Isle of the Dead.
The Alehouse at the End of the World is an epic
comedy set in the sixteenth century, where
bawdy Shakespearean love triangles play
out with shapeshifting avian demigods and
a fertility goddess, drunken revelry, bio-dy-
namic gardening, and a narcissistic, bullying
crow, who may have colluded with a foreign
power. A raucous, aw-aw-aw-awe-inspiring
romp, Stevan Allred's second book is a juicy
fable for adults, and a hopeful tale for out
troubled times.

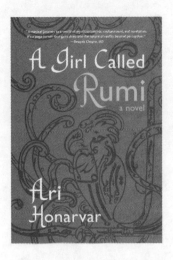

Kimia, a successful spiritual advisor whose Iranian childhood continues to haunt her, collides with a mysterious giant bird in her mother's California garage. She begins reliving her experience as a nine-year-old girl in war-torn Iran, including her friendship with a mystical storyteller who led her through the mythic Seven Valleys of Love. Grappling with her unresolved past, Kimia agrees to accompany her ailing mother back to Iran, only to arrive in the midst of the Green Uprising in the streets. Against the backdrop of the election protests, Kimia begins to unravel the secrets of the night that broke her mother and produced a dangerous enemy. As past and present collide, she must choose between running away again or completing her unfinished journey through the Valley of Death to save her brother.

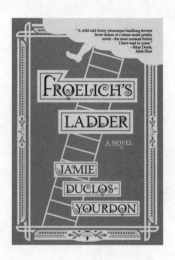

When Froelich disappears from his permanent perch atop a giant ladder, his nephew embarks on a madcap quest to find him in this nineteenth century adventure novel, set in a reimagined Pacific Northwest landscape inhabited by resolute young women who outwit their guardians, skittish Civil War veterans, hungry clouds, and a few murderers, all seeking their own versions of the American dream.

Queen of Spades revamps the classic Pushkin fable of the same name, transplanted to a mysterious Seattle-area casino populated by a pit boss with six months to live, a dealer obsessing over the mysterious methods of an elderly customer known as the Countess, and a recovering gambler who finds herself trapped in a cultish twelve-step program. With a breathtaking climax that rivals the best Hong Kong gambling movies, Michael Shou-Yung Shum's debut novel delivers the thrilling highs and lows that come when we cede control of our futures to the roll of the dice and the turn of a card.

FOREST
AVENUE
PRESS